Callous

By

Kerry Barnes

Copyright

This is a work of fiction. Names, characters, places, and incidents either are the product of the author's imagination or are used fictitiously. Any resemblance to actual persons, living or dead, events, or locales is entirely coincidental.

ISBN 978-1-7393019-9-6

Callous by Kerry Barnes

For more information, address: kerrybarnes999@gmail.com.

Publishers Once Upon A Book

www.authorkerrybarnes.co.uk

Dedication

To all the readers who have supported me. I am forever grateful.

Book in this series

Nemesis

Malice

Callous

Acknowledgement

My editor, Robert Wood, has worked relentlessly on this last volume in the Georgie Deacon series. Over the years, he has spent countless hours editing all twenty-one novels and has been a fantastic source of encouragement as well as an honest sounding board for me. And now I'm looking forward to working with Robert on the next twenty-one books.

CHAPTER ONE

November 2022

Georgie poured a generous helping of gravy over the roast lamb, stood back, and smiled. It was so different cooking in a swish kitchen with all the latest gadgets and with the space to have a family of four all standing in the room simultaneously. It was a far cry from her little kitchen in her old two-up two-down house. She honestly thought she would have missed it. After all, she'd brought up her daughter, Dixie-Lee, there. But along with all the sweet memories, there were some very bitter ones too.

***

She remembered the day Rohan, her fiancé, had surprised her with the new house in Chislehurst. It was not too far from where she had once lived but it was so vastly different. It was six months ago. The sun was shining, and Rohan blindfolded her. She'd been ecstatic with excitement and anticipation. He guided her from the car to what seemed to be a long path up to the front door.

Once he removed the blindfold, she was flabbergasted. Not only was this modern Georgian property enormous but it looked sharp and impressive. From the size of the door, and the two gleaming white pillars on either side of it, to the large multi-paned windows, the house looked remarkably like one of those houses she'd seen a year ago on *Grand Designs*.

Rohan opened the door, and she stepped inside to marvel at the extra wide hallway with a chequered tiled floor. The entrance was at least twice the size of her whole living room at her former home. Looking up to a vast staircase, which dominated the centre of the house, she could barely see any of the six bedrooms. The ground floor was absolutely enormous. Some of the key features included an annexe for Rodney Potter, a state-of-the-art kitchen with every modern appliance one could think of, a grand dining room, and a huge lounge with windows to the front and back.

***

When Rohan finally convinced her to move, he made sure to be considerate of her needs. The main one was letting her late husband's girlfriend's father, Rodney, live with them. The bedrooms all had en-suites and there was a guest bathroom as well. Dixie-Lee had what every girl dreams of – a walk-in wardrobe – although, in fairness, she would more than likely have filled it with books.

Using a tea towel to grip the hot plate, Georgie waddled into the hallway and tapped on the door opposite their lounge. The door opened, and Rodney dressed in a tracksuit and with a beaming smile, quickly relieved her of the mountainous dinner. 'Gawd, Georgie, girl, you do know how to spoil an ol' man.'

She followed him into the annexe and inwardly smiled. It was clean and tidy. The living room-cum-dining room was all neutral colours, with a two-seater sofa and two high-backed armchairs surrounding a log burner, and on the walls were photos of his grandson and his daughter as well as one of her late husband. She didn't mind. It was all in the past now. But even though she had moved on, she felt obliged to take care of the old man. Besides, her daughter loved him and treated him as though he was her own grandfather, although, in actual fact, he was her half-brother's grandfather.

'Aw, didn't Dixie-Lee look a million dollars in her blue suit.'

'Yeah, Rod, she did, but you shouldn't have spent so much money on that brooch. Pearls and rubies in the shape of a heart are so unusual. Still, they matched the necklace I'd made for her eighteenth.'

'Yeah, I know. I had it made. It's one of a kind. Anyway, how do you know how much it cost?'

''Cos the receipt was in the box.'

'Oh, was it? Bloody hell, and I turned this place upside down looking for it in case she wanted to change it.'

Rodney placed the hot plate down on his small table, which was surrounded by four chairs. On a Sunday evening, they all came in here and sat around for chicken sandwiches and a catch-up. However, today, being Monday, everyone was busy and so he had expected to spend this evening alone.

'I wanted to give her something she can keep.'

'I saw her face light up when you gave it to her.'

'Yeah?'

'She will wear it whenever she goes to work.'

Rodney's cheeks went bright pink. 'Well, Georgie, this looks a treat. I'm sure you are trying to fatten me up.'

'You could do with a bit more meat on ya bones.'

'I'll have you know, I've gained four pounds in as many weeks.'

She pinched his cheeks and made him blush.

'I bet you can't wait to see how her first day went, can ya?'

'Hugh reckons she will fit in really well. Apparently, two barristers, Cathy McGowan and Steve Elison, will be taking her under their wing. Hugh speaks highly of them, so I know she'll be in expert hands.'

Rodney pulled out a chair and sat down heavily. 'Join me?'

Georgie hesitated because she wanted to spend the evening with Rohan. Still, like her daughter, she had warmed to Rodney. 'I'll fetch mine over.'

'Sorry, what about Rohan? I mean, I don't want to get in the way.'

'Rod, I keep telling you, you're *not* in the way.'

Georgie returned to the kitchen, collected her meal, which was a much smaller portion, and rejoined Rodney. 'She will be home shortly.'

After half an hour of small talk, Georgie heard the front door open. 'That'll be her,' she said, jumping up from her chair.

However, as soon as she walked into the hallway, she only caught the back of Dixie-Lee hurtling up the stairs. 'Dixie-Lee, are you okay?'

'I'll be down in a minute,' she replied, but Georgie noticed the flat tone in her voice.

Hovering at the bottom of the stairs, Georgie wondered if she should go up and check on her daughter. After deciding better of it, she swanned into the kitchen and put the kettle on. Her daughter was partial to a cup of tea – mainly the funky fruit flavours – and she had explained to her the benefits of each one. However, Georgie had switched off when Dixie-Lee got to beetroot. As she poured the boiling water into the cup of chamomile, she felt Rohan's hot breath on her neck before a gentle kiss on her cheek.

'Darling, let her be. She's nineteen, not nine. She'll be down soon enough, and if she wants you to know about her day, she'll tell you.'

Georgie sighed. 'I know. I've got to let her grow up. She's a working woman—'

'Yes, and as tough as you are.'

'But I can't help worrying about her,' she said, as she subtly fingered the scar that ran inside her hairline.

'You're anxious, babe. I can feel it. What's really going on?'

'Nothing. I'm fine.'

‘Okay.’ He kissed her cheek again, grabbed his dinner plate, and with the evening newspaper under his arm, he wandered into the dining room, leaving Georgie with her own thoughts.

She still couldn’t get that incident at the graveyard out of her mind. Even though it was several months ago now. She’d tried to brush the thoughts off as a vision caused by tiredness and delayed shock, but the figure of a man who had ducked behind that gravestone made her go cold. Trying to explain it away had forced her to consider the past – her mother, the men, and the fight.

When her mother died, she had a proper burial, which surprised Georgie at the time because as far as she’d believed, her mother had no money. She was a drunk who had spent years trying to get off the booze and the drugs, only then to fall back into the habit.

Georgie shuddered when she thought back to those horrific years of searching the bin for food and begging the neighbours to use their phones to call an ambulance when her mother was unconscious. So many times, she had regretted calling the paramedics. Really, she had wished she’d simply let her mother choke on her own vomit. Maybe then she could have had a decent childhood, a happy one with sweet memories, instead of harsh ones that turned her stomach and served only to remind her of those dark nightmares that forced her upright in her bed dripping in sweat and gasping for breath. However, in her dreams, she wasn’t an adult. She was only a child. The men – and certainly one in particular – seemed enormous, threatening, and overpowering and worse than any monster she had seen in a horror movie because the fear was so real. So real, in fact, she could write a book on fight or flight. She had done both – not only in her dreams but in real life.

‘Hi, Mum,’ came the gentle tone from her daughter.

Georgie spun around and noticed that Dixie-Lee had changed into her pyjamas; it wasn’t much past six forty-five.

‘Are you okay, sweetheart?’

Dixie-Lee nodded. ‘Shattered, overwhelmed, confused, and I have the worst headache and period pains.’

‘I’ll grab you some paracetamol. Here, drink some chamomile tea.’

‘I had some just before I left the chambers, but since you’ve made it, I’ll drink it,’ Dixie-Lee said, with a sigh, as she took the mug from her mum.

The enormous kitchen had a dining table and a central island with four tall stools along one side.

Dixie-Lee took a seat while Georgie leaned with her elbows on the central island. ‘So, the word *confused*. What’s that all about?’ She smiled and moved a loose lock away from her daughter’s face.

‘I guess I was expecting to be among the busy chaos, courtrooms, juries. I don’t really know. Maybe I was carried away with the drama side of the legal system.’

Georgie frowned. ‘Well, you had a lot of experience working with the team on Rodney’s case, so what’s made you suddenly disillusioned?’

‘It’s the office work. I am finding it so uninspiring. I have been treated quite dismissively and I’ve been pushed from pillar to post carrying and fetching and searching for files like I’m a gofer.’

Georgie grinned. ‘Dixie-Lee, it was your first day at the chambers. Give the job a chance. And I didn’t bring you up to believe that you would expect to start at the top. You have to work your way up. Listen, when Hugh had you on the team, it was like work experience. They allowed you to be in among the thick of it, and believe me, baby, you shone. But come on, Dixie-Lee, with McGowan and Elison, you have a huge opportunity. With them sponsoring your degree course, this apprenticeship as a legal executive will eventually give you everything you need to be a barrister. Don’t you think they all started at the bottom?’

As Dixie-Lee sipped her tea, her eyes cast down.

'And what else do you need to tell me, Dixie-Lee, because I ain't buying into that story. What's going on?'

Looking up from under her long lashes, Dixie-Lee smiled. 'I don't think Steve Elison likes me much. I just can't make him out. One minute he is side-eyeing me, and the next, he waves his hands for me to move out of his way, like I'm an annoying wasp or something.'

Georgie straightened up. 'Side-eyeing you? What does that mean?'

'I don't know. He kind of looks me up and down when he thinks I can't see him, but I saw him doing it from the reflection in the window.'

'Listen to me, you are a very beautiful young woman, and men will look at you like that, but if he says anything that makes you feel uncomfortable, you tell him and then walk away. And if anyone so much as—'

Dixie-Lee chuckled. 'I get it, Mum. I'm not stupid. I am polite and as helpful as I can be, but if any of the men act inappropriately, they will get a swift kick in the bollocks.'

'That's my girl.' Georgie laughed. 'Now, as for being dismissive, well, he may just be very busy. And let's be honest, he may not want a pupil. It was more Cathy's idea. What is she like?'

'Oh, wow, so you would never believe she is a barrister. She looks like a supermodel.'

'No, really?'

'Yeah, she is tall with legs up to her armpits, long blonde wavy hair, and she walks with so much confidence. I want to be just like her. Honestly, Mum, you want to see her. It's like everyone stops what they're doing when she passes them. Even her secretary – his name is Marlow – has a cup of coffee in her hands before her backside even touches her office chair.'

‘Hugh fancies her.’

Dixie-Lee turned to see her uncle in the doorway. ‘Hi, I was just saying how lovely she looks.’

‘The ice maiden, apparently, but yep, she is very beautiful,’ he said, as he walked towards his niece and kissed her forehead. ‘Not as beautiful as you or your mum, though.’ He looked up and winked at Georgie.

However, Georgie wasn’t smiling back. He had called another woman beautiful, and it was like a knife in her stomach. She chewed the inside of her bottom lip. Only just then did she realise she was jealous.

‘So, have you met her, Rohan?’

‘Of course. We all have. She is our barrister. Hugh often engages her services, so if we have any legal issues with our clients, she’s our go-to.’

The knife was now penetrating her heart because while Rohan had referred to Cathy as beautiful, she could only accept it as though saying an actor was beautiful. This was different, though. He knew her.

She had to smile wider than she would have because she didn’t want Rohan to think she was jealous. Their romance had been complicated to start with, considering he was her late husband’s brother. But now, following the death of Dixie, and all the family in support, they could live their life properly and not hide their affection for each other. She couldn’t afford to spoil what they had.

As Rohan joined Dixie-Lee at the central island, Georgie turned to the sink. And noticing how dark it was outside, her eyes flicked towards the clock on the wall. It was approaching eight o’clock. She glanced out again and suddenly sensed a presence. She froze momentarily and had to blink a few times. She was convinced she could see a dark figure looming just by the tall maple trees that bordered the garden perimeter.

'So what do you say, Georgie?'

Georgie pulled away from her terror and pivoted to face Rohan. 'Sorry, what? I was miles away.'

'I said we should go and see the new Marvel film at the cinema on Saturday.'

'What? Yes, yes, why not.'

Rohan laughed. 'See that look on yer mother's face. She isn't feeling it, is she, now, Dixie-Lee? Maybe we'll leave her with her soaps and go alone. More popcorn for us.'

Georgie turned back to the window and glared at the maple trees. But it was so dark, she wondered if her mind was playing tricks on her.

'Ro, are the sensor lights working?'

'I think so,' he said, as he crept up behind her and placed his hands on her shoulders.

But she flinched so dramatically that Rohan turned her around to face him. 'Hey, what spooked you?'

She lowered her eyes. 'Nothing. I thought I saw a fox, and the lights didn't come on.'

'I'll have a look at the weekend. Right, I'm going to take a bath. Early start for me. I'm off back to Ireland. Mac has a client who needs my suave demeanour and dulcet tones.'

Georgie laughed. 'Suave? Dulcet tones? Mind you, I suppose compared to Mac, they could consider you more refined.'

Dixie-Lee got down from her stool. 'Now, no picking on my Uncle Mac. He may be like a bull in a china shop, but he is a big teddy bear, really.'

'And I thought *I* was your favourite uncle.' Rohan poked Dixie-Lee in the side.

‘It’s on a rotation, Uncle Rohan. Whoever spoils me the most is my favourite, and right now, actually, it’s Grandpa Rodney. I’m going to take my tea in there and leave you two alone.’

As soon as Dixie-Lee was out of sight, Rohan whispered, ‘Are you really all right?’

Georgie ran her hands through her auburn hair feeling the scar. ‘Yeah, I’m fine, honestly.’

He kissed her lips gently before walking towards the hallway, leaving her alone with her thoughts again. She glanced back to the kitchen window and looked outside. Her heart was rampaging, her mind trying to force back to the past, but, for some reason, the image of that man hiding behind the gravestone had been like opening a can of worms in her mind. Dismissing the past was probably not the best of things to have done. Perhaps she should have taken up the offer of therapy when it had been offered to her. Which had been firstly when she was in foster care when her mother was under the not so watchful eyes of social services, and then secondly, during her time in the British Army. But she was a private person and reluctant to trust outsiders. So the idea of talking to a complete stranger about her past was out of the question. She chewed her thumbnail and gingerly looked out of the window again, wondering if the ghosts of the past were ready to prey on her, now she was settled and – dare she admit it – ecstatically happy.

CHAPTER TWO

Georgie didn't realise she was in a dream. Or was it a nightmare? The images were so realistic; the feeling of dread and terror was overwhelming. He was there in her room swaying in the doorway, overweight, greasy, sweaty, and stinking of cheap vodka, soggy roll-ups, and vile urges. She could hear his animalistic panting, like a wild pig snorting for truffles. But there just visible and lurking behind him was a skeletal man. The man with the gaunt ghoulish face, whose eyes penetrated her soul and sucked out any bravery she held. And when he said, 'Jump', and her mother and the fat man said, 'How high?' his menacing tones just added to her fear of him.

As young as she was, she knew it was all about the money. And the skeletal man had a lot of it. The enormous gold watch, the Armani suit, and the fat cigar, which looked like a huge dog turd shoved in his mouth, said it all. She could smell his aftershave; it was a potent trigger for her. That smell mixed with cigars always made her want to run.

Even as a kid, she was able to process the dynamics of the situation. She knew what the skeletal man wanted. He was a voyeur; he got off by watching others taking part in vile acts.

Georgie could hear his high-pitched voice; he sounded like a girl screeching, 'Get her clothes off, get her clothes off.' He was chanting, even clapping his bony hands, to a sickly tune of 'get her clothes off'. She was staring at the fat man in his black slacks with the buttons undone because they were resting just under his colossal beer belly. She pushed herself back, digging her hands into the old duvet speckled with mildew stains. It was *her* duvet, this was *her* room, and it should have been *her* safe place. She could smell the black mould growing up the wall under the cracked window; it was like the shadow of a demon, every week growing in size. The sun had faded the threadbare carpet, and the wallpaper had peeled away at the seams. Her only wardrobe was barely a shell with one door where there should have been two. And all that hung on the rail with wire hangers were second-hand school uniforms donated by social services, a couple of T-shirts, a pair of jeans, and a dress that didn't fit.

Her eyes flashed to the gap between the fat man and the skeletal man, but the gap was closing in as her mother filled it.

She was laughing and clapping along with the skeletal man, chanting, 'Get her clothes off, get them off, get them off.' And as she chanted, her gnarly fingers were gripping the wad of money.

Georgie stared again at her escape route, but the gap was too small to get through. Suddenly, as she tried to get up from the bed and run, she found she couldn't move. She felt paralysed. Her fight-or-flight reaction had left her body. In fact, she couldn't talk, never mind scream. Gasping for breath, she was desperate to fill her lungs enough to beg her mother to stop the men.

The scream came, and she couldn't stop it until she found herself fighting off the fat man, who no longer smelled like vodka and cigarettes. He smelled like fresh limes. His hands were gentle, and his words were soothing.

'Hey, it's okay. You had a bad dream. I'm here, Georgie. I'm here, now.'

She took a few deep breaths, and as she allowed Rohan to hold her close, she was now becoming aware of the sweat dripping down her chest and staining her silk nightdress.

He blew cold air onto her face. 'You're safe.'

Another voice pierced her brain. It wasn't high-pitched, not that of the man in her dream, but a girl's voice – it was her daughter's.

'Mum, did you have a nightmare?'

Georgie could make out her daughter's silhouette against the light outside from the chandelier on the landing.

'Sorry, love, did I wake you?'

'As long as you're okay, Mum, it's fine.'

Georgie felt a sudden burst of pride, which she often experienced when her daughter was so kind and thoughtful. *How did I manage to produce such a special child when I am so fucked up?* she thought.

'Go back to bed, sweetheart. You need to be fresh for this new job of yours.'

'Hmm, yeah, I suppose so,' Dixie-Lee replied, in a flat tone, before she sauntered away.

Rohan flicked the side lamp on. 'What was the nightmare about?' he asked, as he moved onto his side to face her.

'Oh, just monsters and ghosts.'

'You are so independent, but you don't have to be a closed shop.' He ran his finger down her nose. 'I love you, Georgie Deacon. I want *your* problems to be *my* problems. I want you to trust me. I won't let you down, I promise you.'

'I know, you won't, and just so you know, I don't have any problems to share. I mean, I have you, I have Dixie-Lee, and I have this beautiful home. I have a job I love at the bakery, and I have a . . . actually, I'm not sure what he is, but he's part of our family now, ol' Rodney. So I have no problems.'

Rohan clocked that her smile was fake. It never even reached her eyes, but he wasn't going to get her to open up about how she really felt because he knew how Georgie could quickly shut down and become distant. She was cold at times, although not to him but in general she was. And yet he also knew how loving she was, and that could only mean she'd had it tough. Her time in the Army had been a cruel period for her, and he sensed there was more to her past than she fought to dismiss. Having seen her fight, he assumed her rage and strength weren't gained from being in the military. It was from another time. One day, maybe, she would tell him. However, he needed to show her that she could totally trust him first.

'I am fine, love. You can turn off the light.'

Rohan turned over, flicked the switch on the base of the lamp, and rolled back to hold his future wife, sensing she was putting on another one of her fronts.

Georgie grabbed his hand while he embraced her, but she couldn't close her eyes; she stared ahead, trying to get that awful image out of her mind. It was amazing how the fear stayed with her. However, if she didn't know the skeletal man and she met him today, she could easily crush him, snap every one of his spindly bones, and wipe that sneer off his face. Yet even though she was a grown woman, the thought of him still terrified her. And as for that fat man Bruce, she would love to slice his neck open and watch the blood coat his chest like a vast red bib. But then she wondered if she ever met him face to face, she would do what she almost always did – run for her life and leave her dignity behind.

***

It was six o'clock the next morning when Georgie climbed out of her bed. Rohan was already dressed and making coffee, and the inviting aroma wafted up the stairwell and into her bedroom. Hearing chattering, she guessed her daughter was also up and ready for day two at her new job. With her satin robe draped around herself, Georgie descended the stairs and joined Rohan and her daughter in the kitchen. 'Hmm, coffee smells good.'

Rohan passed her a cup. 'Here, take mine. I must shoot. I can't miss the flight.' He quickly kissed her on the cheek, grabbed his jacket from the back of the stool, and scooted out of the kitchen. 'Good luck today, Dixie-Lee,' he called out, before they heard the front door close.

Dixie-Lee was staring at her phone. 'Right, the Uber's arriving any minute now. I guess I'll see you tonight. I bloody hope I'm not pushed into the dark underworld of the never-ending filing system. Christ, you would think that most of it would be digital now, wouldn't you.'

Georgie peered over her cup of coffee. 'Well, old files don't do it all by themselves.'

Dixie-Lee smiled. 'No, I guess not. But I just want to get my teeth stuck into some really thought-provoking case.'

'I know you do, babe, but you're not qualified yet. Don't try to run before you can walk. Remember, you're a newbie.'

'Oh, not you as well! That's what *they* call me. It seems to be my office nickname.'

'Newbie?'

Dixie-Lee nodded. 'Anyway, I will see you tonight.' Before she scooted away completely, she spun back around. 'Oh, yes, I forgot to ask. Are you over that nightmare? I mean, you really did scream loudly. I thought someone was trying to kill you.'

'I'm fine. Go on. Get off. The Uber's outside.'

Georgie waited until the door closed behind her daughter before she went into the lounge and opened her laptop. She was no computer nerd. Far from it. She'd never needed to be, not really, not since she had worked in the café before she became part-owner of the bakery-cum-coffee shop with Henry. So she wasn't glued to a screen all day. And even her phone wasn't a smart one. But things had changed. Now she was living with Rohan in the new lavish home, with all the mod cons and computers, she felt she needed to catch on fast.

She googled the name Linda Marshall only to find reams of information but nothing to do with her mother. Searching old newspapers going back to the date her mother had died also drew a blank.

For a moment, her fingers hovered over the keyboard, before nervously tapping the name Bruce Kern. She hoped to see his obituary. But, to her absolute horror, he appeared as if the photo was taken for her own benefit. His dark narrow eyes glared at her with contempt. And even the corners of his mouth resembled a cruel smirk. She swallowed hard, and yet her mouth was as arid as the Sahara Desert. He wasn't dead. He hadn't drunk himself into oblivion, jacked himself up, and overdosed on drugs. He'd miraculously survived prison. And now he was out on parole. Shit!

This was like reliving the Major Ashby scenario. She had never believed he would have escaped from the Taliban and come for her, but he did, and he almost killed her daughter. So, after that experience, she thought anything was possible. Now Bruce Kern, another monster from the past, who had been convicted of her mother's murder, was alive and out there somewhere. And probably seeking retribution.

She had to look away and take a few deep breaths. Her eyes glared towards the window overlooking the garden. Was that him out there last night lurking in the shadows? Or was she becoming a victim of her own paranoia? And had she even seen a man hiding behind the gravestone? Was it purely her fear creeping up on her, or was he real and back for revenge? She fingered the scar that indented her scalp while staring back at the photo of him.

Something was off. He looked the same as she remembered him, but that was at least twenty years ago. Surely, he wouldn't look so young now; besides, he must be in his sixties. However, she had no idea how old he was. In fact, she wasn't sure how old her mother was when she died. All she ever recalled was the social worker saying that Linda was a child having a child, so perhaps her mother was around sixteen when she gave birth. She didn't want to imagine that her mother could have been any younger. Her desperate need to get away and join the Army had pushed any thought of her mother to the back of her mind. At the time, she'd had no interest in her mother's age, although it was probably on her birth certificate if she could be bothered to find it. So perhaps Bruce wasn't so much older than she imagined. It was simply that he appeared older in the photograph.

An unexpected tear irritated her cheek, but she quickly brushed it away. She was done with making excuses for her mother's behaviour. That chanting in the dream wasn't so much a nightmare as a flashback to the past. Her mother may not have chanted the words repeatedly, but she had definitely said them. Emphatically so.

Georgie gulped the lump lodged in her throat. How could her mother have done that to her? She couldn't imagine allowing any man to touch her Dixie-Lee. She herself would die for her daughter. Why couldn't her mother have just let her go back into care, or, for that matter, leave her in care? She wouldn't have been happy about that, but at least she would have stood a chance of being adopted. She wiped away another tear and wondered where they were coming from. Was it from anger, frustration, or the fact that what her mother had done to her had made her into the cold person she'd become? Or was it from the guilt she now felt for that night – the fight?

The unexpected beeping sound from the oven and the alarm system made Georgie jump. She glanced around and noticed that all the appliances were off. Her heart began to beat fast, her palms felt sweaty, and she was again in a fight-or-flight mode. He was here. He'd turned off the electricity and the alarm. Instantly, she ran to the knife drawer and retrieved the largest one. He wouldn't come for her again and get away with it. Not this time. She was different now. She could take down the biggest and ugliest of men, and her training in the Army had helped with that. Slowly, she snuck behind the central island in the middle of the vast kitchen and waited.

She heard footsteps outside in the hallway and the door to the cellar opening. She swallowed hard and listened. Why was he going to the cellar? Suddenly the American-style fridge-freezer light started to flash, and the oven timer came on. She sighed with relief and chuckled at her own stupidity.

'There you are, love.' Rodney beamed. 'You know what? I think that new kettle I bought is faulty. That's twice I've tripped the electrics . . . Georgie, are you all right, my love? You look a bit pasty.'

'Yeah, sorry, I didn't sleep very well.'

'Worried about Dixie-Lee and her new job? I shouldn't be concerned. It's all new to her, and she'll get used to it. I think youngsters today have it different from when I was a kid.'

Georgie smiled. 'You are right, Rod. Anyway, I must get dressed and ready for work. Henry has hired a new staff member, so I'd best get off.'

'Right you are. Now, shall I sweep up the leaves, or is there anything else you want me to do?'

Georgie understood Rodney wanted to feel useful and contribute to the chores.

'Yes, please, and could you deadhead the flowers.'

Rodney's smile lifted his cheeks and made his dewy eyes sparkle. Giving him extra chores always made him feel needed, and not like a spare part left on the compost to rot.

***

It was gone nine o'clock by the time she arrived at the bakery-cum-coffee shop to be greeted with an overzealous smile from Henry. 'Glad you could make it, Georgie.' His attempt at sarcasm failed because his smile said otherwise. 'Come and meet Sarah Boil. She's out the back kneading the bread, and she's very good, I might add.'

Georgie shoved her leather oversized bag on the shelf under the till and smoothed down her loose satin blouse. 'You've checked her CV, haven't you?'

'Georgie, it's only a little bit of baking and serving the customers. I haven't asked for a degree. Besides, she's not a kid. She's older than us.'

'But you want to check if she has a criminal record, surely?'

Henry tutted and shook his head. His long fringe bounced, and he blew it away from his eyes. 'We need an assistant, and when you interview them, it's not *us* who turn the applicants away, it's *you*. They don't want to work for you. So, anyway, she is fine, so don't piss her off.'

Georgie decided not to pursue the issue and followed Henry into the back room, where the huge oven, the preparation table, and the racks were kept.

Sarah had her back to Georgie. She was navigating the considerable shovel that eased the rolls into the bread oven.

Once she was done and had closed the oven door, she turned around slowly as if she was about to reveal herself. At least, that's how Georgie saw it.

As soon as she was facing them, Georgie felt her blood run cold. There was something about the woman's eyes that appeared to be tugged down at the sides, and she wore a half-smile in a look of contempt.

Sarah stepped forward and offered her hand. 'So you must be Georgie, Henry's partner.'

Georgie shook Sarah's hand and nodded. 'Yes, that's right,' she replied, unable to take her gaze away from the woman. She had seen her before but where? At that very moment, her stomach was in knots telling her that whatever the situation was when they'd last met, it hadn't been a good one.

'Do we know each other, Sarah? Only you seem to be familiar to me?'

Sarah shook her head. 'No, I don't think so.'

Georgie frowned. She knew the woman was lying. 'Are you sure?'

When the reply came it was quick. 'No, we haven't. I'm sure.'

As soon as Sarah turned to talk to Henry about the bread and the oven temperature, Georgie managed to study the woman's face. She was probably in her sixties, judging by the crow's feet and side wrinkles, and her hair was an even auburn, evidently straight from a bottle, and her teeth were false. Yet she looked a little young to have a complete set of false teeth. Her cheekbones were prominent, and the lines around her mouth were deep. It was all evidence that she was a smoker and possibly a drug taker. In fact, she came to that perception because she reminded her of her own mother.

As Sarah continued the conversation, Georgie clocked the 1980s sweatbands on the woman's wrists. Working in a room where the temperature was so hot, she wouldn't have thought much of a sweatband. However, she could see Sarah was perspiring. Strangely, she didn't automatically wipe the sweat away with her wrists. As a trickle of moisture ran down the side of the woman's face, she instinctively used her apron to wipe it away. Georgie wondered if the sweatbands were hiding something. Was Sarah a self-harmer, or was there a mark, a scar, maybe a tattoo, that she wanted to remain hidden?

Once again, Georgie had to consider the possibility that, for some strange reason, she was suffering from paranoia. Her past haunted her but thinking that everyone was out to harm her was surely absurd. At that point, she even wondered whether a shrink would probably section her if they could see inside her head.

CHAPTER THREE

The train was late and it sent Dixie-Lee into a panic. The cold air burned her chest as she ran from Charing Cross railway station to the offices. Having been given the opportunity to work in the chambers on a legal executive apprenticeship fast tracking her career with continued studies, she couldn't afford to be late, not on the second day. Her mother had always drummed into her that there was no excuse for being late unless your legs were blown off. And she would never get better training than with McGowan and Elison.

As she pulled open the sizeable heavy glass door that had the name of the chambers eloquently etched into the frosted glass, she took a deep breath in through her nose and gently let it out before composing herself.

Standing by the reception desk in the small foyer was Clifford Jenson-Baine, one of the junior barristers. Initially, she assumed he was talking to Natalia Beaumont, the barristers' clerk, who appeared to be in her early forties. She was of slim build and immaculately dressed in a fitted grey trouser suit, a pretty pink blouse, and high-heeled shoes. Besides managing the barristers' workloads and assigning them their clients, Natalia also manned the main desk.

Dixie-Lee offered Natalia her widest smile and was acknowledged by a gentle wave from the clerk who flicked her remarkably shiny chestnut-brown hair over her shoulders. 'Good morning, Newbie. I'm surprised you even made it before nine. I heard the trains are all up the wall again.'

Dixie-Lee chuckled as she glanced at the clock. 'I only made it on time because I ran like the clappers.'

Clifford spun around and hissed. 'Shush, will you. I'm on the bloody phone.'

Natalia looked at him and then back at Dixie-Lee before rolling her eyes and shooing him away from the reception desk. 'He is late for court.'

Dixie-Lee watched him wipe a few beads of sweat from his forehead as he stormed off in his black robe as if he were stomping across the stage performing in *The Phantom of the Opera.*

'Ignore him, Newbie.'

'I just want to get on with everyone. I really don't want to be in the way.'

'You're not in the way. Once that filing system is in order' – she tutted – 'and we've all had to do that job at least once in our careers – anyway, once that's done, they will have you working on a case with them. It's not as if you haven't the ability. I heard how you worked with Hugh Shields on securing Mr Potter's release.' She nodded in Clifford's direction. 'Ignore him. He is a know-it-all who actually knows sod all. He's just a right pain in the arse.'

Dixie-Lee's eyes widened at Natalia's terminology.

'He thinks he is a cut above everyone else, what with his privileged background. Daddy's a judge.' She laughed. 'It's okay, he knows we only tolerate him because of who his father is and even *he* knows he's useless. Still, Cathy promised to entertain him. Oops, I mean, have him on board.'

'Oh, I know Hugh asked for a favour. Am I—'

'Just being entertained? No, Newbie, I have read your essay on the jury system, and I was impressed. You're clever. You found loopholes in the law and the failings in the system. We could do with fresh ideas. We need enthusiasm instead of snotty-nosed, entitled dicks like Clifford.'

'Thank you, Natalia.'

'What for?' She smiled, showing her perfect white teeth.

'Making me feel welcome and just being nice, you know.'

A beacon of positivity, she cheekily smiled again. 'There are many personalities in this company, and as the barristers' clerk, I have the pleasure of managing them all. And that, of course, includes Cathy and Steve.'

Dixie-Lee looked down.

'Steve's bark is worse than his bite. You will get used to him. And Cathy takes her work so seriously she doesn't tend to have too much time for niceties and small talk. But when she is in the courtroom, well, she's a sight to behold.'

'I just don't think Steve likes me.'

'Steve pretends to dislike everyone until he is ready to show he likes them. It's complicated. *He's* complicated.'

Having realised she had probably said too much, Dixie-Lee smiled again. 'I'd better get started on the filing.'

Natalia nodded. 'Have breaks, though, won't you? The tearoom always has coffee and cold drinks to help yourself.'

Dixie-Lee nodded and walked to the staircase leading to the lower level. As soon as she was inside the room, where she had spent most of yesterday, she removed her woolly hat and her lightweight knee-length mac and dumped her bag on the old leather office chair. The smell of polished floors reminded her of her primary school days. This part of the building was in marked contrast to the modern offices upstairs. There, the rooms were light, airy, and modern, the walls were filled with vast contemporary artwork, and the windows framed the London cityscape. Down here, though, there was wall-to-wall oak panelling with expansive wooden shelves. If there were no metal filing cabinets here, all the rooms could easily be as they were a hundred years ago.

When she arrived yesterday, she was given such a brief tour that she could hardly recall who worked in each office. But, fortunately for her, the names were on the doors. Nevertheless, it was like going from 2022 to 1922. However, being alone in the filing room wasn't too bad. She could do her work and listen to what she wanted using her AirPods. And it was warmer down here. They had left the heating on permanently because they didn't want to risk any possible issue with mould, given that the building was so old.

While working on the second filing cabinet, ensuring it was all in order, she didn't hear anyone enter the room. So she jumped out of her skin when two hands touched her shoulders. Instantly, she spun around to see who it was.

Steven Elison was wearing a dark navy-blue suit, a crisp white shirt, and a blue tie. His eyes were expressionless as he stared at her.

Dixie-Lee was now frozen to the spot; Steven, it seemed, looked angry.

Without asking, he removed the AirPods from her ears and inspected them. 'I called you, and you didn't hear me. Too busy listening to music, I suppose.'

'I'm sorry, but I wasn't aware of you calling me.' She paused when she saw his eyes narrow. 'I, er . . . I'll put them away.'

He placed the AirPods on the desk and stepped back, looking her up and down again. 'Hugh told me that you have a lot of potential.' He smirked. 'He said you weren't like other young ladies. That you are exceptionally smart.'

Dixie-Lee sensed he was being sarcastic and mocking her.

'And I understand that you are a family friend, so I am doing Hugh a favour because he gives our chambers a lot of work through your uncles' clients, I believe.'

At hearing the word 'uncles', Dixie-Lee looked up and nodded.

‘And you might be smart, but having observed you yesterday, I can see you’re spoilt.’

Wow, she thought. *That hurt.* She bit the inside of her bottom lip. She knew more than anyone else that her upbringing hadn’t been easy but her mother had done everything she could to protect her. All her life, she had never asked her mother for anything unless she knew it was within her reach. They were poor. End of. But they got by.

‘Oh, and would you look at that. I’ve just hit a nerve. Obviously, you are not used to being down the pecking order, are you.’ He waved his hands, indicating she was down here in the depths of the company. Then, he laughed in her face. ‘Because your mummy put you on a pedestal, didn’t she?’

Dixie-Lee’s eyes widened at that cutting remark. But as he stepped closer, into her personal space, she stepped back. She took a defensive stance in case he tried to attack her. Because, after all, he wouldn’t be the first man to do that.

Instead, Steve scratched his chin and tilted his head to the side. ‘I know that stance—’

He was about to continue when Dixie-Lee interrupted him.

‘I’m not spoilt.’

‘You know I’m your boss, Newbie, and yet on day two of your employment, you answer me back.’

‘I apologise if I have offended you, but I think you should know I’m not spoilt. I’m not a privileged child.’ Even though she could feel her cheeks burning, she wouldn’t stand by and allow this man to insult her. She hadn’t been brought up that way.

‘Did you think I meant materialistically spoilt?’

He folded his arms.

‘Yes, I did.’

‘No, I mean you are spoiled with attention, smothered, and you’re in no hurry to cut the apron strings.’

Dixie-Lee imitated him by folding her arms. 'I was and I am very much loved. I've never been smothered, but, yes, I was and I still am absolutely loved and protected.'

'Ah, and that's the next thing. You were protected. Your mother was in the Army. I understand she was quite the soldier.'

Dixie-Lee didn't know where this conversation was going, but the fact that this stranger, albeit her boss, was now talking about her mother like this was raising her heckles. 'I don't understand what you are getting at, but I promised Hugh I would work hard and do my best because I want to be a lawyer, so if I am doing anything wrong, please be honest with me. I really would like to do well in this firm.'

Steve rolled his eyes and picked up the AirPods. 'This isn't a nightclub, Newbie. You cannot dance around the office listening to the charts.' He shook his head. 'And I thought you would show dedication to the task.'

Although Dixie-Lee was polite, kind, and inoffensive, the one thing she couldn't stand was to be accused of doing something that she wasn't.

'I wasn't listening to music,' she said, as she retrieved her phone from her pocket and showed Steve what she was listening to. It was a book that he had written for students. She didn't pout or give him a contemptuous look; she merely glanced away.

'Hmmm. So tell me, did you think that would earn you brownie points?'

'No, I hoped to learn from it, along with many other legal books on my to-be-read pile.'

'So you are telling the truth?'

'I don't lie.'

'Hmmm, I can see that.' He coughed. 'Unless you have reached the chapter that covers body language and how to spot if someone is telling porkies.'

She looked up and smiled. 'No, that's my next chapter.' She hoped he would return the smile, but he didn't. He nodded and walked out of the room, leaving her to relax her shoulders and take a deep breath. She wondered if she would ever be able to work him out, *and*, more to the point, if she would ever be able to work with him.

***

At one o'clock, Dixie-Lee could feel her stomach rumbling, so she left the room and made her way upstairs to the foyer. There, she noticed Clifford, and with him was another man who she assumed was also a barrister – because he was holding his wig – congregating near the door. They appeared to be in deep conversation with their heads bowed down slightly to hear each other's low mumblings. Dixie-Lee guessed the conversation was not only secretive but grave.

'Oh, there you are, Newbie. I was wondering if you had fallen asleep down there. You've not been up for tea or coffee, and it's past lunchtime,' said Natalia, who was searching through a file for something.

'I am going to the sandwich takeout across the road. Would you like anything, Natalia?'

'No, no, I'm fine! Actually, Newbie, you may have the rest of the day off,' she replied, but Dixie-Lee noticed a hint of concern in her voice. She glanced back at the two junior barristers, one of whom looked her way.

Her appearance had clearly caught his attention. He straightened up and then nudged Clifford. 'Who is that?'

Clifford waved his hand as if she was a nobody. Still, the young man with striking hazel eyes and a distinctive jawline, who looked like he was a model for Hugo Boss, ignored him and took a few steps towards Dixie-Lee, holding out his hand. 'Are you the new recruit, by the name of Dixie-Lee Deacon, by any chance?'

Dixie-Lee could feel his eyes all over her, and his smile and raised eyebrow made her think he was assessing her, but not for her intelligence. She smiled politely. 'Yes, and you are?' She held out her hand.

'Sorry, Dixie-Lee,' said Natalia, who still appeared flustered, as she looked for something in the grey file. 'I should have introduced you to Oliver Minster. He works with Cathy or on his own. He is one of the barristers who you may be working with in the future.'

Dixie-Lee shook his hand. 'Lovely to meet you.'

'Stop flirting with Newbie, Ollie. We need to talk,' urged Clifford, who was growling under his breath and narrowing his beady eyes. 'You can chat to Dixie later.'

'Er, sorry, it's Dixie-Lee,' she said.

'*What?*' he snapped, now clearly irritated.

'My name is Dixie-Lee, not Dixie. Dixie was my father's name.'

'Yes . . . right, fine. Well, it doesn't matter. You're to be called Newbie because you are the new member of staff,' said Clifford, while glaring longer than he should with a hint of a lazy eye, deliberately making her feel uncomfortable. At that moment, with his huge gawping eyes and a small yet distinctive hooked nose, which resembled a beak, he reminded her of an owl. His nasal voice was like a gruff squawk and probably not ideal for an advocate, especially in the courtroom when every word needed to be clear and precise. And his oversized tongue left his mouth gaping most of the time and it exaggerated his lisp, which lent itself to a potential comedy sketch.

Turning back to face Natalia, Dixie-Lee said, 'Are you sure I should go home?'

Natalia nodded. Her face was now flushed.

However, as Dixie-Lee pulled open the door, she felt someone close behind her gripping her shoulders again.

'Hurry up,' Steve said, while pushing Dixie-Lee out of the building. He had his key in his hand and a bulky briefcase under his arm. 'Come with me, now,' he hissed.

She stopped for a moment and glanced back to the chambers, hoping to see Natalia give her the okay to go with Steve. But she was out of sight.

'Hurry up, girl,' Steve snapped, as he grabbed her elbow, steering her towards a Land Rover Discovery. He pressed the key fob unlocking the door. 'Get in.'

Dixie-Lee didn't have a chance to question why. She simply did as she was told. After all, he was her boss, he worked with Hugh and her uncles, and, surely, he wouldn't try anything funny with her, knowing the strength of her family.

As soon as she closed the door, he tore off, and minutes later, they were in the middle of London, blending in with the rat race of it all.

'First of all, stop looking at me as though I'm going to rip your fucking clothes off.'

Dixie-Lee was surprised to hear him swearing because she thought lawyers didn't use that kind of language.

'I would claw your eyes out if you did,' she replied, feeling she could say that, since they were no longer in a professional environment. They were in his car tearing around London as though he'd stolen the bloody vehicle. 'So are you going to tell me why you have me in the car and why Natalia said I could go home now and why—'

'Enough of the whys.' He sighed heavily. 'Listen to me, I appreciate that you are new, and, yeah, you helped with Rodney Potter's case, and so, in some respects, you are a celebrity.' The sheer volume of traffic forced them to remain stationary. 'I read the headlines, and I followed the case. I think a lot of it was done for the benefit of the newspapers because it was clear that the nation liked to follow your story. The reporters make the news or make up news, which sells papers, so reporting on your role in the case was exactly what the public wanted to hear. One paper read . . .' He paused and gestured headline news with his hands. 'Coma patient Dixie-Lee Deacon runs rings around the prosecution in Rodney Potter's case.' He laughed. 'Runs rings. I swear, people are so stupid. You were a pupil, nothing more.'

'I know I was, but I worked hard. And I didn't claim to be anything other than the general dogsbody. Is all that stuff in the papers the reason why you don't like me?'

He stared at the congested traffic and sighed. 'So, as it looks like I am stuck in this poxy jam with you, I guess it's time to be honest with you. I didn't want you in the chambers. You would be a distraction. We have four, sorry, two top barristers in our offices, and I want our chambers to maintain its excellent reputation.'

Dixie-Lee felt her world imploding. She had just told him she hadn't wanted the publicity. And she certainly hadn't wanted to be in a coma or in a fight to save her life against Ashby. She had never wanted any of it. Fast forward several months, and now all she wanted was to be a lawyer and to be judged on her own merits. After everything her mother had sacrificed for her, she needed to make her proud. An unexpected tear filled her eyes and one toppled down her cheek; instantly, she brushed it away.

But Steve clocked it right away, and for a brief moment, he felt he may have gone too far with his criticism.

'I understand you think my presence will draw attention to your chambers for the wrong reasons.' She swallowed hard. 'I could say that I would keep a low profile. But you're right. The media love to hear about my life. I probably need to rethink my career choice. I'll get out here, and thank you, Steve, for being honest,' she said, as she tried to open the door. But it was locked, and an unexpected spasm of panic rose in her chest.

'Automatic lock, sorry. Don't get out just yet. I need to think this through.' He turned slowly to the side to face her. 'Look, I am sorry. When I said you would be a distraction, I think I was probably being sexist and inappropriate.'

'I can't help the way I look. I don't wear anything to be provocative. Hell, I don't even wear make-up.'

Steve stared at Dixie-Lee for a moment and realised that she was right; this woman wasn't the type to focus on her appearance. It certainly wasn't her fault that she was blessed with such staggeringly good looks. She just happened to be very attractive without even trying. Clearly, he had misjudged her, yet again. But, in fairness to himself, he'd wanted to test her to see if she was a pushover. It seemed she wasn't. And he liked the fact that she stood up for herself, and she did so in a professional manner.

'Right, here's the deal. I am going to trust you with some information.'

Dixie-Lee suddenly felt exhilarated.

'The judge's son, Clifford, who, by the way, is a fucking moron, has agreed to take on a case. He insists that Natalia handed it to him. However, she swears she didn't. The solicitor who supposedly gave her the case is a chap called Bernstein, who we don't frequently work with because he is a drip. Anyway, the result is that Clifford – the bloody moron – has taken on the case and thereby committed us to representing her.'

Dixie-Lee stared. She was waiting for the rest of the story, because, so far, she couldn't see anything wrong with what he'd just said.

He delved inside his suit jacket pocket and handed her a page from today's newspaper that was folded four times. Without hesitation, she unfolded it and stared at the headlines.

Mrs Bianca Malloye arrested for the murder of her husband Tommy Malloye.

'Who is she?'

'She is now the widow of the infamous Tommy Malloye, who, by the way, your uncles will know very well. In fact, the whole of southern Ireland will know the family. They are Dublin's version of the Kray twins, and then some, in their case.'

'Ah, so representing the woman accused of killing the infamous Tommy Malloye will have its risks. I guess you're concerned that on the one hand if the Malloye brothers think Bianca is innocent, they will do everything to get her name cleared and will support your chambers in any way they can. But if they believe she killed their brother, then whoever represents her is potentially signing their own death warrant.'

Steve's eyes popped wide open, and the corners of his mouth turned up only slightly, but Dixie-Lee spotted the admiration.

'Yes, I'm afraid Clifford is easily led, and dare I admit it to you, he isn't cut out for this job. He wants to inherit his father's money and the only way he will do this is by swanning about in a wig and a robe and acting like the twat he is.'

Dixie-Lee smiled. 'Thank you, Steve, for trusting me enough to talk freely. I promise you I won't let you down. I really want this job. I want to be the best, and I will work hard and do whatever it takes.'

As he stared ahead, now getting ready to move through the lights without getting caught in the yellow boxes and being issued with another fine, he said, 'I know your past and your mother's, and I like to think I'm a good judge of character. I also like the idea that you are not like some of the poncey barristers we have in London – all toffs, scoffs, and complete wankers. You're authentic, Dixie-Lee. You're from the real world. Just don't let me down. Oh, and I'm not a soft touch either, so step out of line, and that's you for the boot.'

CHAPTER FOUR

Georgie was desperate to get to know the new employee. She was still baffled as to where she'd seen her before. And she really wanted to remove the sweatbands from Sarah's wrist. So much so, her eyes were utterly drawn to them every five minutes, which was distracting her from her work. She had already got two orders wrong and given Banger Billy, the most loyal and regular customer, a custard tart instead of one of Henry's famous cream-filled doughnuts.

'What is it with you today, Georgie? You know, I've never criticised you, but I can sense you are not that keen on our new staff member. Why is that? What's she done to you?'

'I don't know what you're talking about, Henry,' Georgie replied, with an icy tone.

'Georgie, I've known you for years, and, yes, you can be cold at times, but come on, girl, you're staring at Sarah and giving her harsh looks. You've done nothing but criticise everything she does.' He pulled the tea towel off his shoulder and placed it on the counter. 'Why don't you go home? It's quiet, anyway.'

'Henry, in case, you've forgotten, I also part-own this place. So I will decide when I go home, thank you very much.'

'That's very true. But as a friend and not an *equal* partner' – he emphasised the word equal – 'I suggest you go home and come back tomorrow with a fresh personality. Because as your friend, I will tell you now, you're not being particularly gracious.'

Georgie flared her nostrils before she took a deep breath. 'Henry, you don't know that woman.'

'And neither do you,' Henry quickly responded.

'Look at her, Henry. Just look at her. She must have been a druggie or an alcoholic or both. She is wearing fucking sweatbands. What is she hiding, eh?'

Henry shook his head in disbelief. 'Georgie, stop! You of all people—'

'Of *all* people? What the hell's that supposed to mean?'

'Sorry, Georgie, I mean you've had a rough past, and we all have, so if Sarah was on drugs or had turned to drink at some point in her life, then who the hell are we to judge.' He folded his arms and stared at her. 'Give her a fucking break, will you, or go home. I don't know what's got into you, but it's unpleasant.' Suddenly, he lightened his tone. 'So whoever you are that has invaded our Georgie's body, give her back.'

Georgie smiled, realising that Henry was one of the few people who could actually say that to her without her biting his head off.

'I'm sorry, Henry. I think I do need a break. Are you sure you can manage?'

He raised his eyebrow as if to say *are you kidding*?

'Sorry, yes, of course, I can.'

As she was about to remove her pinafore, the door opened and in barged Sheila Marx, shocking both Georgie and Henry. Sheila looked smarter than ever and a good ten years younger. Her thin hair, which tended to have a mind of its own, was cut into a trendy modern style, being shorter at the sides and longer on the top, with a longer straightened fringe tucked behind her ear. The colour was a silver grey and shone like glass. Georgie was silent as she admired Sheila's made-up face, which had taken years off her.

'Wow.' It was all Georgie could say before Sheila gave them both a twirl.

'My Yasmin did this. It was her project at college. And the good news is she passed her exams and is now qualified.'

'That's amazing,' said Georgie, as she stared at Sheila's transformation. 'She has worked wonders.'

Suddenly, Sheila's smile abruptly changed. 'What d'ya mean, you cheeky mare?'

'Sorry, Sheila. I meant she's done a great job. I love that style. It really suits you.'

'Yeah, I'm chuffed to bits. So I wanna celebrate my Yasmin's success. I thought how about a nice cake.' She looked at Henry. 'I know, I know. You want the money upfront, don't ya?'

Henry laughed. 'No, Sheila, I don't, love. And I'll make a cake for you on mate's rates. How about that?'

Sheila frowned. 'Really? How much are we talking about?'

'A tenner to you.'

'A tenner? What is it, a fucking cupcake?'

He laughed again. 'No, I fancy making a theme cake, and I have a new member of staff who can help me. She says she decorates cakes, so your cake will be the guinea pig.'

'I was thinking along the lines of a pair of scissors on the top of a plain pink one, but I reckon a guinea pig will have to do. I'll take anything at that price.'

'Scissors and pink it is, then.'

''Ere, you never mentioned you were looking for staff. Fuck me, I would love to work in a place like this. I'd be good with the customers. I bet I know most of them anyway.' She gave a quick side-eye to Banger Billy and then looked back at Henry. 'I can make proper tea, not gnat's piss, and I can use that fancy coffee machine. My Yas and my Riley will tell ya. I pick things up quick, me.'

'Yeah, Sheila, and that's what the Ol' Bill said when they caught you tea leafing up the high street.'

'Oh, shut ya mouth, Billy. That was a long time ago. Can't a person change?' She lowered her gaze and her voice. 'I'm trying, ya know. I've even had my hair done. And I don't drink or smoke. Well, I vape, but, anyway, I'm trying.'

Billy looked up from his paper and realised he had hurt the woman's feelings. 'I was only joking, Sheila, and, yeah, love, you was a right handful a while back, but I ain't deaf or blind, and I certainly ain't stupid. We do know you've changed.' He looked at Henry. 'Any work going for Sheila?'

Sheila smiled from ear to ear because never in her wildest dreams would she have thought that someone like Banger Billy would ever stick up for her.

Henry glanced at Georgie, who gave him a cocky wink. 'We could do with another pair of hands on a Saturday.'

'You wouldn't have to pay much. I just want—'

'I get it, Sheila,' said Georgie, now understanding the woman's reasons. She wanted to be a productive member of society and to be seen as one, and what better place than at Henry's.

'Actually, Georgie's right. Saturday is busy, so come along, and Georgie will show you the ropes, but please, Sheila, leave the profanities at home.'

Sheila laughed excitedly. ''Ere, now, that's a good name for your next fancy cakes. Cream-filled profanities.'

Even Banger Billy laughed.

'I suppose I'd better introduce you to our newest staff member, if you're sure you want to work here. And, of course, you will be on a probationary period.'

Sheila nodded so fast that she looked as though her head was about to fall off.

'Sarah, would you come to the counter, please?' Henry called out, while smiling nervously at Sheila, wondering if he had made a colossal mistake. However, how could he go back on his word? Only moments ago, he'd more or less told Georgie that everyone deserves a chance.

Sarah walked from the back room and hovered in the doorway. Her head was down, and she appeared uneasy.

'Well, I'll be buggered. It must be, what . . . twenty years ago since I last saw you.'

Georgie felt her skin come alive with goosebumps. *So the mystery was about to unfold if Sheila knew who the woman was.*

'Sorry, love, I think you have the wrong Sarah.'

Sheila glanced at Georgie and frowned before she looked back at the woman. ''Ere, listen, I ain't holding no grudge. It was so long ago, and, look, I forgive ya.' She huffed. 'As long as you forgive me for the larruping, I gave ya. So you don't have to pretend you're someone else. I ain't about to leapfrog the counter and give you another shiner.' Sheila sighed. 'And the truth be known, looking back, I should have let you have me ol' man. He was a prick, a nasty rotten, stinking, fucking prick.'

Banger Billy almost choked on his tea. 'Now that's a changed woman, and I thought you worshipped your ol' man, Sheila?'

'Yeah, well, everyone thought I did, but he was a bully and a nasty piece of work,' she replied, as she watched Sarah saunter off to the back of the shop.

'Oh, sorry, Henry, did I say something wrong?'

Henry and Georgie looked at each other in surprise before Henry called Sarah to come out to the front.

She returned looking very wary and removed her apron. 'Sheila, it was a long time ago. The fight was nothing, and your husband was just a, well, he was a . . .' She paused and looked at all the eyes on her. 'Never mind.'

'He was a paying customer,' said Sheila, trying to be tactful.

'Something like that.'

Henry coughed and waved Sarah to return to the back room. 'Introductions over. Let's get back to work,' he said, clapping his hands but feeling thoroughly awkward.

Sheila beamed and rubbed her hands together. 'So this Saturday, yeah? Henry, what time?'

Henry was still trying to figure out what to make of Sarah. It was all very well forgiving a person's past, but a prostitute? *Maybe Georgie was right, and he should have asked for a CV. Then again*, he thought, *how would you word that*? 'Yes, er, nine o'clock on the dot, and please, Sheila, be careful with your language. Colourful, it may be, but it's not everyone's cup of tea. Know what I mean?'

Sheila gave a salute and laughed. 'O' course I do. I will be nuffin but professional.'

As Sheila left the coffee shop, Georgie snatched her bag and ran after her. 'Wait up, Sheila.'

Sheila stopped and turned around. 'Oh, please don't say you've changed your mind. I really need this job.'

'No, the job is yours, and if you do well, we could increase your hours.'

'I will, Georgie. I won't let you down.'

Georgie pointed to her car. 'Shall I give you a lift back?'

'Yeah, why not. The bus I got on earlier stank of shit and old people.'

A small chuckle left Georgie's mouth before she opened the car door and gestured for Sheila to climb in.

As soon as she pulled away, Georgie said, 'Sheila, do you know Sarah well?'

'Nah, not really. I *kind* of knew her from when I used to go to Sidcup. She was an old bike back in the day, tossing off any ol' geezer for a pound note or a packet of fags.'

'Including your husband, by the sounds of it.'

'Yeah, I caught her once poncing drinks off the ol' man, and then when he thought I was drunk, he fucked off outside with her. The dirty bastard had her in the alleyway. I made out I didn't see him 'cos he would have belted me one. But I fucking got hold of her the next day and beat the granny out of her. She hobbled away, she did, with a fat lip, a black eye, and a wet pair of drawers because she pissed herself when she saw me. I never had much time for her. We knew each other before. You know, about town, at the working men's club, and in the pubs. It was back in the day when everyone knew everyone. So that is about as much as I know about her, and she served time at Holloway many moons ago. Oh yeah, I forgot about that shit.'

Georgie sensed the concerned tone in Sheila's voice. 'Go on, tell me, what was she in the nick for?'

'Well, at the time, I thought, in fact, a lot of people thought, that the police just wanted her and a few of her associates off the streets, although I understood she worked from a brothel. But, anyway, listen, I might have this all wrong, but there was a suggestion that she was involved in child porn or something. I really wouldn't like to say for sure, and it's a fucking bad, bad thing to be labelled with. Anyway, you have one of those laptops, I'm sure. No doubt, you can google her.'

'Yeah, I will do that. Do you know where she used to live?'

'Er, do you know, I can't remember, but she lived in Sidcup. Why the interest?'

'I think I have seen her before.'

'Well, Georgie, Sidcup ain't a million miles from The Crays now, is it?'

'No, I guess not.'

'Funny, but I don't remember you living around The Crays, but, then again, you were in the Army, and I wouldn't have known you as a kid. I barely knew any kids until they were eighteen. I didn't like kids much, and mine kinda had each other, so the only youngsters in and out of mine were teenagers, and, besides, you were a bit older.'

'I moved back to the area after I had Dixie-Lee. I left when I was sixteen to join the Army, and we lived in Sidcup.'

'And your muvver let you sign up so young, did she?'

Georgie laughed bitterly. 'She was drunk when she signed the paperwork, and I was gone before she sobered up.' Quickly changing the subject, Georgie said, 'So I'm pleased Yasmin is a qualified hairdresser now and doing well. And what about Riley? He doesn't visit so much now.'

Sheila fiddled with her gold chain around her neck. 'He is doing well at college, and to be honest, I don't think there is going to be a wedding between your girl and him. He is, er, well, he's sort of keeping his options open,' she replied and turned to gaze out of the side window.

'He is seeing someone else, isn't he?' said Georgie.

'Yeah, I guess you heard. I know he tried his best to let Dixie-Lee down gently. He really loved Dixie-Lee, I know that, but they are so young.'

'Yeah, Dixie-Lee said they had decided to be friends and date other people, so I am pleased they're still mates because they do get on well, but it explains why he hasn't been about lately. So is his new girlfriend nice?' Georgie asked, showing an interest. However, inside, she was laughing. Dixie-Lee had already told her that she had called the close friendship off, and the truth was they were better as mates; it was just more comfortable that way for her.

'She's okay. Not as pretty as Dixie-Lee, but she's a paramedic, so they have that in common.'

As Georgie parked the car outside Sheila's house she said, 'Do me a favour. If you remember anything else about that woman, let me know.'

'I will do but what's the real reason you want to know about her, Georgie?'

‘Because when I look at her, I see something dark. It’s as if she did something bad to me. I don’t like her and yet I can’t place her.’

Sheila’s eyes widened, and her skin paled. ‘Oh Christ, what if the rumours were true? I mean, she didn’t kidnap you, did she, or give you to any strange men, or . . .’ She shook her head. ‘Nah, sorry, Georgie. My mind is running away with me. The best thing is to just ask her, and if that don’t work, ask her again with a knife at her throat. It might loosen her tongue.’

Even though Georgie knew that Sheila meant that as a joke, it would be a typical move on her part. However, right now, she was going over Sheila’s words. *Give you to any strange men.* If she wasn’t being mentally thrust back into the past, she would have pushed Sheila for more information about the rumours. Still, her legs were shaking and all she wanted to do was to get home.

CHAPTER FIVE

As soon as the traffic began to move, Steve turned away from Dixie-Lee and put his foot down on the accelerator.

'Where are we going? The station is back there,' said Dixie-Lee, pointing her thumb over her shoulder.

'We are going to our old office. I need you to help me find a file.'

'Oh, I see,' she replied, flatly.

'I heard that dissatisfied tone in your voice. Don't pout like a spoiled child.'

'I wasn't pouting, and again, I'm not spoilt. I understand that I work for you, Steve, and also Cathy, but don't prejudge me, please. I was disappointed because trawling through files is boring. Reading the files, though, is another matter.'

'Okay, okay, I won't call you spoilt again. And . . .' He paused for a moment. 'I need you to help me find files on the Malloyes. Everything we have. Since Clifford, the twat, has taken on the case, the Malloyes will know by the end of the day that it's McGowan and Elison who have been charged with the work, because we have the means. I can guarantee the Malloyes will have someone watching the police station in which she's being held to see who is representing her. Now, the one person they won't know is you.'

Feeling totally intrigued, Dixie-Lee held her breath.

'Once we've got the file I want, I need to takc it to a safe place. And then we need to go to the police station to have a word with *Mrs* Malloye.'

Dixie-Lee noticed the emphasis on Mrs and wondered about the reason behind that.

'Damn it! The stupid woman, why the hell did she get her lawyer, the prick, to engage our company and to use Clifford, the thickest barrister in London?'

'May I answer that?'

Steve turned to the side and frowned. 'Yes,' he replied.

'Perhaps the solicitor wanted to score points with the judge by engaging his son, Clifford, to be the advocate in what I can assume will be a high-profile case.'

'Yes, that would be a feasible explanation.'

He said no more, leaving Dixie-Lee to wonder if there was more to this than Steve was prepared to let on. She decided not to force the issue; besides, she was new and was only merely touching the surface of Steve's character.

***

The old office was part of a Victorian building that had been added to over the years and modernised at different stages, making it appear a mismatch of designs. The only way in was via a wrought iron external staircase to a steel door.

Dixie-Lee followed him up the staircase. She didn't like heights and was annoyed that she had to grip the railing so tightly that her knuckles turned white. A gust of wind blew through the gap between the two old brick buildings, and when she caught her breath, she gasped. Her legs were shaking from the cold weather and the fear of falling.

Steve hadn't noticed. He was clearly intent on getting inside, and once he had the door unlocked, which was a process in itself, because it had more locks and coded security systems than Fort Knox, he used his foot to give it an extra force to push it open.

A musty smell hit them. Steve was obviously used to the office and walked straight in before bolting the door behind them.

Dixie-Lee realised they were inside a room that she barely got to see before they were in total darkness. Her heart was beating fast as the dark and the silence spooked her. She heard a click, and suddenly the lights were on, and then she could see the office clearly. It was basic, with just the one window, which had heavy-duty security bars on the outside.

Steve immediately lowered the blind to black out the room. There were three Formica desks and a few chairs scattered about, and along the whole stretch of the longest wall, there were grey filing cabinets.

Dixie-Lee thought she had stepped into an early version of *Minder* or *The Bill*; the old-fashioned landline phones, tongue-and-groove panelled walls, and the Formica desks were typical of the 1980s.

She shivered, and right on cue, Steve walked around the office and switched on the electric heaters. 'It should warm up fairly quickly if the bloody things don't trip.'

Dixie-Lee removed her hat and mac and placed them on a desk, along with her bag. 'So what am I looking for?'

Steve raised the blind to look out of the window before lowering it again. He leaned against the window frame with his legs crossed and his hands on the windowsill. He sighed, tilted his head to the side, and looked Dixie-Lee up and down.

She immediately looked away, feeling uncomfortable.

'You are very beautiful.'

A tightening in her throat stopped her from answering; this wasn't a good situation. Steve had the keys, and the door was locked. No one knew where she was, and she didn't know Steve well enough to feel totally comfortable in his company.

'And what makes you so attractive is that you really don't see yourself that way, and you don't look at beauty as an attribute either, do you.'

The sense of the conversation changed slightly; his tone was not so much flirtatious but merely factual.

'I guess it's not important unless you go into the beauty business or become an A-lister or a model. Or anything like that. You need to actually look quite beautiful. Me, I'm not into fancy hairstyles or make-up. I just want to use my brain for my job because beauty doesn't last forever. Besides, it's boring. I would much rather be known for my intelligence than my appearance.'

'Yes, and that sounds all very admirable, but as you get older, you will realise that your good looks will also open doors for you. A word of advice: use them when you can.' He laughed. 'Cathy does.'

Ignoring the comment, Dixie-Lee said, 'Where should I start with the file? Could you tell me again what we're looking for?'

'I saw what you did,' he replied, quickly diverting the conversation. 'But that's fine. So what I want is a file that contains the name Malloye.'

'Well, that should be easy. Why don't I just look at all the files listed under M?'

'Do I look that stupid? If it was that simple, Newbie, I would collect the file myself. It would be easy to look under M. But the issue here is that the Malloye file is not under M because then it would be easily accessible. It's hidden away somewhere and I don't know where it is.' He sighed heavily and then tutted. 'The problem is we had a secretary who . . .' He paused and pushed himself away from the windowsill. 'All I can say is this secretary thought she could be more than a secretary, if you know what I mean. When we sacked her, she got her own back by mixing up the filing system to make our work so much damned harder.'

'Right, so it's down to me to find it.' She looked up at the clock. 'Do you mind if I call my mum to tell her I will be late?'

Steve threw his hands in the air. 'And there, Dixie-Lee, we have it. I rest my case. As I said, you're mollycoddled.'

'Look, I understand that you seem to think I'm a mummy's girl attached to my mum's apron strings. However, you have no idea what my mum went through while I was in a coma and also when I was kidnapped. So if you've done your homework, like you say you have, you would completely understand why I don't want her to worry unnecessarily. Not when it takes just a brief phone call to put her mind at rest.'

Steve sniffed the air, mumbled under his breath, and walked over to the first filing cabinet. 'Okay, I'll start at this end. If you start at the other, hopefully, we will meet somewhere in the middle with the Malloye file.'

Dixie-Lee was surprised that he was actually going to help and was even more astonished by how fast he could move; it was as if his eyes could process the files like a counting machine.

As she searched for the missing file, she realised that this secretary had evidently left the firm with a raving hump because the files were deliberately in disarray.

After an hour, Steve slammed the filing cabinet shut and paced the room with one hand on his hip and the other combing through his hair. 'Right, I need a coffee. You carry on, and I'll get some food or something. Is there anything you don't like?' He waved his hand for her to hurry up with an answer. Clearly, patience wasn't his strong point.

'Flat white for me, please, and I eat anything, thank you.'

As soon as he left the office and she heard him running down the staircase, she felt the tension leave her shoulders. He was so unpredictable, and, in some ways, a little scary.

She opened the second drawer to the third filing cabinet, eager to find the file she wanted and then to get off home, when she was met with resistance. She tugged a little harder, but something was jamming it. Searching for a pen or an envelope opener was hard because this wasn't a working office. It was only used for storage. Looking to her right, she spied a set of drawers visible from the edge of the desk. She hurriedly opened the top drawer and grinned when she clocked the bottle of Scotch, a few paperclips, a ball of elastic bands, and a hole puncher. When she opened the second drawer, she found a letter addressed to Steve Elison. It was old and faded, but it was unsealed. Holding the letter, she listened for any sound that suggested he was coming up the staircase. There was nothing but silence. She slowly removed the letter from the envelope, knowing this was not a good thing to do. The note was handwritten and quite beautifully scribed.

To my forever Stevie,

I hope you know how much you broke my heart the day you said we were done. But I know you didn't really mean it. One day, you will see how much I love you. I will make a home for us while you work hard to reach the top. I know what I have to do, and one day, when I build up the courage, I will do it, and we will be together again.

I love you, Stevie, and I always will.

Forever yours

Noting the fact that the letter wasn't signed, Dixie-Lee turned it over to see if the sender had put their name on the back, but they hadn't. Popping the letter back into the envelope, she then returned it to its spot beside the hole puncher before she continued searching for an instrument to help her open the filing cabinet drawer.

After she exhausted her search for a useful implement, she pulled her phone from her bag and texted her mother to let her know she would be late home and not to worry. Just as she replaced her phone in her bag, the door opened, and with two cartons of drinks in his hands and a bag gripped between his teeth, Steve barged in.

She hurried to relieve him of one of the coffees. Then she watched as he emptied the contents of the bag onto the table. He had bought sandwiches, doughnuts, and bananas.

'Help yourself,' he said, while snatching the beef sandwich and taking a massive bite as if he was starving.

'Filing cabinet three, second drawer down is jammed.'

With a full mouth, he mumbled, 'Bingo.'

His briefcase was on the table, and he dived in and pulled out a screwdriver, compelling Dixie-Lee to raise a questioning eyebrow before she chuckled. 'I guess that comes in handy.'

His expression took Dixie-Lee by surprise; his whole face was smiling, and she noticed that he was quite good looking for an older man. And she was not shocked now that someone had referred to him as *forever Stevie*.

Dropping the remains of the beef sandwich onto the desk, Steve dug the screwdriver into the tiny gap and levered the drawer open with brute force. The file that was jammed ended up falling down the back of the drawer. He instantly opened the bottom drawer and pulled it completely out to retrieve the file that had caused the jam, and there, sure enough, was the name 'Malloye'.

He slapped the file down on the desk, grabbed his sandwich, and again ate it as though he was starving, but then he stopped midway when he read the first sheet of paper and then the second before frantically searching the entire file. 'Bollocks!' he said, as he turned back to the filing cabinet, removed each folder, and checked inside, before, finally, he threw the last file up in the air. 'This is someone else's. The actual file has to be back at the office, probably filed under Mercstone and Amble.'

'How do you know?' Dixie-Lee asked, before taking a swig of the coffee.

'Because the file with the Malloye name on it was inside the Mercstone and Amble file. And that was moved to the new office because the case was reopened with fresh evidence. Bollocks!'

'May I ask why the Malloye file is so important?'

Steve sighed and drank his coffee to wash down the sandwich now lodged in his throat. 'Fucking indigestion! Right, the file contains Tommy Malloye's last will and testament and a key code to a safe deposit box. He was a very rich man. Obviously, the file was important because he insisted I kept everything safe – hence here is where we keep our archives, away from the chambers. Although I am not sure I have managed to do that. The fucking file isn't here. That damn secretary.' He stared at her. 'You have no idea how dangerous these Malloyes are, do you?'

She shook her head. 'No, not at all.'

'Like I said, they are well known, an Irish family who live in London and Ireland. I've known them to get away literally with murder, and, again, if they believe Tommy's wife killed him, they will come for whoever is representing her. And as it just so happens, Newbie, they haven't asked me to defend her. Now, that is strange. If they wanted her out, believe me, they would get her out. So it tells me either they want her inside, or they have no idea she has asked for our help – and via that drip Clifford. Sorry, Newbie, no disrespect to your twaddle . . . I mean theory on it regarding the solicitor sucking up to the judge.'

Dixie-Lee shook her head. 'Oh gosh, don't worry about that. It's all so intriguing. So what now? Do we go back to the office?'

He raised the blind again. 'It's looking pretty dark outside. I think we need to pay Mrs Malloye a visit at the station.'

Shocked but excited, Dixie-Lee grinned. 'You mean me? Am I going with you?'

Steve rolled his eyes. 'I suppose so. Actually, yes, I need you to do some acting for me. If any of the Malloyes are watching the station, they won't think we're there to see Bianca. They will think I'm accompanying you to report a theft.' He looked her up and down. 'You don't look like a lawyer. Yet. You will look like my daughter, who has just had her handbag nicked and was at the station to report the incident.'

They finished their coffees, and Dixie-Lee scoffed down the cheese and ham sandwich, followed by a banana because she was so hungry, and she had no idea when she would eat next. Still, the evening was becoming exciting, and it was also nothing how she imagined the life of a barrister to be.

Just as Dixie-Lee was putting on her mac and her hat, Steve's phone went off. He had a strange birdy ringtone, and yet she'd heard his phone ring before, and that one was a straightforward bog-standard tune.

He stared at the phone. 'Fucking moron, calling me now.' He shook his head before answering the call. 'Yes.'

'Steve, Clifford here. I have just been informed by Cathy that you will be overseeing the Malloye case. Well, just to let you know, her solicitor has been involved in a car incident. I'm not sure of all the details, but he was run over and his secretary Janey called me to let me know. I was supposed to have a meeting with him tomorrow. Anyway, I am going to meet with Bianca Malloye later this evening. I think, in this case, two's a crowd, so I'll fill you in first thing in the morning.'

'Clifford, before you make another huge cock-up, do *not* go and visit Mrs Malloye. You weren't supposed to take the case on, and I have no idea why you seem to think you are qualified. How many sodding clients have you represented in a murder trial?'

'Well, I, er . . .Well, I have to start somewhere, so . . .'

'So you think you are equipped to take on the Malloyes, do you?'

There was silence as Dixie-Lee listened for an answer.

‘I thought not. Now *I* will pay Bianca a visit at the station, and *you*, Clifford, will wait for my instruction in the morning. Got it, sunshine?’

‘Now hold on a minute, Steve. I have been assigned the case and—’

‘No, you were *not* assigned the case. There was obviously a mix-up, and no way, not in a million years, would Natalia assign you that case, so I think we both have a pretty good idea, don’t we, Clifford, who did.’

‘Whatever the path the case took to be in my hands doesn’t matter. Steve, I—’

‘It absolutely *does* matter. You bloody well assigned yourself. As your senior, you will listen and listen well. The Malloyes are worse than the Colombian cartel, so if you want to keep your hands attached to your wrists, then leave Bianca to me for now.’

‘Steve, are you threatening me?’

‘Oh, grow up, Clifford. I wasn’t threatening you. I was warning you about how dangerous the Malloye family are. Jesus Christ, if I gave you one brain cell to match the other, you’d be bloody dangerous.’

‘All right, all right, er . . . is Newbie with you?’

‘Yes, Clifford, why?’

‘Shouldn’t it be me?’ he asked nervously. ‘I mean, really, she is not much above admin, so I can’t see why she is shadowing you.’

‘Clifford, fuck off.’

Clifford didn’t argue back. He ended the call.

‘Prick!’

‘So are we to meet Bianca tonight?’

‘Yes.’ He looked at her oversized bag. ‘I hope you have a notebook in there.’

‘I do, of course.’

'Great because when we get to the station, like I said, I want you to go in like a kid and look like you are reporting a theft. I'll be empty-handed, and I'll try my best not to look like a lawyer of any kind. We lawyers tend to stick out like sore thumbs, you see, and I really do not want to risk any of the Malloyes seeing us. Tommy's dead, and I don't think the others would recognise me, but I need to be careful. I am concerned because it wouldn't surprise me if they have already got to the solicitor. It could be a coincidence, but I don't believe in those.'

Just as they were about to leave, Steve scooted back to the drawers under the desk and snatched the bottle of Scotch and the letter.

Dixie-Lee watched him shove the letter inside his suit jacket before he glanced her way and narrowed his eyes. She looked away before he could sense her guilt.

'Right, come on, then. Let's see the black widow.'

'Do you think she killed him?' asked Dixie-Lee, excitedly.

He paused and gripped her shoulder. 'Listen to me, this may seem exhilarating to you, but I need you to understand that I am dropping you in at the deep end. Hopefully, your uncles won't have my guts for garters.'

'No! They understand this is my work now.'

'They also know who the Malloyes are.'

'You said I am mollycoddled. Well, I might not want my mum to worry but this is my life and my career. Only I can make the choice, and, furthermore, I'm not a fragile teenager with fancy ideas, you know. I've, well, you know I've killed a man!' She quickly added, 'In self-defence. But, anyway, I just wanted you to understand how serious I am about this job.'

He opened the door for her, and as they headed out onto the external staircase, he squeezed her arm. 'I know you are. I just hope I'm not putting you in harm's way.'

‘My choice, Steve.’

‘Hmm, yes, but if you get caught in any crossfire, firstly I’d live with never-ending feelings of guilt, and secondly, your uncles will probably string me up. Both outcomes would be awful.’

‘Whoever helps you, Steve, could be caught in the crossfire, so why not me?’

He chewed the inside of his bottom lip and pondered for a second before he shut the door and hurried around to the driver’s side.

‘Let’s do this, Newbie,’ he said, as he gunned the engine.

CHAPTER SIX

'Where is Bianca Malloye being held?' asked Dixie-Lee.

'Bromley Police Station.'

'That's near where I live, and, sadly, I know that police station only too well.'

'Yes, I know you do, Newbie. As you will be aware, I obviously carried out a background check on you. And you would have been familiar with the station because you live within the area, just like Bianca does. She lives in Leaves Green, in Keston.'

'A rich area, then,' said Dixie-Lee. Guessing Bianca was from new money – it appeared she was another one who had benefited from ill-gotten gains – she thought for a second or two before she looked over at Steve.

'So, do we have any more information on the murder other than Bianca being in the frame?'

'Nope, nothing. But since her drippy solicitor engaged our services, I have the right to go in and speak with her to find out what the hell has gone on.' He huffed. 'We really shouldn't be taking this on, you know. Damn! I wished we had a choice.'

There was an awkward silence, and Dixie-Lee felt the urge to fill it. 'Do you have any hobbies, Steve, like golf or scuba diving?' She assumed lawyers, bankers, and businessmen played golf.

'See what you did there, Newbie? You asked a question and then offered answers. Don't do that, okay? You have one mouth and two ears. Use them in that proportion. With anyone, be it the client or a witness, you should ask an open question, but then you need to remain silent while you wait for them to answer.'

'I understand, thank you. So, do you have a hobby?'

'Newbie, you know everything I want you to know about me.'

'Okay, sorry, I was trying to get to know you, that's all.'

'Well, don't. We're not friends. You work with us, and that's it.'

The man's rudeness raised Dixie-Lee's heckles. 'Okay, fair enough. But it seems to me you know a lot about me. Don't you think that's a bit one-sided?'

'One-sided? Seriously? Newbie, you work for me. I don't work for you, so, like I said, you know everything about me that I want you to know.'

'Sorry, I just . . . well, sorry,' she replied.

Dixie-Lee looked out of the side window, now annoyed with herself for being far too presumptuous and naïve. That said, she had already done her homework on him. So she wasn't in the dark. She knew he had been a solicitor and had owned his own firm for many years before he became a barrister. So the man was a hot shot. She couldn't imagine anyone getting one over on him. He won far more cases than he lost, and there were waiting lists for his services. He had been described as not your typical barrister type with a plum in his mouth and an air of entitlement. She could see he was a man of mystery and it appeared he had little time for unnecessary niceties.

'Tell me, why did you say scuba diving?'

'In your office there is a photograph of a sea turtle. I assumed that a picture taking pride of place on your desk meant that you took it yourself, and, clearly, it was underwater, so I kinda guessed that you liked scuba diving.'

'And you never thought, perhaps, I liked photography?'

'Maybe, but your office has just the one photograph, so I thought you were showing the beauty of the turtle.'

Unexpectedly, he laughed. 'Yes, well, okay, you're right. I like scuba diving, and as it so happens, I spent some time in the water with that turtle before I photographed her. It was a memorial trip, so that's why I have the photo in my office.'

Dixie-Lee smiled to herself; at last, she was getting to know the man behind the steel façade.

'You have a good eye for detail and an interesting method of qualifying a situation.'

She didn't know if that was a compliment or not; she would be shocked if it was. 'I also saw your key ring and the fish. I mean, who has a fish unless it means something.'

Pulling up in a side road, Steve popped the boot. 'Time for a wardrobe change,' he said, before he reappeared, having removed his jacket and tie and replaced it with a leather bomber jacket and a scarf.

Dixie-Lee exited the car and smiled. 'You definitely don't look like a lawyer now.'

'Good, that's the plan. I don't want any of the Malloyes noticing me.'

He stopped talking and pulled out his phone. 'I need to get straight into the interview room. No hanging around,' he said, before whoever he called answered. 'Ah, hello, Fitzgerald, it's me, Steve Elison.'

Dixie-Lee could just about follow the conversation and she knew who was at the other end of the call. She was aware of who Fitzgerald was, and she recognised his deep husky but sharp voice.

'I take it your firm will be representing Bianca Malloye? I, um, just heard that her solicitor was mowed down. So the Malloyes are up to their tricks again, are they?'

'Seems that way, Fitz. Anyway I'm coming in with my assistant Dixie-Lee Deacon. You know her, I believe.'

'Of course I know her. But is that a good idea, Steve? I mean, her uncles are built like brick shithouses, and if anything happens to her, they'll come for you.'

‘Never mind that. If the Malloyes are watching the station, I need to appear as if I’m her dad reporting a theft or something. I’ll be at the station in ten minutes. Could you have everything ready for me?’

‘Yes, sure. Rajesh Raj is our best guy, and Dixie-Lee knows him. He’s in charge of the case. A right bloody mess it is too. I’ll have Raj on standby, ready for you.’

‘Great. I wish that bloody moron of ours – Clifford Jenson-Baine – hadn’t taken the case. I mean, the drip couldn’t handle anything this big.’

‘You don’t mean the judge’s son, do you?’

‘Yes, I do. Anyway, how is the solicitor? Is he alive or . . .?’

‘Barely, but I’ll keep you updated. Maybe Hugh should be taking over. The woman has to be represented, and I don’t fancy assigning a duty solicitor.’

‘No, I’ll speak with Hugh about it, but, for now, I just need to get the facts from her before we decide what to do.’

‘Good luck with that.’

Steve ended the call and rubbed his cold hands together.

‘I’m going to put my arm around you.’

‘Sure,’ she replied, surprised he’d even asked.

They walked casually along the side road, then onto the high street and into the police station.

The entrance and waiting area were quiet, with only a few drunks and a snooty woman demanding to speak to the chief superintendent. Dixie-Lee took a seat and watched as Steve approached the desk and then pointed to her. As he did so, she clocked a menacing-looking young man strolling into the station. He was big built with cropped fair hair and brown bags under his eyes. He licked his lips, flared his nostrils, and glanced her way.

‘Dad?’ she called out, really getting into her role.

Steve looked over his shoulder. 'We won't be long, sweetheart. I think one of the detectives will be taking a statement very soon.'

Dixie-Lee nodded and pulled her hat over her ears before she looked back at the man, who hovered only momentarily in the doorway, before he left.

Raj appeared from a side room and acted as if he didn't recognise her, which was best considering the circumstances. Inside, she was feeling quite exhilarated by the whole process.

'Follow me. This way, sir, madam,' said Raj.

With that, Dixie-Lee leaped up from her seat and swiftly followed Steve and Raj through the door and into a corridor. She looked back to ensure no one could see them.

'We haven't met before. I'm Detective Sergeant Rajesh Raj,' he said, eager to shake Steve's hand. 'And I know this one. Hello, trouble, how are you doing?'

'I'm good, Raj. I'm working with Mr Elison from McGowan and Elison.'

With his hands on his hips and his face beaming, Raj said, 'Hugh told me. I'm thrilled for you, Dixie-Lee. We all know you're gonna make a great barrister.' He looked back at Steve for a reassuring nod but there was no response at all from him.

'Raj, is Bianca Malloye ready to be interviewed?'

'Oh yeah, sure. Would you like a coffee, tea?' He peered down at Steve's hands, noticing that he didn't have a briefcase. 'Pen and paper?'

'I had to come empty-handed. I didn't want to look remotely like a lawyer. Best to be careful, considering we're dealing with the Malloyes.'

Raj nodded. 'Yes, for sure. So would you like a drink? I was going to get Mrs Malloye one.'

Steve nodded. 'Two white coffees, no sugar, thank you.'

They reached the interview room and then Raj left them to arrange the refreshments.

Steve turned to Dixie-Lee. 'Good piece of acting, but now . . .' He paused and sucked air in through his teeth. 'I want you to watch her as I ask the questions. I need you to be the other half of my brain.'

Dixie-Lee could only guess what he meant. 'I'll observe and write notes. Got it.'

'You notice tiny details, and I think you are good at it.'

He looked at his key ring and the contemporary piece of art. No one else would have guessed that the moulded pieces of metal were triggerfish, a reminder that as pretty as something looks, it can still kill someone if it bites them and in the most vulnerable spot too. He felt a tingle shoot down his leg.

'Oh, and don't underestimate her. What I mean by that is don't judge a book by its cover.'

Dixie-Lee removed her hat and shook her hair. 'I never do, Steve. I not only learn from my mistakes but from my mother's as well.'

Steve nodded and looked her up and down again, biting his lip. 'You know, you are proving me wrong at every turn.'

'Is that a good thing?'

'Yeah, I think you'll be an asset to the firm. Well, let's see how you do this evening.'

Dixie-Lee would have loved to have jumped up and down and clapped her hands, but she was too old for that, so she did it mentally instead.

Moments later, while Steve and Dixie-Lee were waiting outside the interview room, Raj returned with a tray of drinks including an array of biscuits. Raj nodded for Steve to hold the door open.

Knowing Raj from past experience, Dixie-Lee wasn't at all surprised by his hospitality. Raj was one of the good guys.

As the three of them entered the interview room, Dixie-Lee cast her eyes on an officer guarding a woman. On one side of the room was a glass wall, which told Dixie-Lee that this was one of those interview rooms where suspects could be monitored by officers from outside. The wall was in effect a two-way mirror. As soon as she was familiar with her surroundings, Dixie-Lee looked at the woman. From what Steve had told her on the way over, she seemed like a gangster's moll.

Steve's words: 'Don't judge a book by its cover' rang in Dixie-Lee's ears. Because judging by her looks, she certainly was striking.

Bianca was not a woman to blend into the crowd. Far from it. Dressed in a black satin blouse that showed enough cleavage to see she had undergone a boob job, she was more than likely to stop traffic whichever street she was walking down. Her skin was tight and tanned. Her perfect nails, long and a deep red, were clearly not her own.

Dixie-Lee wondered if her hair was even her own. It could be extensions, professionally applied. It was jet black, dead straight, and hung over her shoulders like a satin curtain. Her lips were filled to the maximum, but, weirdly, they suited her, and her skin was so taut that there was no doubt in her mind that Bianca had had Botox treatment. So, she concluded that Bianca was eager to look good and remain young.

It was hard to judge her age, but Dixie-Lee assumed she was at least forty and so she'd had years to build up that level of confidence or arrogance. What was missing was the expensive jewellery, the gold watch, and bangles, but they would have been removed while she was in custody.

'Steve, it's a relief to see you.'

They knew each other! But that really didn't surprise Dixie-Lee. However, the way in which she smiled and tilted her head coyly told her that Bianca's relationship with Steve was more than just a business one.

But what seemed more interesting was how Steve deliberately pulled his chair a foot away from the table to sit down, as if he could die by her touch. He was silent as he sat heavily before removing his scarf. Ignoring her, he sipped his coffee while he stared at her.

Raj nodded to the officer and they left the room.

The moment the door closed behind them, Dixie-Lee pulled a chair, which was against the wall, over to the table and sat down. She carefully positioned the chair next to Steve's so that she could watch the conversation play out like a game of tennis. After removing a notebook from her bag, she held her pen at the ready.

Bianca gave Dixie-Lee a contemptuous grin as she turned to face her. 'So, Steve, who is this?' Her long red fingernail pointed disapprovingly at Dixie-Lee.

Saving Steve the trouble of replying, Dixie-Lee replied, 'I'm a trainee legal executive at McGowan and Elison. My name is Dixie-Lee Deacon. I'm pleased to meet you. So I'm here to take notes,' she said, extending her hand. But by the look on Bianca's face, she knew her offer to shake hands wouldn't be taken up.

Right on cue, Bianca ignored the gesture and looked back at Steve. 'Are you serious? Christ, Steve? She's a fucking kid?' She peered up at the clock. 'And a trainee, yeah? Well, she's working a little late for a trainee.'

Dixie-Lee watched Steve smirk. It was as if they were playing a game. Either that or she was one jealous bitch.

Steve sipped his coffee, not saying a word, which clearly irritated Bianca because her cheeks reddened ever so slightly and her lips twitched.

‘Why did you get your solicitor, Bernstein, to contact us? And do you know he has been run over and is lying in a hospital bed fighting for his life?’

Bianca nodded. ‘Of course, I know. Detective Sergeant Raj told me. But let’s speak about Tommy. As the accused, I have the right to legal counsel. I should think Hugh Shields may take over, since most of his work goes to your firm.’

Steve shook his head. ‘Really? So why didn’t you ask for Shields before asking that dipstick Clifford?’

‘Shields would have played the *far too busy card.* I’m not stupid. But now your firm is representing me, it’s only right that Shields acts as my solicitor.’

‘Doesn’t it bother you that your solicitor has been run over?’

‘So I’m a heartless bitch. Is that right, Steve? Is that what you’re suggesting?’

‘Maybe. Anyway, did you kill Tommy?’

‘See, you haven’t lost your solicitor’s touch. Straight to the fucking point. Did I kill Tommy? You tell me, Steve. Do you think I’m capable?’

Dixie-Lee was shocked when he looked her way to answer the question. She straightened up and coughed. ‘Anyone is capable of killing someone. It’s under what circumstances that matters. Was it an accident, self-defence, or did you just want to kill him because he was a prick?’

Bianca glared with her eyebrows arching as if Dixie-Lee was insulting her. ‘Don’t you dare question me. You’re just a kid. And this, darling, is a grown-ups’ meeting, so why don’t you take your coffee and fuck off.’

Dixie-Lee stood up. ‘With pleasure, Mrs Malloye. I’m here at Steve’s request to help, but I’ll be honest – you may be older than me, in fact, more my mother’s age, but you’re not my mother, and I don’t deserve to be spoken to like that, and so, yep, I’ll fuck off.’

Unexpectedly, Steve chuckled. 'Well, Bianca, you have just managed to piss off my protégée.'

'Protégée?' she snarled, looking Dixie-Lee up and down as though she was scum. 'Steve, Tommy is dead, and I'm in the frame for his murder, and you come here with a bit of a kid as if this case only warrants the skills of a youngster on work experience.'

'You can always sack us and use another chambers.' He held up his hands. 'I would gladly allow it because the truth is, Bianca, representing you is going to be a fucking nightmare for the reason you already know.'

Bianca looked the girl up and down again, minus the snarl. 'What makes *her* so special?'

'Dixie-Lee Deacon has got an eye for detail, something your barrister Clifford lacks.' He watched her smile. 'You knew I didn't like Clifford, didn't you? You did your homework, and that's how you got me here because I can't have that moron fuck up my firm, that you' – he viciously pointed in her face – 'know I worked hard to build.'

Her face softened, and even her voice changed. 'Stevie, I didn't kill Tommy. As much as he was a bully, I didn't kill him. I walked in, and he was on the floor with a knife wound to his chest, and as you can imagine, my first reaction was to see if he was dead. I got on my knees and grabbed his shoulders trying to get him to answer me while I was screaming his name. He let out a gasp, but it might have been his final breath. Who knows . . .' She stopped and covered her face with her hands, and then, when she removed them, there were tears in her eyes. 'It was awful after I called the police. They came and carted me away, so here I am.'

Steve shook his head. 'I didn't ask for an account. I asked if you killed him.'

'No, I didn't kill him.'

'You don't look covered in blood. If you went over to him and grabbed his shoulders like you said you did, there would be claret all over you.'

She shot him a look of spite. 'You sound like that detective. FYI, I got changed before they arrived. I couldn't stand being drenched in his blood.'

'Where was the weapon?' Dixie-Lee asked, but as soon as she did so, she froze when she realised she was going beyond her remit. *But strangely*, she thought, *Steve didn't seem the slightest bit concerned by her question.*

'I don't fucking know. The person who killed my husband probably ran off with it. And my money is on Tyler, his son.'

Dixie-Lee nodded. 'But if there is no weapon, what exactly do they have on you?'

Rolling her eyes, Bianca bit her bottom lip.

'Bianca, why do they think it was you?'

'Because the lucky bastard had won the fucking lottery. I mean, he had a lot of money, and he had already started divorce proceedings.'

Steve suddenly sat up straight, and Dixie-Lee clocked the blood drain from his face. 'Why?'

She raised an eyebrow. 'Why do you think?'

Dixie-Lee was not only watching Bianca's body language but Steve's too. This was much more complicated than she'd imagined, and she wasn't sure if her being here was appropriate.

'Stevie, you still have the instructions, don't you, if Tommy ever died? Tell me, did he update them recently?'

Steve combed his hair with his fingers. 'I can't tell you that, Bianca. You know I can't. But I can guarantee your family will be after what he has. And the will is to be opened when he dies, regardless of the circumstances.'

'Well, he is dead, and I am technically still his next of kin.'

Jumping up from the chair, Steve growled, 'Tell me, did you know what was contained in that file?'

'I heard him telling someone on the phone. So I know he had money and his bleedin' diamonds are stashed away in a safe deposit box somewhere and he left the key code and details, which are in that file.'

'Did you inform Bernstein what you thought was in Tommy's file?'

It was Bianca's turn to look uneasy. Dixie-Lee saw her swallow before she slowly nodded and bit her lip again. 'Is that a problem, Steve?'

'Yes, you stupid woman. Of course, it's a bloody problem. If Bernstein informed Clifford about the value of that file, then I can guarantee the idiot will be at the old office searching for it as we speak. He knows that my files *especially* are kept there. He is a walking disaster. If Clifford has an inkling that the content of the file is worth a fortune, he could well be tempted to get his hands on it himself.'

Bianca's eyes widened. 'What? But he is the son of a judge. And he's a barrister.'

'What he is, Bianca, is not only a sly, greedy, useless pain in the arse but he's also a fucking liability! A waste of space who should have been put down at birth.'

'So, it's true, then. The file does contain Tommy's last will and testament and the key code to the safe deposit box. Er . . . does the deposit box contain his diamonds?'

Steve threw his hands in the air. 'You don't give up, do you? I don't *bloody know* what is in the box but evidently it is valuable enough for him to keep the key code to it at our chambers.'

He turned to Dixie-Lee and lowered his tone. 'It's late, but if I give you the keys, will you return to the basement at the chambers? You know where the file will be, don't you?'

Dixie-Lee took the office keys and nodded. 'Yes, under . . .' She decided not to repeat the name but smiled instead. 'Yes, I do.'

'Are you okay to do that? It's already nine o'clock.'

'It's fine. The station is virtually next door, and a train will get me into London in under an hour. I'll call you once I have the file.'

'Get a cab, a black cab, back to here. I think I should open the file in front of the detective.'

Bianca rolled her eyes again. 'For fuck's sake, couldn't you just let me see it? Technically, it's mine now, isn't it?'

'You know what, Bianca, sometimes I think you are an intelligent woman, and at other times I think the hamster's fallen off the wheel.'

Her fiery copper eyes snapped. 'You are a bitter man, Steve.'

'Am I, and . . .? You listen to me, Bianca Malloye. Whatever I am, it makes no difference to your case. Just so we understand each other.'

Dixie-Lee managed to catch the last few words before she closed the door on her way out of the interview room.

'Stevie, please understand—'

'Oh, Mrs Malloye, I understand perfectly.'

CHAPTER SEVEN

Dixie-Lee left before she could even say goodbye to Raj. She only had a few minutes to catch the train, so she ran down the stairs to the platform at a speed of knots just before the doors closed. Although she had never been on a train so late at night going towards London, she was, nevertheless, surprised at how empty it was. The whole experience was eerie and somewhat scary. Regardless of her own paranoia, though, she had to concentrate on the job at hand and prove her worth. It was all becoming very exciting, and this was her opportunity to make a name for herself.

Charing Cross railway station was hustling and bustling with late-night workers rushing to get home and the odd drunk begging for spare change. Dotted about in recesses or shop doorways, the homeless, who were trying to sleep in their makeshift beds, shivered from the bitter cold. She wanted to give them some notes she kept in case of emergencies, but she had to get to the chambers first and then back to the police station.

As she turned into the street leading to the McGowan and Elison chambers, Dixie-Lee paused only for a moment. The road was not well lit, so she could not see who lurked in the doorways. Pulling her hat below her ears, she marched on ahead and tried not to look at the dark shadows. Of course, she kept her head up high to maintain a confident posture. It was something her mother had taught her to do, among many other things. *Never look weak.*

When she reached the premises, she noticed the lights were on. She was curious to know if this was always the case. What puzzled her, though, was the fact that the door was unlocked. A momentary feeling of dread whipped through her like an electric shock.

Holding her breath, she listened for any sound. The thought of the Malloyes inside rummaging around compelled her to reconsider entering the building. But perhaps someone had left the door unlocked by mistake. She recalled earlier in the day that everyone seemed to be in a panic and she now knew that was because Tommy Malloye was dead and he had been a client at the firm. So someone could easily have left the front door unlocked or maybe one of the cleaners had. After taking a few deep breaths, she decided she would head to the basement. She knew it would only take five minutes to locate the file; it would be filed under Mercstone and Amble.

Placing her bag, her mac, and her hat on the reception desk, she thought for a moment that she could hear someone in the offices upstairs. She hurried down the staircase to the room she had spent most of the last two days in. The moment she turned the light on, she froze on the spot. There were files strewn all over the floor, the filing cabinet drawers were open, and it was clear that the place had been ransacked. Her first thought was that it was someone from the Malloye family who had been in here. From everyone's reactions, they were evidently very dangerous people, so if she stuck around and they saw her face, or, more to the point, she saw theirs, she figured there was a good chance they would kill her.

With her mind now running in all directions at once, a voice behind her said, 'And what the hell are you doing here?'

The sudden relief on hearing Clifford's voice put a huge smile on her face before she spun around to greet him.

Nonetheless, when she faced him, her relief was replaced with concern. He looked different. With his shirt undone to his chest, he appeared less than daisy fresh. In fact, he stank of booze and body odour, and as he stepped closer, she could smell traces of cigarette smoke on him.

'I left something behind, so I came back for it,' she replied nervously, sensing his predatory stance.

'Liar!'

'*What?*' she replied, as she stepped back. He was too close, and his expression wasn't friendly.

Licking his lips and looking her up and down, Clifford hissed, 'Steve's tart, no doubt. Well, join the queue. You won't be the first, and you won't be the last.'

'*Tart?* I'm not anything like that. I'm here to work.'

'Sleep your way to the top, you mean. Because with an accent like yours, who will take you seriously, eh? I know your game, Newbie. Sucking cock to get to the top.'

'*How dare you!*' she snapped back, hoping he would back off. But when he stepped closer, and before she could get around him, he gripped her shoulders, forcing her against the wall.

'I bet he's already been inside your knickers, hasn't he? Admit it!' he hissed, exhaling his hot stinking breath in her face. The foul smell of his dry tongue mixed with garlic and fish made her turn her face to the side.

As his lecherous glaring eyes drilled into her, he used one hand to hold her in place while he ripped open her blouse with the other. For a second, she couldn't move; fear had paralysed her. But when he thrust his hand up inside her skirt, pulling her knickers away viciously and grabbing her between her legs, Dixie-Lee turned from an angelic young, graceful woman to a beast that foamed at the mouth.

He knew he had made a mistake as soon as she launched into attack mode. And when he caught sight of her expression, he was thrown back to the past when his older brother made him watch *The Exorcist.* This girl was fighting him with such fury, she was like a volcano suddenly erupting.

The first assault was the headbutt. She caught him precisely across the bridge of his beaked nose. He barely had time to feel the pain before she clawed at his face and caught the corners of his eyes. He staggered back, totally aghast that this sweet girl could be so vicious.

But there was no way that this stupid tart was going to hurt him. She would be done for assault, and he knew that his father would see to it that she would be behind bars, and that would leave Steve Elison, the man who everyone aspired to be, questioning his own sanity. Seeing egg on Elison's face would be the icing on the cake for him.

Surged on by combating his own humiliation, he lunged forward and brought his fist back and punched her in the side of her face. The force knocked her to the ground, and before she could get up by herself, he kicked her in the ribs. 'You dirty whore,' he spat, as he held his bleeding nose, before he reached down, grabbed her by the collar of her blouse, and tried to lift her up. However, he wasn't as strong as he thought he was. When she grabbed his arm and sank her teeth into it, he was horrified.

Now gasping in agony, he ripped at her hair for her to let go, but she wouldn't. Her eyes were red with rage. She bit deeper, making him scream like a child.

Her mother's words went around in her mind. *Use everything you have, no matter how animalistic it seems.* And right now, she was like a rabid dog tearing into his flesh.

Too late, Clifford realised that he had taken on a girl who was even more strong-willed than himself. It compelled him to punch her in the face once more to stop her, but that just made her sink her teeth in even deeper.

'Get the fuck off me, you biiiitttch!' he screamed, before he suddenly felt an unforgiving and excruciating pain. She had kicked him between the legs so hard that his eyes couldn't focus. The pain was now curling from his stomach up to his spine.

As she unclenched her mouth, she watched him double over in agony and fall to the floor, rolling around as though he was on fire. Desperate to escape, she attempted to crawl away from him, but even though he was in agony, he still managed to grab her hair and pull her back. She punched and scratched him, but he was on to her, his stinking breath almost suffocating her. But his mistake was that he came too close.

She grabbed his ears, and in a flash, she pulled his left cheek to her mouth and bit him again. Her jaw locked tight this time, and she savagely tore a chunk of skin and flesh from his face.

He sat up, still straddling her. With one hand clutching his cheek, his eyes widened when he saw the amount of blood pouring off his face. Then he watched as she spat out his flesh. Seeing this slip of a girl doing this made him scream so loudly that if anyone was in the building, they would surely have come to the rescue.

Dixie-Lee knew he was weak from the pain, and she pushed him off her.

He fell to the side and began vomiting, coughing, retching, and then throwing up.

She could hear him choking as she got to her feet. She then discovered that in the fight, he'd ripped her skirt up to her crotch. Her face throbbed like hell. And all she could taste was his blood. But on the floor right by him was the file. The label read: Tommy Malloye. The thought in her head told her to take it. But she didn't. She was so terrified he would catch her, she tore up the stairs into the foyer, grabbed just her bag, and headed for the exit door.

But once she was out of the building and hurtling along the street towards the station, she could hear footsteps behind her. So he was catching her up, was he? She was so frightened, she couldn't even scream. She had to reserve all her energy to escape the moron, the monster, the potential rapist. As her brooch hit the pavement, she heard the clanging sound, but she couldn't bend down to pick it up. She had to get away. Out of breath and feeling sick, she soon realised she had outrun him and briefly turned back to check. All she saw was a man running back towards the offices, but it wasn't Clifford; this was a younger man with broad shoulders, but he was too far away to get a proper look at him.

***

With her stomach hurting, and her lungs feeling as though they were burning from all that running, she knew her body couldn't take this punishment for much longer. Spotting an alleyway between two buildings further along, she stopped and leaned against the wall to take a deep breath to slow her racing heart. With her hands shaking uncontrollably, she searched for her phone. She had to call someone, but who? Steve? Her mum? Or the police? She fumbled around inside her bag before tipping it upside down. Her phone was missing. But so was her purse. *Where the hell were they? Her bag was always zipped up. Who had taken them?* She wondered if that moron Clifford had rifled through her bag before he came into the basement. Then her mind switched to the state of the room that had been ransacked. What were the perpetrators looking for? And who had done it? The most likely culprit, she suspected, was Clifford. After all, he hadn't accused her and hadn't acted surprised. And that file with Tommy Malloye's name on it was there by Clifford's side.

Her whole body was now shaking, not just her hands. She slid down the wall and hugged herself tight while her teeth chattered so hard, she believed they would break unless she could stop them. Now her hands and feet were turning to ice, and her throat closed up. She gasped and gasped as if she couldn't breathe. A million thoughts stampeded through her brain. Had she been poisoned? Was this shock? Was she going to die?

‘All right, love, wanna earn a score for a quick blow job?’

As Dixie-Lee looked up, she saw two men, possibly in their thirties, who’d clearly had a skinful.

‘Fuck off!’ she yelled, not thinking straight.

‘Aw, come on, girl. Look, I’ll give you a fifty-pound note,’ said the man, his face red from the cold and his pure white teeth glinting in the moonlight.

‘Fuck off, I’m no prostitute,’ she said.

‘You could have fooled me,’ said the man, as he unzipped his flies. ‘’Ere, go on, earn yourself a wage for the night.’

The other grabbed his arm. ‘Come on, Giles, leave the girl alone. She looks like the last punter’s got his money’s worth.’

‘Get off, Geoffrey,’ growled the red-faced man, pulling his arm away. To make the point he was angry, Giles began urinating over Dixie-Lee.

‘You bastard!’ she squawked, before jumping up and lashing out by fly-kicking him in the chest.

In his drunken state, he fell back and off the kerb, soaking himself in his own urine.

Snatching her bag, Dixie-Lee legged it up the road. Once she was out of their reach, she stopped in front of a shop window. Her reflection gave her the fright of her life. Her hair was sticking out in all directions, her blouse was torn and covered in blood, her jacket pocket was hanging by a thread, and she was missing a shoe. And worse, her skirt was ripped so badly that her underwear was on show. The blood on her cheeks and around her mouth looked like dirt. No wonder those men assumed she was a streetwalker.

There was no way she could walk around looking the way she did. The fear of another man touching her made her blood run cold, leaving her with a tightening feeling in her throat. Crouching down in a doorway, she hoped no one could see her. She needed a moment to think straight. Without her phone and purse she was up shit creek. There was only one thing for it: she would have to head to the railway station and chance her luck in finding a taxi driver to take her home. Mentally, she would have to ignore how she looked and just go for it, or she would be alone in London and freeze to death in the depths of winter. Turning her skirt so the slit was now at the side and not showing off her knickers, she tied her blouse in a knot at the front and ripped the pocket completely off her jacket. She smoothed her hair and wiped the tears from her eyes because feeling sorry for herself wouldn't get her home.

Holding one shoe in her hand, she hurried towards the station where she was relieved to see a few black taxis lined up awaiting their next fares.

Running to the first taxi she came across, Dixie-Lee tapped on the window.

The driver, who was reading a newspaper, quickly folded it up. He stared at her for a moment before he sighed. 'I want the money upfront, and you'd better not be sick in my cab.'

'Please, I'm not drunk. I've been attacked. I need to get home to Bromley, Kent.'

'Oh, hold up, love, that's quite a way. You could catch the last train, though. It will be so much cheaper 'cos I will charge you a lot to take me away from here.'

'I don't care how much it costs. I swear to you, my mother will pay it.'

He sucked his back teeth. 'Nah, if you do a runner, I'm outta pocket and . . . Oh shit, don't cry. Please, get in.'

Dixie-Lee hurried into the back of the taxi and was instantly relieved when the warm air relaxed her body and she felt the vehicle pull away from the taxi rank. Sliding the glass partition ajar, she said, 'I really appreciate this. I swear my mum will pay you. Look, if you have a phone, I can call her. She'll give you her card number now, if you'd like. Just please get me home.'

The man in his sixties glanced at her in the rear-view mirror. She had a pretty face which was red and bruised, but she looked terrified. He could see she was telling the truth about being attacked. 'I'll get you home, don't worry. I've got to call into the coffee shop on the way, though. I need a hot drink to keep me awake.'

Dixie-Lee nodded and smiled back at him, now so grateful he was taking her home.

After five minutes, he pulled into a parking space in front of a row of shops and hurried into a café. When he returned, he was holding two steaming cups of coffee and a bag of buns.

He opened her door and smiled. 'Here, I've got you a drink. You look terrible, darling. Are you hungry?'

She shook her head; her body was still trembling, although she wasn't cold.

He patted her knee. 'You rest your head, sweetheart. I'll get you home safe and sound.'

She nodded and gratefully took the coffee. He was a real gentleman – a five-foot angel – with a subtle Greek accent.

'Is that your blood?' He pointed to her face.

She shook her head. 'No, it's from the man who attacked me.'

'I have some baby wipes in the front.'

She sipped the hot coffee, and moments later, he returned with a pack of wipes. 'Let's get you home.'

She touched his arm. 'Thank you so much.'

'No problem. I have a granddaughter. She looks like you.'

Safe in the taxi, Dixie-Lee felt drained. Her brain was exhausted, but she couldn't close her eyes, and she wouldn't until she was in her own bed.

By the time she reached her house, her legs felt heavy, and panic rose again in her throat. She didn't want to worry her mother, not this late at night, and yet she needed to pay the taxi driver.

'Don't worry about paying me.' He pointed to her face. 'Call the police. No man should hurt a woman like that.'

Dixie-Lee wanted to laugh out loud. *If only he knew what she had been through*, she thought.

CHAPTER EIGHT

Apart from the hallway light, the house was in darkness. Dixie-Lee crept up the curved staircase, tiptoed into her bedroom, and gently closed the door behind her.

'Is that you, Dixie-Lee?' Georgie called out.

'Yeah, it's me, Mum.'

'I know it's late, but your dinner is in the fridge, if you're hungry, and there's a teabag in the cup.'

'I'm . . . fine, Mum,' Dixie-Lee said, trying to keep her voice on an even keel because she knew her mother would sense any hint of pain, distress, or anxiety in her pitch. That was how it was with her. And she could also look at her face and know instantly what was going on.

'Goodnight.'

Leaning against her door, Dixie-Lee looked down and wondered why the hell she was still holding her shoe. She dropped it like a hot brick. The vision of Clifford's face and the smell of his breath plagued her mind.

'How the hell could he do that to me?' she whispered to herself. It was as if he had so much hate for her, but she'd never given him a reason to. Christ, she'd only met him a couple of times. Pushing herself away from the door, she took a closer look at herself in the long mirror. Instantly, she ripped her clothes off and threw them into the clothes basket, walked into the en-suite, and switched the shower on. Usually, she would wait a minute or so for the water to hit the right temperature, but not this evening. She didn't care how hot or cold it was; she had to wash away all remnants from the attack on her. The sharp spray of the fast-flowing water stung her like hot pokers, but she didn't care. The quicker the blood and urine were washed away, the better. Tears streamed down her face. It was only now, now that she was alone in the shower, that she could feel sorry for herself. How could she go back to work? She'd let Steve down by not returning to the police station, and who would believe *her* over the judge's son? After all, he hadn't raped her. She had none of his semen inside her to prove it. All she had were bruises. Her throat tightened up again. Nonetheless, she had hurt the man. She knew that. She'd sunk her teeth into his arm, kicked him in the balls, and bit a chunk out of his left cheek. As a result, she wondered if he would press charges against her for what would undoubtedly be classed as a serious assault.

After the fourth all-over body scrub, Dixie-Lee stepped out of the shower and sat on her bed, still wrapped in her towel. She thought she could still smell the urine, but that was probably because the smell was embedded in her memory. An hour passed while she mentally went over and over everything before she slipped into her pyjamas and got into bed. Her last thought before she fell asleep was one of regret: she should have taken the file.

***

It was ten o'clock and Georgie woke up late. Her alarm hadn't gone off. Still, she wasn't keen to go to the coffee shop, not after Henry had asked her to go home. Assuming Dixie-Lee had already left for work, she made some porridge and turned the radio on to check the morning news. However, when she filled the kettle, she noticed that the cup with the teabag inside was still there. Concluding that maybe Dixie-Lee was running late and had not bothered with tea or breakfast, she thought no more of it. Peering out into the garden, she noticed Rodney collecting the dead leaves. He was wrapped up warm and was so stuck into his work that he didn't see her staring out of the window.

Just as she was about to pour more milk onto her steaming porridge, she heard a commotion at the front of the house. A heavy banging at the door then followed and a man with a deep voice called out, 'Police! Open up!'

Georgie hurried to the front door and peered through the long glass side window. Sure enough, there were police officers and two were armed. Her heart was in her mouth, and right away, her thoughts immediately went to each member of her family. She knew Rohan hadn't done anything wrong. Rodney was an old and fragile man and had been here all the time. And Dixie-Lee was working in London. That left just her! Suddenly, she was gripped by panic. Had the police discovered the truth about the murders of Todd and Eve Marx? With her mouth as dry as a desert, and her hands shaking uncontrollably, she opened the door.

Without a word, one officer pushed her aside, while another man, clearly a detective in a cheap suit, said, 'Where is Dixie-Lee Deacon?'

'*What?*' shrieked Georgie, in utter shock. 'Why do you want to know? What's going on?' She followed the tall middle-aged man into the lounge. 'Er, do you have a warrant? You can't just walk in here. What the hell's going on?'

The man spun around to face Georgie. 'I'm Detective Inspector Sparks!' he said, with a look of contempt on his face.

Georgie noticed how his complexion was white and insipid-looking against his distinctive narrow dark-brown eyes. His hair was unevenly peppered with grey and the black tufts of hair protruding from his ears sent a message that he didn't care about his looks.

She watched as he pulled a piece of paper from his pocket.

'I am here to arrest Dixie-Lee Deacon. Now, stand aside. This warrant allows me to search the house.'

‘Wait, she’s at work. What on earth . . .’ She looked at the two armed officers and the number of police cars outside. ‘What in God’s name has she supposed to have *done*?’

Sparks glared at her. ‘If you are hiding her, you will also be arrested. Now, I recommend you tell me where she is or step aside and allow us to search the property.’

Georgie was shaking from head to toe. There was no way these police officers were here to arrest her daughter for a minor offence – not with armed officers storming through her house. This was either very serious or they’d made a colossal mistake.

As she stood helplessly watching the officers march through, moments later, a scream alerted her to the fact that Dixie-Lee was still at home. Instinctively, she pushed one of the officers out of her way and bolted up the stairs to find two female officers trying to handcuff her daughter.

‘Get your fucking hands off her. I know the law.’

Ignoring her, the two officers bent Dixie-Lee’s arms behind her back.

‘I said, get off her. You don’t need to manhandle her like that.’

‘Mum, what’s going on?’

Sparks, who had stormed into the lounge, was now in Dixie-Lee’s bedroom. He roughly pushed Georgie aside. ‘Dixie-Lee Deacon, I am arresting you on suspicion of the murder of Clifford Jenson-Baine.’

Georgie knew immediately that her daughter was innocent because the complete shock on her face was enough to convince her that the police had arrested the wrong person.

‘Wait, she didn’t kill anyone. You’ve made a grave mistake.’

Georgie looked back at her daughter’s face. Dixie-Lee looked terrified. Tears filled her eyes, ready to plummet down her cheeks. Then she clocked the bruise around her daughter’s cheek. ‘Oi.’ She poked one of the female officers. ‘Did you do that?’

The female officer grabbed Georgie's finger. 'Poke me again, and I'll arrest you for assault.'

'I asked you a question! Did you do that to my daughter?'

'No, Mum, she didn't.'

Instantly, Georgie surmised this was a self-defence move. 'Right, say nothing, Dixie-Lee. We'll have you out of the police station in no time. I'll call Hugh Shields.'

She could see that Dixie-Lee was struggling with her predicament. Still in her satin pyjamas, her head was down, as if she was carrying the weight of the world on her shoulders.

But the female officer closest to her was indifferent to her plight. She yanked her as though she was on a dog lead.

'There is no need for that,' spat Georgie. 'And I will be making sure you don't harm a hair on her head, lady, or I will call the press, and you know how much they love my kid.'

The female officer, whose hair was bright ginger and cropped close to her head, merely smirked. 'Well, they are sure gonna love this story.'

'Cocky cunt.'

'What did you call me?'

'I called you a cocky cunt.'

'I'll arrest you under the Public Disorder Act, if you say that again.'

Georgie grinned. 'You can't, you idiot. You're in my home, so, darling, I'll call you what the fuck I like.'

She looked at her daughter, who was shaking her head as tears streamed down her face. 'It's okay, darling. Listen to me: say nothing until you have spoken to Hugh Shields.'

Dixie-Lee nodded.

As her daughter was being taken to a police car, it took all of Georgie's willpower not to run at the two officers and tackle them to the ground. Instead, she held her cool and tried not to cry in front of her daughter. She had to show she was on top of the situation and not look like a crumbling wreck.

***

Dixie-Lee was shaking in the back of the police car. She was between two female officers. They didn't take the cuffs off and weren't kind to her, either. As snot and tears ran down her face, she was peeved that neither officer helped to wipe her face.

The ginger officer laughed at her. 'Dixie-Lee Deacon, who'd have thought it, eh, but you've killed before, so perhaps you've developed a taste for it.'

Dixie-Lee was trying so hard to recall how she'd managed to kill Clifford. Had he choked on his own vomit? Had he bled to death? Surely not. Then her eyes widened when her mind cast back to the man she saw running towards the chambers. So, okay, she didn't see him go inside the building, but he was heading that way. Then again, she could have imagined a two-headed beast, in the state she was in. Nothing seemed to make sense. Why was she being dragged in for Clifford's murder? She knew she hadn't killed him, but how the hell was she going to explain it? She bowed her head again and cried. Not for herself, but for her mother, who would be devastated.

The car pulled into the police car park, and the two officers frogmarched her into the building, along the corridor, and into the custody suite.

The custody sergeant looked Dixie-Lee up and down and frowned; he then turned to the arresting officer Detective Inspector Alan Sparks. 'Really?'

Sparks nodded. 'Can you get her booked in? I want her in interview room four.'

The two female officers removed the cuffs. 'Empty your pockets!' said the ginger officer.

But Dixie-Lee shrugged. 'I am in my pyjamas. They don't have pockets.'

'Right, let's take your prints and a mugshot, and we will also need a DNA sample,' she said, in a sharp tone.

Dixie-Lee felt utter humiliation. Her whole world of becoming a barrister had gone out of the window. Now experiencing at first hand how the police treated a suspect as if they were guilty before being proven innocent, she knew, then, that this lesson would be one that would serve her well in the future – if she ever got to become a barrister. But looking at the predicament she had just found herself in, she knew it would be a very long time – if at all – before she could ever hold her head up high and see herself in a role that she instinctively knew she would be very good at.

The smarmy smirk remained slapped on the ginger woman's face, all the time she was degrading her suspect.

But Dixie-Lee remained calm and silent and did as she was asked.

Afterwards, she was taken to interview room four, where she was joined by the ginger WPC and Detective Inspector Sparks.

Sparks pointed to the chair. 'I am DI Sparks. I and Officer Brenton will be asking you some questions, and you know you are under arrest, and I have read you your rights. We will record the interview through a video recording.' He leaned across and turned on the record button. 'For purposes of the recording, I am DI Sparks and with me is WPC Brenton. We are interviewing Dixie-Lee Deacon. It is ten forty-five a.m. on the thirtieth of November 2022.'

Sparks paused and smiled. 'So I want you to tell me the events of yesterday which took place on . . .' He looked at his dull stainless steel watch. 'The twenty-ninth of November. Start with when you left home to go to work.'

Dixie-Lee sat up straight and coughed to clear her throat. She knew they should have offered her legal representation. So she stared at both Sparks and Brenton without saying a word.

'Look, Miss Deacon, it will be better for you, in the long run, to give us a full rundown while it's fresh in your mind.'

Dixie-Lee looked at the door, hoping to see Hugh, their family solicitor and friend. Her cheeks began to burn with fear, but she wouldn't cry. She was determined to hold her emotions in check. She didn't want them to see it as a sign of guilt.

'So you left your home to go to work. Did you drive, walk, or take the train? What did you do?' asked Officer Brenton, her green eyes beady and daring.

But Dixie-Lee just sat back and stared at her. Finally, she said, 'I would like to speak with my lawyer.'

'He isn't here, and why would you need a lawyer if you're not guilty?'

'Because as well as being not guilty, *I'm not stupid.*'

DI Sparks's eyebrows lifted. 'See that tone, there.' He pointed with his pen. 'That tone tells me that the innocent look you gave us was just an act. You're quite a confident woman, aren't you, Miss Deacon. Confident enough to kill a man.' He paused for effect. 'Now, Miss Deacon, I don't know the circumstances around this murder, and you may well be justified. But let me tell you straight up, we know you killed Clifford Jenson-Baine. That's not in any doubt. However, what we don't know is why. So, as we said, tell us what happened while it's all fresh in your mind.'

Dixie-Lee stared at the door, willing Hugh on to walk in. But when she looked back at Sparks, she only got a smirk.

'It doesn't look like he is coming, Miss Deacon, and time is ticking by. Now, let me ask another question, but before I do, I want to show you something.'

The moment he left the room, Dixie-Lee lowered her gaze because she wouldn't give Brenton the satisfaction that she was scared.

'Nice designer pyjamas. I bet you are used to getting exactly what you want, and when it doesn't go your way' – Brenton threw her hands up – 'you lose your temper, throw your toys out of the pram, and even resort to violence.' She leaned back on her chair. 'You left a right mess, didn't you? But you did so with Major Ashby as well. He bled to death, didn't he? Seems to me, Dixie-Lee Deacon, you know exactly how to kill. I know your mother does because she was in the Army. Like mother, like daughter, eh?'

Dixie-Lee had a sudden urge to laugh. This situation she had found herself in. It was so insane. Everything was. The whole idea of it all. So, when she raised her head, she did so with a smile.

The change in Dixie-Lee's demeanour momentarily made Brenton twitch and wonder who she was actually dealing with.

When Sparks returned, he was holding a clear plastic evidence bag, which he slapped onto the table. 'Yours?'

Dixie-Lee couldn't help but look. It was her brooch inside the evidence bag and the brooch was covered in blood. However, she was shrewd enough to keep her head down and not show any emotions.

'I take it that's a yes?'

With the sudden heavy rap at the door, Sparks showed his annoyance by sighing deeply before rising from his seat. He had a good idea who it was, and so when he opened the door, he did so with agitation.

Hugh Shields, who didn't wait to be invited in, pushed past Sparks and flicked his thumb at his colleague to hop it.

Brenton acted like a child and rolled her eyes before storming out of the room.

‘Tut tut, my client asked for a lawyer, but here you are, with the tape on, I see.’ He switched the tape off and then he handed Dixie-Lee a bag.

Sparks glared. ‘What is that you’ve given our suspect?’

‘You didn’t even give this young lady an ounce of dignity. I’ve brought her a tracksuit.’

Sparks, now embarrassed, replied, ‘We have alternatives on their way.’

‘I want time with my client before you question her. And I will make this very clear. You will not be questioning her without me present. Is that understood?’

Sparks’s jaw protruded, exaggerating his underbite, before he picked up the plastic evidence bag and left the room.

‘Sorry, I’m late Dixie-Lee. I was talking with Steve Elison.’

Looking up, she frowned. ‘Does he know what’s going on?’ Her eyebrows snapped together into a worried frown.

‘Well, when you didn’t return, and he couldn’t reach you because your phone was dead, he drove back to the office and found Clifford dead.’

She momentarily threw her hands to her mouth. ‘Oh no. Did he think I killed him?’

Shields shook his head. ‘No, well . . . He was actually more worried that he couldn’t find you. His theory was that someone from the Malloye family killed Clifford and then you.’

‘I sense a *but* in there, Hugh.’

Running his hands through his hair, he sighed. ‘He naturally called the police.’

She nodded, urging him to continue.

‘The police found a brooch in Clifford’s hand.’ He stared into Dixie-Lee’s eyes.

‘My heart brooch with blood on it? Yes, I know. It was in the evidence bag that the detective was holding.’

Shields nodded. 'They told me they found Clifford gripping it.'

'Look, we had a fight, Hugh. He tried to . . .' Her eyes filled with tears as she swallowed hard and recalled the events.

'Go on, it's okay. Tell me everything that happened.'

'I went to the office to collect a file . . . Clifford was there being rude and then he pinned me against the wall, and he put his hands . . .' She looked away, her cheeks burning red.

'He tried to rape you?'

She nodded. 'So I kicked him between the legs and bit his arm and his cheek, but please believe me, Hugh. I didn't kill him.'

'So why did you bite him?'

'I was frightened. I thought he was going to . . . Well, I just didn't know how else to stop him.' The tears cascaded down her face.

'Hey, it's okay.' Shields took his handkerchief from his pocket. 'Here, it's clean.' He smiled.

'How did he die?'

Shields knew that question was completely genuine, and he also knew then that Dixie-Lee hadn't killed the barrister.

'Someone killed him by using a long-pointed instrument, probably a knife. He was stabbed in the neck.'

Dixie-Lee put her hands over her face, leaned her elbows on the table, and cried heavy sobs as if she was choking.

Shields put his arm around her. 'Listen, I believe you. You didn't kill him.'

She wiped her eyes and turned to face Shields straight on. 'You may believe me, Hugh, but you've also taught me far more about how the law really works than what I am learning on my degree course, so I know what's going to happen now.'

He frowned.

'Clifford is the judge's son. The police will have to prosecute someone, and the judge won't want delays, will he? They will gun for me because they already have evidence that I assaulted him. There is blood on my clothes and my unique brooch – which I now recall I dropped on the street as I fled from the scene – in his hand. More than that, a dental impression will prove I bit him. How could I ever prove I didn't kill him?'

Shields was speechless because the facts were starkly ominous: unless they had the real killer, what Dixie-Lee had just told him was utterly true.

CHAPTER NINE

It was late Wednesday evening when Georgie's phone eventually died. She'd been in the police station all day. There was nothing she could do about it until she could get back home to charge it. Here she was in the police station with a lukewarm cup of coffee and not a soul to talk to. Hugh had been kind enough to keep her updated. But, even so, the frustration of being so helpless flew around her veins like a never-ending loop of poison. She and Hugh knew that Dixie-Lee would not have killed Clifford Jenson-Baine. But that was not to say she hadn't attacked the bastard. She wasn't her mother's girl for nothing. From what she had been told, the guy deserved everything he'd got – and more!

Of course her daughter would have injured him if he was trying to sexually assault her. She had brought Dixie-Lee up to use everything she had to fight. It was obvious to her that her daughter had fought for her dignity but had left before he was killed. A lump lodged in her throat because she couldn't get her daughter's expression out of her mind when Officer Sparks arrested her for murder. That look said it all – she was innocent.

Just as she rose from the hard plastic chair bolted to the wall to stretch her legs, the main entrance door to the station opened and in marched a tall blonde woman. She was dressed in a long blue fitted cashmere coat that wasn't buttoned up to reveal a blue suit and a satin blouse underneath. She had a briefcase in one hand and a takeaway cup of coffee in the other.

Georgie stared at her because she thought she had seen her somewhere before. It was the way she walked with such confidence that suggested this tall leggy blonde was the famous barrister Cathy McGowan. If she was, was she here for Dixie-Lee or for someone else?

Straining her ears, she listened hard.

'Would you call the custody desk and confirm you have a Dixie-Lee Deacon in your custody? I am one of her legal representatives. Cathy McGowan KC.'

The police officer looked up, and Georgie clocked the surprised expression on her face.

'KC?'

'Sorry, was I not loud enough for you.'

Georgie wanted to smile; the woman had balls, that was clear.

'Yes, of course . . . Er, your client is Dixie-Lee Deacon, you said?'

Georgie noticed the barrister move impatiently from one leg to another. It seemed to have the desired effect on the reception officer, who suddenly became flustered.

'Dixie-Lee Deacon has a legal representative, a solicitor by the name of . . .'

'Hugh Shields,' said Cathy, finishing the woman's sentence for her.

'Yes.'

'Well, I know that! I am her *barrister*.'

'Yes, please wait a moment. I'll make that call.'

As Cathy spun around, Georgie, who was now on her feet, was surprised when their eyes met. 'I'm Dixie-Lee's mother.'

Cathy stepped forward, held her drink in the same hand as her briefcase, and extended her other hand. 'Pleased to meet you. Georgie, isn't it?'

Georgie was instantly captivated by the barrister's demeanour. The woman, who was clearly in her forties, had a youthful appearance. Her lips were plump, and her skin glowed, but it was her green eyes that were so enchanting. So much so, she half-wondered if she fancied the woman herself. However, she concluded it was probably a case of being in awe of her.

'Yes, I am. Look, she didn't kill him.'

Cathy nodded. 'Right, well, my colleague Steve Elison is too involved to represent her.'

'What do you mean by *too involved*?'

Cathy gestured they should move away from the front desk. 'Apparently, he asked Dixie-Lee to go to our offices, so he is effectively a witness. In what aspect, we don't know. So it is easier to engage my services. Changing the subject, is Dixie-Lee okay? Does she need anything I can take in for her?'

'I gave Hugh a tracksuit for her, so she's comfortable, and she now has her washbag. They dragged her out of bed still in her pyjamas.'

Cathy nodded again. 'I'm afraid they would have done so because she is potentially a murder suspect.'

'No way—'

Cathy put her finger to her lips. 'I need to speak to Hugh and Dixie-Lee.'

Georgie frowned. 'Do you believe her?'

'It's irrelevant what I believe.'

'No!' snapped Georgie. 'It's not. It's bloody *not*!' Her words were said so firmly because although she saw how Cathy could be very intimidating, she could be too.

Cathy tilted her head to the side, making it clear that she had noticed Georgie's anger. 'Georgie, if I may, you need to understand this. Dixie-Lee has two options: one, she pleads guilty to manslaughter in self-defence, by which she will have to prove she used reasonable force to defend herself, and two, she pleads *not* guilty to murder.'

Georgie flared her nostrils. 'She'll plead not guilty. There's no way she would do anything else.'

Cathy nodded again, in acknowledgement. 'And that being the case, whether she is guilty or not, I will be representing her as innocent until proven guilty.' With that rejoinder, she returned to the front desk, leaving Georgie speechless.

But before Georgie could respond, Cathy spun on her heel and returned to where Georgie was standing. With a genuine smile, she said, 'I'm not going to patronise you, Georgie. I appreciate that it is *your* daughter they have in custody. I don't have children, so I won't pretend to know what it feels like. But that's not my job. My job is to have her walking out of the courtroom as a free woman and back in my offices as one of our employees.'

'And this judge's son. He was one of your employees, wasn't he?'

'Yes, he was. But he is dead, so he obviously won't need our services. However, Dixie-Lee will, so it is what it is. Oh, and by the way, Dixie-Lee may *not* want me to represent her, which is her prerogative.'

Georgie was gaining the measure of the woman. Although Cathy was so mesmerising, she was also no pushover, and Georgie thought she might well be one of the best barristers for the job.

'Now I have spoken to you, I am sure she will want you.'

'But, again, Georgie, she is an adult, so it is *her* choice.'

That comment put Georgie in her place. However, she didn't argue back because it was the truth. And when Rohan referred to Cathy as the ice maiden, she could see why. Another thought flew through her mind, and it was that underlying dismissal of her moments ago. She could not forget that Cathy had been quick to shake her hand but equally as fast to make it clear that she had no interest in anyone other than Dixie-Lee.

Georgie now felt suddenly insulted. As much as what Cathy McGowan had said was true, it was also said in such a way as to be dismissive of the mother of the accused. She decided there and then to put this woman in her place.

'Before I go, Ms McGowan, I want you to know that Dixie-Lee and I are very close, so do not be surprised if she wants to run anything by me first.'

Georgie was dumbfounded when Cathy looked her up and down and smiled using one side of her mouth, which was more like a smirk. 'I can see why Rohan likes you. You're a very confident woman.'

Feeling the blood rush around her body, Georgie chewed the inside of her mouth to stop herself from giving this woman a piece of her mind.

'Look, I am sure Dixie-Lee would want to run everything past you first, but understand this: it is not how it works. If your advice is the opposite of mine, we have a problem. And I do believe I know best because that's my job.' Even though her voice was sharp, her smile counterbalanced that.

It was a clever move, thought Georgie.

'Anyway, you should get some rest and be ready for Friday.'

'Friday?'

'Yes, they'll want to keep her another day to grill her and collect any other evidence. You know how it works. I should think the court listing will be for ten o'clock and I know the magistrate will remand her in custody and bail will be denied.'

Georgie was trying to digest everything Cathy was saying.

'Don't look so shocked. As far as they are concerned, she killed a man, who happened to be the son of a judge, so unless in the next few hours we find proof that she didn't kill him, then, I am afraid, she will be before another judge first thing on Friday morning.'

The realisation hit Georgie that her sweet daughter could end up behind bars and there was nothing she could do about it. For the first time in her daughter's life, where she had protected her through thick and thin, Georgie felt a complete loss of control.

The side door opened, and Shields emerged, escorted by an officer.

Georgie expected him to hurry to Cathy and greet her; yet he appeared to have a frown on his face and a slight tilt to his head. *Why was he confused?*

'Hugh,' Cathy said, walking towards him. 'Steve can't represent Dixie-Lee, so I thought I should, considering the circumstances.'

Even though Cathy had her back to her, Georgie could still hear her and see Hugh Shield's response. She watched him excuse himself and hurry towards her.

'Georgie, you should go home and get some rest. Rohan is flying back from Ireland as soon as possible.' He looked around and lowered his voice. 'Brodie and Mac are staying behind at their family home. They want to talk to a few people.'

'Who?'

Shields shook his head. 'Listen, I'll come over tomorrow and meet with you and Rohan. I want to get as much out of Steve and Cathy about this file, and then we can go from there.'

'File?'

'Shush, I'll talk when we're alone, okay?'

Sensing Hugh was on to something which seemed to be a secret, Georgie smiled. 'Okay. Oh . . . is Raj looking after her?'

Shields shook his head. 'He is not on her case. A prick called DI Alan Sparks is.' He wiped his brow. 'You go home, okay?'

'Look after her, Hugh. She'll be frightened.'

Shields hugged Georgie. 'You know I will, but she's okay. She's a tough nut, just like her mum.'

Georgie smiled and left before she couldn't hold back the tears any longer.

***

Dixie-Lee nervously fiddled with the stretched cuff of her black velvet tracksuit. She was grateful that Hugh had made such a fuss to force Brenton to allow her to wear it. It was her favourite. Her grandmother Finella had bought it for her. She'd said it was ideal to wear on her flights to Ireland.

Stroking the soft material, she wondered if she would ever get to fly to Ireland again. This situation would undoubtedly cause her family pain, especially her grandmother, and she wondered if they would believe her or if they would just pretend to because she was family. She knew, though, she couldn't live with herself if they had genuine reservations.

A gentle tap at the door shook her from her thoughts. She assumed it was Hugh, but as she peered up, she saw not only Hugh but Cathy McGowan. The first thing she noticed was that Cathy looked fresh; her make-up was immaculate, and her hair looked as if it was newly washed. There was not a crinkle in her suit or even a speck of dust on her cashmere coat.

'Dixie-Lee, how are you?' Cathy asked, before she sat down and placed her drink on the table and her briefcase beside her.

'Numb, I guess. I am so very sorry, Cathy, about Clifford. But I want you to know I didn't kill him.'

'Hugh briefly filled me in.' She narrowed her eyes and pointed to Dixie-Lee's cheek. 'Have the police photographed that bruise?'

'They took a mugshot.'

'No, I don't mean that. Have the police taken a medical photograph showing your injuries?'

'No.'

Cathy turned to Shields. 'Why didn't you question it?'

'I did, and they said they had.'

'A bloody mugshot isn't the same thing.'

'Do you have other injuries?' She held up her hand to stop Dixie-Lee from jumping in. 'I mean any small scratches, bruises, or anything like those?'

Dixie-Lee blushed and looked at Hugh. He picked up on it right away.

'I'll organise some refreshments and leave you two alone.' Promptly, he left the room.

'My left breast is bruised. Clifford grabbed me there, and he tore my knickers. And he also scratched the inside of my leg.'

'When you got changed into your tracksuit was an officer present?'

Dixie-Lee nodded. 'Yes, WPC Brenton was.'

'But she didn't take a note of the injuries? Is that right?'

Dixie-Lee shrugged her shoulders. 'I don't know. She didn't comment. She only stared, making me feel . . .'

'You don't need to go into details. Look, I won't accept that, so I will ensure they take her to task. Now, first things first, I will arrange for a doctor to come in and for photos to be taken. We need those.'

Dixie-Lee sensed that Cathy's mind was more on the purpose of her own visit to the chambers.

'Good, now we can talk about the events of last night. You obviously went to our chambers. Tell me what happened when you got there.'

'I left my things on the reception desk and then went downstairs into the basement to look for a file. Steve wanted me to find a specific one. The Tommy Malloye file. He thought at first it was at the old office. But when we searched for it there, we found a manila folder with Tommy Malloye's name on the cover. Inside were the Mercstone and Amble files.'

'Why were the Mercstone and Amble files inside Tommy Malloye's folder?'

Dixie-Lee shrugged. ‘Steve said the previous secretary purposely rearranged the files out of spite. So he guessed that Tommy’s file would be at the chambers filed under Mercstone and Amble.’

‘Right, so that’s why you went to the chambers. Now tell me, were you successful in finding Tommy’s file?’

‘Well, yes and no.’

‘Oh, what do you mean, Dixie-Lee? Try and stay focused.’

Dixie-Lee was amazed that Cathy was showing practically no empathy whatsoever. Instead of asking her about what had happened to her down in that basement, all she was concerned about was this sodding file!

‘So, the file. Did you find it?’

‘Well, I didn’t exactly find it. It was there lying on the floor.’

‘Why didn’t you take it, then?’

‘Look, Cathy, a lot was going on last night. I was attacked, for God’s sake. Shouldn’t you be asking me about *that*?’

Cathy shook her head in annoyance. ‘Dixie-Lee, this file is of the utmost importance. Whatever happened to you personally yesterday evening, you are alive to tell your version of events. Tell me this: did you see anyone else besides Clifford in the building?’

‘No, I didn’t, not in the building. But when I ran out of there, towards Charing Cross railway station, I heard someone chasing me, and that’s when my brooch fell off. The footsteps stopped, and when I looked back, I saw a younger man. He was running back towards your offices. That’s all I saw.’

‘So let me get this straight. Clifford attacked you while you were in the room searching for the file. And you saw the file on the floor. Did he ask you why you were there?’

Dixie-Lee nodded. ‘Yes, and I made up some silly reason that I had left something in the room. He didn’t believe me. And then he made a move on me. He was really nasty. He was belittling me. He grabbed me and pushed me against the wall. But I could smell the drink, and I couldn't . . . I couldn't . . . Oh my God, it was awful . . .'

'Okay, that's enough for now. I'll call the doctor and get your injuries photographed,' Cathy said, as she rose from her seat. 'Tell me, Dixie-Lee, is your plea one of not guilty?'

Dixie-Lee glared at Cathy. 'Of course it is. Why would you ask that?'

'Because it is going to be hard to prove.'

The blood drained from Dixie-Lee's face as her world imploded. Never would she have expected Cathy to say that. Knowing Cathy and Steve were the best, she assumed that she would have at least been offered a smidgeon of hope, but there it was in black and white. She could be faced with a murder charge.

Before she could verbalise her own fears to Cathy, the barrister left the room and a PC entered; it seemed to her that he was guarding her as if she was some kind of serial killer. At least, that was how it felt, at that very moment.

As soon as Shields returned, laden with drinks and biscuits, courtesy of Detective Raj, he found Dixie-Lee as white as a ghost and tears running like rainwater running down a downpipe in a storm.

'Hey, what on earth is the matter? Where's Cathy?'

Dixie-Lee tried to talk in between sobs, and it was then that Shields saw her as just a child. 'Slow down. Take a deep breath. What did she say that made you so upset?'

'She said she is going to call a doctor to examine me and to get someone to take photos of my injuries, and then she said it will be hard to prove I'm innocent.'

Shields sat beside her and put his arm around her shoulders, nodding to the police officer to leave the room. 'Listen, it is difficult, but you know that you're a bright girl, and what happened to you doesn't mean it's over for you. We won't sit back and do nothing. I promise you, we will fight tooth and nail to prove you didn't kill Clifford.'

Dixie-Lee wiped her eyes and took another deep breath. 'This will upset my mum so much, knowing she can't do anything for me.'

'She will be fine, and so will you. Now, I need you to tell me everything from start to finish, and—'

'Well, that's something, Hugh. Do you know what? Cathy wasn't interested at all in what happened to me last night.'

'Hmm, Cathy is known for lacking empathy with her clients. I'm sorry you witnessed that.'

Once Shields heard Dixie-Lee's version of events, he finished up by saying, 'Look, we will make sure you see a doctor before . . .' He paused. 'Before you have to go to court.'

She looked up. 'It is going to come to that, isn't it?'

Shields nodded and hugged her again. 'I can't lie to you, Dixie-Lee. The evidence against you is formidable. And you are not pleading self-defence, which, under the circumstances, would have been feasible.'

She straightened up. 'You don't believe me either, do you?'

He sighed. 'I'll be honest with you. I do believe you, Dixie-Lee, because I know you're not lying. And there is certainly a lot more to this. So, know this, sweetheart. I'm on your side. As I said, I will fight hard for your freedom and to bring to justice the person who killed the judge's son.'

CHAPTER TEN

As Brodie Deacon exited his car, he saw the black clouds rolling towards him. The bitter cold air stung his cheeks and froze his gloveless fingers, so he dug his hands deep into his pockets as he stormed towards the old lock-up garages. It was a secluded area that was once a street full of two-up two-down houses thriving with families, with probably too many to occupy the small dwellings. However, now there were only a handful of houses and a few garages left. Most of the homes had been condemned and pulled down. As for the garages, they were left standing, although only a couple were in use; in fact, the two had been knocked into one and used as an office. Surrounding this area was an old unkempt road with rocks still piled high from the demolition project.

With his head held high, Brodie pulled his shoulders back as if the Malloye family, with their vicious reputation, were nothing to him. Opening the door to the double garage, he walked inside. The air was impregnated with a hostile stench. With it hung a thick grey pall of cigarette smoke.

Scanning the room, Brodie clocked a number of men who had their backs against the walls as if they were hiding in the shadows.

Michael Malloye, the head of the family and the breeder of pure evil, sat on a wooden chair behind a table facing the door. His legs were outstretched, and he leaned on the table with one arm. A blue wisp of cigarette smoke left his mouth and clouded his face.

'So, Brodie Deacon. You called the meeting, and we are here.' Michael Malloye's Irish accent was thick and harsh and would have intimidated most men, but not Brodie. 'So, you had better have a good fecking reason because, as you have probably heard, we have a funeral to arrange and we' – he pointed around the room with a long bony finger – 'we are very busy people.'

'Oh, I have a very good reason to call the meeting, Michael.'

'Er, now, lad, you need to show your fecking manners. It's Mr Malloye, to you.'

'Oh, is it, now? Well, you have a short memory. It was not that long ago you were calling me *Mr Deacon*.' Brodie stepped closer. 'It was when you needed *my* fecking help, if my memory serves me correctly.'

Michael Malloye's sudden movement as he sat up straight stirred the other men. They pushed themselves away from the walls, ready to protect him.

Brodie laughed. 'You see, there, Michael, your lads, all on guard, ready to wade in, and you don't even know why I'm here. That tells me you have a lot of enemies. Correct me if I'm wrong, but at the last meeting, your boys weren't ready to pounce on me like a pack of fecking hyenas. Not when you were begging for my help.'

Michael flared his nostrils. 'And if my memory serves *me* well, you were paid handsomely for the work.'

Brodie smirked. 'And so I should. You hired my services, which, Michael, meant that you managed to hang on to your fecking head and your lads were still able to shit out of their own arseholes.'

Michael nodded slowly. 'But you were paid good money.'

'And you're still alive. So next time you have a dispute with the likes of the fecking Colombians, find another firm that will be the negotiator, 'cos I'll not do it again, you ungrateful cunt!'

Michael jumped up from his seat, and, suddenly, Brodie was staring down the barrel of a gun. But he didn't flinch or blink, which unnerved the old man.

'You, Michael, are just so fecking predictable.'

'Stop with the idle chatter, Brodie. Tell me why you've called for this meeting and with *all* of us Malloyes to be here.'

Brodie lifted his hand and moved the gun away from his face. 'Pointing a fecking gun in my face is insulting. I haven't given you reason to, so don't act like a fecking bully in my presence.'

'Or what?'

'I thought you had more brains than to ask me *or what*? How the hell did you think I got you off so lightly with the Colombians?'

Michael screwed up his face and squinted his beady eyes. 'So they're fecking pals of yours, are they now?'

'I wouldn't say pals, no, but they show me respect, and you know what comes with respect.'

Michael had got the message that Brodie Deacon was no idiot. 'Just tell me what you want, Deacon.'

Brodie gazed around the four walls and checked every face in the room.

'What are you doing?'

'One of your lads is missing.'

Michael sat back down and placed the gun on the table. 'Our Tommy's dead, fecking murdered. But you already know that, so why state the fecking obvious?'

Brodie shook his head. 'No! I don't mean Tommy.'

'Who *do* you mean, then?' Michael suddenly shifted uncomfortably in his chair.

'Your gobshite grandson Tyler.'

'Yes, he is my grandson. But you said *one of your lads*.'

'Fair enough, but I know you, and I know that little shit, and he would be here now with the rest of yous. Anything for a bit of action. So where is he, Michael?'

Brodie concluded that Tyler was in London after seeing the unease written all over Michael's face. So he decided to put his theory to the test. 'Get him here, Michael.'

'Now why would I do that?' Michael's eyes glared and his jaw protruded like a bulldog.

'Because I want to eliminate him—'

'You fecking what?'

'Don't worry, I'm not going to kill him. Not yet, anyway. I was going to say before you interrupted me that I wanted to eliminate him from my list of potential suspects.'

With his hands hovering over the gun, Michael looked up. 'Take a seat, Brodie.'

Smiling, Brodie sat opposite, and even when seated, he dwarfed the room. He was easily a good foot taller and broader than any of the men here.

'What is this about, Brodie?' Although Michael's hand wasn't far away from the gun, he couldn't look Brodie in the eye.

'One of yous – and my guess is it's your grandson Tyler' – he pointed a finger at Michael – 'has gone and made a big fecking mistake – a huge blunder.'

Michael's eyes widened, and he licked his lips. He then took another drag from his cigarette before he realised that he had smoked it down to the butt. Snatching the packet off the table, he sparked up another cigarette.

'Blunder? What's he supposed to have done?'

A grin spread across Brodie's face. 'I think you *know* what he's done.'

'Well, I don't, so don't waste my time. Just tell me now.'

'He was looking for a file in one of the London barristers' chambers.'

Michael took another drag and respectfully blew the smoke to his left. 'Is that it?'

Brodie sucked air in through his teeth. 'No, he killed a barrister who happened to be a judge's son, no fecking less.'

'Right, okay. Now, you don't know that was my grandson, for one, and two, what the feck has that got to do with you?'

Brodie hissed through gritted teeth, his eyes round and raging. 'The little cunt planted evidence on the man to incriminate my *niece*!'

When Michael slowly looked up, clearly shaken, his complexion paled, and Brodie clocked how he struggled to swallow.

'Your *niece*?'

Instantly, Brodie was alarmed by Michael's reaction and snatched the gun, pointing it at him.

Putting his hands up, Michael yelled to his sons. 'Don't fecking move, boys, because this fecker will shoot me!'

'Good, Michael, *now* we have an understanding. I will give you time to put your guts back in your arsehole and loosen that tongue to fill your mouth with truthful words. Do we fecking understand each other?'

'Yes, so now, will you put the gun down, you fecking eejit.'

'I'll put the gun down' – said Brodie, as he waved it around the room – 'but if any one of yous thinks they can get smart and act like Billy Big Bollocks, then, believe me, you will fecking kick yourselves afterwards, that you will.'

Lifting his chin, Michael waved his hands at his sons. 'Put your tools away, boys. Brodie here is not a fecking eejit.' He turned to Brodie. 'I'm guessing you have a guarantee in place that gets you out of here alive, don't you?'

Brodie slowly nodded. 'Aye, and she is happily sharing a cake and a cup of tea with the big boy. He is good at showing his condolences.'

'*Mac?*'

'Yep.'

Michael jumped up. 'If he fecking—'

'Reel your neck in. You know Mac. He is a big softie. Your missus will be deep in conversation with him by now and serving a cream tea, and Mac will be attentive, kind, and the best company. For now, that is. But, you know how it works. If I *don't* get out alive, you'll be going to *two* funerals.'

Retaking his seat, Michael sighed. 'Fair play.'

'Now, when I mentioned that the girl who was set up was my niece, your face told me everything. You had no idea that the girl was related to me, which actually tells me much more, and that is you knew that your grandson went to London to retrieve some fecking file and killed a man in the process because your instant reply was "*your niece*." See, your first reaction should have been to say I don't know what you're talking about. But you do know what I am on about. So now you're shitting it, ain't yer, Michael. Because that girl, who is being held in a police cell back in London as I speak, is our Dixie's daughter, the only thing left of our brother. And I want you to know we would all die for that kid. Just so you understand me clearly enough.'

Michael ran both his hands through his thinning greasy hair and again glanced around the room as if he was looking for help from his sons. But it was soon apparent they weren't even used to wiping their own arses, let alone capable of making decisions. He had always been the front runner and then the next in line had been his Tommy. Tommy had more or less taken over; the others merely acted as the brawn, the foot soldiers. They could fight and would give someone a good hiding, but they needed a hands-on leader, now Tommy was dead.

The silence was uncomfortable for everyone except Brodie. He felt confident knowing he was barking up the right tree. So all he needed to do was to convince Michael to get Tyler to hand himself in.

'He has to do the right thing, Michael. My niece is a kid who is just starting out in life, and she has been through enough shit to put anyone in an early grave.'

'I didn't say he killed anyone. You only assume it was him.' Michael sat up straight. 'In fact, Brodie, you are assuming a lot. Why would Tyler be after some file from a lawyer's office, and why would you think it's to do with us . . . well, our Tyler?'

'You have dishonesty written all over your face.' Brodie smiled. 'The last thing I want to do is hurt you and your boys, but it's still on the list.'

Michael remained silently brooding, but Brodie didn't fill the silence for the sake of it.

From his right-hand side, Gilead, Michael's middle second-born son, a man in his late thirties, a thickset guy with a thick accent and a rasping undertone, stepped forward. 'You are nothing but a negotiator undoing wrongdoings and all that shit, so are you here with threats of violence or are you negotiating? Because I believe you need to make yourself clear, you cocky wanker.'

Although Michael rolled his eyes, he didn't interfere.

Brodie got up from his chair and stepped towards Gilead. 'Wanker, yeah? You need to crawl back into the shadows and shut the fuck up.' He looked down at the baseball bat in Gilead's hand. 'And you'd better know how to use that, or I will take it off you and shove it up your fat hairy arse.'

Instantly, Gilead's short temper hit the roof. He lifted the bat, but as much as he was a size, he wasn't as fit as Brodie or as fast.

Brodie threw a left-handed uppercut, which no one saw coming, and certainly not Gilead. He didn't have time to put his tongue firmly back in his mouth, and, ultimately, his jagged bottom teeth managed to sever the tip of his tongue clean off.

Before he even realised what had happened, Brodie ripped the bat out of the man's hand and beat him about the ribs. And for good measure, he managed to catch him in the throat.

Gilead fell back. Blood poured down his chin, and as he put his hand to his mouth, he let out a blood-curdling scream.

Martie Malloye was the other middle brother with a serious reputation for being so violent that when he was in prison, he'd spent most of his sentences in solitary. The only person who could stop him was his father, but he didn't have a chance this time. Martie launched himself off the wall and grabbed Brodie in a headlock. The next youngest brother Cameron ran at Brodie and threw his best punch, and as he made contact with Brodie's chest, he could feel the rock-hard muscles.

Before Cameron had a chance to throw another punch, Brodie managed to flip Martie over onto his back and fly-kicked Cameron across the table, knocking the old man onto his arse.

'Stop!' bellowed Michael. 'Yer fecking eejits.'

Bran, who was the youngest brother, tried to help Michael to his feet.

Meanwhile, Brodie snatched the gun and pointed it at Gilead and the other three brothers. 'Now, back the feck off and shut your mouths.'

Martie, who was also back on his feet and about to have another go, stupidly believed that Brodie wouldn't use the gun. It proved to be a big mistake.

Brodie fired it like a shit-hot marksman and the bullet pierced through Martie's ankle.

'Now that's fucked up your chances of auditioning for *Riverdance*, you muppet.'

The shock of Brodie firing the gun at one of the brothers had the men with their ears ringing and suddenly recoiling in fear.

As soon as the pain hit Martie, he was gasping for breath. It was the worst pain he'd ever experienced.

'Now, back off or I will shoot the fecking lot of you. I came in peace just for answers, but you lot have just made another mistake.'

He turned to face Michael, who was dumbstruck staring at his injured sons. 'Don't look so shocked. This isn't business – this is fecking personal. And like I said, I would die for my niece, so you'd best take me seriously.'

Michael nodded.

'You tell me, Michael, what's in the file, and don't try to fecking lie. I know they have Tommy's missus in the nick.'

'How the feck do you know all this?'

'Because she hired Steve Elison who worked for Tommy. Whose majority of work comes via Hugh Shields, our lawyer, who you fecking know. Christ, Michael, is your memory shot to shit? I introduced you and Tommy to Hugh Shields.'

Michael's eyes widened. 'Hang on, is Steve Elison representing that fecking whore?'

'Oh, come on, you knew he was.'

'I sent Tyler to watch that police station to find out who she had representing her, and who was going in to see the dirty fecking whore. He didn't tell me it was Elison, the two-faced bastard.'

Brodie tilted his head to the side, but Michael was distracted by his sons' moans and groans. 'Go outside. You're doing my head in, you fecking useless lot.' He nodded to Bran to join them and turned to Brodie. 'I see you've put on some muscle and learned to fight like a fecking pro.'

Brodie shrugged. 'I only get angry when I am set upon. You know me and my brothers may stay on the right side of the law, but when fecking needs must, I will fight as good as any of your boys. And you can't kid me, Michael. Your reputation stands because you have an unruly bunch of lads, well, men, who fight as a pack. But they aren't any good one on one. However, you see, me brothers and me, we can have a good ruck when it's man to man. And like I said: this *is* personal.'

'Okay, you've made your point.'

'I want to know what this fecking file is all about!'

Michael shrugged. 'I don't know. Tommy apparently gave someone a file containing, I assume, his last will and testament.'

'And so Tyler will go to such great lengths – even murder – to get it, will he? Hmm, I think there is more to this than a last will and testament.'

'Listen to me, Brodie, I don't know exactly what's in that file. For all I know, it could contain information on the whereabouts of Tommy's diamonds. Now, they are worth a fortune, but whatever it says in that file, his son – our Tyler – will probably know more than us. But what I do know is this: Tommy's bitch of a wife was fecking every man and his brother who had a twelve-inch cock, and when my Tommy found out about her adultery, he filed for divorce.'

'So what's that got to do with anything?'

'*Everything*, Brodie. My Tommy was fecking murdered *before* he was divorced, and considering he was worth a lot of money and that dirty no-good murdering whore is his wife, she will now get the lot.'

'Right, so now it all makes sense. You lot wanted the file destroyed so that she couldn't claim it because without a will and with him having filed for divorce, she wouldn't automatically get the money.'

Michael slowly nodded.

However, Brodie felt his anger reach a pitch. 'So your shit cunt of a grandson broke into the chambers, killed a barrister, and framed my niece all over fecking *money*? Is that *right*?'

Michael sank back into his chair knowing that the way Brodie addressed it made it sound so cold-blooded, which is what his family was known best for. Still, he was more worried by the angry look on Brodie's face and the gun in his hand.

He had known the Deacons for years and he had to take his hat off to them. They were good men who ran a decent business. He was truly grateful when they managed to cut a deal between him and the Colombians over a drugs racket that had gone terribly wrong. He and his sons were all facing inevitable death following horrific torture. The deal meant he would lose his house and car but he could keep his cottage, and his sons had to work as runners for the Colombians for a year and a day. They stuck to their end of the bargain, and all escaped with their lives. The Deacons were paid fifty grand, and that was that.

He admired the Deacon brothers in as much as they always held themselves well. They were big men who knew their own value. They possessed such quiet certainty that when they entered the room, heads would turn, and when they spoke, their level of intelligence captivated their audience. Which was why they were so successful at what they did. Yet they weren't averse to getting their hands dirty, like Brodie had done just now. If he was honest with himself, Brodie had more intelligence than his lot put together. His Tommy was the brains, and Tommy's son Tyler was the reckless one who would go that one step beyond what was asked of him.

But when Tyler eventually came home, he would have the living shit beaten right out of him. All he was asked to do was to watch the police station and find out who was representing her. Then, they could have a few words with this lawyer, put the fear of God into them, and leave the whore without representation of any clout. She would die, hopefully in a stinking jail – where she belonged.

The news that Steve Elison was representing her shocked him since he now suspected Steve was holding Tommy's file and the plan to retrieve it had not been put in place. Yet how could Brodie really know that Tyler had gone there to get it? Tyler, being the mental bastard he was, probably did kill the barrister, and if this girl was collateral damage, so be it. But there hadn't been any intention to frame Brodie's niece!

Deep down, as much as Tyler was his eldest grandson and his grandmother's favourite, he was aware that the kid wasn't wired up right. If a psychiatrist properly assessed him, they would diagnose him as a psychopath. He felt a lump in his throat. He was still grieving over Tommy. It had been forty-eight hours, and his death still hadn't sunk in. He was pushing it out of his mind and concentrating on getting revenge because he believed in his heart that Bianca *had* killed his son. Flaring his nostrils, he stared at the gun in Brodie's hand. 'So, what now?'

'I want you to get your grandson to hand himself in.' He looked at his watch. 'Right, it's now midday. With today being Wednesday, Tyler's got until midday tomorrow because there is no way my niece is going to jail on Friday for that little fecking cunt.'

Michael nodded in agreement. In his heart, he knew he probably wouldn't have a choice, but that was only if Tyler agreed, and the chances of that happening were zero to none. 'I'll be honest wid yer. I will call Tyler, and I will tell him to do that, but he is a little bit independent of us, if you get what I mean. He may not do it.'

'Oh no, then find a fecking way to *make* him, because if my niece ends up in prison, I'll forget I'm a law-abiding citizen. I'll put aside my work ethic, and I will come for each and every one of you, and you will wish the Colombians had ended your life, by the time I'm done.'

Michael could feel the threat deep in his stomach. This man wasn't acting tough with words. He meant every one of them.

'I'll be in touch at five this afternoon, and I will want to know what's happening.'

Michael nodded. 'I understand.'

Brodie's family phone, the only one he had brought with him, buzzed with a text message. He pulled it out of his jeans pocket and stared at the screen. The text was from Hugh Shields, and he could hardly believe what he was reading.

Get away from the Malloyes, like now. Tyler Malloye has just been found dead.

Without showing any visible trace of nerves, Brodie said, 'Right, I'll be in touch, but I'll take this gun for safekeeping. At some point, I might give it back to you. But that depends on you doing what I want.'

Michael nodded, but Brodie didn't hang about. He knew that any time now, Michael would get the same message. He hurried past the men, who were either moaning or mumbling under their breath, and picked up the pace the nearer he got to his car. At the first opportunity, he looked in the rear-view mirror and saw everyone was now looking at their phones. Putting his foot down, he sped off.

CHAPTER ELEVEN

At six o'clock on Friday morning, Steve entered the police station, having heard the news that Tyler Malloye had been found dead not far from his chambers in London. Tyler's throat had been slashed, but there were no signs of a struggle. Even though Steve had hardly slept during the last two days, he was still bright-eyed when he marched into the police station with confidence.

Sparks greeted him with an acknowledging nod, followed by a smirk.

'Is the interview room ready?'

Sparks nodded. 'Your client's lucky, ya know, that we can't pin Tyler's murder on her. But only because she was here at the time.' He chuckled.

'And you find that funny, do you?' Steve stopped in his tracks and glared at the officer. 'Because the murder of a young man is hardly a comedy sketch, is it.'

'You know what all of the Malloye family are like.' Sparks stood cockily. 'They're all trouble. From Ireland to here, they've left a long line of victims.'

'Oh, I see, and you are not only a comedian but the judge and jury and no doubt the executioner too. With so many strings to your bow, I'm surprised you're not the bloody chief commissioner. Which room is my client in?'

Sparks ground his teeth and pointed to room one.

'Thank you, officer, and could you arrange some refreshments since I will probably be in there for some time.'

Feeling inadequate and truly put in his place, Sparks walked along the corridor and ordered one of the PCs to organise the drinks.

As soon as he stepped into room one, Steve noticed that Bianca wasn't looking at her best. She had washed her make-up off and was now dressed in a standard police tracksuit, which was so big and baggy, it now made her look less than sexy. In fact, he stared longer than he should have because he had never ever seen her without make-up. Her eyes looked so much smaller and her skin tone so uneven that it seemed she had a severe skin condition.

'How are you doing, Bianca?'

'How the fuck do you think I am doing? Look at me, Steve. Fucking look at me. I'm being treated like a common criminal.'

Steve raised his brow. 'I've got some news. Whether it is good news or bad news depends on your perspective.'

'Go on,' she said, as she leaned forward.

'Tyler Malloye has been found dead.'

The grin that tugged at the corner of her mouth said it all as far as Steve was concerned. She looked so pleased, she must have really hated him.

'I see you're happy about that.'

'Well, he was a right vile git. I won't lie and hide the fact that I hated him. Tommy spoiled the little shit rotten, yet he could never see that the boy had something not quite right about him. I would have said that his scruffy, stinking, lowlife mother gave him some of her genes. She wasn't right in the head, either, but Tyler, well, he'd make the Devil look good.'

'I know he was in and out of prison.'

She rolled her eyes. 'He would have been inside a lot more if his father hadn't kept organising alibis for him.' She sighed and looked up to the ceiling. 'He was wicked to me, hated me, he did. The little bastard was a little too premeditated for a young teenager. He did things for a laugh, but they weren't funny. They were cruel.'

'Like what?' asked Steve, now genuinely interested. For the first time, he could see the hurt on her face; he'd never known her to have that expression. She was as hard as nails and such a cold person. Apparently, back in Ireland they called her the Black Widow because she turned up at her second husband's funeral dressed in red and spat on his grave. And, heartlessly, she'd had her first husband cremated so fast that by the time his family had got wind of the fact that he'd died, she'd already had the funeral, leaving his ageing mother devastated.

'He unpicked the seams of all my beautiful designer dresses, and when I wore them out, they would literally fall apart on me. And he Photoshopped photos of me with other men.' She suddenly stopped and looked down. 'He was bloody determined to break me and Tommy up. Then he went too far and told Tommy I was making a play for him, but the truth was it was the other way around.' She sniffed the air and looked away, before she stared down at her hands. 'Well, he's dead now. Fucking good riddance to bad rubbish, is what I say. If there is an afterlife, then, hopefully, Tommy will give him the beating he deserves.'

Showing no compassion whatsoever, Steve moved his chair back from the table, before sitting down. 'Right, so do you know who killed Tyler?'

'Of course I don't fucking know who killed Tyler, but, clearly, it wasn't me, was it.'

'Did you pay anyone to kill him? I mean, you hated him that much.'

'But I would hate prison more, so no, numbnuts, o' course I didn't pay anyone to kill him.'

'And did you see any other men behind Tommy's back?'

She peered up at Steve. 'That's irrelevant. When am I getting out of here, Steve?'

'The issue is this: I have been informed by Detective Inspector Sparks that the police have enough evidence to charge you. You didn't tell me you'd rinsed his current account before he was killed. And you also didn't tell me that you'd renewed his life insurance two weeks ago, when you were also made aware that he was filing for divorce. You can't deny it because you had the paperwork. It was hand-delivered to you. Tommy was found dead at your house. There is motive. So, the troublesome issue I have is that right now, Bianca, I don't believe you.'

'You bastard, you owe me.'

Those words had Steve sitting up straight with a deep frown creasing his forehead. '*Owe you?* How could I possibly owe you?'

She nodded. 'You liked me. You know you did. We had a—'

'We had nothing, Bianca. It was all in your head.'

'Fuck off, I'm not a nutjob. It *wasn't* in my head.'

'Yes, it was. Whatever it was you felt for me, it definitely wasn't reciprocated. We had a friendship, and that's all.'

'Bollocks, I know it was more. You were going to wait for me. I was going to leave Tommy for you. But then you changed your mind.'

Chewing his bottom lip, Steve contemplated what her words would mean if she were to tell anyone else. If she did, he could be disbarred.

'I was your husband's lawyer, that's all, and you leaned on me for support, but there was no me and you. It was all in your head.'

There was another expression he'd not witnessed before: it was hurt, possibly even shame.

'Did I really get it all so wrong, Stevie?'

He coughed and loosened his tie. 'Yes, you did.'

'So that's it then, is it? They have enough evidence to convict me of my husband's murder, and my lawyer, who I really thought I could trust, is practically on their side.' Her voice cracked and squeaked. 'How convenient for you, Steve. You won't have to see me, talk to me, even. *And* you can push all thoughts of me to the back of your mind, and I can't say a word to anyone to hurt your pathetic life. You will still be the well-known lawyer, and as for me, I'll be the mad woman – the black widow – left to rot in some stinking hellhole.' A tear trickled down her nose, and she gracefully wiped it away. Then, her chin wobbled, but she took a deep breath and looked away, determined not to let him see her cry.

'Right, Bianca, are you still pleading not guilty?'

Suddenly, her eyes were like a blazing fire as she flashed a glare his way. 'Of course, I'm pleading not guilty, you prick. I'm *not* fucking guilty.'

The backlash made him flinch. 'Okay, I'll be in court with you first thing. And unless you have any other evidence that will help your case, I will see you then.'

She watched him rise from his chair and grab his briefcase. 'How can I put together evidence stuck in here? Will you push for bail for me?'

'Yes, but you are a Malloye, and so I'm afraid it's implausible you will be given bail. The money you do have wouldn't cover it. The house, the other assets – in fact everything – were in Tommy's name. But, right now, the file, which includes details of his last will and testament, is missing.'

'I heard about the kid. Your protégée killed the barrister, 'cos he tried to rape her, so I heard.' She smiled smugly, knowing it would send Steve into a fury. 'Not such a protégée after all, was she.'

He slammed the briefcase on the table and lunged forward. 'Shut your mouth, or you will find yourself being represented by a duty solicitor.'

'You have accepted the challenge. I believe you will need a bloody good reason not to see it through.'

Steve smiled and then gave a fake cough. 'I do believe I am coming down with something.'

Her eyes pinged open. 'You bastard.'

'Reel it in, Bianca. I will see you tomorrow.'

He left before she could say another word.

***

Hugh Shields was outside the interview room hovering around, but, unlike Steve, he was dishevelled, sporting the start of a beard, and his hair was dull and lifeless.

'Steve!'

'Oh, hi, Hugh, I'm in a bit of a rush. My client, Bianca Malloye, is pleading not guilty, and I am stumped as to what I can say in court tomorrow that will keep the judge from sending her to Bronzefield or Peterborough since Bronzefield is becoming quite full up these days.'

'This Malloye kid, Tyler. What are your thoughts on his murder? Only, Sparks is trying to link his murder to Dixie-Lee, although it seems he is desperately clutching at straws.'

'Dixie-Lee?'

'Yes, since they have evidence suggesting she killed the judge's son, and they won't consider it a coincidence that Tyler Malloye's body was found by some dumpster raider, in the back alley by the bins, only a few metres away from your chambers.'

'But what would be her motive?'

Shields shrugged. 'The obvious, I suppose. Tyler witnessed her killing the judge's son.'

‘Oh, for goodness’ sake! Really? So they believe that this kid – ’cos let’s face it, she’s just a student on an apprenticeship – goes and murders her colleague and then murders a well-known hardcore villain with the strength to slit his throat without any struggle. I just don’t buy that scenario.’

‘I know. It’s all bloody ludicrous. I guess Sparks is looking for promotion. Raj might have been of some help to us if the boss didn’t think he wasn’t too invested in the family. So, as Dixie-Lee’s solicitor, what I am asking you is this: has Bianca said anything about Tyler?’

Still stunned, Steve nodded. ‘She said he was evil. She hated him, but she didn’t mention Dixie-Lee, apart from revelling in the fact that she has been nicked for the murder of Clifford.’

‘Why would she do that? She doesn’t even know Dixie-Lee.’

‘No, but Dixie-Lee was there when we interviewed her, and Bianca is such a jealous bitch, she took an instant dislike to her . . .’ Steve paused and tapped his lip. ‘Did they find Tyler’s blood on Dixie-Lee’s clothes or her hair? Anywhere that could link her?’

Shields stared, now in deep thought.

‘I thought not. So Sparks is either gunning for that promotion, or he has a vendetta against Dixie-Lee. But, surely, there can’t be yet another bent copper in the station, can there?’

‘Well, Sparks is showing an unhealthy level of determination to pin both murders on the girl.’

‘I’d look into him if I were you, or get Raj to. She’s hardly a well-known gangster who Sparks should naturally want to throw the book at, is she.’ Steve tapped the side of his nose. ‘Do some digging and get hold of the forensics report. So is Cathy with Dixie-Lee now?’

‘No, she was only here briefly, yesterday, before she had to leave.’

‘Look, if these cases are connected, as I am also a witness, I can’t help to represent Dixie-Lee. Off the record, I can, though. I can give advice if you need it, Hugh.’ He patted his shoulder. ‘Anyway, I must get off . . . Oh, did they find any paperwork on or about Tyler’s person?’

Shields shook his head. ‘You mean Tommy Malloye’s file?’

Steve nodded.

‘No.’

CHAPTER TWELVE

Friday morning, Georgie descended the stairs biting her thumbnail as tears streamed down her cheeks; she had never in her life felt so helpless.

Rodney seemingly loitered in the hall, but he stepped back when he saw Rohan coming in through the front door. 'She's in a right old state, poor thing.'

Rohan, who was a good two feet taller than Rodney, patted his shoulder. 'It's okay, mate, I'm home. I can drive her to court.'

'Do you think they will let our Dixie-Lee out?'

Rohan slowly nodded. 'Hugh and Cathy will do their best, I'm sure. They are the elite.'

Rodney gave Rohan a compassionate smile and retreated to his annexe.

After taking his coat off and hanging it on the sleek black modern coat hook and then dumping his suitcase on the floor, Rohan walked into the kitchen. Instantly, he could see that Georgie was miles away and staring off into oblivion. She hadn't even heard him enter the room.

Rohan came from behind her and slid his hands around her waist. 'They are doing their best, darling.'

When Rohan returned from business in Ireland, she would normally throw her arms around his neck, but today, she didn't have an ounce of happiness to throw at anyone. Unable to rid her thoughts of the unimaginable, she stared out of the window and allowed her tears to fall. She couldn't speak; the lump in her throat was choking her.

‘Mum’s waiting in the car. She came back with me for moral support, I guess.’

Georgie snatched a tea towel and wiped her eyes. ‘I can’t get my head around it. She could go to fucking prison. If that Tyler hadn’t been murdered, I would have killed him myself.’

***

The mood was sombre, at the very least, by the time they all arrived at the court. The place was buzzing with reporters. Sparks had deliberately informed them about considerable press interest, even though the chief superintendent had told his officers to keep the incident out of the press. But Sparks had obviously wanted the notoriety as the arresting officer in the hope of increasing his chances of promotion. However, he didn’t know Fitzgerald, the chief superintendent, very well, and also he hadn’t realised that going over the chief superintendent’s head like that would go down like a lead balloon.

‘For feck’s sake, they are like fecking vultures. Look at them. Just fecking look at them,’ hissed Finella, who appeared as if she had just stepped out of a Prada advert for the mature woman.

No one would have guessed that she had been up since two in the morning and flown in from Ireland because she didn’t even have a hair out of place. Storming through the throng, she looked as fresh as a daisy and could have been mistaken for a solicitor or someone of importance.

Georgie didn’t care about the reporters. However, Rohan was moving people out of her way until a reporter shoved a giant microphone in her face. ‘What do you think about your daughter being charged with the murder of a barrister?’

Rohan glared at the young cocky-looking man, with eagerness proudly penetrating from his eyes.

‘Move!’

Ignoring Rohan, the reporter pushed the microphone even closer to Georgie. 'Mrs Deacon, do you know why they arrested her?'

'I said move,' growled Rohan, as he tried to push Georgie past the persistent reporter.

'Come on, Georgie, give us a clue.'

The fact that the reporter had ignored Rohan and then had the cheek to call Georgie by her first name pushed Rohan over the edge. 'I said move, you prick.' With that, he shoved the man out of the way with such force that the reporter tumbled back. But in doing so, when he grabbed Georgie's top to stop himself from falling, it led to her being pulled onto the pavement with him.

Rohan's anger quickly turned to rage. He grabbed the man by his hair and lifted him off the pavement before he could knock some sense into him.

Then Finella got involved. She swung her handbag so hard it knocked the reporter over. This time, he didn't have a chance to get to his feet. She walloped him repeatedly, while yelling, 'How fecking dare you put your hands on my daughter-in-law!'

Rohan swiftly pulled his mother away, while Georgie, who seemed to be racked with grief, tried to adjust her clothing.

The waiting gathering parted as Hugh Shields came charging through. He grabbed Georgie by her coat and pushed her through the central court main doors. 'Jesus, Georgie, are you okay? I saw what happened outside through the glass doors.' He looked at Finella, who was out of breath, huffing and puffing. 'I shouldn't think that reporter will want to get in anyone's face again. How's the handbag?' he asked, as he tried to make light of the situation.

'It's a designer one and well-made, unlike that reporter with a cheap suit and a mouth that needs filling.'

Rohan glared back through the glass doors and bared his teeth at the reporter, who looked down in embarrassment.

The reporter knew the public supported Dixie-Lee ever since the media had first followed her story from her time spent in a coma. But now, he hoped, another reporter could turn that around, especially if the altercation was filmed from an angle that made it appear as though he hadn't intentionally pulled her to the pavement.

As Shields tried to hurry Rohan, Georgie, and Finella through security, Steve Elison appeared and he looked less than pleased. Then again, Shields knew Steve to have a solemn expression most of the time unless he was performing in court, and then he could fool anyone. He checked the time. Dixie-Lee's case wasn't being heard until eleven.

'Ah, Steve.'

'Where is Cathy?' Steve asked.

Shields shook his head. 'She's not arrived yet. Why?'

'*Why indeed?*' said Steve, raising his voice.

Steve looked at Rohan, Georgie, and finally at who he assumed was Rohan's mother. 'She is supposed to be representing a member of our chambers. To wit: one Dixie-Lee Deacon. She should have been here way earlier to see to that poor girl being held downstairs in a bloody cell, who hasn't a clue, by the way, what the hell is going on.'

Georgie suddenly broke out of her sorrowful daze. 'Is my girl here already and *alone*?' Her eyebrows snapped together in fury. 'Will someone tell me. Is Cathy actually any good, or do we have the wrong Silk for the fucking job?'

Steve was shocked at how scary Georgie was. 'I can't represent her. It's not allowed since I would be a witness in the case,' he said, lowering his tone and adding a little empathy, which, to be fair, was something he had very little of. However, he did care for Dixie-Lee. 'Hugh, go down to the cells, will you. Make sure that the girl is okay.'

Shields nodded. 'Certainly, but before I do, tell me, Steve, did Bianca get bail?'

'Of course not! Sparks shoved her record as an accomplice to the Malloyes' earlier crimes in front of the judge, and as soon as he realised she was related to the Malloyes, he banged her up for her safety as well as the public's.' He shrugged his shoulders. 'I'm not surprised, though. Anyway, forget her, Hugh. Go and see Dixie-Lee, as I am sure she's . . .' He looked back at Georgie, who was hanging on to his every word. 'Well, she's probably in need of a little support.'

'They haven't hurt her, have they? I mean, I know what coppers can be like.'

'I only saw her briefly, but not to talk to, but, no, she's not been hurt. I think she is in deep contemplation.'

'You ain't suggesting she is guilty and—'

'Good God, no! I certainly don't believe she is guilty, not for a second. Sorry, that was badly worded, Mrs Deacon. Look, please know this. Even though I can't represent her, I will work from the sidelines with Hugh.'

Georgie nodded. 'Thank you.'

'Cathy is good, though, isn't she, Steve?' asked Rohan, quickly stepping in. His aim was to put Georgie's mind at rest, but he also knew he'd said the wrong thing the moment he'd said it.

Georgie gave him a look of annoyance. 'Well, she's clearly not good at timekeeping, is she.'

Rohan could have kicked himself. He knew he had said the wrong thing.

As Steve left the main court, Shields showed them to the first floor where courtroom two was. 'The hearing will begin in about ten minutes. I will go down and make sure Dixie-Lee is all right.'

'Tell her that we are all here.'

Shields smiled at Finella. 'Of course I will.'

On the first floor, through the double doors, there were two courtrooms and rows of plastic seats screwed to metal frames. The Deacons wouldn't have to wait long before they could go inside courtroom two.

Rohan tried to put his arm around Georgie's shoulders, but she shrugged him off.

Finella noticed it and glared at Rohan, now wondering what he had done to upset her daughter-in-law.

'This Cathy has an attitude problem that, to be honest, I don't much care for, and you sticking up for her when the woman is late and should be here, quite frankly, it pisses me off.'

'I was only trying to put your mind at rest, that's all.'

'Hmm, really? Well, anyway, I won't argue. My girl's liberty is at stake here, and that's all I am really concerned about.'

Georgie suddenly choked on her words and took a deep breath; she couldn't cry anymore. It was ridiculous. Dixie-Lee would want to see her upright and strong, to show her that there was nothing to worry about. In her heart, though, she knew it would be so damned tough if her daughter was given a prison sentence.

The main double doors opened, and everyone looked up to see what was happening.

Georgie was surprised to see Sheila hurtling towards them. Her long black coat, fur boots, and black hat would have been perfect for a funeral but her attire seemed distinctly out of place for a court appearance.

'Oh, fuck me, I thought I was going to miss it.' She stopped talking then and removed her gloves.

'You only just made it, Sheila. Five minutes and we go in.'

'Poxy place, Georgie. It's swarming with reporters, ya know. How is Dixie-Lee?'

Georgie shrugged. 'I haven't seen her. Apparently, she is in quiet mode.'

'Always happens. Ya know you sit there quiet, thinking and worrying, not about yaself, like, but more about your family and how they will take it all. So, listen to me, 'cos ya know I've been in your shoes many a time, what with my unruly lot, and I've been in Dixie-Lee's shoes too. I'm not proud, but I've served bird.' She stopped talking to take a breath and smiled at Finella, who was intrigued by what Sheila was saying.

'When she comes into that glass box, you look her in the eye and tell her you love her and that everything will be all right. Don't, for fuck's sake, cry or yell or even call out if, and I mean only *if*, she does have to go on remand. 'Cos your hooting and hollering will play on her mind, and your face will be imprinted on her brain. Got me?'

Georgie smiled and hugged her newfound friend. 'Thank you, Sheila, that's good advice.'

'Yeah, well, I should have been a counsellor, what with my history, and I'm known for being able to put people at ease. My Yasmin's always saying how good I am with words.'

Georgie wanted to laugh because of all the careers suitable for Sheila, counselling wouldn't be one of them. Before Sheila could rattle on anymore, the court usher waved Georgie in.

'The gallery will fill up as soon as they open those doors. Do please take your seat first.'

Georgie then realised how big this case would be. It hit her that now her daughter was on trial for killing the judge's son, there was no way on Earth that Dixie-Lee would get bail.

The usher wasn't wrong about the enormous interest in this case. Within minutes of her taking the front-row seat, the doors opened again, and people piled into the gallery. The noise was like a flock of seagulls finding an uneaten wrapping of fish and chips.

Georgie couldn't hear what they were saying, but whatever it was, it was loud and excitable.

However, as soon as the usher shouted out 'All Rise!', the judge entered, and the courtroom was silent. Wearing thick Coke-bottle glasses and a yellowing beard, Judge Althorp took his seat and scrutinised the paperwork before him. He peered below where the prosecution and defence barristers were sitting.

On one side was the prosecution barrister. He was a middle-aged man whose eyes were pretty wide apart but who seemed to sit with an erect posture. His movements were quick and precise as he flicked through his paperwork. Beside him was a junior barrister.

But on the other side of the aisle, to the left of him, the judge frowned when he saw two empty chairs.

The judge's confusion was not lost on Georgie, who was observing proceedings with laser-like thoroughness. 'Where the fuck is she, Rohan?'

Georgie could feel his heavy sigh. 'I don't know, darling, but please try not to get uptight. You heard what Sheila said.'

The judge leaned forward and whispered something to the usher, who promptly left the room. The only sound now was the rustling of paper.

Moments later, everyone heard footsteps, and to the delight of some onlookers but to the consternation of Georgie, Dixie-Lee appeared in the glass box.

Georgie's heart began to beat so fast, she thought she would be sick, but Sheila's words were at the forefront of her mind, and she looked over to her daughter with a broad smile.

Dixie-Lee instantly sighted her mother, and she nodded.

Georgie mouthed the words 'I love you. We're here, darling.' But what she wanted to do was to smash the glass box and rescue her kid. She tried to keep her smile plastered on her face, but it was so hard. Seeing her daughter in a suit she'd previously sent in, and with her hair pulled back, she looked like a kid dressing up playing bank tellers. Her sweet dainty face was so white, and dark brown rings circled her eyes. The bruise on her cheek was still apparent.

Georgie wanted to run to her and hug her, and if she could swap places, she would have. This was all wrong. How could she be there in the dock when she was the one who was sexually assaulted? Her daughter had only fought for her dignity as she had taught her to do. If only she hadn't trained her to fight, maybe she wouldn't be in the dock. Instead, she might have been at home playing with her cat.

The lump in Georgie's throat was back again and threatening to choke her. And it was as if Rohan sensed it. He squeezed her hand and whispered, 'Be strong.'

After a few seconds, Georgie was dragged from her thoughts when the door opened, and in waltzed Cathy as if she was the main attraction. Georgie could see how she commanded attention. She carried herself with absolute conviction, laced with elegant charm.

'I do apologise, Your Honour.'

Georgie looked at the judge, who, to her surprise, seemed to blush.

'Take a seat. We haven't begun yet,' he replied, with a smile, as if she was the only woman in the courtroom.

The prosecution barrister shot a look of distaste at Cathy, who merely smiled back in utter contempt.

Feeling her heart jumping out of her chest, Georgie tried to listen and lipread when the judge called the two barristers to the Bench. She didn't like the look on the prosecution barrister's face. He was smiling.

The barristers returned to their seats, and the judge presided. 'In view of the evidence against the accused, the Crown will have grounds to remand Dixie-Lee Deacon in custody until the trial date. Are there any extenuating circumstances we should hear for grounds to oppose bail?'

‘Your Honour,’ said Cathy, standing up and using her clearest tone, ‘Dixie-Lee Deacon neither has a criminal record nor does she have reason to abscond. If it pleases Your Honour, I would respectfully suggest that she be monitored using an electronic tag. I can assure you that Miss Deacon is an upstanding citizen. In fact, she is training as a legal executive to eventually become a barrister. She is unlikely to leave the country before she is found innocent of this dreadful murder. It is truly a case of someone being in the wrong place at the wrong time.’

Georgie stared, scrutinising the expression on the judge’s face.

He didn’t answer. He looked at the prosecution barrister, who abruptly rose from his seat and said in clear, precise words, ‘Your Honour, Dixie-Lee Deacon is charged with the murder of a bright barrister with an impressive record. So, in light of the circumstances of the murder, and this being most vile, and’ – he pointed to Dixie-Lee – ‘on account of the fact that the accused hasn’t denied that there was a fight between them which led to her biting chunks out of his flesh, the prosecution would be concerned about the Court granting bail. This is no shy, retiring young woman. At best, she is unstable, and at worst, a premeditated killer. We find no reason for her to be granted bail, and we strongly oppose it. She has family in Ireland, who are not, shall we say, on the poverty line. She will have the means to abscond if she chooses, so we, the Crown, object to bail.’

‘This is a rather sensitive case, considering the accused was also the victim’s colleague.’

The prosecution waved something at the judge. ‘May I approach the Bench, Your Honour?’

Georgie saw the prosecution barrister hand several sheets of paper to the judge.

He studied the photographs and then mumbled, 'Yes, rather gruesome. Bail is denied. Please take Miss Deacon into custody until the trial date is set.'

'Committal first, Your Honour?' asked Cathy.

'Yes, quite, quite. Sorry, until the committal date.'

Georgie couldn't process the words quickly enough before Dixie-Lee was escorted back towards the cells. She only just managed to get a glimpse of her daughter's smile, and she knew Dixie-Lee was only doing that to put her mind at rest.

'All Rise!' shouted the usher.

But Georgie couldn't. Her legs were too weak with shock, and her mind simply couldn't register that her daughter was now being taken to prison. Surely not?

Rohan tugged at her arm. 'Come on, love, let's go. The usher said we can leave via a different entrance.'

Georgie looked at Rohan, who was standing and towering over her, but her mind wasn't focused on getting out without the reporters seeing her. She was determined to catch Cathy McGowan.

Just as Cathy collected her papers and slid them into her briefcase, Georgie got up, shuffled past Rohan, and marched straight over to her. 'What the hell was that all about?'

Cathy snapped her briefcase shut. 'You didn't think I could wave a magic wand and, poof, Dixie-Lee would walk free, did you?'

'Don't be so fucking facetious.'

'Excuse me, Mrs Deacon, but I represent your daughter, not you.'

Cathy looked over Georgie's shoulder and smiled in acknowledgement of someone.

Georgie spun around to see Rohan smiling back. Georgie was already devastated, and the woman's nerve, along with Rohan's lack of support, made her furious.

'Well, I'm fucking glad, Rohan, that you can smile at a time like this. When our, I mean my Dixie-Lee is getting ready to go to a fucking prison.' She looked back at Cathy. 'You didn't say much to defend her or to push for bail. Useless! Fucking useless!' she spat, looking Cathy up and down.

Shields quickly intervened. 'Come with me, Georgie. This will do no good, love.'

He grabbed her arm and looked at Cathy. 'Can we talk later?'

Georgie noticed his voice was firm, and, at that moment, she knew he was as angry as she was.

As Georgie and Hugh Shields walked towards the door, Cathy called out, 'Mrs Deacon, it was a foregone conclusion. They were never going to agree to bail. I knew that before I walked in. This was just a formality, and as much as I am a barrister, I'm not the bloody judge. They want blood, Mrs Deacon. Clifford was actually a judge's son. I'm sorry.'

Georgie turned around and shook her head. 'Not good enough. You should have shown my girl that you were fighting for her regardless of how well you knew the fucking outcome. My daughter will go off to prison thinking that you never had her back. Just like I do.'

CHAPTER THIRTEEN

As Dixie-Lee was finally escorted off the prison van, her hairband broke, and her loose waves blew freely around her face. It wasn't lost on her that her final moments of freedom were about to end. She was now just a number.

Her hesitant steps were compounded by her playing over in her mind the final conversation with Cathy. *Had Cathy not believed she was innocent?*

The guard's words were firm and cold, enriching the gravity of the situation. 'I haven't got all day, you know.'

Before she walked into the imposing building they called Bronzefield Prison, she took one last look at the outside and the looming dark clouds that seemed to have followed her all the way to her impending doom. Her actions were now on autopilot.

It seemed that every officer merged into one. Going from one security check to another, she was finally given her prison clothes to wear and taken to a room to change from her courtroom attire. The prison-issue grey tracksuit was two sizes too big for her, ridiculing her frame, in that it gave her the appearance of a fragile and seemingly vulnerable woman. But that, it seemed, was the least of her problems. She had yet to meet the inmates.

Every officer's words appeared to go in one ear and out the other, so preoccupied was she by her own sense of helplessness, so she couldn't remember the exact details. And as for the rules and procedures, there were just too many to take in. But what did it matter if she got the rules wrong? It occurred to her that she would have years to get them right. Being charged with the judge's son's murder, she would probably be found guilty. She would be lucky if she was younger than forty-five before she saw the outside world. Would her mother even be alive then?

Gripping a clear plastic bag in her right hand, which held everything she would need for her time inside, Dixie-Lee was led towards a spur, as it was called, to a room they called the cell, which she would share with a stranger. As she walked a foot behind the officer, she passed other inmates and was immediately uneasy. Everything was unfamiliar: the smell of bleach and disappointment, the women's faces carved with defiance – some with resignation and others with unadulterated hardened anger – and the terrifying realisation that there would be no one in here she could call a friend or someone to help her when needed. And she knew she would need someone. She had heard stories about prison life from her new grandfather Rodney. He had spared her much but she wasn't a fool. Reading between the lines, she knew you had to keep your thoughts to yourself. Never have a friend – because that friend would be someone's enemy.

She lowered her gaze, terrified to look these inmates in the eye and become the woman they would bully because what clout did she have? None. She had to keep herself to herself and hope they would leave her alone.

But in her heart, she surmised that she would be a target. Rodney's stories of life in prison – and the very little information she had managed to glean from her mother – weren't the only font of all knowledge. She understood and had even studied many books on women behind bars, all part of her online degree course. So she recognised that many of them had been bullied themselves, some abused by their partners and even their fathers, and many women were inside for minor property crimes such as shoplifting and simple assault. So the hardened expressions scarred on their faces were explicable. Even the women with the over-the-top smiles and wild eyes that were ravaged by drugs, life, and finally coping with prison through mania brought on by prescribed drugs.

It wasn't until she was told to go inside her room that she looked at the officer, a tall woman with strawberry blonde hair and freckles.

This officer wasn't wearing much of an expression. She seemed indifferent to the new inmate's plight. 'This is your room. Bottom bunk locker on the left and shared bog. Lunch is in ten minutes.'

'I, er . . . I'm not hungry. May I have a cup of tea?'

Suddenly, the officer, whose lanyard read 'Officer Nora Sheen', seemed to come alive, and her expression changed instantly. Spiteful eyes replaced dull ones and her poker-faced expression was replaced with a cruel, spiteful smirk. 'Cup of tea! This ain't a hotel, Deacon. This is a prison, so no one makes you tea. There's no waiter.' She pointed to the clear bag. 'In your bag are a few teabags, a small carton of milk, and in those two flasks is hot water. Make your own tea.'

Dixie-Lee nodded. 'Thank you,' she replied.

'And you need to go over to the canteen area now to get your lunch. Get used to the times or you will starve to death, and our medical wing is full to the brim, so don't you add to it, 'cos I won't take too kindly to you doing that. D'you hear me?'

'Yes, er . . .' She looked closer at the officer's lanyard. 'Mrs Sheen.'

'Good. Get unpacked and head back along the corridor, past the education wing, and into the central hub. You will be signed off at the queue. And one final thing: I'm not Mrs Sheen to you. Call me Officer Sheen, in future.'

Dixie-Lee didn't argue. She nodded politely and waited for the officer to leave before she unpacked the plastic bag. After emptying the contents onto her bunk, she stared at the cheap toiletries and the stiff bedding. She'd never been spoilt and hadn't been used to anything remotely luxurious for most of her life, so the meagre lifestyle she was now going to have to get accustomed to wasn't so daunting to her. It was only comparatively recently, when her grandmother, Finella, came into her life, that she experienced anything at all that smacked of real class. But the plastic bag made her feel so lost in it all. A tear rolled down her cheek, but she instantly brushed it away when she heard a voice in the doorway.

'For fuck's sake, I said I wanted the cell to *myself*!'

Dixie-Lee spun around to face a woman in her thirties. She was skinny with a gaunt face and round bulbous eyes.

'Hi, I'm Dixie-Lee. Sorry.'

The woman crossed her arms, leaned back, and laughed. 'What are you? American or somink?'

'No.'

'What are you in for?' sniggered the inmate.

'Sorry, I thought. I mean . . . I was told we can't ask that question.'

'Oh, fuck me, we've got a jobsworth 'ere, 'ave we. Don't tell me. Whatever you were accused of, you didn't do it. Am I right?'

Dixie-Lee looked the skinny woman up and down.

'Oi, Miss USA, don't look at me like that. I'll wipe that pretty look clean off ya fucking face.'

Staring at the woman, Dixie-Lee didn't care what she had to say. And out of the blue, she felt an inner strength and confidence. Where it came from, she didn't know, and neither did she care. Having reached the abyss in her life, perhaps there was only one way to go for her and that was up. She smiled, thinking what her mother would do because she certainly wouldn't stand any shit from anyone, and if she had even an ounce of her mother in her, she would stand her ground. Without replying to this inmate, she merely smirked at her.

It prompted an instant response. The wretched-looking woman straightened her shoulders and smiled. 'Look, me and you have to share this cell, so best we get on, yeah?'

Dixie-Lee suddenly sensed the level of power she had just gained and smirked again. 'Sure.'

'My name is Andrea Bowman.'

Dixie-Lee nodded confidently. 'So you're on the top bunk, then. Yeah?'

'Yeah, er . . . have you done bird before?'

Dixie-Lee shook her head. 'No, it's the first time.' The moment she said it, she clocked the cockiness creep back into Andrea's eyes.

'Stick wiv me, Dixie-Lee, and you'll be fine and fucking dandy. I know everyone in this nick. I've got loads of mates, and 'cos you're me cellmate, they'll leave you alone.'

Dixie-Lee wanted to laugh because she'd passed a few inmates who would scare a caged lion. Andrea, on the other hand, was, in her eyes, pathetic. Her long bony arms, scarred from injecting heroin, and her nails bitten down to the quick, told her so much about Andrea, that respect for her out of fear wasn't going to happen. Not now, not ever.

'Great,' Dixie-Lee replied, sarcastically, although if this situation had happened on the outside, she might have been grateful. In prison, though, it was all a game of cat and mouse – like mixing on a school playground full of groups and bullies.

'Yeah, er, listen, Dixie-Lee, there's a woman in here. She likes to meet the newcomers, yeah. She'll tell you how it works and how you can make your life easier for yaself. And if you want to get ya hands on a bit o' gear, like, well, she'll take you under her wing, kinda thing, and see you all right. You wiv me?'

Dixie-Lee didn't answer her. But she let Andrea know she wasn't enthralled by her comment by dismissively turning away and picking up a teabag from the few that had fallen out onto her bunk and snatching the prison-issue mug. She dropped the teabag inside and nonchalantly poured the hot water from the flask into it. She then used a teaspoon from the small table to stir it.

All the while, Andrea watched her. 'So, anyway, this woman, uh, she wants to meet ya. She kinda runs the prison, like.'

Dixie-Lee sipped her tea and then looked casually up and replied, 'Oh, but, Andrea, I thought *you* ran the prison.'

'Who? What? Me?' She poked herself in the chest before she laughed. 'Nah, mate, not me. I just, well, I kinda work for her, but don't get me wrong, I'm not her gofer Anyway, you stick with me, and no one will touch ya.'

'Andrea, look, with respect, I want to be left alone, right? I need to get my head straight for my trial, so, thank you, but I don't need to meet anyone. I'm not into being part of anything, so thanks but no thanks.'

With one hand on her hip and the other rubbing her forehead, Andrea's eyes flicked nervously around the room. 'Nah, see, you have to meet her, right? It's not an ask, it's a demand. Listen, just have a quick word, yeah, and then it's job done.'

Dixie-Lee gulped the last of her tea and sighed. 'No, Andrea. It ain't going to happen.'

'Oh, fuck me, what ya doing to me, Dixie? She will fucking give me such a beating.'

'My name's *not* Dixie, it's Dixie-Lee, and your problem isn't mine. I said, I don't want to meet anyone, be friends with anyone, or talk to anyone. I just want to be left alone. I appreciate we must share a room, but that's where our relationship ends.'

With her face now burning red with anger, Andrea tapped her foot. 'You will be sorry, you fucking idiot, and if she beats me up,

I'm coming back to beat you up, Miss Fucking USA, and believe me, darling, I will scar that pretty face of yours.'

As soon as Andrea stormed off, Dixie-Lee was able to relax her taut shoulders and bring her heartbeat back to normal. Although she may have overdone the cockiness, she was pleased she had shown Andrea that she didn't want to be bullied. Her mother sure as hell wouldn't have been. Pushing everything that was on her bunk onto the floor, she curled into a ball on the stained mattress. Then, holding in the tears, she tried to figure out a way to survive this shithole and how to deal with these inmates who were all eager to take a piece of her. She would fight to save her sanity and dignity and work hard to think of a way of escaping from this mess.

After a few minutes, there was a tap at the door, even though the door was open. 'Deacon, I told you to go to the canteen. Like I said, I ain't taking anyone who faints – because they're starving – to medical. Now, get up and get in that canteen and eat the shit you're served.'

Dixie-Lee uncurled herself and sat up as straight as the bottom bunk would allow. She didn't answer. She stared at the officer before standing up. Having been polite the first time, which had achieved nothing, she decided to do as she was told and not to say a word this time. It seemed that being courteous and pleasant got you nowhere in this place.

She followed the officer to the central hub where the food was being served, only to find a hive of women all nattering and stuffing their faces.

As soon as she arrived in the room, the place turned scarily silent. She then learned what it was like to take in the real grim stench of prison. It wasn't the smell or the dull fake lights but the atmosphere of pure hostility. There wasn't a friendly pair of eyes in sight. Scanning the room, she could tell that this was nothing like a school canteen, where there was a buzz of excitement about the place. Instead, she found herself in a setting where survival of the fittest played out at every table, with each group huddled together, pacts already established, and the pecking order certified.

High-pitched giggles came from a few thin women who looked like Andrea's clones; they were so easily recognisable as drug addicts.

Dixie-Lee could see they were laughing at her as if they knew something she didn't. They reminded her of hyenas. Instantly, she looked away and stared at the first woman serving the food. She was a large Asian woman with a blank expression and she was holding a ladle already heavy with lumpy mashed potato.

Collecting a tray, a bowl, plastic cutlery, and a bottle of water, Dixie-Lee looked back at Officer Sheen.

'Go on, get your food, and find a seat. Once you're done, you can return to your cell.'

Relief came when the chattering began again, and she was no longer the centre of attention. Placing her bowl under the ladle, she watched the woman, who, like a robot, dropped the food into her bowl. In the next section, a Chinese woman, who seemed to have a permanent grin on her face, slapped a pie into her bowl before saying, 'You're not a vegetarian, are you?'

Shaking her head, Dixie-Lee moved to the next section. This time, with a sour face, another Chinese woman dropped a ladle full of overcooked discoloured carrots into her bowl. A feeling of sickness came over her. The food wasn't so bad, but it was all a shock to her system. Only a few hours ago, she was in court, and now, here she was faced with eating her food in a canteen with a hundred strangers all ready to eat her.

Steadying her hands to hold the tray, she was careful not to give away the fact that she was inwardly shaking. Her heart was back to thumping loudly and fast, echoing her nervous energy, but she lifted her chin and acted as if she wasn't afraid. Her eyes roamed the area, looking for the right table to sit at, like the characters in *Goldilocks and the Three Bears* – not too quiet, not too rowdy, but just right. To her far left was a table with three women. One looked to be in her late seventies, another was pregnant, and the other was a soft-faced middle-aged woman.

As she headed towards them, she was suddenly met with a startled look from the older woman, who then became evidently very agitated. Then, the pregnant woman flicked her hand as if shooing away a fly. Something was unnerving them, but she wasn't going to retreat and look weak. So she sat down at the end of their table with her back to the wall. The three women then moved along to the other end of the table, as far away from her as possible, as though she had a contagious disease.

A lump lodged in Dixie-Lee's throat. Not only was she locked up in this monstrous place, but she was also being treated like a leper.

Just as she was about to put a spoonful of lumpy potato to her lips, she heard a woman shout, 'Oi!'

The room fell silent, but Dixie-Lee didn't see where the voice was coming from. Glancing at the two officers standing together, who were clearly whispering to each other, she could see they were obviously ignoring the pervading hostility in the room.

When Dixie-Lee heard footsteps heading her way, she couldn't resist looking up.

It was Andrea, who was seemingly flustered. Stopping in front of Dixie-Lee, she said, 'Dulcie Forest wants a word!' Then she leaned closer, and whispered, 'I fucking told you, didn't I? Now you're in trouble. No one fucking breathes in this nick unless she says so.'

Dixie-Lee scanned the room, taking in every pair of eager eyes, until she realised who Dulcie was. It didn't take more than a second or two to lock eyes on her. And then it seemed that the whole room full of inmates were focused on the interaction between her and Dulcie.

Dulcie's table was full. She sat at the end as though she was sitting on a throne, and the inmates surrounding her all looked cocky, ready for a fight. Dulcie wasn't a huge woman, but she was heavily built. It was hard to distinguish her heritage, but Dixie-Lee guessed she was Hispanic. And surrounding her were women of all colour. Curling her finger, Dulcie beckoned Dixie-Lee.

Why aren't the officers doing anything? Dixie-Lee fretted. Was it true that this woman who Andrea called Dulcie was, in fact, the boss here? Instantly, she assessed her situation. For a start, there was too much evidence against her to fight for her own freedom. And so the chances were that she was going to be in this prison for a long time. All too many thoughts flashed through her mind just then. Snippets of conversations she'd had with Rodney and her mother, both of whom had served time. If this was going to be her new life from now on, she needed to make a quick and irreversible decision about her plight and her future. She had two things going for her that the rest of these inmates were unaware of. She had her mother's resourcefulness and her guile. She would use those qualities. They should serve her well. One thing she definitely wasn't going to accept was to become a pathetic runner or gofer, or, worse, a sexual partner for a woman who looked old enough to be her mother. She had read about that too in her studies.

So she was left with two options: to submit herself to the cruelty of these women and Dulcie in particular, or to stand up to them. The second option would mean one of two things: she would either be killed, or she would come out on top; the latter was probably more through hope than a real possibility.

Using her plastic knife and fork to cut into the rock-hard pie, she totally ignored everyone, including Andrea, who was now sitting in an agitated state by her side. However, as she glanced at the officers again, she saw that they now had their backs to her. It told her one thing: they knew something was going to kick off, and they weren't going to witness it. Her moment of bravado was suddenly dismissed, and frissons of regret and fear began to creep in. Her heart thumped, and she tried to swallow the mashed potato that had sucked every drop of moisture from her tongue. When she tried to open the lid of the bottle of water, her sweaty hands were shaking.

'Just go over there. She will fucking kill you, otherwise,' urged Andrea. Her tone had changed as if it was friendly advice she was giving. 'See, she's got nuffin to lose. She's in 'ere for five counts of murder, so killing you will just be another crime to add to her time in prison.'

Out of nowhere, Dixie-Lee replied, 'She ain't the only one. Now, just fuck off!'

The minute she said it, she wondered who the hell had just invaded her body. Opening the lid, she downed the water before she found the guts to get up and leave. However, just then, the main door burst open.

Dixie-Lee hoped it was back-up in the form of officers to end the brooding and impending violence. Yet, to her amazement, she was shocked to the core when she saw Bianca Malloye strolling in and being escorted by two officers. She had to look twice. They weren't treating her like an inmate: they were fussing over her like a celebrity. One officer found a tray for her, while the other was joking and laughing as though they were old buddies.

Dixie-Lee almost jumped out of her skin when there was a sudden rapturous applause. As all the inmates cheered Bianca, Dixie-Lee's blood ran cold. Bianca was known here; of course, she would be. She'd served time before. And being Tommy Malloye's wife, she was now on the inside again with women she'd probably ruled while inside for her previous conviction. She would have had it easy and still would.

Having studied many of the sociological issues affecting women during their confinement in prison in her degree course, Dixie-Lee had become familiar with inmate hierarchy and how it was achieved. Bianca was rich, and her husband had been powerful. The officers would have been bought, securing her a cushy time inside. She would have got her hands on drugs and phones and all manner of contraband, which would assure her the position as boss – a woman who ran the wing or the entire prison.

As Bianca collected her food, she sauntered over to Dulcie's table and was greeted with hugs and pats on the back.

Dixie-Lee gazed around to see most of the women waving and nodding. Someone called out, 'Good to see ya, Bianca.'

But there was a small group who didn't look up. They caught Dixie-Lee's attention for no other reason than they appeared to be too busy eating to be bothered by all the fuss that was going on around them. One was a big woman, probably three times the size of Dulcie. Dixie-Lee decided it was time to head back to her cell and hopefully not get jumped on.

But, as she took two steps, Andrea grabbed her by the shoulders. 'Don't walk away, for fuck's sake. Dulcie will muller ya and . . .' She lowered her voice. 'She'll do it to show off in front of *The Widow*, Bianca Malloye.'

Dixie-Lee spun back. '*Don't* fucking touch me. I'm not worried about Bianca.'

'You should be. She'll have you killed in the blink of an eye. Please, Miss America, just go over there. Do it for me.'

'No, I'm not doing a thing for anyone in here. I don't owe you, Dulcie, or Bianca Malloye anything.'

'Well, well! If it ain't the solicitor wannabe!'

Dixie-Lee's blood ran cold. She looked across the room to see Bianca glaring wildly with a sneer slapped across her face and her hands on her hips.

Dulcie jumped up and ran towards her with another woman in her twenties. She was stocky with tattoos covering both arms.

Dixie-Lee suddenly felt so overwhelmed. The lunatics were running the asylum. All she could think to do was to run, but, in a flash, one of the officers hurried to the door.

The feeling of terror gripped Dixie-Lee around the throat. She felt as though she was actually choking. And her head felt like a million ice spears poking her scalp. Enveloped by fear, she was suddenly rooted to the spot. Her breathing stopped. Staring ahead, she knew she would never be able to fight this woman and her sidekick.

'Bring her to me, 'cos that little bitch killed my stepson.'

Those words were so alarming that Dixie-Lee's mouth dropped open, and yet her tongue was paralysed. No words would come out.

Before she could do anything, Dulcie stormed across the room, swung her arm, and held Dixie-Lee in a tight headlock.

Despite seeing the girl struggling to breathe, Dulcie didn't let up. She squeezed tighter and tighter.

All Dixie-Lee could do was to claw at the woman's meaty arm, desperate to be able to breathe. She knew that Dulcie was going to make her victim number six.

Her ears felt at first as though there was a swarm of bees buzzing inside them. It made hearing anything very difficult. But then, when Dulcie released her grip fractionally, she heard Bianca cackling away. 'See, Dixie-Lee Deacon, now you're fucked.'

From nowhere, another voice yelled, 'Get the fuck off her!'

Through blurred vision, Dixie-Lee saw an enormous woman come bounding over like The Hulk, except she wasn't green. Before she managed to blink, a punch was thrown in her direction.

Assuming the punch was being aimed straight at her, Dixie-Lee then closed her eyes. The next thing she knew was that Dulcie was falling backwards and dragging her down too.

The colossal woman pulled Dixie-Lee away and turned to take on anyone who would dare to stop her.

'Now, back the fuck off. Any of yous touch this kid, and I'll 'ave ya!'

Dixie-Lee coughed and spluttered and blinked to get her focus back.

'None of your business, Patsy,' said Bianca, as she walked towards her.

'Oh, believe me, bitch, Dixie-Lee Deacon *is* my fucking business. You may have had clout in this nick once upon a time. But me, I don't need fuck all from you now and I never did back then. No baccy, no drugs, no nuffin. So you have jack shit over me.'

She spun around to face Dulcie, whose nose was swollen and dripping with blood. 'And as for you, Dulcie, you take your scaghead mates with ya and fuck off.'

Dulcie wiped her nose and backed away, but Bianca stood her ground. 'You'll be sorry, Patsy. Fucking sorry.'

'You don't run this joint, Bianca. Look at ya. You're a fucking washed-out bit o' trash.'

Patsy Dewhurst looked around the canteen. The officers were now on the perimeter, waiting to step in.

'You lot are as thick as shit. She's in here for killing her ol' man. If you think she's gonna run this place now, think again. She's skint, and the Malloyes won't back her now! She only killed their big brother!'

Dixie-Lee clocked how everyone was now looking at each other as if the penny had dropped.

'You know nothing, Patsy, and you've made a big mistake. Another thing. See that bitch. She killed my stepson. You think she's gonna get away with that?'

Patsy turned to Dixie-Lee. 'Did ya kill her stepson?'

'No.'

'See, Bianca, she didn't kill him.'

Bianca was glowing red. 'You know fuck all, Patsy.'

'If Dixie-Lee Deacon says she didn't kill him, she didn't fucking kill him. End of. And if you fucking dare harm a hair on her head, I'll turn ya into the fuck-up fairy and curdle your blood after I've shit down your scrawny neck. Now, take your paper army and back off.'

Bianca looked at the officers, hoping for an intervention. But Patsy's words were resonating with everyone because the inmates went back to their tables and the officers were taking no notice of what was happening. Even Dulcie was merely mumbling threats under her breath.

'D'ya wanna speak a bit louder, Dulcie, or are you too chicken? Either way, amigo, I will fuck you up.'

'I said I'm sorry, Patsy.'

'It ain't me you wanna say sorry to. It's Dixie-Lee.'

Dulcie's bottom lip quivered as she wiped her bloody nose again. She looked Dixie-Lee up and down and grinned. 'You've got bravado, I'll give you that. Who is she, Patsy?'

'This, Dulcie, is Georgie Deacon's daughter. And believe me, Dulcie, this kid is one you won't wanna fuck over, not if you have loved ones on the outside. 'Cos, see, her family will make your life and your family's a bloody nightmare.' She looked at Bianca. 'I bet the Deacons have already paid your family a visit.' She paused and laughed. 'Of course, you wouldn't know that 'cos I bet they want your head on a plate for killing a member of their family.'

Everyone saw the sudden look of fear distorting Bianca's face.

'Huh, see right there, Bianca, you've just lost your arsehole, haven't ya.'

Unexpectedly, Bianca looked at Dixie-Lee. 'I apologise.'

'Nah, not good enough, Bianca, but you'll be in here long enough to make amends. Now, who is sharing a cell with my Dixie-Lee?'

'Your Dixie-Lee?' said Dulcie, still intrigued.

'I'm as close to an aunt as she'll get in here, so' – she pointed around the room – 'if any one of yous even looks at her the wrong way, remember this: you are fucking with Patsy's niece. Got it, 'ave ya?'

Dixie-Lee was surprised to see everyone nodding.

'I'm sharing with Dixie-Lee. I'll look after her. I'll see her all right, Patsy,' said Andrea.

'No, you won't, you crackhead. You are swapping with Ginty.' She looked over at an officer, who rolled her eyes but nodded.

Ginty Conway, who was a skinny woman with dark cropped hair and as bright as a button, appeared smiling. 'It was nice, Patsy, sharing with you, but family comes first.' She nodded to Dixie-Lee out of respect.

Dixie-Lee couldn't smile because she had just stared death in the face, and her saving angel was a woman who was the size of a house with a tattooed neck and spiky hair. But she wasn't dressed in white with feathered wings, that was for sure.

'Sit, back down, Dixie-Lee. Let's have our lunch in peace now.'

'I'm not really hungry.'

'No worries, I'll eat yours. Me, I'm always starving. Look at this physique. It didn't get like this by eating carrots.'

As if the atmosphere had instantly changed, Dixie-Lee giggled nervously, contemplating the prospect of sharing a cell with Patsy Dewhurst.

CHAPTER FOURTEEN

By the time Georgie got home, her mind was full of dark thoughts. And no matter how much she tried to get herself together, she couldn't get the vision of her daughter being carted away out of her head. She knew what prison was like, and recalling how she was initially treated and the horrific physical altercation she'd had inside, she now felt sick with worry for her daughter. Dixie-Lee was a kind girl and she could defend herself, but she didn't have the same genes as her, and so she felt her daughter could easily be the girl the inmates picked on. All she could tell herself was that she shouldn't underestimate her daughter because she had shown she could fight if need be.

Georgie paced the bedroom floor, unable to go down to the kitchen to face Rohan and Finella. In fact, she wasn't sure how she felt about Rohan right now. Seeing him smiling at Cathy when she herself was breaking her heart over her daughter didn't sit well with her. And as for Finella trying to say everything would be okay, well, how could it be? Clenching her fists, she wanted to lash out at someone, and the one person she hated right now – and for no other reason than that cocky smile and dismissive attitude towards her – was Cathy McGowan.

Deciding to stop pacing the bedroom floor, Georgie stared at herself in the mirror. What she saw didn't lift her spirits one bit. Her youth had gone. She was now a woman heading towards middle age. Her fresh look was dull and even spiteful compared to Cathy's. No wonder Rohan was smiling; he probably fancied the pants off her, and she clearly liked him. She was jolted out of her doldrums by the phone ringing – her mobile – which was in the kitchen. Taking the stairs two at a time, she was met by Rohan who handed her the phone. She looked at the number and knew it was her daughter. As she answered it, the automated voice said: 'This is a call from a prison. If you do not wish to accept this call, hang up now.' Georgie was shaking, holding the phone to her ear.

'Put it on speakerphone so we can all hear,' said Rohan.

Georgie wanted to hog the phone and keep her conversation with her daughter just to herself, but seeing the pleading look on Rohan's face and Finella hovering in the background, she decided to do as he asked.

'Hello, Georgie.'

For a moment, Georgie frowned. 'Er, hello.'

'Listen, girl, it's me, Patsy. The screws have allowed the one call and then you're gonna have to wait for your number to be put on to Dixie-Lee's pin. I've got her in a cell with me, so now you don't need to worry about her. I'm taking care of her. I'll hand her over, babe.'

'Dixie-Lee, how are you, darling? Do you need anything? Are they treating you okay? When can we visit?'

'Slow down, Mum. Look, I'm fine. Patsy . . . well, Auntie Patsy, should I say, is being really good to me, apart from eating my chocolate biscuits.' She giggled.

The more Dixie-Lee spoke, the better Georgie felt. Her daughter would be safe because Patsy Dewhurst was a woman of her word. She would look after her child, because unbeknown to anyone else, she was looking after Patsy's little ones. It was a promise she had made on her last day in HMP Bronzefield and she had kept that promise to the letter. Every Friday, she would send a cheque to Patsy's mother for Patsy's children in order to keep them out of social services' care.

'Tell Nan Finella and Uncle Rohan I'm okay.'

'We're here, darling,' said Finella. 'Now, listen. You put a list together of whatever you need, and we'll get it to you. And your mother, here, is fine, so you'll not be worrying about her now, d'you hear me. And your Uncle Rohan will be liaising with Cathy McGowan. They've worked together for years, so you don't have to worry about the legal stuff either, now.'

Georgie suddenly felt a little stupid. Why had she been so worried about that smile on Rohan's face? He knew Cathy. They had obviously worked together, and presumably, he was just being polite. *Had the shock of seeing her daughter being marched off to prison been the catalyst for setting off her insecurities?* she wondered.

As soon as they were about to finish the call, Patsy came back on. 'Listen, Georgie, a woman in 'ere called Bianca Malloye is bandying it about that Dixie-Lee killed her stepson. Now, she used to have clout in prison a while back, but she don't anymore, but I just wanted you to know what she's saying to everyone here. But, this is the thing: Bianca is still peacocking about, and I'm not sure that's because she was so used to running her wing. Perhaps habits die hard, or, more likely, she has a good reason to.'

'Understood, Patsy, thank you. I can't tell you how relieved I am, though, that my girl's there with you by her side.'

'Well, I had no idea until Bianca called out her name. It's such an unusual one that she could *only* be your girl. She's got balls like you, though.'

'Is she all right, really, Patsy?'

'It's all new, but she's smiling and eating, so don't worry, and again, thanks for helping me kids. You know how much it means to me. I can do me bird and not have to worry.'

***

While Finella ordered an Indian takeaway, Georgie remained downstairs. She had stopped giving Rohan the cold shoulder, but now he was quiet. Maybe he didn't like her jealous side. She couldn't really blame him.

Rodney joined them for dinner but it seemed the mood music was even affecting him as he was quiet himself. In fairness to him, he knew exactly how things played out in prison and he had hated every minute of it. He didn't want to vocalise his concerns and tell everyone he couldn't imagine how Dixie-Lee would survive. They didn't want to know that!

'I couldn't eat another thing,' said Finella. 'Do you mind if I go to bed? I'm drained.'

Georgie nodded. 'You know which is your room.'

Finella smiled. 'Look, let's address the elephant in the room. Dixie-Lee will be okay, Georgie. She's a fighter. You know that.'

But it was Rohan's words that really threw Georgie. 'Yeah, she'll be okay if you don't piss off her counsel.'

Before Georgie could respond to that, Finella intervened and tried to shut down her son's provocative comment. 'Well, actually, Rohan, I'd have said the fecking same. I am also concerned about Cathy McGowan. Cathy may be the best there is, but *being* it and *showing* it are two very different things. So I think our Georgie is right. Cathy should have shown she was up for fighting for Dixie-Lee. At the very least, she should have given the poor child some hope.'

'It doesn't work that way, Ma.'

'And while I am on this subject, you, my son, should show some compassion as well. Can't you see what our Georgie is going through, eh?'

Georgie expected Rohan to soften as he always did and say he was sorry, but he didn't. Instead, he rose from his chair and threw his napkin onto the table. 'She's not the only fecking one.'

Feeling hurt, Georgie snapped back the only way she knew how to handle situations like this. 'So you think more of that woman than you do me, yeah? Is that right, Rohan?'

Just as she was about to jump up and storm off, Rohan grabbed her arm.

'Stop it, will you? Why do you make it so hard on us all? We are here for you and Dixie-Lee and have been since we all met you, but you seem to think you can snarl, holler, and get nasty because of *your* feelings, *your* worries, and *your* pain.' He poked himself in the chest. 'Have you ever considered ours, eh? Look at me mother. She has been to hell and back, yet she fusses over you like you're her daughter, but you don't return the love. And as for me, I'm there for your every want and need, and yet earlier today, you shrugged me off because I smiled at the barrister.' He glared angrily. 'I smiled at the fecking brief and now I get all this!'

'Rohan, stop, please,' said Finella.

'No, Ma, it's not fair. We *all* love Dixie-Lee. Georgie doesn't own the patent on that.'

As he stormed away, Georgie sat back down. Staring out of the French windows to the garden, she held back the tears.

Finella rubbed Georgie's back. 'We're *all* anxious. That's the truth of the matter. I suppose Rohan's tired and probably needs a good sleep, and you do too. Things will seem more apparent in the morning.' Kissing the top of Georgie's head, Finella left to go to her room.

In the prevailing silence, Rodney cleared the plates away before he returned to the dining room. Giving a slight cough to clear his throat, he gave Georgie a wary look. He didn't like dramas at the best of times, but, worse than that, he was really concerned for Georgie.

'Georgie, no one will ever understand what it's like to be a single parent. I do, my love. Raising my daughter by myself, I felt every laugh, tear, and pain, and when she hurt, I hurt, and when things went wrong for her, I felt I was to blame, and unless you are in those shoes, you won't understand.'

Georgie looked up and met the ice-blue pools of compassion as his tear-filled eyes appeared drenched in sadness.

'You're right, Rod, but I guess Rohan is too.'

He smiled and hurried away before his tears poured down his cheeks.

The house was suddenly silent. There was not a hum or a buzz, nothing, just the silence.

Georgie got up from her chair, stared out to the end of the garden, and thought again she could make out a person down there. The only light came from the moonlight, but she was sure there was someone nearby. Then, her notion was confirmed when she saw a plume of warm breath that looked suspiciously like cigarette smoke. She stepped closer to the French doors, and this time, she wasn't afraid. Her biggest fear had been anything happening to her daughter, and now it had.

Although Georgie was grief-stricken, she was angry as well, so confronting a trespasser in her garden was no big deal; in fact, if they tried to harm her, she would beat the living shit out of them, and release her anger, which was mounting at a rate of knots.

Unlocking the doors, she stormed across the lawn towards the trees at the end of the garden. Surprised at how light it was, even though the sensor lights hadn't come on again, she hoped to get a clear view of the person she was convinced was stalking her.

A fox screamed and made her jump, yet her nerves weren't on edge. She would have it out with whoever it was lurking like a psychopathic serial killer. She blinked to focus, and what she thought was a person soon became the outline of a bush. The closer she got, the more she realised she had been seeing things. So she turned on her heel and sauntered back, now feeling stupid.

However, she then heard a rustling, and she froze. Her gumption had suddenly left her. She thought she could hear heavy breathing, even the soft padded sound of footsteps creeping up on her, and then the sensor lights came on as a scruffy urban fox ran past her. She sighed with relief. But then her mind was confused. Had a fox startled her or had it been startled by someone? Even though her heartbeat had slowed down, she still turned to look again at the bushes with bated breath. And she was sure she could see a dark figure moving and even a plume of night breath dissipating in the calm evening.

***

After returning to the house and locking the French doors, she climbed the stairs, scooped up her satin nightdress, which was draped over her velvet chair in the bedroom, and stared for a moment or two at her fiancé sleeping. He looked beautiful even while asleep. An unexpected lump lodged in her throat. Had she pushed him too far away, this time? She knew she had a habit of doing that to people. It was her defence mechanism and it had served her so well for all the years she could remember. But she'd really hoped she'd let him in. Perhaps, though, that wasn't enough, and Rohan had taken all he could. She removed her clothes and allowed the soft fabric of the nightdress to cascade over her body before gently lifting the duvet and climbing in. She hoped he would wake up, slide his arms around her, and kiss her, which she had become accustomed to. He didn't this time.

She lay there with her mind going over the day's events, until, when she thought of her daughter safe with Patsy, sleep finally arrived.

Her dream took her to the garden again. This time, the bushes were men, all led by Bruce Kern. He was smiling, his teeth black like his eyes, and he marched towards her while the men by his side were waving wads of cash.

'She's a virgin,' he repeated, over and over, like the beat of a marching band.

Georgie couldn't move. Her feet were stuck in the thick gloopy mud, and every effort to pull herself out only sucked her back in. Drenched in absolute terror, she tried desperately to pull herself free to run and escape, but it was impossible, and now here he was with the syringe in his hand and a crooked smile on his face.

Suddenly, she was paralysed, and when Bruce saw her in that state, he forced a canvas sack over her head. He was binding it tighter and tighter around her neck. She couldn't breathe or scream. His hand was on her top, feeling her breasts, and then she felt the needle plunging into her arm. Suddenly, she found her voice and screamed.

This time, she could move. Because, she realised, this was now no nightmare. Sitting upright, she found herself dripping in sweat and gasping for breath.

The bedside light came on, and Rohan was there, trying to comfort her.

'You had another nightmare, Georgie, that's all.'

She detected his voice was flat, almost matter-of-fact, even.

'I'm sorry, I, er . . .' She took a few deep breaths to steady her mind. 'I'm sorry.'

Rohan wiped the sweat from her forehead and pulled her close. 'Do you want to talk about it?'

'It was just a nightmare, that's all.'

'See, Georgie, I know it's not just a nightmare, but will you ever really let me in?' He pulled away and turned on his side before he switched off the bedside light.

She remained silent, digesting his words. As much as she wanted to let him in, she really didn't know how to. How could she explain that part of her childhood memory was missing? There were chunks gone. She rubbed her arm as if she could still feel the needle going in. How could she tell Rohan what had happened in her past if she wasn't sure herself? She was brainwashed into believing the lumps and sores on her arms were gnat bites, but somewhere in the depths of her memory, there was a vision – Bruce, the syringe, her mother, and the skeletal man.

Her mother may have been able to excuse away the marks on her arm, but how could she account for seeing half her body naked in those dreams? And there were times when she woke up so dazed that she was convinced it wasn't a normal sleep.

The anxiety of living in her mother's house compared to a never-ending roller-coaster ride of emotions. She recalled the filthy, vile men who came and plied her mother with drink and drugs, acting as though they were her friends, until that was they took her upstairs and left her on the bed naked, with money on the side or a bottle of spirits.

Even on a school day, her mother would walk around the house half-naked in a see-through negligee, with a cigarette dangling from her mouth and her breath foul from stale whisky. There was no ice-cold milk poured onto a bowl of cereal or a lunchbox with a cheese sandwich and a Penguin biscuit. She even remembered spraying her school uniform with air freshener because her mother hadn't dried her clothes and they stank of damp.

So she was left for most of the time to drag herself up. Some turned their predatory eyes her way, and that's how she learned to fight and run. But there in the shadows was Bruce. It was always Bruce. He watched her with his roaming eyes.

A cold shiver ran through her body. Was her past catching up with her? Had she not buried it deeply enough? Had her time in purgatory come home to roost? She shuddered again, forcing the reality away.

Of course, I was a virgin when I met Dixie. It was a dream. There was no syringe.

She had fought for her dignity. It was all she'd had because her mother had nothing to give her to make her feel good about herself. She was only handed back to her by social services because her mother had pretended to clean up her act. But it was all a lie, and she had to live in that 'house of ill repute', so the neighbours called it, in order that her mother could claim the welfare benefits.

Another vision hurtled past, and a feeling of dread instantly crept into her bones. If only she had stayed away. Her mother had signed the papers for her to join the Army, and so she had, but she had to return because her mother was so sick, she was dying, so they said. She wished the military had not insisted on her returning to see her mother and she regretted doing what she did at the time. She really thought she could bury her memories, but now it was as if the ghosts from the past were like zombies coming for her, racking up the events of the sick, turbulent life of running and hiding to evade those disgusting men.

But had she done so? The big question was this: had Bruce drugged her and sold her time and time again? From the skeletal voyeur to the stinking, greasy, perverted druggies, her mother had never once attempted to save her. She suspected that she had done that knowing that if she was forced to face the truth for what she had become, it would send her insane. She collected the family allowance and discarded her as a daughter.

She shuddered again. This time, her stomach began to churn. She simply couldn't get Bruce out of her head. Every time she closed her eyes, he was there, along with his paying cronies. But he wasn't the only one. There were others. Her mother, obviously, was there too, pissed and cackling like a witch. But there was a third person – a younger woman – who looked on from the shadows.

Georgie got up from the bed and hurried to the toilet before she was sick. A burning sensation came from the pit of her stomach and up through her throat before she choked and coughed. Gasping for breath, she closed her eyes again. There she was: it was that woman again.

In a eureka moment, Georgie crystallised that time all those years ago. It was a real memory because she now recognised the woman. She was so much younger back then.

With her blood rushing around her body as though it was opening the floodgates to hell, Georgie got up from the floor, wiped her mouth, and gargled a handful of water. As she turned around, Rohan was there. He looked exhausted.

'Are you okay, Georgie?'

She nodded, her face pale and drawn. She had just spent an hour fighting her past but she knew now she had lost the fight. Her memories were returning, and she knew it wouldn't be okay anymore. There were more demons she would have to face sooner rather than later.

'Rohan, I will tell you about my nightmares.' She bit her bottom lip, and her eyes welled up.

'Not now, eh? Let's just sleep, and when you're ready, you can tell me.'

She nodded, and he placed his arms around her, before he guided her back to bed.

CHAPTER FIFTEEN

It was the strong aroma of coffee wafting upstairs that woke Georgie up. She opened her eyes to see the sun shining through the bay window, so she knew then it was late. After the sleepless night disturbed by recurring nightmares, she wasn't surprised to have eventually fallen asleep, but she slept later than she usually would.

Running her hands down the back of her neck, she could feel the sweaty grease. She couldn't face a day without a hot shower to clear her mind, although the one vision that she couldn't shake off was that woman in her dreams the night before. A sudden rush of anger tightened her mouth, and she bolted into the en suite bathroom and turned on the shower. She was on a mission, not caring now if the water was hot or cold. The ice-cold spears took her breath away, but she braved them until the water became warm, and she was then able to take a few relaxing breaths and mentally figure out what she would say or even do to this woman. Violence was not the solution, but, nevertheless, she wanted to hurt her.

With so much on her mind and Finella saying that things would be more apparent in the morning, Georgie gritted her teeth because she hadn't woken up feeling any better. In fact, she was probably even more confused, stressed, and angry than before she went to bed.

Gingerly, she stepped into the kitchen believing that Rohan would be there waiting for her, but he wasn't, and neither was Finella. However, there was a plate with croissants and some coffee in the percolator. A note was scribbled on the fridge magnetic board. It read: *Auntie Rae, Ma's sister, has been taken sick, so I'm taking Ma to the airport.*

Georgie had met Rae only once. The elderly woman was Finella's older sister – her only sister – and she had various conditions. They were all treatable, but she needed to be in a nursing home. Knowing how much Finella loved Rae, she understood how important it was for Finella to be by her side if she was sick.

And knowing Finella so much better now, she realised that Finella would have told Rohan not to wake her because she was a kind woman. Rohan was right about what he'd said to her yesterday evening. Finella *had* treated her like a daughter. After pouring a coffee, she took a bite of the pastry, gulped a few mouthfuls of her drink, and searched for her car keys.

The woman's face came into her mind again, spurring her on to get going. After she picked up the keys in a bowl on the hallway console table, where she always put them, she glanced at the clock. It was nine-thirty. The Saturday morning rush to the shops would be over by now. She gripped the keys, her hands balled into fists, and her lips tightened over her teeth.

The sun had disappeared behind dark clouds, and then the heavens opened, and it poured down. She should have taken her foot off the accelerator and driven sensibly, but the woman's face kept appearing. At one point, she imagined her sneering, her eyes filled with excitement. Well, today, the woman wouldn't be smiling, that was for sure. Parking her red Audi A1 at the back of the coffee shop in a space reserved for her, she fought with the seatbelt before clambering out of the car. Her neck was once again burning, and her anger was increasing. Violence was back on the menu.

As soon as she entered the rear of the shop into the room where all the bread and cakes were baked, she clapped eyes on Sarah – the new recruit – the woman in her nightmares.

With a tray of rolls ready to slide into the giant oven, Sarah turned to see who was there.

It was the look on Sarah's face that made Georgie certain that this was the young woman in her dreams. There was no mistaking that fact. It was her face she saw lurking in the shadows. The level of anger had forced her stomach acid into her throat. Flaring her nostrils, gritting her teeth, and balling her hands into fists again, she marched towards Sarah.

Sarah instantly recognised the rage and froze, with the tray still in her hands. Too afraid to move, she hoped Georgie would be all words and not get physical because she knew what Georgie was capable of; she'd seen it for herself a long time ago.

In one fluid movement, and using one hand, Georgie flipped the tray out of Sarah's hands. The noise echoed as it hit the floor. But Georgie didn't jump or flinch because she had her hands around Sarah's throat and was dragging her towards the oven. 'You disgusting bitch!' she screamed.

Sarah realised that Georgie was going to carry out the unthinkable. She knew how hot that oven was, and if she put her hands or, worse, her head inside, she would be scarred for life – if not killed.

'Please don't!' Sarah screamed. Having felt the strength of Georgie, her battle now was with her own fear and weakness. She found herself sliding towards the oven because her shoes couldn't grip the tiled floor. With one hand seizing Georgie's, she used the other to pull Georgie's hair. But her efforts were in vain.

Riled to the point where she wanted to kill the bitch, Georgie pulled her fist back and viciously punched Sarah in the face, compelling her instantly to let go of her hair.

Staring into the begging eyes of the woman meant nothing because she had beseeched her with her own once upon a time. Now, she wanted to kill her. She didn't know or care whether it was the pain from the past catching up with her or the past just adding to the ingredients in the messed-up cocktail of what was now her life. Her anger was boiling, and this woman was there when those men hurt her. She was watching her from the background, and now she'd had the audacity to get a job in her coffee shop. Rubbing salt into the wounds came to mind. Just as she was about to shove Sarah's face into the oven, she felt an arm around her chest and she was wrenched back.

'What the fucking hell! Stop, Georgie, or you'll kill her!' yelled Henry.

Sarah managed to break free and staggered back, now out of breath and crying from relief. All she saw was the red glow of the inside of that oven and she felt the heat as if her face was being toasted.

'Jesus, fucking wept!' came another voice.

Georgie suddenly snapped out of the raging trance and looked around her. Henry had positioned himself between her and Sarah, and Sheila was pulling her away by her arm.

'It's all right, Henry, I'll see to Georgie,' said Sheila. 'She's having a bad time of it, that's all.' She put her hand up at Sarah. 'You're all right. No harm done, eh?'

Sarah stood shaking all over.

'I said no harm done, right!' repeated Sheila, reinforcing that it wasn't a question but a statement.

Henry had his mouth open in disbelief. But before he could ask Sarah if she was okay, she'd fled, slamming the back door behind her.

Just as Georgie tried to pelt after her, Henry blocked her path, and Sheila pulled her back. 'What the fuck is going on, Georgie? Calm down.'

'*Calm down!*' Georgie looked at Sheila and then at Henry and realised they were both in a state of shock.

'I'll close up,' said Henry, hurrying to lock the shop door.

Sheila put her arms around Georgie. 'I thought you were gonna kill her. Listen, babe, you've been, I mean, you're going through a tough time. I get it, Georgie, but, wow, you need to get your brain into gear. Taking your anger out on that old crackhead won't make you feel any better.'

Georgie was still shaking but her temper was easing. 'Okay, okay, I'm calmer now.'

'My arse, ya are. Now, go and sit down. I'll make us all a cup of tea. Fucking hell, I need a snout now.'

Georgie suddenly took a deep breath. 'No, don't, Sheila. You've done well giving up the cigarettes. I'm fine.'

They walked through the door to the counter and into the coffee shop to find Henry shooing out the last customer. Once he had turned the sign to 'closed' and spiralled around, he leaned against the door, his face like thunder.

'What in God's name is *going on*?' He waved his hands to stop her from answering. 'Forget it. I don't want to know, Georgie, but one thing I do know is you have changed so much, I don't even recognise you anymore. The way you've treated that woman, for example. You can damn well see she is on the bones of her arse. And if I hadn't stopped you in time, she would have been burned alive. I can't handle this, Georgie. I think I'm done. You can buy me out or sell the place!'

Georgie sat on a chair. All the weight of her emotions were pulling her down. 'No, listen, Henry, it's *you* who doesn't understand.'

‘Give her a chance, Henry,’ Sheila said, taking a seat beside Georgie.

‘*A chance?* I gave her a chance but only because she wanted us to turn this place into a coffee shop together. I wanted to expand and to be able to share my recipes and create masterpieces, but all that seems to have been created here is a fucking monster.’ He pointed at Georgie. ‘Don’t be surprised if the police don’t show up and cart you away. You could have killed her.’ He pulled his apron off and threw it on the floor. ‘I’m going, Georgie. Do what you want with the fucking shop. I’m done.’

‘Hang on, Henry. Look, Georgie’s in a state. They’ve just locked her girl up, and she’s all over the place. Don’t be so harsh, mate.’

Henry’s shoulders dropped. Slowly, he picked up his apron and shook his head. ‘I understand that. And don’t get me wrong. I love Dixie-Lee, and we all want her home, but, Georgie, taking your frustrations out on Sarah is *insane*. You need to see a professional. Your moods are up and down like a fucking yoyo. One minute, you’re all sweet and well, and everyone loves you, and the next, you bring a dark cloud to the shop, and no one wants to stay for second helpings. And, honestly, even though I think you, Sheila, have a foul mouth at times, you at least bring something different to the shop other than Georgie’s doom and fucking gloom.’

Every word resonated with Georgie; she had to admit she had been all over the place. And with the recurring nightmares, she was certainly having her own internal battles. Perhaps Henry was right and it was affecting everyone around her. Henry, though, was one of the last people she wanted to upset.

She peered up, her face changing from being sullen to showing some contriteness. ‘I’m so sorry, Henry. Maybe you’re right. Perhaps I do need to get help.’

Sheila rubbed her back. 'Or a few of them happy pills. Maybe you're depressed.'

'Depressed, she's fucking bipolar.'

Henry looked at Georgie. He expected her to bite back, but when a tear escaped her eye, he was utterly surprised. He'd never seen her cry. Ever. She wasn't the type. It was then when he realised that something was seriously wrong.

'What's really going on, Georgie, love?'

Georgie looked at Sheila and then back at Henry. Her words were circling in her mind, ready to fall out of her mouth. At this pivotal moment in her life, she knew that her fears needed to be addressed.

'I think I was abused as a kid. That woman . . .' She began to shake, almost like a convulsion.

Henry instantly sat beside her. 'Okay, okay, slowly, tell me, love, what is it about that woman you so dislike?'

'I, er . . . well, I knew I'd seen her before, and attached to that thought was something dark, if you know what I mean. She was linked to my past, and I know something bad happened to me, and she was somehow in the middle of it.'

'I'm sorry, love. 'Course I had no idea.'

'No one knows anything about this except you two.' She let out a short laugh. 'Christ, not even Rohan knows. I think he is angry with me too. He put me in my place yesterday. I suppose I'm pissing everyone off.'

'Well, you've not been pissing rainbows, but it's understandable,' said Henry. 'Now tell me, Georgie, if this happened a long time ago, why is it affecting you now? Has something happened? Is it because Sarah reminds you of someone?' he asked, in his most compassionate voice.

'No!' she snapped. 'She doesn't *remind* me of someone from the past. She *is* the someone from my past. It's her. I *know* it is.'

‘You’ve never recognised her before. So why now?’

‘Look, something happened to me as a kid, right. I believe I was drugged and abused, and she was there. I know she was. I’ve seen her in my dreams.’

Henry chewed his bottom lip and looked at Sheila to see if she was thinking the same as him.

‘Ya know what, girls, sometimes when things are pretty shit, we block ’em out for a while. We can then change the story to block out the bad bits, but then they can get mixed up and the good guys become the bad guys, and, before you know it, you’ve got a whole other storyline going on.’

‘No, I know she was there. She was definitely linked in some way to the abuse.’

‘Listen,’ said Sheila. ‘When my ol’ man was abusive to me, I pushed it to the back of my mind. And when my kids joined in with the abuse, I suppressed the real truth about what they did to me as well. So it wasn’t until they were killed that the shame of what they did to me reared its ugly head. Ya see, I’d suppressed all the bad memories. So maybe, Georgie, you are suppressing everything that happened to you. Sarah may have been there, or she may have just been a neighbour. Anyway, she’s fucked right off now. I can’t see her coming back anytime soon. You shit the life out of her.’ She smiled sympathetically. ‘Some day, girl, the truth will out. Until then, we’ve got ya back. Ain’t that right, Henry?’

Henry nodded, deep in thought, while he watched Georgie mulling over what Sheila had just said.

After listening intently to Sheila, Georgie found it so strange to hear Sheila giving her the benefit of her life experiences considering she wouldn’t have pissed on her a couple of years ago if she’d been set on fire. Then her mind went off to the time she was drugged and raped by Lieutenant Marston-Smith. Was her memory messing up what happened to her as a child to what was happening to her as an adult?

Marston-Smith had fought her before he stuck that needle into her arm, and when she came around she was sore down below. There was no doubt about her being raped. And, by more than one man as well.

She rubbed her arm. Had she seen her mother inject her, and that was where the notion that her mother's friends had injected her had come from? She started to breathe fast and shake again.

Henry jumped up and poured her a glass of water. He grabbed a paper bag and rejoined them. 'Georgie, you are having a panic attack. Breathe into the paper bag, and it will pass.'

Taking the bag, she did as he said, and, after a few minutes, she began to settle down. 'Henry, I'm so sorry for today. I need to get myself together and figure out what's going on in my head before I kill someone.'

Henry reached across and placed his hand on hers. 'I don't want to see you back here until you are well. And you know me: I can run things okay without you, for now, but please, get some help. After everything you've been through, no one would be surprised if you need a little therapy, a counsellor maybe.'

'Or a course of knock-out tablets.'

'Yes, Sheila.' Henry nodded. 'Anyway, go and see your doctor and get help. You are too nice a person to let whatever this is turn you into a bad person.'

Georgie smiled. 'If I don't get help, I'm heading down the road of paranoia, and I don't want that. I will lose everyone who cares about me, and especially for Dixie-Lee's sake, I can't afford to do that.'

'The other thing, Georgie, is you could be right. That skinny-arsed bird may well be a dodgy figure from your past. In which case, you ain't paranoid, but you are mentally suffering, girl, so

Henry's right. Go and see the quack. I'll help Henry, so don't worry about that.'

Georgie nodded and glanced at Henry, who playfully rolled his eyes.

'I'd best be off, in case the police turn up.'

'I dunno. I've got a feeling she won't call them. And you're right, Georgie: she does have a secretive vibe about her.'

'Or she could just be shy,' Henry suggested.

'Oh, leave off, Henry. There's shy and then there's fucking sly. I reckon she's on the sly side, like a fucking mangy fox. They reckon if you see a fox during the day, it's on crack cocaine. See, I reckon she's either still on drugs, or she's got something she's hiding.'

***

As Georgie drove aimlessly away from the coffee shop, she felt ashamed. What if the poor woman was a figment of some warped imagination in her past? She'd nearly burned her face off, and she knew that if Henry hadn't stopped her, she would have. 'Fuck! Fuck!' she yelled to herself.

Driving towards St Mary Cray, she realised she was going in the wrong direction. She didn't live there anymore. Maybe, she thought to herself, she was simply on autopilot, but then, as she hit Sevenoaks Way, ready to go towards Chislehurst, she turned right, aiming for Star Lane. And before she knew it, she was heading for the cemetery. She parked the car and hesitantly stepped out as if she was actually visiting her mother's house. Except her mother wasn't there: she was in the graveyard, six feet under.

As she slowly walked towards the grave, she expected it to be overgrown with weeds, but to her surprise, it wasn't. The headstone was wonky, but that was to be expected. They often tilted over time. As she got closer, she saw a bunch of red roses, and so she assumed that someone had left them on the wrong grave. She scooped them up. Inside the cellophane wrap was a card. Her pulse quickened. It read: **I'll make sure to do the right thing. You at least deserve that. I couldn't keep the promise before, but I can now. I haven't forgotten you, my angel.**

Those words were like spears of ice piercing her chest. She dropped the roses and watched them fall apart, all over the grave.

CHAPTER SIXTEEN

Brodie checked his phone; it was bang on twelve o'clock. He had arranged a midday meeting with Michael Malloye in a public place, namely, a coffee shop.

For his family's safety, he wanted to meet with the man and thrash out what had ended up being a hostile situation. But he suspected the meeting might prove volatile. Not only was Michael and his family grieving over the fate of Tommy but they would be incandescent with rage over the demise of Michael's golden grandson Tyler.

The wind had an icy edge, so he lifted the collar of his Crombie coat and rubbed his hands together. When he saw Michael's Range Rover pull up slowly outside the coffee shop, he instantly peered up and down the street before he surveyed the inside of the car. There was only Michael sitting in it, which made him smile inwardly with relief. Even though he had beaten up three of his sons in one go, he would never underestimate that family. They hadn't gained their vicious reputation for nothing.

As Michael got out of his car, he looked Brodie in the eye and kept his stare there until they were inside the shop. Michael was the first to sit down, and as he did so, Brodie clocked how stiff and old the 'godfather' of the family had become. It was only a few years ago, when he had been relatively fit; then, he could easily handle himself as well as any man in their prime.

A waitress hurried over and beamed at Brodie. She was in her twenties, with the thickest eyelashes that cast a deep shadow over her narrow eyes. Her red lipstick was dripping, and her orange make-up looked as though she had applied it with a brick. 'What can I get yer?' She fluttered her eyelashes, and giggled, not even pretending to be subtle. Her flirting was off the charts.

Brodie gave her a warm smile, although, inwardly, he refrained from laughing at her. The dramatic eyelash flutter had somehow caused the top set of her false lashes to tangle up with the bottom set, leaving the girl struggling to open her eyes.

'Two coffees. Bring the milk. We will do our own thing,' he said, sparing the poor girl any further embarrassment.

Trying to pull the eyelashes off, she nearly wrenched her eyelids off in the process. 'No, you have to place your order. We do the making. We know how to do it, yer know.' She again tried to smile and would have winked if her eyelids were stable enough.

'Darling, just fetch two black coffees, some sugar, and a glass of milk, then. How about that?'

'So you want a glass of milk?' she said, as she managed to pull off one of her eyelashes. But all she succeeded in doing was to make the other one that was still attached look as though it was fanning her face when she blinked.

'Yep, a glass of milk and two black coffees and some sugar.'

'I would have thought you were sweet enough. But would you fancy something to nibble on?' One drawn-on eyebrow raised an inch.

Brodie stared. 'Listen, darling, that chat-up line is used by men, not women, so don't lower yerself. There's a good girl.'

'I was only trying to be friendly.'

'Hmm, so was I with some advice,' Brodie replied, dismissively. 'Now, again, two coffees, one glass of milk, and sugar, please.'

When he looked back at Michael, he saw the broad smile. And he was grateful to the waitress for turning what might have been an antagonistic meeting into something more laid-back.

Brodie laughed. 'Imagine getting on the drink and waking up next to that in the morning.'

Michael's smile turned into a giggle. 'I think I've experienced that a few times. She wouldn't be so bad compared to some of the mooses that dribbled on me pillow.'

There was a silent pause before Brodie sighed. 'This is a fecking mess, Michael.'

'It is that, Brodie.'

'Would you say I am a man of my word?'

Michael looked out of the window, rubbed his bristly beard, and nodded. 'I think I would, aye.'

'Right, so believe me when I say we didn't murder your Tyler. I'll tell you for why. Firstly, we assumed it was Tyler who killed Clifford Jenson-Baine because we thought you had sent him to find the file. But we didn't kill Tyler. In fact, we needed him alive because otherwise our niece was going to take the rap for killing the barrister and that is what is very likely to happen. And secondly, we – as in my family – were here in Ireland. The police informed us that Tyler was murdered around the same time as the barrister, and not very far from him, so—'

Michael quickly interrupted. 'Right, but listen. We sent Tyler to find out about Bianca's counsel, and then we were going to make a plan to get our hands on the file. And before we knew Steve Elison was Bianca's barrister, we considered bribing him to hand us Tommy's last will and testament. But the plan wasn't confirmed yet. I mean, to bribe a man like Steve, we would need a lot of money, so I was looking into that, and, of course, the other option was to break into the offices and steal the file, but, again, that's not something I would have asked Tyler to do alone.'

Brodie nodded and was about to speak when the waitress appeared with a tray of two cups of steaming coffees, a tall glass of milk, and sachets of sugar. Both men looked straight at her eyes and noticed how different she looked without the false eyelashes. Brodie was about to compliment her on her fresher-looking face, but in the end, he decided not to. She was giving him the eye again, and he wasn't in the mood.

She didn't speak; she merely placed the tray on the table and sauntered away.

'You know it wasn't us, right?'

Michael nodded resignedly. 'I knew. Of course, I knew.'

'So, we're good?'

'I wouldn't say good. I can't speak for Gilead. He's still in the fecking hospital. His mouth is all swollen and he'll never speak right again. And Martie will—'

'I know, okay, but what did you expect me to do? Stand there and be attacked by your lot, did you now?'

Michael didn't answer. Instead, he sipped the black sugarless coffee, delved into the pocket of his thick sheepskin coat, and pulled out a hip flask before pouring himself a generous helping of Irish whiskey.

'Would you like some?' He poked the silver engraved flask under Brodie's nose.

'Not for me, thank you. So, then, apart from the injuries following a fair fight, are we good?'

Michael raised his brow and stared. 'Er, Brodie, you want your niece out of jail, I take it?'

Brodie nodded and leaned forward, responding to Michael's tone, as if he had an idea.

'Well, I believe that whoever killed my Tyler also set up your niece, unless . . .' He sipped his coffee and shook his head. 'Unless this niece of yours killed the barrister and then my Tyler because he saw her do it.'

Brodie stared in disbelief that Michael could come up with such an absurd theory. He reached into his pocket, pulled out his phone, and scrolled through the photos before he came to the one he wanted. 'Take a look at this photo. I took it only last week.'

Michael took the phone and held it close to see the photo clearly. He smiled. 'And this bonny-looking young woman is your niece, I take it?'

Brodie nodded. 'She is a sweet girl, inoffensive, hardworking, and not the type to murder a barrister even though the dirty bastard tried to rape her. She didn't kill him because, Michael, if she had, she would have had a good reason and a solid defence if the CPS decided that the case should go to trial.'

'I see where you're going with this, and she looks a sweetheart, but even the cutest of kids can kill. Don't you watch the fecking TV?'

Brodie shook his head. 'Not really, I prefer to read. Look, I think we are on the same track. You believe whoever killed your Tyler also murdered the barrister. Dixie-Lee is not that person. She is studying to be a barrister. Hugh Shields reckons she is bright and will sail through her exams, and believe me, she is clever. Now, if she killed him because he tried to rape her, she would have a defence. But she said she didn't kill him, and I know her. If she said she didn't, she didn't. She has no reason to lie to me.'

He could see that Michael was mulling everything over.

'And another thing: she had blood on her clothes, but none of it matched Tyler's, and I'm sorry, Michael, but I know how he was killed. The blood would have spurted out like a spray gun.'

Michael nodded in resignation. 'Okay, Brodie, I want whoever killed my Tyler just as much as you want your niece out of prison. I guess what we need to do is to work together.'

'Yes, Michael. For starters, we must share what we know. You see, I can get a lot of information from the police station in England.'

'Oh yeah?'

‘Our solicitor is pals with a detective in there, so we can cover that side. As long as you cooperate and give me what you know from your family’s perspective – like what the hell is in that file and why it is so important – then we will be able to sort out this mess.’

Michael leaned back and shrugged his shoulders. ‘Did you know that Tommy was worth a lot of money?’

‘Well, you were all well off until the drug mishap.’

‘Yeah, we piled a lot of money into the venture and got badly fecked over. Thanks to you, the Colombians let us off lightly. I know they did, Brodie, so I’ll take back what I said the other day. After losing Tommy and Tyler, I realise now that life is worth more than anything, especially money. But Tommy won big, millions, in fact. The lad’s lucky numbers came up on the lottery.’

‘So this file contains his last will and testament, does it?’

He nodded slowly. ‘It also has information as to the whereabouts of the code to a safe deposit box where he keeps his diamond stash. Again, they’re worth a fecking lot of money.’

‘You never said that before.’

Michael smiled. ‘I didn’t fully trust you then.’

‘Fair enough. Anyway, I take it, all of you want to get your hands on it?’

Michael shrugged again. ‘I’m not bothered now. We wanted to see what was in that file ’cos we already knew about the key. And here’s why. That bitch Bianca was seeing someone. Tommy knew it. He filed for divorce and the next thing is he’s dead. I don’t think he had a chance to change his will, and that could mean that he left everything to Bianca, but the rightful heir should have been Tyler, his son.’

‘Surely, Tommy would have left something in his will for Tyler anyway?’

Michael took another mouthful of his coffee and sighed. 'Hmm. You would think so, wouldn't you. But there was a falling-out. Bianca claimed that Tyler came on to her. And our silly bollocks Tommy, who, believe you me, was besotted with Bianca, chose to believe her, and so Tyler came to Ireland, to stay with me. Bianca, the cheeky mare, accused Tyler of killing Tommy. But we believe it was her.'

Brodie shrugged. 'Well, that's easily proved away. If he was at yours, here in Ireland, he couldn't be in two places at once, could he?'

While rubbing his bristles again, Michael's eyes seemed drawn down at the sides, as if he was exhausted by it all. 'He wasn't in Ireland. He was in England. He wanted to prove to his father that he didn't make a pass at Bianca and he would find out who she was seeing. Tommy suspected she was seeing someone, but, in his heart, he didn't want to believe it. But he had to save face and be a man, so he filed for divorce.'

Michael took a final sip of his coffee before he continued.

'After what Bianca had said about our Tyler, it left the lad raging that she had the fecking brass neck to accuse him of coming on to her, and, worse, that his father believed her. So Tyler wanted to bring her down and expose the whore for what she was. Before he left, he said he had an inkling who she was seeing, but he didn't say who it was. Then we got the news that Tommy had been murdered. No way did our Tyler do it, though.'

Having known the Malloyes for years now, especially the old man, Brodie was surprised to see Michael's eyes well up. Unimaginable grief had stripped away his brutal gangster façade. Michael had always been the hard one who had taught his sons to fight and steal. To the outside world, he was a heartless bastard who would rob his own granny of her pension, although he would never do that.

‘Our Tyler loved Tommy, and that Bianca is toxic, like a witch poisoning Tommy’s mind. It kills me to think that he died believing that his own son had tried it on with his wife.’ He swallowed hard and breathed heavily through his mouth before saying, ‘And our Tyler died believing his dad didn’t love him anymore.’

Those words hit home to Brodie but not as much as they would do to the man saying them.

Unexpectedly, Michael coughed, and his face flushed red as he tried to stop the tears. He never cried – ever – and now he was a wreck in front of Brodie Deacon.

But Brodie wasn’t one to take the piss. He got up and walked around to Michael’s side and put his arms around him. ‘Let it out, mate. I’ve got yer.’

He could feel the built-up pain of grief as the man sobbed and sobbed, his rib cage shaking as he let out the pent-up emotion.

The waitress deliberately came over at the wrong time and asked, ‘Is there anything else you would like?’

Brodie craned his neck and glowered at the woman, mouthing the words ‘Fuck off’ at her.

She quickly retreated to her counter, and Brodie helped Michael to his feet. ‘Come on, mate, let’s get out of here.’

Michael wiped his eyes and stared at Brodie. He sniffed and then smiled. ‘You’re a good lad, eh.’ He smiled again. ‘This company of yours, undoing wrongdoings. I know why it works so well now.’

‘Go on.’

‘You don’t personally hold a grudge, do you? You genuinely are impartial, and that, my friend, gets you the truth, and that’s why you’re so successful, isn’t it.’

‘That’s about the sum of it.’

‘Did you never want to be a detective, Brodie?’

‘We play that game in our work, but . . .’ He chuckled. ‘We get paid a fecking lot more.’

‘Yeah, I remember parting with the fifty grand.’ He winked. ‘But it was money well spent. And now, Brodie Deacon, it looks like you and me have a mystery to solve.’

CHAPTER SEVENTEEN

Having experienced a genuine sense of relief, Dixie-Lee spent the afternoon learning more about her mother from – of all people – Patsy Dewhurst.

Dixie-Lee listened absolutely gobsmacked to hear Patsy's account of how single-handedly her mother had fought two women inmates, who had a brutal reputation in the prison. And not only that but how she had used her brain to stop Patsy herself in her tracks from intimidating her.

At least, Dixie-Lee thought, she had her mother's ex-enemy, now her friend, for protection. Because, deep down, she hadn't envisaged prison life to be so challenging.

It was time for the evening meal, and although Patsy patted her back, telling her everything would be okay, Dixie-Lee suddenly felt unsettled. Maybe it was the fear of walking back into the dining area where, earlier, all eyes were on her.

Dixie-Lee could tell that Patsy was starving, so she hurried along behind her to the 'chow hall'.

As soon as they joined the queue, Dixie-Lee clocked Bianca already there with her food piled high on her tray. She was seated in a prime position, at the head of the table, and holding court with a group who all seemed to be engrossed in what she had to say.

When Dixie-Lee eyed up the food on Bianca's tray, she was impressed. Bianca was eating a breast of chicken with a selection of roast potatoes and steaming vegetables. *Maybe prison food wasn't so bad after all*, she thought.

The food at lunchtime had been horrible, but if the evening meals were like the one that Bianca was eating, she figured she wouldn't starve to death. However, when she reached the serving section, there was nothing on the menu comparable with what Bianca was eating. Instead, she was looking at chicken legs that had originated from anorexic chickens and cooked until the meat was just like dry string cheese.

Dixie-Lee grabbed a bottle of water because she knew she would need it to get the chicken past her tonsils. The vegetables were peas with a mix of pea shells, another throat irritation adventure, and the roast potatoes were more like fat-burned chips. Still, she wasn't stupid enough to refuse what was on offer. She had to keep going and nourish a fresh mind and a healthy body. But the only nutritious food she could see were the apples at the end of the serving segment. She decided to take one of everything offered. She could swap her pudding – rice or semolina – or whatever it was supposed to be. She couldn't actually tell. But she knew that Patsy would eat it. She ate anything on offer, bless her.

At that moment, Patsy was bartering with the server for a better piece of chicken and more peas. When it came to the potatoes, Patsy said, 'For fuck's sake, give me that ladle. That ain't enough spuds to feed a fucking toddler.'

The server, an Asian woman, didn't answer. She let Patsy help herself, and then, as the server was about to take the ladle back, Patsy scooped another helping and slapped it onto Dixie-Lee's plate. 'She ain't on a fucking diet either.'

Dixie-Lee wanted to laugh because Patsy was such a no-nonsense woman. The officers didn't intervene. They were too busy talking to each other.

Dixie-Lee followed Patsy and accepted what was given to her by the servers. But all the while, her mind was on Bianca. Suddenly, her insides felt as if they'd turned over. Her hands shook, but not enough to spill her food.

She followed Patsy to the table where the older woman and pregnant woman she had seen yesterday were having lunch.

Both inmates ignored her again, just as they did on the last occasion, but then she realised that they were also ignoring Patsy as well.

'All right, Deidre?'

The older woman nodded fast but didn't speak.

Patsy sat up straight and stared. 'What the fuck's the matter with you today? Has someone given you a hard time, love?'

Deirdre glanced across to someone at another table before she shook her head sharply, without even looking at Patsy.

As if the penny had just dropped, Patsy spun around and spotted Bianca.

Dixie-Lee watched Patsy and knew then that she had clocked the same thing as her. Bianca was acting as though she was the big pin, and her followers were hanging on to her every word.

Patsy turned back and glared at Deirdre. 'I'll give you one chance to fucking tell me. How the hell has Miss Fucking Bougie Bianca suddenly become the main attraction in this shithole of a place?'

Deirdre's eyes widened. She shrugged her shoulders. 'I, er, I dunno.'

'Yeah, ya do, Deidre, so now you'd better tell me.'

It was evident that Deirdre was afraid of something. 'I don't know, Patsy. Please leave me out of this.'

'Out of *what*?'

'I dunno whatever the beef is, but whatever it is, I ain't nuffin to do wiv it.'

Patsy leaned forward and gently tapped Deidre's face. 'You fucking *owe* me. I've let you off twice now, and so you'd better fucking start singing like a canary, or I will be pulling your lungs out through your arsehole. *Speak!*'

Deidre's face paled. 'Bianca is running the wing.'

'Oh yeah, and how's she doing that, then?'

Deidre glanced at the two officers and then back at Patsy.

Patsy had followed her eyeline and nodded. 'Shit, she's bought the fucking screws, has she. Well, if the stupid tart is going to fill their thick heads with IOUs and fucking promises, then more fool them—'

Patsy stopped when she saw Deirdre look over at Bianca. She then turned to see the number of women gathered at her table. She had been in prison long enough to be able to tell that business was taking place.

'Don't look at them, Deirdre, but tell me this. Is she supplying?'

Deidre nodded.

'Not false promises?'

'No, she's got gear in here. She's top dog, Patsy, so please, I've told you now. I can't get involved.'

'Fair enough.' Patsy smiled sweetly at Deirdre before her face turned deadpan and threatening. 'What gear?'

'Please, Patsy, leave me out of it.'

'I fucking asked you: what gear?' she growled, under her breath.

'Brown, MDMA, and cocaine.'

'How?'

'Oh, come on, Patsy, I don't know how. I only know the addicts are on a buzz, and she has assured them of a regular supply.'

'So now the bitch has an army, and I'm probably a target.'

Dixie-Lee had sussed it out as well, the minute she'd clocked eyes on Bianca, and now it was confirmed.

There was silence as Patsy pushed her food around her plate, but Dixie-Lee ate hers. She knew she needed to keep up her strength because if there was trouble, she had to be ready for it. However, the feeling of dread had already crept up her spine. She couldn't help but look over at the looming threat.

Patsy hissed in her ear, 'You need to watch my back, kiddo. If they come at me, warn me, babe, 'cos they will shiv me on the sly, the dirty cunts.'

Dixie-Lee got up, walked over to the displayed bottled water, grabbed one, and headed back to the table. This time, she sat opposite Patsy, so that she could keep an eye on what Bianca and her lot were doing.

'Not that I'm experienced at this kind of thing, but, Patsy, ain't it better to let them know we know?'

Patsy smiled. 'You are like your mum. She was always ready for everything.'

'They are looking over,' Dixie-Lee said, without moving her lips. She smiled back at them, waving her hand, as if she was taking their glares as friendly acknowledgements.

'What are you *doing*, for fuck's sake?'

'Oh, I'm just being polite. It tends to throw people the wrong way.'

'Or rile them up the wrong fucking way.'

'Oh . . . sorry, I'm not used to prison or the prison etiquette.'

'I need to think, 'cos right now, kiddo, we are up shit creek without a paddle. Let's go back to the room. We're safer there.'

'How's that going to work out?'

Patsy replied, 'Have you seen the fucking size of me? I take up the doorway. They have to get past me to get to you.'

Looking down, Dixie-Lee whispered, 'You don't have to protect me, you know. It's not your job.'

'Oh, babe, you have no idea. Your mum, God love her, is keeping my babies out of the system, and I hope you will never have to understand that. But, anyway, keeping them out of care is keeping me alive too, ’cos, believe me, if my kids went into a children’s home, I’d probably kill myself anyway. I couldn’t live with the guilt.’

Deirdre uncharacteristically slid her hand across the table and tapped Patsy’s arm. ‘Listen, girl, you have clout in here ’cos people fear you ’cos you can have a right good tear up. Bianca can only buy people, and look at ’em. Most of ’em are like me, ol’ scagheads – thin and fragile – and they can’t fight their way out of a paper bag.’

Patsy looked back at Bianca and realised that she might be surrounded by the druggies, but there were one or two who would fight, including Dulcie, the Brazilian, and two of her sidekicks. Although fighting probably wasn’t the correct terminology – assassination was more their thing.

Dulcie’s intense stare told Patsy that Dulcie was gunning for her. She’d shown up earlier today and left a threat saying that she would be sorry. Patsy was now considering that might well be the case.

***

Patsy quickened her pace as Dixie-Lee hurried beside her towards their room at the end of the wing. As soon as they were inside, Patsy shut the door behind them and snatched a wooden crucifix from the wall above the table.

To Dixie-Lee’s surprise, she removed the top section of the cross to reveal a blade. ‘There she is.’ She turned to face Dixie-Lee. ‘I made this in my last prison. We had a woodwork lesson. The teacher left his tool on the side, and I thought it might come in handy.’ She turned the weapon around in her hand and sighed. Her face had fallen into deep sadness. ‘Dixie-Lee, promise me something.’

‘What?’

'If they do stab me and I die, promise me that you will make sure your mum continues to look out for my kids.'

'They won't kill you. I mean, that's going a bit OTT. It was just an argument and a couple of punches.'

Patsy shook her head. 'Babe, this is a prison. Dulcie ain't ever getting out. She doesn't *care* if she kills me. Returning to court on another charge of murder will just be a day out for her.'

Dixie-Lee bristled as reality kicked in. 'You really do believe she would go that far?'

'Yeah, I do. Now, get up on the top bunk. You'll have an advantage,' she said, as she pushed the table against the door.

There was silence for a moment as Patsy picked up a rabbit mug. It was really cute with a daddy and a mummy on it. She seemed trancelike as she turned it around in her left hand. 'You promise me that you will tell your mum to look out for my kids, won't you?'

The solemn tone was enough for Dixie-Lee to understand the gravity of this situation. Patsy was going into battle and expecting to lose. Before she had a chance to speak, Patsy smashed the mug against the concrete wall. When the bulk of it fell on the floor, she was left holding a jagged piece of pottery that was still attached to the handle.

Dixie-Lee knew that that mug had meant the world to Patsy. It had probably been a gift from her children that she had somehow snuck into the prison. Dixie-Lee was aware of how the prison protocols allowed the staff to strip everyone of everything, even their dignity. So she suspected that Patsy may have paid a screw to let her keep it. Now, she had painfully sacrificed it to be used as a weapon.

'Look, if they come to fight, why don't we shut the door and call the officers?'

Patsy twisted her head to look up at Dixie-Lee perched on the top bunk. ''Cos, this ain't how it works in here. These screws are bought. A prison officer's wage is fucking peanuts. O' course they would turn a blind eye for the right money. And believe me, babe, someone is looking after Bianca.'

'How do you know for sure, though?'

'Your mother never told me you ask a lot of questions.'

'Sorry.'

'No, don't be, love. Understand this: inside here, drugs are worth more than money. If Deidre is telling the truth, and I have no reason to doubt her, then Bianca becomes the top dog. I can see for meself that the scagheads are buzzing off their scabby nuts, and it ain't their methadone time. So the bitch has got someone on the outside, someone with weight, to get her a decent supply of whatever.'

'Fucking hell!'

Patsy raised her brow. 'No need to talk like you're a jailbird. You're better than that, Dixie-Lee.'

Feeling her cheeks burning, Dixie-Lee knew she probably did sound out of place by swearing like that. 'I can't just sit up here if they are going to barge in and start . . . well, whatever they're going to start.'

'You do nothing.' Patsy looked one more time at the broken mug and handed it to Dixie-Lee. 'If it comes to it, you protect yourself. But don't, and I mean *don't* jump into the fight. Only protect yourself if they attack you.'

'But why will they try to hurt you?'

'Dixie-Lee, listen, you can't make threats in here without carrying them out, right? If you do, you lose face. A woman like Dulcie has nuffin except respect from inmates. Okay, it's born out of fear, but, nevertheless, it's respect all the same. For her to hold her head up and have the little runners doing her dirty work for her, she needs to have them shitting bricks if they don't do as they're told. Most girls in here, the skinny bitches, will do the running around for her and sucking up to her for protection, right, but, see, me, I don't need anyone. Dulcie hates that. One on one with no tools, I will have her on her back in a few seconds. She knows it, but when she says *I'll be sorry*, she means it. I guarantee you that that lunatic will bustle her way into this room with a load of skinny-arsed limpets with her.' She pointed a warning finger. 'And with Bianca backing her, Dulcie will recruit a couple of the harder bitches.'

'Harder?'

'Yes, harder!' Recognising her tone of voice sounded harsher than she'd meant it to, she softened her tone. 'So there's a few other women in here. They keep themselves to themselves. But when they get wind of the fact that there are drugs or any other smuggled goods in here, they'll crawl out of the woodwork and place themselves in a position where they will fight for a piece of whatever's going on. Bianca knows that, and she's also aware that they will be in her room now bartering for gear, and she will use them to get at me. That bitch hates me 'cos she can't control me. She couldn't before, and she ain't gonna now, either.'

Dixie-Lee didn't want to know any more. Her heart was thumping in her chest at such a terrific rate. As she ran her index finger along the jagged edge of the remains of the mug, she had just one thought on her mind: it was to stay alive, at all costs.

CHAPTER EIGHTEEN

Georgie decided to busy herself in the kitchen while trying not to make too much noise for fear of missing a phone call from Dixie-Lee. It was now seven o'clock in the evening. *Why hadn't she called?* she wondered.

Rodney offered Georgie a cup of tea and was even happy to cook her a meal, but she seemed clearly in a state – not in the mood to talk, let alone eat.

Georgie's eyes flashed to the landline phone, just in case she had somehow miraculously missed the call. But with no flashing light on the answerphone, she knew her daughter hadn't left her a message.

'Georgie, you'll wear the floor out at this rate, love. Go and put your feet up. You *will* hear your phone. Christ, even the neighbours will hear it with the volume turned up so loud.'

'She should have called by now, Rod.'

'Love, you know how it is in prison. Everything that *can* go wrong *will* go wrong. Sod's Law. They may have the phones down, repair works, anything. It used to happen to me. She may even have been called to the office to finish her induction. You just don't know. Still, if she wasn't all right, then they would let her use the phone to call you.' He held up his hand before Georgie could protest. 'And if, God forbid, anything has happened, then your mate Patsy would have made the officers call you. So stop worrying. You'll give yourself a heart attack. Like I said. Go and sit down and I'll make you a sandwich and a cuppa.'

Georgie was about to walk away when she stopped and eyed Rodney. 'Have I changed, Rod? Like, have I got nasty?'

Rodney placed his discoloured veiny hands on his hips. 'Look, time has a way of healing, but *only* when you've accepted what caused your pain and stress in the first place, love.'

She smiled, but Rodney could see the sadness hidden behind that smile.

'It's like pushing old rubbish at the back of a drawer, isn't it? It just doesn't go away. It's there gathering dust, and if you keep adding to that drawer, one day, you won't be able to close it, or it will break. I only know part of what you've been through and how you handle situations. You just throw your shoulders back and carry on.'

He walked towards her and gently ran his hand down her arm. 'You have probably shrugged off more than most. That's why you have this tough exterior, but I also know that you are troubled by something that's blighted you for a long time.' He rubbed her arm again. 'I've heard you call out in the night. Lots of times recently. No one has nightmares that bad that they have to rush to the bathroom to be sick.'

Out of nowhere, her throat suddenly ached from emotion. The unspent tear made her eyes glisten before two huge streams poured down her cheeks.

'It's all right, girl. You can cry. It'll do you good, but so will talking about it, and believe me, I'm a good listener.'

Georgie coughed to hide her emotion, wiped away her tears, and allowed Rodney to hug her.

'Let's get a cup of tea, shall we, love, and you can start by talking. Go on, take a seat. I'll bring it in.'

She glanced at the phone again and then nodded. 'Okay, my mouth is parched, anyway.'

Georgie had never had a father and had never really wanted one. She'd loved only one man – that was Dixie – until Rohan came on the scene. In fact, apart from Henry, her business partner, she'd shied away from having men as friends. But Rodney was different; he was gentle and sweet. He had been to hell and back – much like herself. So once he'd handed her a cup of tea, she decided that now was as good a time as any to confide in him.

He listened as she began by telling him how it was for her growing up, which, if he was honest, wasn't unlike how he grew up. However, the era was different for him. But, nonetheless, poor was poor, and he was one of the many shoeless kids running along the streets with bread and jam for supper if he was lucky.

But for Georgie, it shouldn't have been that way, he thought.

Every so often, he nodded, letting her know that he was listening to everything she had to say, and yet, so far, all he was hearing was that her mother was a drunk and often took drugs, and Georgie had nothing to be proud of, not in the way of clothes. And food was either all or nothing. She could have an evening when her mother splashed out on a large cod and chips that would fill her empty belly and bring colour to her cheeks. But the next day, there would be nothing – not even a crust of bread, although there would be a bottle of vodka on the table.

What Rodney couldn't understand, though, was why Georgie would find the past cause enough to give her these frequent blood-curdling nightmares. That was until the penny dropped. He straightened up, slid his hand across the sofa, and covered hers. 'Did she beat you?'

Georgie was silent for a moment. 'Yes, she did, Rod. When I was tiny she did and up until I was around ten, although I did spend a lot of time in foster care. I wished she had left me there. She didn't give me a chance.'

Rodney was still baffled. He couldn't imagine her childhood upbringing was horrific enough to cause those nightmares. He had noticed that Georgie had shrugged off the memory of her mother beating her. That being the case, he wondered if she had harboured a grudge against her mother because she had been given the opportunity to live in a better home. If so, was Georgie pointing the finger at her mother because Georgie had wanted the finer things in life?

He soon had that notion quashed.

'She didn't just drink and take drugs, though, Rod. She . . . er . . . she.'

Seeing her bottom lip quiver, Rodney assumed her mother was also selling herself.

'It's okay, Georgie, I understand now. So your mother had her own way of paying for her drugs, then? Is that right?'

With eyes wide like saucers, Georgie stared at Rodney. 'It was worse than that, Rod. I think she *sold* me.'

As if he had just been bitten by a false widow spider, he pulled his hand away and stiffened. 'Christ almighty!' He suddenly realised that his reaction wasn't helpful in any way. 'Oh, darling, I'm so sorry. I had no idea you were going to say that.'

Unconcerned by his reaction, Georgie carried on. 'I don't know what to think anymore, Rod. You know about Marston-Smith injecting me and what followed, don't ya?'

Rodney nodded. 'Yes.' They all did in the family. It wasn't a secret.

'I'm so confused, Rod. I have these nightmares about my mother and her boyfriend or whatever the fuck he was . . . Oh, yeah, and there was another man. I remember him as well. He looked like a fucking skeleton, but here's the thing. It's all a blur. I am sure they injected me and then did things to me.'

Rodney remained quiet, listening, concerned he may say the wrong thing.

'But what if I'm wrong and I'm getting what Marston-Smith did to me mixed up with what my mother did?'

'Did you ever speak to your mother about it?'

Georgie rubbed her throbbing temples. 'No, we never spoke much. As I grew older, I learned to dodge her. I hated her, Rod. I hated her. And I hated *him* – her boyfriend – and the other men who came and went. I hated my life so much that I ran away and joined the Army.'

Georgie took a few sips of her tea as she stared down to the end of the garden.

'I really had no aspirations to join. There was no burning ambition. I didn't see myself as a soldier. But, and this is the point, it was my only way to escape. I knew I would be good because I could run. I was fit, then. I had to be. My mother's paying customers often thought they could get a piece of me, so I learned to jump through the fucking windows and land without breaking my ankles. I could summersault, backflip, and fight, so all the army training was easy for me.'

'Did you visit your mother when you were on leave to talk to her? You know what I mean. Like as a grown woman?' Rodney asked.

That question, which Rodney thought was a pretty low-key one, quickly stirred up something inside Georgie. Her entire face turned ghostly white, and he could see the subtle dilation of her nostrils.

Quickly, she shook her head. 'No, but they let me know that she was sick. Too many drugs, I guess. I saw her briefly before she died.'

'So you never had the opportunity to ask her about what happened to you?'

Georgie shook her head again and placed her hands around her cup as if for comfort. 'I think I know I was abused, but I have wiped away the memories – maybe for my own sanity – and now, I don't know what is true and what is not.'

'But you're sure you were abused, are you?'

Georgie nodded and used her index finger to wipe away an escaped tear.

'There's something else, Rod. This woman, Sarah, who has just started working at the coffee shop, keeps occurring in my dreams. I am sure she was about when I was younger, much younger. I feel like she was connected to the abuse.'

'So, have you asked her outright?'

Feeling a little foolish, Georgie shook her head. 'Well, no, not exactly. I nearly put her head into the oven, though, the other day. She's gone now from our café, and I doubt she'll return. But to get back to the point of this conversation, I am sure I saw someone at the grave when we laid Dixie to rest. And I think I've seen someone at the end of the garden.'

'Who?'

'My mother's boyfriend. I thought he would be dead after all these years. I assumed he'd died in jail.'

'So he went to prison, then?'

'Yeah. Anyway, he's out. And there's something else, Rod. I went to my mother's grave, and there was a bunch of roses with a message.'

Delving into her back pocket, Georgie pulled out a scrunched-up piece of paper.

'Here, read it.'

She handed him the note.

He read it twice before he peered up. 'That could mean anything.'

'I know it could, and I hate bloody riddles. It makes me think that Bruce – that's his name, by the way – is around somewhere. He may even be watching me.'

'May I just say this Bruce, who obviously frightened you as a child, must be very old now. He can't hurt you anymore, Georgie.'

A deep frown furrowed Georgie's forehead. 'You don't understand. That man will get revenge, by hook or by crook. I *know* he will. He was evil.' The moment she said those words, her eyes widened.

'Revenge? For what?' Rodney shook his head, showing his confusion.

'Well, er . . . I, um, I suppose because I left my mother. I ran away to the Army while he was away.'

'Oh, I see. So you were in the Army when he went to prison, then?'

'Yeah, well . . . er, no . . . he went to prison just after Mum died.'

Her hesitation was too profound. It was so unlike her, and Rodney sensed there was more to this story than she was telling him.

'Georgie, you can tell me anything. You don't have to hide anything from me.' He looked around. 'You took me in, put me up in my only little piece of luxury, and treated me like one of your own, and you didn't have to do any of that. So please believe me when I say you can trust me.'

She looked up at him and stared for a moment. The words that had never left her mouth – because they were too painful to say out loud – were now on the verge of falling out. Her lips partially moved, but the hesitation was too great. She could see Rodney perched on the edge of his seat, holding his breath, but just as she took a deep breath to speak, a noise from the hallway made them both turn their heads.

'Bloody traffic!' yelled Rohan, before he bowled into the lounge with a vast bouquet of roses.

'Coffee?' asked Rodney, wanting to give the couple a few moments together.

Rohan, dressed in a navy-blue polo neck and jeans, looked immaculate. Rodney could see how much he looked like Dixie. And also why Georgie would love him.

'Yes, please, Rodney.'

As soon as Rodney left the room, Georgie rose from her seat and smiled. 'Are those for me?'

'Yes, my sweetheart. I was hard on you yesterday. I'm sorry. You're everything to me, Georgie, and look, I should try to be more sensitive. It's tough for us all but more for you. You're Dixie-Lee's mother. Roses won't change your heartache. It's more a sorry from me.'

Georgie took the roses, placed them on the coffee table, and flung her arms around his neck. 'I'm sorry too. I'll try to be . . .'

He placed a finger over her lips. 'You will be, darling. When we sort this whole mess out and get our Dixie-Lee home, we'll go on a long vacation.'

'Sounds good. I just hope it gets sorted out sooner rather than later. I can't breathe properly worrying about Dixie-Lee, and she hasn't called today either.'

Rohan sat on the sofa and pulled Georgie down beside him. She rested her head on his chest. 'Have you heard from Brodie?'

'Yeah, he met with Michael, and they agreed to investigate the poxy mess. Michael has agreed to join forces, so to speak, to find out who killed his son and also his grandson.'

'What, just like that?'

'Our Brodie is the best when it comes to persuasion.'

'Violence?'

'No, no, not at all. Apparently, he laid down the facts and made Michael see sense. Michael believes that Bianca killed Tommy. Who killed his grandson, though, is a mystery because Bianca was in the station when he was murdered.'

‘But will there still be that doubt in the back of Michael’s mind that Dixie-Lee had something to do with it?’

Rohan shook his head. ‘No, Brodie was sure, and he wouldn’t say that unless he was.’

Georgie nestled her head under Rohan’s chin and closed her eyes as she breathed in his sweet-smelling aftershave and listened to his heartbeat. But her moment of calm was short-lived. They were interrupted by a banging at the front door, compelling her to try to jump to her feet.

Rohan pushed her back. ‘I’ll answer it.’

However, before he got out of the room, Rodney had already pulled the front door open, and there, looking a little out of breath, was Sheila, who didn’t wait to be invited in. She stormed through the wide hallway where she was met by Rohan and Georgie.

‘Shit! Sheila, what’s happened? Are you okay?’

Sheila took a few deep breaths, and without invitation, she walked into the lounge. ‘Oooh, Christ alive, let me get my breath.’

Unbuttoning her coat, she then kicked her boots off and flopped down on the sofa. ‘Shit me, I couldn’t find your gaff for love nor money. That idiot Uber driver. Anyway, I’m here now.’

‘What’s happened, Sheila?’

‘Fetch me a glass of water, or, better still, a cuppa tea. My mouth is like the bottom of a fucking parrot’s cage.’

Rohan hurried to the kitchen and poured a glass of water while Rodney put the kettle on.

‘Listen, my niece . . . ya know, the rough one?’

Georgie had no idea because, as far as she was aware, everyone in that family was rough, except Yasmin and Riley. Somehow, they’d managed to pull themselves out of the gutter, and even Sheila was doing her best.

‘Go on.’

Rohan hurried back and handed Sheila the glass of water as if she needed it to work like a car needed petrol.

'Cheers, babe.' She gulped it back and took another deep breath.

'You know who I mean. My niece, who's serving fifteen years for killing . . . er, anyway.' She waved her hands dismissively. 'She is inside with Dixie-Lee. Now, she phones me, she does, when she needs a little bit of money. Like if her ol' man has spunked all his benefits. I thought she was up in Peterborough. Anyway, it turns out she's inside, with your girl.'

Georgie took the chair opposite, hanging on to her every word. There was no point in rushing a woman like Sheila.

'So she calls me, she does. She recognised the name from, well, you know, when my Yasmin was up in court, and with Dixie-Lee being an unusual name, of course it stuck in her head. Anyway, luckily, she called before she put the boot in and I could set her straight, or Gawd knows what would have gone off.'

Georgie's eyes were on stalks, and her mouth dropped open.

But Sheila waved her hand. 'It's all right. My niece won't touch her now. I explained everything.'

'So, was she going to hurt Dixie-Lee because of the incident with Yasmin? That was sorted out ages ago. They're even friends now.'

Again, Sheila waved her hand. 'No, no, that's not why I'm 'ere. And I could have called ya, but I don't like to talk on the phone, in case they tape shit and that.'

Rodney came in with the tea and a few biscuits on the side and smiled at Sheila.

'Hello, love, thank you,' she said, as she took the cup and saucer and blushed slightly. 'Oooh, look at that. Just how I like my tea. You are a gem, Rodney, and how have you been, love?'

'I'm very well, Sheila,' Rodney replied.

Georgie coughed to get Sheila's attention back. 'You were saying.'

'It was all a bit cloak and dagger, like, and I think I got a bit confused, but the main point is this: my niece, Minnie. Well, she ain't no mini – if ya know what I mean. She's fucking massive, and she fights like a geezer. She's inside for killing a bouncer 'cos he touched her girl inappropriately. But she is a basket case. She will do anything for money, and this is the thing: she's been offered something, drugs or whatever, to annihilate someone called Patsy Dewhurst and leave your girl wide open with no protection.'

Georgie's hands flew to her mouth in horror.

'Are you sure about this, Sheila?' asked Rohan, taking over the conversation.

Sheila nodded. 'Totally. She has no need to make up bollocks, and she's no need to lie to me either.'

'No, I guess not. So what else did she say? Please, Sheila, try and recall everything because I'll call the prison and . . .'

Sheila quickly shook her head. 'This woman, this Bianca Malloye, has the screws bought. She offered my Minnie a lot of whatever to carry out basically a near-death beating. So whatever it is they have against Dixie-Lee, it must be serious. Has she clumped anyone inside?'

'No, of course not, Sheila. Will Minnie call you back? Please tell her not to hurt Dixie-Lee. Whatever they are paying her, we'll double it.'

'No need, Rohan, my niece will do what I tell her to do. We're family. Now, I've told her to make sure no one touches Dixie-Lee, and since this Patsy bird seems to be Dixie-Lee's only protection, my Minnie has been told to stop anyone from hurting her an' all.'

Rohan nodded, taking it all in, but at the back of his mind, he knew why they wanted Dixie-Lee in a state of fear. He glanced briefly at Georgie and he knew he couldn't voice his thoughts, not right now. Georgie's tough exterior was crumbling. He could see the light in her eyes was dimming by the second, and her face was so white, her legs were shaking. She was literally falling apart.

CHAPTER NINETEEN

'I don't think anyone is coming, Patsy,' said Dixie-Lee, still perched on the top bunk and holding the broken mug handle.

'That's what they want us to think, and then they'll storm the room when the fucking chances are I'm on the khazi and you're sound asleep.'

Dixie-Lee looked at Patsy and shuddered. She really didn't want to picture her on the toilet. Still, if she wasn't getting out of prison anytime soon, it would be a possibility. The thought made her stomach churn over. It was true. There really wasn't much left that prison could take from a person because it sure as hell was taking every ounce of *her* dignity.

Patsy started moaning and groaning while pacing the small room.

'Patsy, what's up?'

'Nuffin, kiddo.'

'No, really, why are you pacing?' She could see that Patsy was slightly bent over. 'You need the loo, don't you?'

Patsy's face looked like a beetroot. 'I do. I've always had stomach issues, and I can't ask you to go outside in case they come for you, and I'm on the poxy throne. Agghhh!' she groaned, once more, as she clutched her middle.

Dixie-Lee jumped down from the top bunk. 'Look, don't worry about me. I'll wait outside, and if they turn up, I'll come back in.'

'No, don't! I promised your muvver I would be her eyes and ears here. The last thing I want is for something to happen to you.'

'Patsy, nothing *will* happen. I can easily shoot back inside. I'm hardly going to wander around, am I?'

'Okay, but don't go anywhere else. If they come, get back inside. I'll sling my own shit at them, if I have to.'

That thought had Dixie-Lee almost gagging. But with her mind on her enemies, she slipped outside the room to give Patsy some privacy. However, she had hardly closed the door when she was stunned to find three women leaning against the wall. They had managed to sneak up to her cell without making a sound, and there they were, like a pride of lions, lying in wait and hoping for the monkey to drop out of the tree.

It was Dulcie who moved first. Swiftly, cupping her hand around Dixie-Lee's mouth, she lifted her off the floor and away from the wall to prevent her from kicking and screaming.

But Dixie-Lee wasn't going to go quietly. She kicked back at Dulcie's crotch as hard as she could.

However, one of the other women, a tall skinny blonde, was on the ball. She instantly grabbed Dixie-Lee's ankles, stopping her from lashing out and causing further injury.

Strangely, Dixie-Lee was more angry than scared right now, so she bucked, buckled, and wiggled like Houdini escaping a straitjacket. But the more she thrashed around, the tighter Dulcie held her grip, until she was finally carried into a cell further along the wing and thrown onto the floor.

Dixie-Lee was out of breath, but all that hurt was her knee, where she had landed heavily. So, in the blink of an eye, she jumped to her feet to assess her surroundings. She was in a double room, more significant than Patsy's, with a single bed. It looked more like a bedroom than a prison cell. The bedclothes were blue satin, the chair had a fur cushion, and a heavy deep-blue set of curtains adorned the window.

Standing at the end of the bed by the window was Bianca. She was in prison sweats that actually fitted her and her hair was pulled tightly away from her face. Her arms were crossed while she tapped her foot, and her chin jutted in a daring pose.

Dixie-Lee then peered around to see who else was in the room, but it was only Dulcie and the tall blonde girl because the other one had either scarpered or was keeping a lookout.

Dulcie shut the door and leaned against it while Blondie propped herself against the wall chewing gum like a moody teenager in a playground and trying to act hard. Blondie didn't bother Dixie-Lee, but Dulcie did. She'd already felt her strength.

'What do you want, Bianca?'

'Get you, *Miss Deacon*, the protégée.'

Dixie-Lee glanced back at Dulcie and then returned her gaze to Bianca.

'So, this is what's going to happen. You see, you've probably already gathered that I personally have a lot of influence over the guests in this establishment – even the screws – so there's no point in trying to go against me or my wishes because you will find yourself completely fucked up! Do you understand?' She stepped closer, grinning like a psychopath.

Silence pervaded the room while Dixie-Lee got her thoughts together. 'I'm not sure I do,' she replied, crossing her arms and mimicking Bianca.

'Oh, so, *I* see. A couple of days in the grown-ups' prison, and suddenly you're all cocky and acting hard.' She wagged her finger. 'But the thing is, Dixie-Lee, you're *not* hard, are you? You're just a pretty kid who's probably been used to getting away with everything 'cos her sweet, innocent looks have allowed for that. But, believe me, darling, it doesn't work like that in here. There's a kinda pecking order, shall we say. And you, little chicken, are at the bottom of that order. So it works like this: the little chicks at the bottom do as they're told by the bigger chicks at the top.' She pointed to herself while stepping closer again.

Imagining how her mother would handle this situation, Dixie-Lee smiled. 'I'm not a chicken or a chick or a fucking cockerel. So please, Bianca, say what you want and be done instead of giving me a fucking lecture, which, by the way, you're not doing very well.' She had to swear to authenticate her put-on persona. She was sure her mother would have said a lot worse and probably flattened the three women in the room by now.

Suddenly, Bianca grabbed Dixie-Lee around the throat and squeezed hard. While the shock knocked Dixie-Lee off her act, the fear of being strangled boosted her gumption. Without another thought, she kneed Bianca between the legs twice and with such speed that Bianca was forced to release her hold. It allowed Dixie-Lee to jump up and fly-kick Bianca in the chest, a move her mother had taught her, and one she'd learned well.

Bianca hit the back wall, stunned.

Dixie-Lee was about to fly-kick her again but she was dragged back by Dulcie, thrown against the wall, and punched in the face. The blow caught her high on her right cheekbone, forcing her eye to shut completely.

With her adrenaline now surging through her veins, Dixie-Lee tried hard to fight back, but the blonde girl now joined in and grabbed Dixie-Lee by her hair, forcing her to the floor while Dulcie booted and booted her in the chest.

'Stop!' yelled Bianca, as she brushed herself down and got herself together.

With her eye swelling at a rate of knots and her chest feeling as though it had imploded, Dixie-Lee tried to get to her feet. But every time she did, her legs gave way, and she slid back down the wall. She stared at Bianca with so much hate that she wanted to kill her. She didn't deserve any of this. She hadn't done anything to antagonise the woman.

'You killed my stepson.'

'No, I didn't, and you know I didn't,' Dixie-Lee replied, shaking her head.

Bianca folded her arms again and nodded rhythmically. 'You did, and you killed the barrister as well.'

Dixie-Lee frowned. Where was this going? Bianca wasn't asking her if she killed the barrister. She was telling her. It made no sense. Why would Bianca be so worried about the barrister? She wasn't accused of his murder. She had an alibi. The police at the station could vouch for that.

'Oh my God—'

Bianca's lip curled in satisfaction as she watched the fear slowly creep over Dixie-Lee.

'You know who killed the judge's son, don't you?'

Bianca's face was like stone, with not even a hint of acknowledgement or denial.

'What do you want from me?' Dixie-Lee asked, as she made another attempt to get to her feet.

'Hmm, see, I just want you to be honest, and by that, I mean you need to change your plea.'

Unable to put both feet firmly on the floor, Dixie-Lee leaned against the wall, with all of her weight on one foot. 'What, and plead guilty to something I didn't do?' Confused, she tilted her head. 'Why would I do *that*?'

'Oh, dear, dear, you must know how it works in here. I'm not on the outside to do much myself, but' – she clapped her hands – 'I have friends, very fucking dangerous friends, who will do exactly what I say.'

Dixie-Lee wasn't that naïve; she knew precisely what Bianca was saying, but, still, she wanted Bianca to spell it out. 'And say what?'

'*Say what?* Tell me, Miss Protégée, because you are supposed to be a clever girl. What would it be like to live as a free woman on the outside but have no one to share that freedom with? No Mummy, no Uncle Rohan? Shall I go on?'

'You wouldn't dare. You're not that hard or powerful enough, Bianca.'

Bianca looked at Dulcie and laughed. 'Did you hear that, Dulcie? This little prat said I'm not that hard or powerful enough. What do *you* think?'

Dulcie's laugh was deep, like a man's. 'I think she needs a little taster. So, go on, Bianca, give the order, and I'll do the deed. It's water off a duck's back to me.' She turned to face Dixie-Lee. 'And it will be nuffin compared to what her people will do to *your* family when she gives the orders.'

'Take her ear off for not fucking listening.'

This was far more violent than Dixie-Lee imagined. She had nowhere to run. She couldn't escape. All she could hear was Bianca laughing.

The blonde girl pulled out a knife hidden down the back of her tracksuit.

Even though Dixie-Lee could barely stand, she tried hard to stop Dulcie from pinning her against the wall. Yet Dulcie had the strength of a man and would win. So all Dixie-Lee could do was let out a high-pitched scream.

But it didn't stop Dulcie, who grabbed Dixie-Lee's ear. The moment she snatched the blade from Blondie and was about to slice the ear off, the door flew open, knocking Dulcie across the room and on top of the blonde girl.

Dixie-Lee was again on the floor, but, instantly, Patsy grabbed her arm and slid her away from the other women.

An inmate the size of Patsy and another in her late thirties, who was caked in tattoos and looked as tough as old boots, forced their way through and dragged the blonde girl and Dulcie out into the corridor.

Patsy was holding Dixie-Lee up and trying to get her back to their cell. But Dixie-Lee couldn't resist looking over her shoulder. She saw the tattooed woman smashing the life out of Dulcie. A stream of claret shot up the newly painted wall, followed by a blood-curdling scream from Dulcie, but it didn't stop the tattooed woman. Dixie-Lee glanced at the blonde girl who looked as if she was left for dead. Her body appeared to have been dropped from a great height because she was splayed out at a funny angle like a child's broken marionette.

'Come on, kiddo, let's get you back. I fucking knew I shouldn't have gone and had that shit.'

As soon as they were in their room, Patsy helped Dixie-Lee onto the bottom bunk. 'Oh my God, the fucking state of you. Your muvver will kill me.'

'I'm all right, Patsy. I've just got a few broken ribs, I think.'

Patsy threw her hands in the air. 'A few broken ribs! No, no, this can't be happening. We need to get you to the medical unit. You'll be safe there. Shit!'

Dixie-Lee sat up and lifted her sweatshirt to show Patsy her injuries. 'Are they bad?' she asked, unable to look down because she had also strained all of her muscles kicking Bianca.

Patsy got on her knees and looked at Dixie-Lee's side. It was instantly showing signs of bruising. The skin was like red and purple marble. She then looked at the girl's face. Her right cheek was so swollen it had forced her right eye shut. Without thinking, Patsy put her arms around Dixie-Lee and hugged her. 'Oh, little sweetheart, I should have protected you. I can't forgive myself.'

'Patsy, you saved me because that Dulcie was about to take my ear off, and I don't think they would have stopped there.'

Patsy jumped up, her nostrils now flared and her fists in balls. 'I'm gonna fucking kill them. Three women on a kid like you. So they were gonna cut your ear off, were they? Well, we'll fucking see about that.'

'No! Please don't do anything. The screws will take you away. I'll be alone. I'll be an easy target then.'

Patsy stared at the door, desperate to go and finish Dulcie off. She took a few deep breaths and looked down at Dixie-Lee. 'It was lucky Minnie and her sidekick Muscles were there to help me. Well, that's her nickname.'

Dixie-Lee chuckled. 'I could have guessed that because who would call their little girl Muscles.'

Patsy smiled. 'I dunno if she was ever a little girl.'

'Are those the women you were talking about – the really hard ones?'

'Yeah, I'd just got off the loo when they barged in looking for you. I thought, oh no, they're gonna hurt you, but, apparently, Minnie is the niece of someone called Sheila. Her aunt told her to look out for you and me.' She laughed, and her belly rolled up and down. 'As if I need anyone to look out for me. Mind you, I'd rather have Minnie on my side than against me.'

'Sheila Marx? I know Sheila. It's a long story, but I'm just so pleased that the three of you came to help me.'

'Hmm, I wonder what's happened to Dulcie? She's not well-liked, ya know. She's done bad things to many innocent kids in here.'

Suddenly, an alarm went off; it almost made Dixie-Lee jump out of her skin.

'What's going on?'

'The screws have sounded the alarm for help. I reckon Minnie and Muscles have done a number on Dulcie and even Bianca.'

'Patsy, that blonde one was either out cold or *dead*.'

Patsy looked at Dixie-Lee in amazement. *Why was this kid even bothered?* Shrugging her shoulders, she replied, 'So? She's another low-life scumbag. She's only hard with a knife in her hand. I hope she *is* dead. I hate her.'

Pulling the chair over to the bunks, Patsy sat down facing Dixie-Lee. 'You're brave, and I bet you want to be like your mum, don't ya?'

Dixie-Lee nodded slowly. 'My mum is something else. She's tough. I guess she was always there when I was a kid and fighting my battles. She did teach me to fight, though.'

'Yeah, I can see why she would. She wanted to protect you from the world of the bad and the ugly, and I get it. She taught you to fight to protect yourself, for when she's not around.'

'Yes, she always said if I'm not there and I need to fight, use everything I've got.'

'But listen to me, kiddo, what you don't have is your mother's *fighting spirit*. I, for one, have never seen a woman fight like her. And it doesn't come from army training. She is angry with the world. Something probably from her past made her that way. I've seen it before in some of the women in here. They never tackled their demons until it was too late, and they ended up on a murder charge and are now stuck in here for the rest of their lives. But you, little 'un, don't have that because you're *not* angry with the world. You were loved by your mum so much. And, of course, you still are. But a word from Auntie Patsy. Don't act hard: instead, box clever. Right? You're bright. Your mum told me all about you and with some pride, I've gotta add. You're not like me, Bianca, or Dulcie. You're better than that. So, use your brains. Be smart about stuff in here. Don't try to fight your way out of trouble. Just talk your way out.' She stopped when she saw a tear trickle down Dixie-Lee's nose.

'Hey, are you hurting? Shall I get you to medical?'

Dixie-Lee bit her bottom lip. 'No, it's not that. It's the thought that my mum suffered when she was a kid. I know her mother was a drunk, but she's never really talked about it. I hate to think my lovely mum suffered. I know most people see her as cold, but she's not, you know. She's very kind and has a lot of love inside her. She's always showered me with love. She's a *good* mum.'

Patsy wiped her eyes. 'Stop, you've got me all emotional now. Your mum has a heart of gold, I'll give ya that. A while ago, I honestly thought I would lose my kids to social services. They live with my mum and dad, ya see, who struggle to cope financially. But when I phoned my dad a week or so after your mum was released, he said that a cheque was posted through the door, and then it became a regular thing, and the only person I know who would do that is your mum.' A sudden barrage of tears fell down her cheeks. 'How fucking kind is that, eh? She didn't even tell me she did it, so, on the outside, even with her beautiful face, she may look a bit cold, but really, she's an angel.' She wiped her eyes and laughed. 'No one makes me cry. Now look what you've gone and done.'

Dixie-Lee looked on, disturbed by what she'd heard, but inside, she was feeling such a lot of pride for who her mother was and what she had done for those she loved.

'Right, kiddo, you'd better call your mum. She'll be worrying.'

It took some time before Dixie-Lee was able to get up off the bunk to make the call. However, as soon as she dialled her mother's number, the phone went dead. 'Oh, it's not working.'

Patsy snatched the phone and dialled a different number. It rang, but she replaced the receiver. 'They've removed your pin to call your mum. The bastards, they are playing dirty now.'

'The screws have that power?'

'Yep.'

'Hopefully, Mum will be okay until I see her tomorrow.'

'Tomorrow?'

'Yes, I have a visit booked. I did it at reception when I arrived. I gave them all my mum's details, and Mum booked the visit at her end.'

Patsy frowned. 'Shit, Dixie-Lee, what the fuck are you gonna tell her?' She pointed to Dixie-Lee's face.

'I don't know yet. But I'll think of something. There are a few things I need to work out first.'

'Like what?'

'My plea.'

'Your plea? I don't understand.'

'I may change it to guilty.'

Patsy's jaw dropped. Then, as she worked out the subtext of what Dixie-Lee was telling her, she screwed up her face in anger. Before she had the chance to rip open the door to get to Bianca's room, the door clicked shut. They were locked in. The alarm went off again, indicating that the whole of the prison was now in lockdown.

CHAPTER TWENTY

After yet another restless night, Georgie awoke to find her pyjamas soaking wet. Rohan was already up, and by the time she showered and got dressed, she heard the front door close behind him. Her heart sank. *Was she losing Rohan?* She didn't recall his arms around her when she woke up trembling from another one of her nightmares. *Was all of this too much for him to handle?* The roses were sweet, and he'd hugged and kissed her before he went to sleep, but he seemed distant, and right now, she needed him.

She sighed before shrugging off any further worries about her future husband. She would make things good again – when she could get her head straight, that was. But as soon as she tried to take control of her thoughts, her mind turned to her daughter, and a hot flush enveloped her. *Why hadn't Dixie-Lee phoned her last night?*

After gulping down a coffee, which literally scorched her throat, she slid her arms into her long black coat, zipped up her black leather boots, and checked her purse to make sure she had her driving licence. She didn't want to give the prison staff any reason to refuse the visit, and the lack of any ID would be the first reason they'd use to make her life difficult and turn her away.

The ground was icy this morning, and she contemplated going back inside and switching her boots for trainers, but glancing at her watch, she realised that time was pressing, so she walked quickly towards her car.

The visit today was booked solely in her name and she couldn't wait to get there. She was so anxious to see how her daughter was doing that her chest felt tight, and she was experiencing palpitations. The only thing that lessened her anxiety was telling herself that Sheila's niece – Minnie – and Patsy were there to protect her daughter. Hopefully, though, there would be no reason *to* protect her. She was an innocent kid who had just happened to be in the wrong place at the wrong time.

As she drove to the prison, her thoughts turned to Cathy McGowan. Although she wasn't keen on her, Rohan had insisted she was the best, and if anyone could get her out of prison, it would be this woman. She decided she would pay the barrister a visit herself and apologise for her rudeness in the courtroom, in the hope it would reflect well on her daughter.

Hugh Shields had kept them up to date with any news from the police station, and as it stood, the authorities were not looking for another killer of the judge's son because as far as they were concerned they had Dixie-Lee as their primary culprit and there was no reason to suspect anyone else. However, they weren't putting Dixie-Lee in the frame for the murder of Tyler Malloye because there was a question over the amount of blood at the scene. Since some of Tyler's blood would have been on Dixie-Lee's clothing – the same clothing that had the judge's son's blood on it – that ruled her out as the murderer. So, for that reason alone, she wasn't on a double murder charge.

None of it made any sense, but then again, it was early days, and Georgie hoped and prayed that some evidence would show up soon and prove her daughter's innocence and end this unimaginable situation.

***

Arriving at HMP Bronzefield gave Georgie a strange sense of déjà vu. After all, it wasn't so long ago that she had been imprisoned here.

The entrance to the prison was closed, and so the visitors were left queuing outside in the freezing cold. Georgie would have waited in the car, but she wanted to be near the front of the queue and ultimately spend the maximum time with her daughter.

Standing out in the cold, Georgie stood there shivering, as did all the other visitors. These today were mainly men but a few older women had arrived. One had five little children with her. Naturally, the kids were bored and were making a racket while skipping under people's feet. Georgie could see the older woman was probably an inmate's grandmother; no doubt, she had been left to look after the kids while their mother was behind bars. It was a sad sight. The woman in her seventies looked to be run ragged; she barely had the strength to hold the youngest child who was probably around sixteen months old.

'Jesus, mother of fecking God, you're a lump, just like yer father, that you are. Stop wriggling, would you now.'

Georgie looked at the baby and clocked the earrings and the knee-length socks with bows. All the children were prettily dressed, with styled brown ringlets and piercing blue eyes.

An officer, who was holding his jangling keys, walked along the line asking if everyone had their paperwork. This was standard practice. No one would be admitted unless all the formalities were in place. In any case, today the prison was short-staffed.

When the officer got to the Irish grandmother, she struggled to balance the child and delve into her huge bag.

Georgie tapped the woman on the shoulder. 'Shall I hold the baby for you?'

'Well, there's an angel, if ever there was one. Thank you.'

Georgie took the baby, who seemed to be quite taken with her, and stared at her. She reminded Georgie of Dixie-Lee as a baby, with her dark hair and blue eyes.

Once the officer had finished with the Irish woman, he looked at Georgie, who pulled out her driving licence and visiting code number.

Looking her up and down, he said, 'Who did you say you were visiting?'

'Dixie-Lee Deacon.'

Before the officer could ask any more questions, one of the little girls suddenly kicked him in the shin. 'You've locked me mammy up. Now, you go and let her come home.'

The kick must have been hard because the thin rake of a man hopped and then hollered, 'You, madam, need to keep the children under control or I will cancel your visit.'

''Ere, mister,' said the elderly woman, wagging her finger in his face. 'She's only a little girl, not even fecking five years old, who wants to see her mammy. Now then.'

'Look, just keep them in order.'

As the main door opened, the visitors pushed forward, and the young officer suddenly hurried to the front of the queue.

Georgie grinned, knowing that he would never control a bad situation, not in a million years. He looked so out of place to be a prison officer.

As they went in one by one, showing their identification, a female officer tried to keep the noise down. 'Right!' she bellowed. 'Listen up, everyone. We are very short-staffed, so please bear with us. You're all lucky we didn't cancel the visits today.'

A woman behind Georgie whispered, 'That's a touch. They won't have the staff to watch us like hawks.'

Once seated in the visiting room, Georgie fixed her eyes on the door from which the inmates would enter. The officer hadn't been wrong. There weren't many officers in the room at all. The tuck shop, however, was open. Of course, it would be because there would be a right old stink if it wasn't, especially with all the children here.

As another officer, a large rotund woman with pink hair, unlocked the door, the first bunch of inmates entered. Georgie stared, clocking every one of them. They came into the visiting room in all shapes and sizes – tall, thin, fat, toothless, veneers – but all were similarly dressed in grey tracksuits. They also had a prison pallor about them – a particular look one gained as an inmate. Maybe it was the food or the lack of sunlight, but their faces seemed grey with a hint of yellow. And their hair was darker than it would naturally be: it was a dead giveaway. Georgie's stomach was in her mouth. *Surely her daughter wouldn't look like that, would she?*

There was a break when no one appeared for a few minutes. Georgie felt her heart hammering in her chest. Then, the officer opened the door and smiled at a woman. She was very tall and her hair had been pulled back into a ponytail. She didn't look like an inmate one bit. Her face, which evidently had been cosmetically enhanced, was heavily made-up. Her lipstick highlighted her pout and she had dusted her cheeks with blusher. But it wasn't how she looked that stood out. It was how the officer treated her as though she was royalty. The rotund officer's smile lifted her cheeks, and her hand gesture, with almost a bow from her neck up, spoke volumes. *Who was this woman?*

Then another face appeared. When Georgie saw that it was Dixie-Lee, her eyes nearly popped out of her head and a rage swept through her to the point that she was ready to kill someone.

Dixie-Lee's right cheek was swollen and there was a large bruise around her right eye. And dressed in a tracksuit that seemed to swallow her up, her daughter looked sad, lost, and pathetic.

All Georgie wanted to know was who had done this to her precious child.

The woman with her hair in a ponytail turned and whispered something in Dixie-Lee's ear.

Dixie-Lee's face said it all; she was afraid of this woman. Her eyes looked down, and she held her hands together as if she had done something wrong or was being threatened.

As Georgie immediately jumped up to greet her daughter, who was approaching her table, she noticed how two officers were intently watching Dixie-Lee, before one of them diverted her gaze to the woman with the ponytail.

The minute Georgie put her arms around her daughter, she could feel Dixie-Lee's body stiffen as if in real pain. Georgie didn't ask or wait for her to explain what was wrong with her. She pulled away and lifted Dixie-Lee's top to see the huge bruises on both sides of her ribs.

Dixie-Lee quickly pulled down her top and sat down. 'Don't, Mum. *Don't* make a fuss, *please*,' she whispered.

Georgie scanned the room knowing who was responsible. The woman with the ponytail was clearly the culprit, although she couldn't see who was visiting her. Only that it was a man. But then she noticed the woman's stare. She was like the cat that got the cream.

'Mum, stop staring, *please*.'

'It was her, wasn't it? Who the fuck is she, and why is she grinning at us?'

'Mum, *please*, keep your voice down.'

Looking at her daughter's face, Georgie felt every pain there was. 'I thought fucking Patsy was looking after you?'

'She is, Mum. If she and Minnie, Sheila's niece, hadn't come and got me, I'd be dead. So please don't stop paying for her kids. Patsy's good, I swear.'

Georgie could feel the tears stinging behind her eyes. 'Fucking hell, why, Dixie-Lee? Fucking *why*?'

Knowing how well her mother could read her, Dixie-Lee looked directly into her eyes and with a straight face, she replied, 'I upset a couple of people, but it's all sorted now.'

'Oh, that's all right then, is it. You just upset a few people, did ya,' she answered, in her best sarcastic tone. 'Babe, listen, I want to know what the fuck *happened*. Why aren't you in hospital with injuries like that?'

'I'm all right, Mum. Please, I'm okay. I just upset the wrong person, that's all, but it's all sorted. No one will hurt me now.'

Georgie could feel her stomach churning, her rage bubbling, and it was taking all her strength to hold it down. Her eyes flicked to the woman with the ponytail who was now deliberately smirking at her.

'How did you upset this person?'

'Mum, please leave it, yeah. Tell me, how are Uncle Rohan and Grandpa Rodney?'

Chewing her lip for a moment, Georgie finally answered. 'They're both fine. Now, is there any more news from your barrister? Has she booked a visit or had one of those link-up Zoom-call thingies?'

'Not yet.' Dixie-Lee paused and looked her mother directly in the eye. 'It doesn't matter anyway, Mum. Not now.'

'Of course it bloody matters. We need to get you out of here before any sodding trial. You are not meant to be in here, and if I could fucking swap places with you, I would.'

'Mum, it doesn't matter because I am pleading guilty.'

Motionless, Georgie just stared at her daughter in disbelief. *This couldn't be happening, could it?*

'I'm sorry, Mum. I know it's not what you want to hear, but that's my plea because I have a defence. Clifford tried to rape me, so I won't serve that long. It'll be dropped down to a manslaughter charge.' Dixie-Lee tilted her battered face to the side and smiled gently at her mother.

Georgie shook her head as if she had misheard her daughter. 'Sorry, what? No, this is ludicrous. You're not guilty. You didn't kill him. What the fucking hell's going *on*?'

Dixie-Lee waved and gestured for her mother to calm down. 'Listen, please, Mum. I'm pleading guilty. I want this over with. It's my decision, Mum, not yours, okay?'

'But you didn't kill him. You really didn't.'

Watching closely, Georgie could see that Dixie-Lee's face had now turned deathly white, and her eyes were huge and round, with heavy tears ready to fall. Her daughter epitomised an entirely different person from the one she was hoping to see today.

'Mum, I did. I did kill him.'

The shock made Georgie gasp out loud. 'No,' she said, shaking her head, not wanting to believe her daughter. 'You wouldn't do that. I don't believe you.'

As she said those words, she could sense the ponytailed woman's eyes on her. Glaring back, she saw such a self-satisfied smile on her face that it made her want to go over and punch her lights out.

'Who is that?' Georgie pointed to the ponytailed woman without bothering to hide her annoyance.

With her eyes now even larger, Dixie-Lee pushed her mother's hand down. 'Stop, Mum. Please, you'll get me *killed*.'

'Right, okay, now tell me what the hell is going on because I will go through this visiting room like a fucking tornado, and the first bitch who's gonna get it is that woman, the one who whispered to you when you first came in here. Is it that Bianca Malloye? If she's threatening you, Dixie-Lee, I won't stand by and let it happen. I'll go down myself before I let her hurt you.'

'No, Mum, Bianca is in another prison. Just stop getting angry.'

'I'm not gonna have you bullied. If she is throwing accusations that you killed her stepson, Tyler, I'll give her something to fucking cry over.'

'I'm going back now, Mum.'

A deep frown creased Georgie's forehead. 'What? No, wait, I've only just got here. Let me get you some chocolate from the tuck shop. Anything, but don't go yet, darling.'

But Dixie-Lee was already on her feet. 'Mum, please understand. I'm pleading guilty, and I don't want to fight over it. I want to go back to my room. I love you, Mum, but you seeing me is making you angry, and I can't have you kicking off in here. It will only make matters worse for me.'

Georgie nodded in resignation. 'Okay, I understand, but if you're being bullied into changing your plea, then tell me. We can have you moved to another prison. We can—'

'Stop, Mum. I am going to plead guilty, and that's that. No one is going to hurt me. I've got Patsy. She has been so good to me, Mum, so don't worry.'

'Dixie-Lee, that woman behind you. Is that Bianca Malloye?'

'No, Mum, she's not here anymore. They moved her out. I'm going back to my room.'

Having no choice, Georgie got to her feet and hugged her daughter. 'I love you, my girl. Please don't go yet.'

'I'm tired, Mum. I need to lie down.'

'Oh, er . . . okay. Call me tonight, please. Don't leave me worrying.'

'I won't, Mum, and yes, I'll phone you, if the numbers have been put on my pin. I'm sure they will have by now.'

'And go to medical. You need to have those bruises checked.'

‘They are worse than they look, Mum. Stop worrying. I’m not a kid anymore.’

‘You’re my kid, though,’ Georgie replied, flatly, now thoroughly subdued and feeling utterly helpless as if nothing she could say or do would change the situation. Everything was now so out of her control. Her daughter had begged her not to say or do anything, but her heart was saying: go and smash the life out of the tall woman.

‘I’ll call you later, Mum. Love you, bye.’

Georgie didn’t want to let her daughter go, but something was seriously off, and maybe this would be the one day she would have to back off and allow her daughter to decide what was best. However, her frustration was making her bite her bottom lip. She could easily give the tall woman the beating of her life. But who was she? And why was she whispering to her daughter? It would be understandable if she had asked Dixie-Lee to bring drugs in, but there was no mention of smuggling in contraband.

As soon as Dixie-Lee left the room, Georgie walked towards the exit door to be escorted out, but as they were short-staffed, she had to wait. However, she couldn’t take her eyes off the tall woman, and although she tried to get a look at the man, they had their table placed at such an angle that it wasn’t possible to see him properly. He seemed relatively young and quite athletic from the back view.

After fifteen minutes, an officer approached with the keys in her hands. ‘I’ll take you back to the main reception.’

‘Thank you. The tall woman with the ponytail . . . er, I wanted to thank her. Oh, my head,’ she tutted, ‘I’m all over the place today. What’s her name again?’

The officer looked over. ‘Bianca Malloye, you mean?’

Georgie was speechless. Her mouth fell open. Her daughter had blatantly lied to her. Twice!

‘Sorry, did you have a message for her?’

In shock, Georgie glanced back at the officer. ‘No, no, I’m very sorry. I thought she was someone else.’

As the visitors approached the gate, the young male officer was there again. He flashed a look at Georgie and hissed at the escorting officer, ‘She was supposed to be denied entry.’

Georgie heard what the officer said and spun around. ‘What the fuck did you just say?’

The young officer jumped back, his face pale. ‘Oh, I wasn’t talking about you.’

‘Sure you weren’t, you silly little prick.’

CHAPTER TWENTY-ONE

Trudging to her car, Georgie was still bubbling over with anger. She was now in despair and at the same time exasperated by the way that her daughter had not only cut short the visit but had lied outright about Bianca being moved from the prison.

However, what probably bothered her the most was a feeling of complete helplessness. Having had to witness the pain on her daughter's face and seeing the bruises on her daughter's torso, she wanted to rip through Bianca like a fast train and tear her limbs apart. And the fact that the woman had the audacity to demonstrate her arrogant pleasure through her lip-curling smirks was a complete piss-take.

Angrily, she clicked the key fob to open her car. Then without thinking, she opened the door so quickly, she slipped on some ice and nearly put her shoulder out. 'Damn!' she cursed, before she slowly got to her feet and clambered into her seat.

While she sat for a few moments waiting for the pain to gradually lessen, she was struck by two things. First was the realisation that she wasn't young anymore. That really hit her hard. The second was that Dixie-Lee wasn't a child and so she couldn't fight her daughter's battles for her.

Rubbing her shoulder, Georgie appreciated that she was not getting any younger, and she was obviously lacking the strength and the stamina she once had. She stared at the enormous imposing prison walls that stood like soldiers guarding the place and keeping her daughter away from her. An unexpected tear ran down her cheeks. Her nose prickled, and she sniffed back more tears knowing that crying wouldn't change the fact that her kid was in a hellhole and being threatened and bullied. And to make matters worse, there wasn't a damn thing she could do about the situation.

All she could do was to hope that the police wouldn't wholly leave all their eggs in one basket, but, instead, start to look for other possible suspects. She knew Mac and Brodie were working with Michael Malloye to consider anyone else who would want to get their hands on the Malloye file or anyone who would be working for Bianca; so far, though, nothing was staring them in the face. And she couldn't do anything herself because she didn't know the Malloye family, Dixie-Lee's barrister, or anyone else connected to the case.

It wasn't lost on Georgie that at this precise moment she felt at her most vulnerable since leaving the Army. Not only was everything slowly stacking up against her but it seemed that the feeling of helplessness she had experienced as a child was now returning in spades. It was eating her up inside.

Not one for curling in an emotional ball and having a good cry, Georgie decided to visit McGowan and Elison's chambers where she hoped to meet with Cathy McGowan. But if she wasn't available, at least she would see where her daughter worked. And she thought that perhaps she might find out something in connection with the death of Clifford Jenson-Baine and those of Tyler and Tommy Malloye. At the very least, she needed to feel that she was doing something proactive. Because it seemed those chambers contained the answers – or at least some of them – to what was going on. It was better than doing nothing.

The traffic through London was a nightmare, so by the time Georgie reached the chambers, she was thirsty and had a pounding headache. But, right now, she needed to find a place to park because the empty spaces were for permit holders only.

By late afternoon, she finally spotted a space and quickly squeezed her car in before taking a deep breath and exiting her vehicle. With the cold air helping to ease her headache, she marched towards the chambers, more confident now that the ground wasn't so icy and relieved that her shoulder had stopped aching. She gazed around, taking it all in because this was where her daughter had been coming to work. The building itself looked grand in a professional way. The entrance door was huge, with the name of the chambers etched into the glass.

Georgie hesitated and peered inside the considerable entrance hall with a reception desk at the far end. The interior of the building matched the appearance of the outside façade: it was just as impressive, and she imagined that Dixie-Lee would have felt quite important working in a place like this.

Just as she was about to push the door open, she suddenly froze, before stepping back to hide from sight.

With her heart beating so fast, she felt that her head was nodding of its own accord. Unbelievable! Were her eyes deceiving her? No, they weren't. Standing at the reception desk were Cathy and her own Rohan and both were in deep conversation with each other.

Cathy wasn't dressed in her lawyer attire but in jeans and a red fine knit jumper. Her hair was loose and flowing around her shoulders. She looked even more beautiful in casual clothes; in fact, she looked absolutely stunning.

Rohan was also dressed in jeans and what looked like the same black cashmere sweater she had bought for him as a birthday gift.

They seemed like the perfect couple. No one looking at them now would have thought otherwise. It sickened her to see how well suited they appeared.

Georgie couldn't help it. Jealousy hit her like a punch in the face, and that earlier feeling of despair at the prison car park was now magnified enormously by what she saw going on in the building. Not only did she feel utterly out of her depth, but she now saw herself as unattractive and entirely out of his league. She knew her hair was a bit messy, and her clothes were just what she'd literally thrown on. She couldn't even recall putting lipstick on. But there the pair were, looking as if they were modelling a famous fashion brand for the front cover of this year's Christmas magazine.

Suddenly, Rohan placed his arm around Cathy's waist and steered her away from the reception desk. Slinging her designer bag over her shoulder, Cathy walked beside him with confidence as her blonde locks bounced off her shoulders. Both were still in deep conversation and laughing as they headed to the front entrance.

The scene made Georgie shake with rage. The green-eyed monster had raised its ugly head; it was an emotion that she wasn't used to, and she hadn't realised until this moment that she could feel such intense anger and pain. And betrayal!

Rohan was *her* man. He had pushed for their relationship. Why? Was he only looking for a woman who he perceived as hard to get? Did she even really know him at all? Stepping back into the shadows, she slipped down a side alley a few metres, with every muscle as taut as a rubber band ready to snap.

She was close enough to hear the front door of the chambers close and the schoolgirl-like laugh coming from Cathy, and it took every bit of effort not to confront them. But she didn't. Instead, she leaned against the cold brick wall and felt the sting of new tears as they pricked the back of her eyes.

Rohan had never mentioned to her that he was going to have a meeting with Cathy, so why was he? *Unless he was having an affair with her.* Her mind darted back to the courtroom and his over-eager smile at Cathy. Unable to rationalise anything right now, she wondered if he was gaslighting her? Everything seemed to be such a mess. Now, with her mind all over the place, she was overwhelmed by anger, frustration, and confusion. She wished she had never moved into their big house but instead had stayed in her little two-up two-down in St Mary Cray.

After hearing a car door closing, she emerged from the alleyway and looked across the road. *How had she not spotted Rohan's car?* But there again, she hadn't expected to see him here at the chambers. What was really puzzling, though, was that if he was having a business meeting with the barrister, why were they both dressed in jeans and off somewhere in his car? All she could conclude was that Rohan was secretly dating Cathy.

Forcing back the tears, she flared her nostrils and powered her way towards her car. That was it now. With Dixie-Lee in prison, Rohan clearly entertaining Cathy, and a wavering relationship with her business partner, Henry, Georgie sensed her life, as it was, was slipping between her fingers. Sliding onto her car seat, she slammed the door and tore away, ignoring the one-way sign, before spinning around and heading back along the street. She had to get home – his home – pack her bags, and get out.

However, she only managed to think that far because where could she go? She had no one. All she'd ever had was Dixie-Lee, and now she was in prison and reluctant to talk to her. Perhaps, she had pushed people too far to the point where they'd had enough of her. After all, Henry had implied that, when he said she needed help. It then crossed her mind that maybe she was in a far worse state than even she comprehended, and it was having more of an effect on the people around her than she had realised. Perhaps she did need therapy.

Yet today, she was being confronted with so many unanswered questions. And from the two people who meant more to her than anyone else. First, her daughter: why had she lied so openly to her about Bianca Malloye's whereabouts? Second, Rohan: What was he up to? And what did she even know about him?

For a start, she didn't know very much about his work. So, when Rohan told her he was off to meet a client, she was none the wiser and didn't know what he was doing. For all she knew, he could, as they say, have a girl in every port.

Twenty minutes into the drive home, the outside temperature had warmed up somewhat and now it was raining hard. She drove along the street with the wipers working furiously; in a sense, they replicated her mood of fury and desperation. This had not been a good day.

And unbeknown to her, it was about to get worse. Looking ahead, she saw the traffic was at a standstill. Now her headache had worsened to the point that her head throbbed and her mouth felt parched as if it was full of cotton wool.

Unable to get the images of Rohan and Cathy looking so comfortable together off her mind, Georgie banged the steering wheel in frustration. No longer could she hold back the tears and a deep sob paralysed her throat. Seconds later, with her face in her hands, she cried and cried.

A sudden beep from the car behind compelled Georgie to look up and see that the road ahead was clear. She slowly selected 'drive' and was about to move forward, but the impatient driver in the car behind swerved around her, barely missing her vehicle, before they all came to another stop.

The stupid sod. If she hadn't slammed on her brakes, he would have hit her car. She could see that the driver was a big bald man and he wasn't in a good mood. But he'd just had the audacity to stick his fingers up at her while yelling profanities.

Hearing him call her a 'stupid bitch' made Georgie immediately see red and her anger burned. She opened the car door and got out.

Seeing her getting out of her car, the baldheaded man followed suit.

Yelling and waving his hands only infuriated Georgie more. Marching forward, in one fluid motion, she kicked him between his legs and stepped back when he buckled in half.

Georgie thought that would be the end of the matter. However, the driver in the car behind hers got out, grabbed her, and pulled her back. And he wasn't gentle.

'You think you can hit a guy 'cos you're a woman and can fucking get away with it!' he shouted, almost deafening her. 'You fucking nasty bitch!'

Stunned that this man had her arms behind her back, Georgie writhed about until he let her go. In her frustration, she punched him hard and then kicked him, but he was young, around twenty-five, and made of solid muscle. So when he didn't go down, she attempted to throw another punch; however, this time, he took up a boxer's stance and launched two punches. One caught her just above the cheek and the other on the chin. She staggered back. But now, other drivers were leaving their cars to break up the fight. When someone shouted 'Police!', everyone rushed back to their cars and tore away.

Everyone, that was, except Georgie. She hadn't moved, still stunned. Her head hurt so badly that she saw stars and felt violently sick before she leaned out over the car and vomited. 'God, give me a break,' she said aloud, before wiping her mouth with the back of her hand, getting back into her car, and screeching away.

Her whole body was shivering despite putting the heating on full blast. Blinking furiously, she had to focus. She needed to get home, get a drink inside her, and take some painkillers, and, more importantly, get her head together to make sense of it all.

By the time she reached Bromley, the traffic had eased – as had her mind – and so she decided to pull into a petrol station and buy a bottle of water. Before she got out of the car, she pulled down the vanity mirror. She hardly recognised herself. Her right cheek was swollen, just like her daughter's, and the man who had wrestled with her must have caught her tooth because her lips were also swollen and bleeding. 'What a fucking mess, you are, Georgie,' she hissed.

The cashier stared at Georgie as she approached the counter.

'Is there something up, love?' said Georgie, lifting a bottle of water from the shelf and handing the cashier a five-pound note.

'Did you want anything else?' asked the young woman, ignoring Georgie's rudeness.

Georgie snatched her change, pulled the lid off the bottle, and drank the water as though she had been in a hot desert for a fortnight. After pausing for breath, she returned to her car, looked in the vanity mirror again, and thought that no wonder Rohan was with Cathy. What could she offer? She sure as hell wasn't the life and soul of the party. She wasn't young and dewy looking; in fact, her face appeared miserable, and her attitude probably stank.

She wasn't surprised to find the drive empty when she reached the house. Clearly, Rohan wasn't at home. Taking out her phone from her bag, she stared at the blank screen. Not even a text message. No lights were visible coming from the front of the house, and for the first time since she'd moved into what really was quite a palace, her new home seemed dark, gloomy, and uninviting.

That was until the door opened, and there, with a mug of something hot, stood Rodney.

'I saw you pull up, love. I have just made a pot of tea. How was Dixie-Lee?'

Georgie locked her car, and just for a moment, as she looked about her, the day's events flashed before her eyes. The prison visit seemed like a week ago. But so did seeing Rohan and Cathy together. And then there had been the challenging drive back from London. How she had made it home – and in one piece – she would never know.

As Georgie almost reached the front door, the sensor light came on, and Rodney shrieked, 'What in God's name has happened to you?'

Georgie ran her fingers lightly over her bruised cheek and chin.

'Jesus, let's get you inside and take a look at your face. What happened?'

Georgie couldn't be bothered to even talk. She was so washed out physically and mentally. But as she lifted her bruised cheek in a smile, she replied, 'Just a bit of road rage.'

'Did you call the police?'

'No, I hit out first. I deserved it.'

'And did you give her a good hiding?'

'No, Rod, it was a man. Anyway, I need a couple of tablets for my rotten headache and a lie-down.'

Rodney could see by the way she trudged through the front door and dropped her bag on the floor that she was shattered. He wanted to hug her, but he realised that she was too inside herself to be held. So he handed her a mug of tea and offered to draw her a bath.

'Rod, listen, I'm okay. Believe me, I've been through far worse. I just need an hour or so to shake off this headache and make sense of the day.'

Not wanting to push it, Rodney gave her a sympathetic smile and left her to it.

As she mounted the stairs, he called up, ‘I made a casserole, if you’re hungry. Rohan said he wouldn’t be back until late, so it’s in the slow cooker, if either of you fancy it.’

Heartbroken, Georgie felt a tear tickle her nose as she climbed the rest of the stairs to her room.

CHAPTER TWENTY-TWO

Georgie woke up again, dripping with sweat. Her heart was still pounding from yet another nightmare, but this time, it wasn't only her mother and the skeletal man in the dream but Rohan and Cathy who were kissing and laughing at her. If that wasn't bad enough, there was also confusion added to the mix. Sarah, the woman from the coffee shop, was trying to drag her away, but she was resisting. Sarah was younger and bigger in the dream, not the skinny woman she was now. She had her by her arm, and she was screaming at her, trying to get her away from the house, pleading and begging her to leave.

Georgie sat bolt upright and gasped for air. Was this woman there watching her the night of the fight almost twenty-two years ago. Had she been the one who had helped her escape? What if she had got it all wrong? What if she was now in a cycle of *consistently* getting things wrong?

Feeling that her life was imploding, she knew she had to change things and drastically so. Either she was going mad, or everyone else was, but, in reality, and considering the circumstances, it was probably she herself who was the one who needed therapy.

Gingerly, she turned to see if Rohan's side of the bed had been slept in because she had gone to bed early, having taken some tablets, and slept through until this morning. It did appear that he had slept in the bed because his pillow had the head dent in it. At least he'd had the decency to come home, but what time was that?

As soon as she put her feet on the floor, her head began to throb again. She was also feeling the effects from the fight yesterday. Not only was her cheek sore but so was her jaw where that man had thumped her on the chin. She shook her head in shame. She shouldn't have lashed out the way she had. Sticks and stones and all that meant nothing when she was in one of her tempers, which was another thing that needed to stop. She wasn't twenty or even thirty anymore. Fighting a needless battle could have cost her her life.

Slipping her feet into a pair of slippers while putting on her dressing gown, she turned to look in the full-length mirror. Instantly, she wanted to cry. How could she compete with the likes of Cathy McGowan? Her hair was a mangled mess, her face was hardened, her eyes were narrow and spiteful, and worse, she had let herself go. Unlike Cathy, there was no golden glow, no shiny bouncy hair, and when she peered closer, her skin seemed sallow.

Just as she was about to march moodily down the stairs, she heard voices; they were low, and she suspected for a reason – not for her ears – which infuriated her even more. Still, she swallowed her anger because she was now aware of how heated she could become at the flick of a switch. So, sitting at the top of the stairs, she listened.

'Hugh, do you think Dixie-Lee's version of the events at the chambers is credible?'

'I don't see why not. When they questioned her in the police station, there wasn't a hint of a lie. Her account was black and white and very sincere, and come on, Rohan, we all know Dixie-Lee. She has no reason to lie to us. We would support her and guide her, no matter what. But the police will be rubbing their hands together because with a confession it's a straightforward charge for them. They can close the case. I have to say, Raj has insisted they look elsewhere before throwing the book at her. They agreed. But this will end Raj's petition if she is adamant now that she killed this Clifford guy, and I know that whoever presides over that case will give Dixie-Lee the maximum sentence because, let's face it, Clifford was a judge's son.'

'So, just for confirmation, she told you last night that she wants to change her plea to guilty. Is that right?'

'Yes, it is. Look, I've tried to talk her out of it, and I told Dixie-Lee that whoever did kill him will be free to kill again, but she insisted she did it in self-defence, before she put the phone down on me.'

Georgie stayed where she was, knowing that the two men would be more open if they thought she couldn't hear.

'I went to the chambers yesterday,' said Rohan.

'And did you see or hear anything? That place must be like a beehive. Everyone buzzing over the news. It has so many consequences. How it will affect their business, for one.'

'No, I didn't see anything to make me curious, not really. Natalia seemed quiet. But although she didn't want to talk much, she was kind enough to show me the room where Clifford was murdered. She was shaken up because she was the one who found him dead, and she did say it was horrific, but, then again, she had never seen a dead body, not in the flesh, only in photos.'

'Poor girl. And the other barristers. Did they have anything to say about it?' Shields pressed.

'Well, that newish guy, the pretty-faced barrister, seemed out of sorts. He didn't have time to speak to me. In fact, he stormed past, not even acknowledging me. Looking bedraggled, is an understatement. I've never seen him unshaven. I hardly recognised him. He arrived midafternoon wearing a beanie, sunglasses, and a Crombie. I'm not sure how close he and Clifford were, but I reckon he was red-eyed behind those shades. Who wears shades in the middle of winter? I think it's shaken up the whole firm.'

Georgie was keen to hear what Hugh had to say about Cathy, so she slid down one tread of the stairs and held her breath.

'And Cathy, did you see her?'

'Yeah, now she was a *very* different kettle of fish. She seemed very chirpy, but you know her. She just gets on with her work. I asked her if they had found Tommy Malloye's file, but she said, ''Gosh'', in her posh voice. ''No, that's long gone. Whoever got their hands on that has probably realised that there is nothing there but a bunch of legal papers.'''

'How would she know that?' asked Shields.

'Well, I guess, like most of us, she assumed it just contained Tommy's last will and testament.'

'But it doesn't, though, does it? We know it contains more than that. For instance, the key code to the safe deposit box, so Tommy's father told Brodie.'

'Yeah, but she hasn't been privy to that information.'

'Do you think Steve knew what was in that file? Do you think he had anything to do with it? Because someone killed Tyler and, of course, the barrister. I believe that Tyler killed the barrister, but there was someone else there, and Tyler saw them, so whoever it was, they probably killed Tyler.'

'Steve may well know what was in that file. He was Tommy's brief. But Steve was in the police station at the time of Tyler's murder, so Steve can't be involved. And what would he gain?'

'Whoever killed them did it for the file. I'm sure of it. Bianca was in the police station, so that rules her out.'

'Hugh, wouldn't it be easier to go to the safe deposit box and check the cameras to see who, if anyone, had been there?'

Shields huffed. 'Rohan, do you know how many safe deposit boxes there are in London alone? And where would we even start? No, we need to find the file. It will have all the information, including an address and a code.'

'Oh, I thought Steve would have known all that. I thought he'd have a copy.'

‘No, it was filed the old-fashioned way. Tommy had told Steve to make sure it was hidden.’

‘That’s odd, isn’t it?’

‘Of course, it’s bloody odd. Anyway, Steve assumed that Tommy was paranoid, and he would do, with Tommy coming from a family of crooks. He grew up not trusting anyone, so Steve thought it was just his way of doing things. However, when Tommy was murdered and Bianca was the number-one suspect, as you can imagine, it was a worrying time. Steve knew he had to get the file because of the stakes involved. If that file went missing, then, by law, Bianca, who was still Tommy’s wife, if she isn’t found guilty of his murder, will cop the lot. Every asset he owns. The houses, the businesses, the lottery win, the diamonds, the whole damn lot – lock, stock, and barrel. He was without question worth a lot of money. Enough to kill for. So now, it’s down to who wanted that file *and* who was desperate to kill for it.’

There was silence for a moment, and Georgie wondered if they were whispering until she heard Hugh say, ‘You have something on your mind, Rohan. I can tell.’

‘Nothing to report right now, Hugh. I’m working on something, that’s all.’

‘Are you going to tell me?’

‘No, not yet.’

‘For fuck’s sake, you three brothers are all the bloody same. I wish you would be more open with me.’

‘Hugh, we are, when we have all the facts straight. Okay?’

‘You should have been detectives.’

‘Now, you know that pays feck all.’

‘This, though, Rohan, you won’t be paid for.’

‘Oh, we will, and it will be worth so much more than money. We’ll have our Dixie-Lee home.’

'Yeah, well, not if she bloody insists on pleading guilty. How is Georgie?'

'I'm worried about her, Hugh. She's not the same person.'

Georgie felt her eyes welling up, but she swallowed and then opened her mouth to breathe quietly.

'Rodney told me last night that she got into another fight with a bloke over road rage. Apparently, she admitted it was her fault. It's getting hard, Hugh. She nearly killed the woman who started work at the coffee shop. She doesn't even know her, but she claimed she dreamed about her, and the dream or nightmare was real. I think Georgie is heading for a breakdown. Maybe she needs to go somewhere.'

Hearing those words, Georgie's throat tightened, her fists curled into a ball, and once again, she could feel an intense anger. She was aware of it, so she bit her bottom lip and mentally counted to ten.

'She's been through more than most, Rohan. Maybe with Dixie-Lee getting arrested for murder was the final straw. Be gentle with her, is my advice. She's probably fragile under that tough exterior of hers. Don't you remember when we first met her? She was hard, like she was a whole army herself. And she took everything on the chin. There comes a point when it will have an effect, and I'm afraid if Georgie doesn't get help soon, she may go under, and what comes back will never be the same.'

'That's fecking scary, Hugh.'

'I know, but the truth often is. Get her some help. At least take her to the doctors or a therapist or the hospital. There's no stigma in that. I wouldn't be surprised if she suffers from PTSD from her time in the services.'

'I'll talk to her when she gets up, but you're probably right.'

'Good, listen, I must run. I'm having a legal visit with Dixie-Lee, and I have invited Cathy along. It's all a bit last-minute, but, hopefully, with both of us there, we can swing this around and stop with this nonsense of pleading guilty.'

'Yeah, okay, I've got to get going myself. I've got a lead to follow up.'

'Right, er . . . have you given the lead to Raj?'

'No. It's not that I don't trust Raj, because I do, but here's the thing. Raj will have to pass it on to whoever is on the case, and that, my friend, will probably be filed in the fecking bin.'

'You're probably right. Keep me posted.'

Georgie heard them say their goodbyes, and then there was silence. She walked down the stairs, still angry at Rohan for suggesting he get her help. But when he appeared in front of her, she wanted to cry. His face was filled with so much compassion, it made her lips quiver.

'Hey, darling, look at you.' He pulled her to him, placed his arms around her, and kissed her forehead. 'You're struggling, sweetheart. I can see that. You need a break.'

With her cheek against his chest, she broke down and sobbed. He held her all the while she cried. 'That's it, love, let it all out.'

She stopped and wiped her nose on the sleeve of her dressing gown before peering into Rohan's eyes. She had to see if he still looked at her in the same way.

'Are you okay, physically, I mean?'

She nodded. 'Yeah, my jaw is sore and so is my cheek and I have a cracker of a headache, but I'm fine . . . and mentally, I'm fine too.'

Rohan took a deep breath. 'I'm not so sure about that.' He pulled away and walked into the lounge. 'Come and sit down, love. We need to talk.'

Georgie felt her heart pounding in her chest as she sat down on the sofa. Was her relationship over, or would he have her certified and locked away in an asylum or on a prison-style hospital wing?

That would be one way to get rid of her, so he could have an affair with Cathy. She stared at him, awaiting the announcement.

'You've not been yourself. Everyone has noticed it, love, and that's not your fault. You have been the pack leader, the provider, the boss, and so on, and we all have a limit before we crack under pressure. The nightmares, the aggression, the fights, it's not who you are, sweetheart. It's what life has thrown at you. I think—'

'Oh, now suddenly you are the fucking voice of reason, the one who thinks they know what's best for me, eh!' Her sudden outburst through gritted teeth widened Rohan's eyes.

'See there, Georgie, right fecking there.'

She jumped up. 'Bollocks, fucking bollocks. I know your game, you bastard!'

Rohan didn't move. He remained in the armchair and shook his head. 'Georgie, please look at yourself. This isn't you.'

'Stop it, just stop it. I'm no fool, Rohan. I know what you are up to, and all you fucking had to say was you made a mistake with me – not go behind my fucking back and now send me to some mental hospital.' The veins in her neck popped up, and her cheeks were flushed as she screamed and foamed at the mouth. 'You bastard, you fucking bastard. My kid is in prison, there's nothing I can do about it, and now you start gaslighting me. I have been through far worse, and I'm not going nuts. I'm angry because you have *made* me angry. I am raging with Sarah because she was part of the gang who abused me as a kid, and so fuck off with your allegations that I'm going mad. I have every damn reason to be angry!'

Rohan flew out of his chair and grabbed her, pulling her close, tightening his arms around her. Even though she punched his chest and tried to break free, he wouldn't let her go. 'Stop, please, Georgie, stop.'

Eventually, she dropped to the floor, sobbing again, and Rohan got down with her. 'I'm *not* gaslighting you. I don't want you in a mental hospital or anything of the fecking sort. I was going to get you to a retreat – a spa – where they have therapists for PTSD. Someone you can talk to. Jesus, Georgie, why would I put you in a mental hospital and have you certified? You are my life. You and Dixie-Lee mean everything to me. I want the old Georgie back. I want to help you, not fecking lock you away. Whatever made you . . .' He paused. 'Were you listening to the conversation I was having with Hugh?'

She nodded, expecting him to be cross, but, instead, he smiled.

'No, darling, I was talking about a retreat, a big country house where you can relax, read, paint, or do whatever the feck you do to get better. I love you, my ball of fury, and I don't want to see you hurt, okay? Your pretty face is all battered. It breaks my heart, Georgie.'

'And Cathy?'

'Cathy?'

'Yes, fucking Cathy. What about *her*? I saw you two together yesterday.'

He sat back down in the armchair and a deep frown creased his forehead. 'Were you spying on me? Don't you trust me?'

'No, of course I wasn't spying on you. I went to the chambers to talk to Cathy and saw you with her. She wasn't even wearing a suit. You were both in jeans, and you were laughing.'

Rohan stared at her before he said, 'And?'

Georgie then realised she sounded absurd. 'Well, what were you doing there?'

'I went there to see Steve and to talk to Natalia and anyone else who would talk to me. You have to understand, Georgie, I work with these people. Me brothers and I, we all do. I can go there, and no one will question why I'm visiting the chambers. We bring a lot of work their way. Cathy was off to Hatton Garden, so I gave her a lift, that was all.'

'But you looked . . . er . . . Well, she seemed too comfortable in your presence, and she was . . .'

'Yes, she probably was comfortable in my presence. I've worked with Cathy for a few years. She's good at her job, and we only use the best barristers, but that doesn't mean anything is going on between us. I think in your state of mind, you were imagining the worst, and that's exactly what I'm talking about. Christ, Georgie, think back to a year ago. Do you honestly think you would be having these thoughts?'

She got up from the floor and sat heavily on the sofa, her mind now working overtime. She may have thought differently about things a while ago. Perhaps they were right. Perhaps she did need to see a therapist.

'Can I ask what it is that you are doing? I heard Hugh ask, and you wouldn't tell him, so will you tell me?'

Rohan rubbed his chin and sighed. 'You have to know that we aren't going to sit back and let Dixie-Lee take the rap for this. Something doesn't add up, and so we are looking at everyone who could possibly have a motive, and there are a few. I'm chasing one lead, but I can't tell you, Georgie, not because I don't want to, but there's no point in your mind flying off in all directions. It's my job to chase potential leads, and when we have something concrete, I'll tell you.'

'But I was a copper. Okay, it was in the military. But surely, I can help?'

'Too close to home, Georgie. You wouldn't be clear-headed enough.'

She was about to argue, but what he said was true. 'I just feel helpless, that's all.'

He nodded. 'I know you do, love. I understand. But get any thoughts of me and Cathy out of your head. She isn't my type, and I am not hers.'

Rohan rose from the armchair and kissed Georgie on the forehead again. 'Just trust me. Anyway, I must go. Why don't you try to relax today and let us – me and me brothers – try to work this all out. We usually get good results, yer know.'

Georgie nodded, in resignation. She already had other things on her mind.

CHAPTER TWENTY-THREE

Dixie-Lee lay on her bunk pretending to read a book, while Patsy lined up her chocolate snacks, noting how many she had in case another inmate decided to nick one. She poured coffee from the flasks and tapped Dixie-Lee on the arm. 'I know you're not reading that book, babe, 'cos you ain't even turned the friggin' page. How about a nice mug of coffee and a Penguin biscuit to dip? What d'ya say, hey?'

Swivelling her legs around, Dixie-Lee slowly slid down off her bunk and sat on Patsy's. 'Go on, then.'

Patsy handed her a plastic mug with milky coffee and a chocolate bar. 'How's the ribs?'

'Painful, but I'm okay. I feel bad for Minnie and Muscles, though. Do you think they'll let them out of the block?'

'Maybe, if o' course they haven't decorated the walls with shit in protest.'

Dixie-Lee looked at the melting chocolate as she dipped it into the coffee and shuddered. 'Er, would they do that?'

'Those two? A hundred per cent they would. They can be a right royal nightmare for the screws. I'm just thankful they were on your side.'

'Do you think Dulcie will ever be the same?'

'Nah, not likely. She and old scaghead Blondie will probably walk with a limp and speak with their tongues hanging out of their mouths while they serve out their days, I imagine. Maybe for ever. With no teeth and broken legs, they will think again before crossing you, love.'

Dixie-Lee looked down. 'Bianca will have other troops on her side soon enough. She can buy people.'

When Patsy sat down on the only decent chair in their cell, her butt cheeks hung over the sides. 'I heard a whisper that Bianca said something to you in that visiting room. Be honest. What did she say? You can tell me, love.'

'Nothing much.'

'She said something. I'm not *that* stupid. What did she threaten to do to you?'

Dixie-Lee bit into the biscuit and then shook her head.

Patsy decided there was no point in forcing the issue since Dixie-Lee was determined to clam up. 'Okay, love, but tell me this. Why did you cut your visit short? I can't imagine it was your mum's idea.'

'I needed to lie down, that was all. I didn't feel well.'

'Ah, well, if you don't want to confide in me, then I can't fucking help you. But know this, babe, your mother only lives for you. She worships the ground you walk on. Let me ask you this. When she was inside were you worried about her?'

'Of course I was! I do love my mum, ya know.'

'Imagine how she feels, then. You're her child. Her only fucking kid at that. And you're inside this shithole, which I've no need to remind you, she spent time in, in this *exact* cell. You cannot begin to know what's going through her mind and also how damned helpless she must feel right now. She would have been chomping at the bit to see you. She would have driven like a lunatic through the traffic. She would have been the first in the queue and praying that she would see a smile on your face and hear the words "I'm okay, Mum." Imagine her sitting there with her hands clasped together anxious to see you and then you appear with a bruised cheek and a black eye.'

Feeling totally wretched, Dixie-Lee couldn't look up.

'She would have wanted to hold you in her arms, wishing she could swap places with you. And knowing her, I can imagine she would want to know the ins and outs of a duck's arse regarding your shiner. But you cut that precious visit short, didn't ya? Whatever the reason, I hope you can justify breaking her heart 'cos believe me, kid, that's what you did.'

Hearing the sadness in Patsy's tone, Dixie-Lee tried to hold back the tears; her face turned white, and her bottom lip trembled. 'Look, Patsy,' she said, as a tear tumbled down her cheek, 'I'm a grown woman, and yet Mum wants to fight my battles.'

Patsy nodded. 'Naturally. I'd do the same for my kids.'

'But she can't fight this one. I have to, and I have to do it my way. I had to end the visit because she was getting angry with . . . Well, look at me.' She pointed to her face. 'And I couldn't be bothered to go into everything, so I told her I needed to go back to my room to lie down.'

'And what did she say when you called her last night?'

Dixie-Lee looked away and didn't answer.

'No, she didn't say anything because you didn't call her, did ya? And I bet her number is on your pin now.'

Dixie-Lee wiped away another tear. 'It's best if she forgets me.'

'Oh, shut the fuck up. You don't have the right to be so dramatic. You're not that kinda kid. So don't play me for a fool.' She pointed a finger in Dixie-Lee's face. 'And until her dying day, she won't forget you. I bet she is working her arse off trying to find a way to get you out, and if she can't find some legal loophole, she'll be using a bomb and half the fucking British Army to break down the walls and get you out.'

Suddenly, Dixie-Lee chuckled. 'I always called her G.I. Jane when she used to go over the top.'

A bell rang, and Patsy jumped up from her chair. 'Lunchtime.' She rubbed her hands together.

'You go, I'm not hungry.'

Patsy shook her head. 'Oh no, little 'un, you're coming with me. I can't leave you alone again.'

'It's fine. I know that nobody will hurt me now.'

Patsy stopped in her tracks and slowly turned around. 'There is only one reason you can be so sure of that.'

Dixie-Lee's eyes suddenly widened when she realised what she was admitting to.

'You've made a fucking deal, haven't you?'

Dixie-Lee sank back on the bunk, her eyes looking to the floor. 'No.'

'You fucking have, you muppet. Jesus Christ, what have you done?'

'You don't understand, Patsy. I had to. I had no choice.'

Patsy stared at Dixie-Lee 'What's the deal? Pleading guilty, are ya? Please tell me you didn't mean it?'

'Yes, but—'

'Yes, but? Yes, fucking *but*? What on earth has got into you? And there was me thinking you were a lot like your mother. Well, bugger me, you're nothing like her. What have you done, for Christ's sake?' Patsy screwed up her face and frowned. 'Who were you talking to on the phone yesterday when I came back from the shower? When you quickly ended the call. I mean, I know it wasn't your mum.'

Before Dixie-Lee could say another word, two officers arrived and pushed the door wide open. The larger of the two was Officer Judy Moran, who everyone called Moron because she was a bully and her arguments never made any sense. It was either her way or solitary confinement, with a whack from her baton. Officer Kate

Belcher, however, was softer in looks and nature. She would help the women in here rather than confront them.

'You have a legal visit, Deacon. Your lawyer is here to see you,' spat Moran, with a sneer.

'So it was your *lawyer* you were calling? Wait up,' said Patsy.

But Dixie-Lee had already quickly jumped off the bunk and sidestepped past her.

'Don't you *dare* change your plea. I swear to God, Dixie-Lee, you'll be for it if you fucking do!' she yelled, managing to grab Dixie-Lee's sweatshirt before the girl left the cell.

'Get your hands off her, Dewhurst, and shut up. This has nothing to do with you. If you want your lunch, you'd better get going!' growled Moran, as she stepped in front of Dixie-Lee, blocking Patsy.

'What about Dixie-Lee's lunch?'

'She will have a roll when she returns, and I'll have no more legal talk from you. It's not your place or your business,' Moran replied.

Ignoring the officer, Patsy glared at Dixie-Lee, who went bright crimson and quickly looked away.

But Patsy hadn't finished. She sidestepped Officer Moran, left the cell, and caught hold of Dixie-Lee's arm. 'You will break your mother's heart, ya know. And know this, kiddo, Bianca hasn't got enough clout to do whatever she said she would. Believe me on that one. If your lawyer doesn't talk you out of it, then change your lawyer! Don't sign anything!'

'Get back, Dewhurst, or you will find yourself in solitary confinement.'

'I don't give a shit. That kid has been bullied. Bianca has threatened to hurt her if she don't plead guilty.'

'For the last time, back off, Dewhurst,' said Moran, pushing her back into the cell.

‘You lot are disgusting an’ all. You love it, don’t ya, taking a lamb to the fucking slaughter.’

‘One more word, and you’re nicked.’

‘Arseholes.’

Patsy watched Dixie-Lee being escorted towards the visiting room, hoping she had said just enough to convince Dixie-Lee to stick with her original plea. She chewed her nails while thinking about what she could do to help. She had to devise a way to bring Bianca down because as it stood right now, Bianca did have clout. That was a given. She was top dog in here because she was getting a supply in from someone and whatever she’d threatened Dixie-Lee with, it had worked.

With her stomach rumbling, Patsy hurried to the canteen to ensure she wasn’t left with the dregs. As usual, the room was packed, the queue was long, and once again, Bianca’s plate was piled high with what appeared to be healthy food consisting of steamed vegetables and a decent-sized pork chop. She glanced down the line at the food station and saw the slop they called mashed potato and the burned pies. If she was angry with Dixie-Lee’s situation, she certainly was livid now.

She stared at Bianca who was seated in her usual place at the head of the table; she was pushing her food around her plate and wearing a solemn expression. Even though she had her followers all hanging around her like flies around shit, it was apparent from her worried expression that something was amiss. Then Patsy recognised a woman with her back to her talking to Bianca.

It was Keni Christchurch, someone she’d known for a long time. Keni had been moved from prison to prison and was evidently back here. She smiled to herself because Keni was a friend. They’d served time together and got to know each other well. Keni wasn’t a woman you messed with. She liked straight-up people, with no flannel, and definitely no bullshit.

Seeing Keni talking to Bianca made Patsy smile again because she immediately knew what her old pal was up to. If there was any contraband in the prison, Keni would be all over it; she'd want in on the business. And if Keni wasn't receiving a constant supply of drugs to deal in – not take because she thought she'd been clean for five years now – she would be latching on to the next best thing, and, no doubt, she would pursue the idea of being the second in command. She'd argue that if anyone could carry out the best deals, it was her. And with her reputation, few women were stupid enough to disagree.

Patsy had served long enough to know how it worked, and, in her friend's case, how Keni worked. Keni wouldn't bully or fight Bianca for the gear: she'd work with her and then take over. She was shrewd in that way.

Patsy was not just a friend of Keni's. They had shared a cell together, and Keni had trusted her enough to divulge her life story. She was known to be in cahoots with a few no-nonsense gangsters because she had been a big part of that lifestyle and was well known in the game. Inside for the double murder of two police officers, no less, she'd never said, as far as Patsy was aware, where she had buried the bodies. Patsy recalled seeing the case against Keni on a crime programme, where the producers had wanted to reenact the crime but there wasn't a crime scene to reenact because there were no bodies, so it was based on surmises. The police had interviewed her several times to find out where she had buried them, but she had always clammed up and protested her innocence.

Eyeing the other puppets Bianca had sucking up to her, Patsy concluded that none of them were of any real threat to herself. The most dangerous women in the prison were Minnie, Muscles, and now Keni. Although if you didn't know Keni, you wouldn't think that was the case. But even though she wasn't big like Minnie and

Muscles, she was strong and fiery, and she didn't give a shit about the consequences. And she had the scars on her face and body to prove that. They were her mementoes, she would say, from every one of her fights, even with the biggest and ugliest men and women. She would tear in like an Exocet missile, regardless of whether her opponents were wielding knives because her rage saw through weapons as if she was invincible. She was fast and fearless, and with no one on the outside to care about, Keni was very dangerous. If you weren't her friend, then you were her enemy. Fortunately for her, they were friends. *A sudden idea came to mind. It would be risky, but it was worth a try*, she thought.

Patsy stared, hoping to catch Keni's eye, and there it was, as if an invisible line of communication had sent psychic messages between them.

Keni clocked Patsy grinning. Instantly, she left Bianca in mid-sentence and walked over to Patsy. 'Hello, you're still here then, Patsy.'

Patsy smiled. 'Good to see you, Keni. How've ya been? I've missed your ugly mug.'

'Same ol', same ol'. So what's been happening since I've been away?'

'Fuck all, to tell ya the truth . . .' She paused and looked over Keni's shoulder. 'But we need a catch-up. Some information has come to light that I think you need to know.'

Keni leaned in. 'You've got my back, Patsy?'

'Always, Keni. You know me. I'm loyal. We've always been good, me and you, but listen,' said Patsy, as she peered over Keni's shoulder again and clocked Bianca, who was still looking more than a little worried, 'I don't like to interfere in people's business. I like to get on and do me bird without any aggravation. But me and you go way back, Keni, so just be a bit careful. Don't let ya guard down and let your personal dealings slip.'

‘What’s that supposed to mean?’ said Keni, as she shifted from one foot to the other.

Patsy stepped away from the line, and Keni followed. ‘I spoke to a mate of mine on the phone. Her hubby’s a copper. Like a high-ranking knob.’

‘Yeah, and?’

‘She reckons they put a plant in here to get you to talk, you know.’ She lowered her voice to a mere whisper. ‘About the dead bodies.’

‘And what made her tell you that, Patsy?’ said Keni, her eyes narrowed in suspicion.

Patsy had to think quickly and respond in the most matter-of-fact way she could. ‘She hates the wanker. He beats her, and ’cos he’s a copper, there’s fuck all she can do about it.’

Keni’s face turned a deathly white, and slowly, she turned and looked at Bianca. ‘Bianca Malloye has only recently arrived here, ain’t she?’

‘She was here years back and ran the place for a while. Her ol’ man had plenty of dosh and could get gear into the nick for her. Anyway, she’s inside for his murder. Supposedly.’

Patsy could sense that Keni’s cogs were whirring.

‘And Bianca is back in here with Michelin-starred food shoved under her nose, the screws wiping her fucking arse, and the scagheads stuck to her like Evo-Stik on a glue sniffer’s plastic bag.’

Keni glanced back at Bianca and turned to Patsy. ‘If she’s supposedly killed her ol’ man, the Malloyes would want her strung up. So how the fuck is she getting gear in here? More to the point, who’s supplying her?’

Patsy smiled and shrugged. ‘Your guess is as good as mine.’

Keni nodded. ‘So this plant can only be Bianca Malloye! Well, what a devious cunt!’

‘Keni, hold up. I’m not saying it *is* her—’

‘You don’t have to. It’s fucking obvious, and there she is, chatting shit to me, and wanting to do deals.’

‘What does she want from you, Keni?’

‘See, there’s another thing. She said she would give me an ounce! A fucking ounce of cocaine a week in exchange for keeping some kid shitting bricks and maintaining a guilty plea. You know what I mean. Little threats here and there.’

‘So for an ounce of Charlie a week, you have to bully a kid?’

Keni realised it sounded harsh. ‘Yeah, that’s about the size of it.’

‘Keni, she could have asked anyone to do that. She’s getting you on her side so that you get pally pally, and then she’ll try and get it out of you where the other bodies are buried. As you say, she’s a devious cunt. Play her at her own game. Take the cocaine and bleed the bitch dry and flip it back. Find out who’s bringing the gear in for her. Oh, and this kid. It wouldn’t happen to be Dixie-Lee Deacon, would it?’

‘Yeah, why?’

‘The police want her to plead guilty to murder, and Bianca is threatening her, so it just confirms the fact that Bianca is working for the police. I bet it won’t be long before she tells the filth everything she has on the Malloyes, and then, they’ll be behind bars, while she’s walking free and getting her lips, hair, and nails done.’

Keni’s jaw jutted forward. ‘I’ll kill her.’

‘No, listen to me, Keni, don’t let on you know. Carry on pretending you’re intimidating Dixie-Lee, and we’ll find out what she’s up to.’

Keni winked. ‘It’s good to see you again, Patsy.’ She grinned. ‘There’s only one person who knows the truth.’

Patsy tapped the side of her nose. 'And it will never leave my mouth.'

'I know because it didn't even when we fell out, so you are and always will be the one woman I can trust. Bianca will get what's fucking coming to her, the sly whore.'

'Keep your cool. Don't let on that me and you are mates.'

'No worries, Patsy,' Keni said, as she glanced across at Bianca. 'She's looking nervous 'cos we're talking.' She chuckled. 'I'll have her skinned alive when I get her to talk. Listen, I never thanked you for standing by me when the shit hit the fan. I owe you one.'

'You know me, I don't call in favours, but would you find out what the fuck she's up to with this kid Dixie-Lee? I get the feeling the bitch knows who killed this barrister. He's the son of a fucking judge, no less. Dixie-Lee is accused of murdering him, but she didn't. Look, it's a long story, but if Bianca tells you anything, let me know.'

With a slight raise of Keni's eyebrow and a little half grin, Patsy knew she had the woman on her side.

'Good as done, Patsy. Now I'm gonna start poking you in the chest like I'm threatening you, all right? Just so that Miss Rubber Lips over there thinks we're enemies.'

'Go on, then, but not too hard.'

Unexpectedly, Keni pushed Patsy very hard. Now nose to nose with her, she tilted her head from side to side as if she was screwing Patsy's face to the wall. 'I'll cut ya throat, you cunt!' she yelled, before lowering her voice and whispering, 'That should do it, mate.'

The sudden action made Patsy nervous at first, but she soon realised it was all an act and wondered if Keni had taken up drama classes during her time in another prison. She watched as Keni stormed towards Bianca, and then she clocked Bianca staring at her. She'd been observing the whole thing. Little did she know that one way or another, Keni would extract information out of her, even if she had to pull it out of her arsehole. She only hoped that Keni would never discover that she had just fed her a string of lies about Bianca being a plant.

CHAPTER TWENTY-FOUR

With an arrogant air of confidence, Cathy took her seat opposite Dixie-Lee. Her high cheekbones shimmered from pink blusher and her lips were coated with subtle gloss; not a single hair strand escaped her bun. To an onlooker, Cathy could easily be ready for a photoshoot.

'Sorry, I didn't bring any refreshments.' She gave Dixie-Lee a sharp, quick smile. 'It's all been rather a mad rush. Hugh Shields informed me you are changing your plea, so I came as soon as possible. This needs to be acted upon rather urgently, to establish mitigating circumstances.'

Dixie-Lee stared at Cathy, wondering why she was even here. She hadn't asked to see her, and as far as she knew, she was expecting Hugh to be coming to the meeting in an hour's time. 'Where is Hugh?'

Cathy removed some paperwork from her briefcase, which was beside her chair, and arranged the documents in order before she fished inside the jacket pocket of her designer suit for a pen. 'Actually, he doesn't need to be here. I can't hang around for your solicitor, Dixie-Lee. I'm a very busy woman. Anyway it's all fairly straightforward.' She smiled again and kept her smile fixed on her client.

'Is it?'

Dixie-Lee's flat tone compelled Cathy to put her gold pen down and look up. 'Listen carefully.' Her smile evaporated, and her words became firm. 'By changing your plea to guilty, I will have to work very hard to secure a manslaughter charge utilising the act of self-defence, and as you know from your training so far, you will probably be released having served what will probably amount to a year. So, I think considering the circumstances, your option to plead guilty to self-defence manslaughter is a reasonable one. There is no question that Clifford attacked you. From the photographic evidence, you clearly were hurt. You had the bruises to prove it. And what I can elaborate on in your favour is the fact that you bit him.'

A gentle frown flickered across Dixie-Lee's forehead.

Cathy huffed impatiently. 'Biting a victim doesn't go with the remit of murder. A jury would conclude that having bit him, you were certainly in an altercation and most likely defending yourself. There is also another mitigating factor, namely, the considerable size difference between you and Clifford. In this case, you could argue that you were using reasonable force to stop him from raping you.'

Cathy paused to draw breath. 'So before I go on, are you happy for me to type up a statement and return tomorrow for a signature and we can have this put to the CPS and be in court by the end of next week for a mention hearing? You understand the legal terminology, so I don't need to waste time explaining it all to you.'

Dixie-Lee nodded, although Cathy was talking so fast, her brain was struggling to process it all. 'And are you sure I will only serve a year?'

Placing her elbows on the table, Cathy steepled her hands. 'I thought you understood the law. I can't promise you that. As you will understand, it's all down to the judge at the end of the day.'

Dixie-Lee chewed her bottom lip but maintained eye contact with Cathy. 'And how do you suppose a judge, any judge, would view me, having killed the son of a judge? Do you not think they will give me the maximum sentence for self-defence manslaughter and sway the jury on the grounds of unreasonable force?'

‘A judge can only preside over the facts. He is not partial, as you should know by now. A judge certainly must be impartial, no matter what case is presented to him.’ She ended with a Hollywood smile.

‘You don’t like me very much, do you? May I ask why?’ asked Dixie-Lee, in a monotone.

With a frown, Cathy leaned back on her chair. ‘I have absolutely no idea why you would think such a thing. But I am not paid to like my clients. I am paid to represent them. Does it matter to you if I like you or not?’

‘I guess it does. I think if you liked me, I would feel confident that you would fight hard for me.’

Cathy tutted loudly. ‘You are delusional, Dixie-Lee. I was told you had a lot of common sense and would make an excellent astute barrister or solicitor, whatever your preference. I, on the other hand, beg to differ. As a legal representative, you need to be able to represent your client, not psychologically support them.’

Cathy’s sharp tone got Dixie-Lee’s back up. ‘But before a client takes the stand, don’t you guide them, encourage, and support them, then?’

Cathy smiled. ‘I see you have changed, Miss Deacon. You seem a far cry from the shy young lady who came to work in my chambers. You really are rather bold. If I were you, I would lose the boldness when you take the stand. Nonetheless, I am sure you have a lot to think about. I’ll get off and write up your statement. All being well, I will be back tomorrow.’

Dixie-Lee nodded but didn’t stand the minute Cathy rose from her chair.

‘Oh, and one other thing, Dixie-Lee. I rarely defend young women, especially in this scenario, and I am doing this as a favour to your uncles, so I will ask one thing in return.’

Dixie-Lee looked up and nodded for Cathy to continue.

‘Do not discuss this change of plea with anyone. I am sure there are people who think they know best and will talk you into changing your mind. But I won’t appreciate coming back and forth to this prison changing statements because the case will absolutely fall apart before it even gets to court. So stay positive and allow me to do my job.’

‘I have not said I want to change my plea back to not guilty.’

‘Good, I will work on your statement to include the mitigating circumstances.’ She smiled. ‘I’m on your side, Dixie-Lee. Allow me to do what I do best.’

‘And what would you say that is?’ asked Dixie-Lee, with a flat, bitter expression on her face.

Cathy stared for a moment, not understanding the question at first. ‘Well, my work, of course.’ The question had not only thrown her initially but now it was ruffling her feathers. She was well aware she was highly regarded in her field. So was this young woman, who’d only recently joined the chambers on an apprenticeship, questioning her ability to act in her best interests? It was hard to work out. No one had ever dared probe her, not anyone from a professional standpoint.

‘What part of your role do you do best?’

Cathy slid her papers into her briefcase and then shot Dixie-Lee a look that said ‘don’t push it’. But her thin-lipped smile and unsure chuckle were an apparent show of uncertainty. She looked up at the camera in the room and then back at Dixie-Lee. ‘What are you getting at?’

Dixie-Lee grinned. ‘Oh, I was merely asking what part of your job you do best. Is it your advocacy in court, playing detective, putting the case together, setting the scene, building a picture, or convincing a jury or anyone else, for that matter?’

Snatching her pen and sliding it into her pocket, Cathy’s face reddened to the point that she glowed more than the shimmering blusher itself. 'All of it, Miss Deacon. I am bloody good at *all* of it, and that's why your family needs me to get you out of this place.'

With a smile and a nod, Dixie-Lee remained seated while Cathy left the room. She could hear the mumblings outside the door between Cathy and the screws and then the confident clip-clop of Cathy's high heels – Louboutins, of course.

***

Shields was absolutely fuming. He glared at the balding officer whose fat rolled over his tight shirt collar and who was in need of a good wash. 'I am supposed to be present. This is a legal visit with both a barrister and myself, so why are you not escorting me to my client?'

'There is no need to get irate, sir. But as far as I have been told, Deacon has had her legal visit and apparently it was with her barrister, who left' – the officer looked at his watch – 'about fifteen minutes ago. So you will have to book another visit and go through the proper channels.'

Shields rolled his eyes. 'I should imagine you wrote on your CV: *I would be a good asset to the prison service because at the very least I'm an awkward cunt.*'

The officer, who had been sitting in a swivel desk chair stuffing doughnuts into his vast stomach for most of the morning, attempted to jump up to remind the solicitor that he could be banned for using that kind of abuse at a prison officer. But when the arms of the chair gripped his hips and stuck to him like glue, it made the whole scenario look like a comedy sketch.

Shields glanced down and was about to laugh, but instead, he continued. 'And I bet added to that CV was *I am as fit as fuck.*'

As Shields stormed out of the waiting room into the cold air, he felt an overwhelming dread for Dixie-Lee. He pulled out his phone and dialled Cathy's number, but the call was instantly diverted to voicemail. Ending the call, he growled under his breath, 'What are you up to, lady?'

Reaching his vehicle, his phone rang. Assuming it would be Cathy, he answered the phone, only to hear another familiar voice. 'Hugh, I've got some news.'

'Raj, mate, hopefully it's good news because we have an innocent kid inside right now.'

'Look, it's *not* good news. As you know, I was pushing for the team to look at Tyler as Clifford's killer, considering there was so much blood on him. But the bad news is that his clothes were too drenched in his own blood.'

Assuming that Raj wouldn't have called to tell him just this, he replied, with his heart in his mouth, 'Go on.'

'If they had found just one speck of Clifford's blood on Tyler, then we could have argued that Tyler killed Clifford, which meant that Dixie-Lee hadn't. However, Sparks believes Tyler didn't kill Clifford, so they believe that whoever killed Clifford also killed Tyler.'

The shocking news compelled Shields to steady himself against his car. 'I see,' he said, exhaling at the same time.

'You obviously know what that means, mate?'

'Er . . . of course I do. So when will Dixie-Lee be charged?'

'They are on their way to the prison right now, Hugh, and that's why I'm calling you. They are gonna bring her in.'

'I'm on my way, Raj. Thank you, mate. I know you tried your best.'

'Are you coming alone, or will you bring Cathy McGowan with you?'

'No, I will come alone. Raj, they didn't find Tyler's blood on Dixie-Lee's clothes, did they, or are they hiding that fact?'

'No, Hugh, but here's the thing. They found Clifford's blood all over her top and her brooch was in his hand. Worse for Dixie-

Lee is that his bite marks match hers, so considering he was knifed and so was Tyler Malloye, *and* his body was found not too far away from the chambers where Clifford was murdered, they have to charge her.'

'But if she had none of Tyler's blood on her clothes . . . Look, I don't understand.'

'They are saying that after Dixie-Lee killed Clifford, and her clothes were covered in his blood, she then put on a coat before she killed Tyler. Apparently, the coat was what they call oversized, so they are suggesting that it may have been Clifford's coat that she wore.'

'What? That's baffling. In fact, it sounds ludicrous. Because, apparently, she wore a short mac over her suit when she went to work. It's such a pity, Raj, that there is no CCTV at the chambers. But there's also no CCTV for this particular street either.'

'Hugh, meet me at the coffee shop. I'll let you know what they know, but listen, they are keeping much of this under wraps. You know I risk getting sacked, not that I'm very bothered. As you know, I'm looking to change my job anyway.'

'I'll be there in an hour, Raj.'

***

On the way to the coffee shop minutes away from Bromley Police Station, Shields flashed and beeped at other cars. He gave the drivers the middle finger ten times and even yelled at the traffic lights for turning red. His eyes flicked towards his phone numerous times. Should he call Cathy? But after a few moments, he decided not to because when he had tried to call her, she hadn't answered. That was an irritation in itself but even more so was that she hadn't waited for him to attend the prison legal visit. He had arranged it for two o'clock, not one o'clock. Why hadn't he received the memo? Now his anger was fuelled by frustration and his inability to make decisions. And he knew it was because he was so close to his client – his pupil – and he felt that her liberty was resting on his own shoulders. He had to do everything in his power to get her out. And time was not on his side.

As he pulled into a permit holder's parking space, he didn't care if he got a ticket; in fact, he didn't care about much, other than finding a way to get Dixie-Lee out of prison. *It was starting to look like a crusade*, he thought. Sitting in the car, he took a few deep breaths before swallowing down the bitter acid that was now burning his chest. As it rose again and burned the back of his throat, he leaned across, popped open the glove compartment, and reached for his indigestion medicine. Usually, he would swig a mouthful, but today, he nearly drank the whole bottle.

The coffee shop was quiet, so after ordering two coffees, he had the pick of the tables. He chose one furthest away from the door, a spot he and Raj preferred.

As the waitress placed the coffee mugs on the table, Raj appeared through the doorway. He was rubbing his hands together before he removed his plaid flannel scarf and unbuttoned his thick grey jacket. 'Fucking taters out there,' he said, as he looked at the piping-hot coffee. 'Cheers, mate.'

He slid along the bench seating and looked at Shields before he shook his head. 'It's a mess, Hugh, a right fucking mess.'

'I know and the Deacon brothers are running around like blue-arsed flies trying to get to the truth.'

'Look, I won't beat about the bush, and you know how this works, Hugh. But Detective Inspector Sparks had his team question employees of the workplaces surrounding the chambers. You know how it is. Many of them go for a drink after work. They use the local wine bars.'

Shields nodded. 'Please tell me they've got a witness?'

Raj handcombed his long fringe away from his face. 'Yes, but not a good one for our purposes, I'm afraid.'

Overexaggerating his tilted head with a look of confusion, Shields asked, 'Why not?'

'This witness said that he had been out drinking with his mate, who also confirmed this. They were heading towards Charing Cross railway station, past the chambers, when they saw a woman crouched down in an alleyway between two buildings. They assumed she was a prostitute, and so . . . Well, you can bet what they offered her.'

'But why did they assume this?'

'These two snobby little Chelsea boy shits thought she was a prostitute because her clothes were messy and ripped – mainly her skirt and blouse.'

'Well, her clothes *were* ripped, and the police have those, so I don't understand.'

Raj looked around him and gestured for Shields to lower his voice. 'These two lads had drunk too much. Anyway, they decided to walk back to their offices because one of them had left his phone behind, and acting like a spoiled brat, he insisted they return. By the time they returned to their offices, they had sobered up. The less drunk of the two, a chap called Geoffrey, realised that they may have made a terrible mistake because they had, in fact, assaulted the girl – well, as it turns out, Dixie-Lee.'

Shields's whole face tightened in anger. 'Bastards!'

'See, the streets of London aren't always a dangerous place because of the down-and-outs. It's pompous pricks like these two who think that Daddy will bail them out. Being so privileged, they believe they can get away with murder, or, in this case, assaulting a young woman. Giles Pritchard, the son of Richard Pritchard, the chief executive of a small banking firm, was reluctant to say too much. But, evidently, his sidekick and university chum, Geoffrey Luton, clearly has a conscience. He said the more he thought about it, the more he realised their actions had been based initially on how the girl they saw in the street was dressed. But, he conceded, she was not typical of a hooker. He had noticed her ripped blouse and skirt and observed that she had already been assaulted, but at the time, his mate, *the bully*, was on a mission. Geoffrey reckons he tried to stop Giles and was successful in part; however, he didn't stop him from pissing all over her. And we know someone did because the presence of urine on her clothes showed up on the lab report.'

Shields blew air through his tight lips as if to calm his nerves.

'I know, Hugh. I wanted to rip their heads off when I found out about this.' He paused and downed his coffee. 'So, as Geoffrey was saying, when he returned to their offices, it took a while to find Giles's phone. He made a strong coffee and practically forced Giles to drink it before they got themselves into any other trouble. And it was then that he suddenly realised something. He had seen the girl the day before when he had been walking to work. He recalled passing her as she entered the chambers and thinking how attractive she was. Anyway, he reckons that particular night, after they left their offices for the second time, they walked past the chambers. Now, bear in mind it was very late. But, anyway, they saw a woman coming from the side alley. She looked like the same woman they saw earlier, and she was wearing a long coat.'

'And that's it, is it? They see a woman coming out of an alleyway close to the chambers wearing a long coat, and so we must assume that the person they saw was Dixie-Lee?'

'That's where we're at, yeah.'

Shields sighed in frustration. 'We know that Dixie-Lee left her mac and hat on the front desk. She was in such a bloody rush to leave after the attack on her by Clifford, that she didn't stop to pick them up.'

'The police won't make much of that, Hugh. They're looking for a woman fitting Dixie-Lee's description who was wearing a long coat. The witness described the coat as oversized – a fashion term. Nevertheless, the idea that it was too big suggests that it may not have been her coat. The possibility is that Dixie-Lee left the chambers wearing what may have been Clifford's overcoat. But since they don't have the coat, we won't know.'

'None of it looks right, but the police are desperate for a nicking. It seems to me, Raj, that they will do anything to fit what the witness saw in the alleyway to suit their own interpretation of what happened on that night.'

Raj showed the palms of his hands. 'That's where my colleagues are going with it, Hugh. They want to clean up a double murder.'

Shields leaned back, his face losing all its colour. 'Jesus Christ, this is insane.'

'And, Hugh, because this is now a double murder, you can imagine what they are doing now. Dixie-Lee was in the press for months, and the public loved her. They followed her story while she was in a coma and during the court case, and they read all the details about how she killed Ashby in self-defence. She was in some ways a national hero.'

'This just gets worse.'

'Hugh, they want a media circus.'

Massaging his temples, Shields looked up. 'So the one thing this tells me is this: the potential killer is a woman.'

'Yes, Hugh, and like you, I don't believe it is Dixie-Lee.' He looked about him again and lowered his voice. 'I've had Petra looking at local CCTV footage for this other woman in the surrounding area at that time of night. You can see Dixie-Lee, though, heading to the taxi rank, and she isn't dressed in a long coat. But there's *no sign* of any other woman in a long coat. And Petra has done her very best. She has watched hours of footage.'

'So should Petra be looking for someone in a vehicle, then?'

‘Yes, we’re thinking along the same lines. Whoever was wearing the long coat must have been driving or being driven. And Dixie-Lee didn’t drive to work. Petra is now trawling through all the cars in that area at that time. She’s checking number plates and any visible images of the drivers, from the CCTV footage. It will take a lot of work, but rest assured, we are on it.’

Raj sipped the last of his coffee and then continued. ‘One more thing. Our surmising won’t stop Sparks from charging her this evening with Tyler Malloye’s murder, and of course, they will let Michael Malloye know, and that may have consequences for the Deacons.’

‘Thank you, Raj, for giving me the heads-up on all of this. You’re a good mate.’

Raj chuckled. ‘I’m after a job. When the Deacons have an opening, let me know.’

‘I will. Anyway, I guess we’d better get over to the station, ready for when they bring in Dixie-Lee.’

CHAPTER TWENTY-FIVE

When Hugh Shields telephoned Brodie to give him an update about Dixie-Lee's change of plea, Brodie almost fell into the armchair. Hugh suggested it might be best for the brothers to lie low in case the Malloye family came for theirs, but Brodie replied, 'Absolutely not.'

Mac stared out of the window of their mother's house across the vast green landscape. 'This situation feels like a set-up.'

'That it does, Mac, that it fecking does. But what can we do now? We've questioned all the brothers and—'

'Not all the family, though,' Mac quickly interrupted.

'Mac, if you're talking about Gilead, he can't very well speak, can he?'

'No, not that wanker. The *stepbrother*.'

Brodie slowly turned to face Mac. 'What?'

'Michael's son, the one he had out of wedlock.'

Brodie placed his hands on his hips and tilted his head to the side. 'Sorry, Mac, who the feck are you talking about?'

Mac looked at his brother, wide-eyed. 'Please, Brodie, tell me you knew about him. Didn't Michael mention him?'

Brodie threw his hands in the air. 'If I fecking knew about him, Mac, he would be on the list to question.'

'Look, Brodie, don't get angry, but I honestly thought you knew. *I* knew. When I was chatting with Nessa, Michael's wife, while you were fighting with the brothers, she mentioned him.'

'What the feck did she say?'

'She is still very bitter. But she did say they have nothing to do with the lad. He lives in England, apparently, and he has feck all to do with the Malloye family. Michael couldn't have him in their life for fear of losing Nessa and his other sons.'

'So didn't you think this lad could have something to do with it?'

Mac shook his head. 'No, I didn't. He was never a part of their family. Nessa gave Michael hell over it, and there were questions about whether this baby was even his.'

Brodie paced the floor for a few moments while Mac watched.

'What do you know about this bloke?'

Mac's cheeks flushed slightly, and Brodie sighed. 'You daft bastard, why didn't you ask her?'

Mac glared. 'I wasn't there to find out about this lad, was I? I was fecking there to keep her company while you spoke with Michael and his feral rats.'

Brodie hung his head and rubbed his bristly chin. 'Come on, we need to see Michael and Nessa and ask them a few questions.'

***

Michael's house wasn't the big mansion he used to own. After the Colombian deal went terribly wrong, he was forced to sell up and move his wife into a modest house. How that had worked out, he couldn't imagine. But he did know that if the same thing had happened to him and he and his brothers had had to start all over again, his mother wouldn't have been best pleased.

Brodie had never met Nessa before but he had heard about her, and he suspected she was more than a little bitter over Michael's unfaithfulness. He decided there and then that tact and subtleness would be the order of the day when he arrived at the Malloye residence. He needed everyone to be on the same side. After all, weren't they all working for the common good?

While Brodie knocked at the door, Mac stepped back, knowing this could go badly. If the police had told Michael that they were now charging Dixie-Lee for the double murder of Clifford Jenson-

Baine *and* Tyler Malloye, Michael and his family would probably look to take out their revenge on their family, starting with himself and Brodie.

When Michael opened the door, Brodie was the first to notice how Michael's face was so drawn and white. Brown rings circled his eyes, and he clearly hadn't shaved. If Brodie had walked past him in the street, he would have obviously assumed he was homeless.

'So, Brodie, what are yer doing here, eh? Are yer going to try to convince me that yer niece is innocent?'

'Yes, Michael, that I am.'

Michael looked behind Brodie at Mac knowing that if he tried to take both brothers down, he would need a gun or a bulldozer to do it. He sighed. He had nothing to lose by listening to their side of the story.

Flicking his head, he invited them in. Instantly, Mac was salivating. The house smelled sweet, just like a bread factory. Showing them into the living room, Michael offered each of the brothers a strong drink.

Mac was about to say 'No, thank you' because he didn't drink. He was on a healthy diet. But Brodie jumped in. 'Go on, Michael, we'll join you in whatever you're having.'

Michael pointed to the sofa. 'Take a seat.'

As soon as he left the room, Brodie went over to the armchair that faced the door. He kept his hand inside his jacket pocket and gripped a gun.

'Mac, sit on the sofa.'

Mac didn't ask why, knowing Brodie would be prepared for an ambush. And he guessed inside Brodie's jacket there was a gun. He sat on the sofa and in the silence he could hear his stomach rumbling.

Within minutes, Michael returned with a tray holding three glasses and a bottle of brandy. His eyes were totally focused on the tray to ensure he didn't knock anything over.

Immediately, Brodie relaxed in the armchair, releasing his hand on the gun. He guessed that Michael had no intentions of taking retribution on himself and Mac. Poor old Michael. He looked so frail, and his hunched shoulders suggested he was carrying the weight of the world on them.

'I've just had the police on the phone,' said Michael, as he poured a generous helping of brandy into each glass. 'I'll be honest wid yer, I'm not convinced by what they told me. Yer see, I've never trusted the fecking Garda or the fecking Metropolitan Police. Something doesn't smell right to me.' He pointed to Brodie. 'And I believe, Brodie, that you're doing your best to help find the truth, and for that, I can only be grateful.' He took a long swig of his drink. 'The sad fact is, my lads are a little wild. They're always on the wrong side of the law and most of them don't have a fecking brain between them. My Tommy was the only one with brains. Not that they counted for much. And my Tyler, as much as he thought he was hard, he wasn't really. He was all mouth, for sure, but he wasn't a fighter, and like Tommy, he never listened to me. I didn't give Tyler the okay for him to go to the chambers to hunt for Tommy's last will and testament. He was only supposed to find out who was representing Bianca.' He sighed loudly. 'I just wish Tommy had been more sensible and handed a copy of that will to me. I'd have kept it in our own safe. Then, again, Tommy trusted no one. I suppose he trusted Steven Elison, though.'

'Michael, I need to bring up something that, as a family, you've probably dismissed and divorced yourself from. It's about your other—'

Nessa, who appeared in the doorway, stopped Brodie in mid-sentence. She was a small woman with rosy cheeks and she had a distinctive grey streak running down the centre of her hair like a skunk. Her milky-blue eyes were narrow, and her thin lips tightened to a harsh-looking smile.

'Your son, Michael, that's who they've come to talk about.'

Michael didn't look up and took another swig of his brandy while staring at nothing.

'That's right, lads, isn't it?' she said.

Mac nodded. 'I'm sorry, Mrs Malloye, but, yes, we have. We only want to get to the truth behind your son's and grandson's murders and get our niece out of prison.'

Nessa glared at her husband, who by now had finished his drink. Suddenly, snatching the glass from his hand, she hissed, 'And that'll not fecking help anyone.'

Michael didn't argue back, which surprised Brodie. He merely placed his hands over his face.

Nessa sat on the arm of Michael's chair and placed a hand on his shoulder. 'It's been hard, lads, very hard. And I don't think for one minute that your niece killed that man – that barrister – or our Tyler. From what Michael told me, she sounds like a lovely young woman with her whole life ahead of her and a career as a barrister. And now I think about it, a young woman brought up like that wouldn't have the wherewithal to be murdering two men, now, would she? I, for one, wouldn't want the girl to be in prison for something she didn't do. And if she is inside, who the feck is running around with my grandson's blood on their hands?'

'Thank you, Mrs Malloye,' said Brodie, with a compassionate smile.

'Call me Nessa, please. I know my Michael. We had a pledge many moons ago, in fact, when the baby was born, that we would never mention it. I believed at the time the baby could have been anyone's. But Michael knew who the whore was and he sent her away. He gave her money and a fair bit, mind you, and that was that.'

Michael gently tapped Nessa's hand. 'It hurt my Nessa. I mean, *I* hurt my Nessa. It was a stupid one-night stand, that was all it ever was. I couldn't risk losing my whole family over a mistake, and a mistake it certainly was. So, I handed over a lump sum for the lass, Anne-Marie, to leave Kilkenny and start a new life away from us. And, in fairness, she did.'

Brodie watched Nessa slide her hands into her apron pocket and pull out a screwed-up tissue. It seemed she had more to say, the way she fiddled with it.

'Did your estranged son ever come to search you out?'

Michael shook his head. 'No, he wouldn't have known our last name. It was part of the deal I had with Anne-Marie: the cash for complete silence.'

But when Brodie looked at Nessa, her face told another story. So he tried a tack that he'd used many times before in dealing with people.

'Ahh, well, if he never came looking for you, then that's an avenue we've no need to look down. He definitely wouldn't have any connection with you, then. Am I right?'

'I'll put the kettle on. I've made some cake. Would you like a slice?' asked Nessa, jumping up from where she was sitting.

Mac couldn't resist. 'Oh yes, please, and could you make it a large slice? I've been on this diet for so long that I'll soon be sprouting long ears and a bunny's tail.'

Mac knew that asking a woman, who took pride in her cooking, for a large piece was a compliment. Irish mothers loved to feed their sons.

She gave him a beaming smile and hurried away to the kitchen.

Brodie, however, was annoyed. He had seen that Nessa had something to say and he'd hoped she would rise to the bait of his question. But Mac had unnecessarily encouraged a distraction to prevent whatever it was from spilling out.

'I'm sorry, Michael, for all this, but you have to know I am doing my best to help us both.'

With his face sagging and his eyes dull, Michael nodded. 'This grieving process will outlive me, so probably the only thing keeping me going is the quest for the truth and to see that whore Bianca sentenced to life behind bars. That is one evil witch. I knew she was putting herself out with someone when I went to England to visit her and Tommy. Nessa and I stayed for a week at Tommy's place but we hardly ever saw the woman. She was always out getting her hair done or going to yogi classes or whatever they are.'

'Yoga,' said Mac.

Michael smiled at the correction. 'Yoga or yogi, she was good at one thing. And that was keeping her fecking dirty whore legs in the air. I mean, who goes to the fecking gym with their hair all done pretty and enough make-up to re-grout me whole bathroom.'

'She may be one of those women who likes to keep herself looking good all the time. There's a lot like that now, yer know,' said Mac, with one eye on the door, eagerly awaiting his piece of cake.

'I know there is, but yer know, she always hid her phone and would sneak into another room if she got a text. My Nessa hated her. It was a woman thing. She said that Bianca thought she was too good for our Tommy. Bianca called him daft and thick one too many times, for my liking.'

When Nessa came back into the room with a tray laden with tea and cakes, she had overheard a good part of the conversation. 'That's right, and by the fecking way, whore is too much of a compliment for a woman like her. I said to her: "My lad might not have a degree or even a GCSE, but he puts designer clothes on your back and he paid for your boob job." And do you know what she said back to me? She had the brass neck to tell me they were for *his* benefit. Even he said he liked her as she was when he met her. I tell you, Brodie, that woman was only with my son for the money, nothing else. She didn't even sleep in his bed with him in the end. So I don't blame him for . . .' She handed Mac a considerable slice of cake. 'Well, for getting comfort elsewhere. Because the man was being rejected at every turn by his wife.'

Brodie ditched the brandy and reached for the cup of tea. 'Didn't Tommy find out who Bianca was having an affair with, if you're sure she was?'

'No, but he did file for divorce. And . . .' She stopped and swallowed hard. 'Before he was fecking murdered. Oh, and I know she did it. Of course, she would have. She would stand to inherit the lot if he died before the final divorce papers. Unless, of course, that paperwork – the file – had something in there that would say otherwise.'

'Like what?' asked Mac, with a mouth full of Victoria sponge cake.

Brodie glared at his brother. 'Manners, Mac.'

'Sorry, Nessa, but this is so delicious.'

She smiled and blushed. 'I'll give you some to take home wid ya.'

'You were going to say, Nessa?'

But Michael answered instead. 'He would have probably left it to his son, our Tyler. Anyway, we'll never know, will we, unless the file shows up.'

Brodie turned to Nessa, his mind on what he'd been fishing for before Mac's untimely interruption earlier. 'I understand this is a very sensitive topic and one I wished I didn't have to ask, but this lad . . .' He paused and looked at Michael.

'Oh yes, him.'

'Tell me, did you ever see him again – a phone call, a visit, anything?'

Michael shook his head. 'No. Like I said, I paid her off, and that was the end of it.'

But Brodie knew it wasn't because Nessa was now nervously chewing her lip. 'Nessa, it's hard, I know, but if you remember anything, I'm sure Michael won't mind you telling us now. We need to find who killed your son and grandson.'

When Michael saw tears welling up in her eyes, she fiercely blinked them away. He looked up at her and frowned. 'Nessa, speak, love.'

She sat down on the sofa, carefully keeping a cushion between her and Mac. Her eyes then flashed towards Michael. 'I did meet him.'

'*What?*' said Michael, in utter disbelief. 'What do you mean?'

She looked down at her hands. 'He came to the house. Our Tommy and Bianca were here, and he wanted to meet you.'

'You never said.'

She smiled sadly. 'I should have because if you'd met him, you'd have wanted him in your life. He is so handsome, and dare I say it, much more handsome than our brood, and he spoke with a beautiful voice. But I was jealous. I hated the fact that *your* son was everything *ours* weren't.'

Michael seized Brodie's glass of brandy and downed it in one go. 'What did you do, Nessa?'

She sat up straight and looked Michael in the eye. 'I demanded he leave. I said he was a phoney, some kind of chancer, and that you never had a son. But he stood there trying to argue with me, and then you know what our Tommy was like.' She shook her head. 'Tommy saw I was angry, and so he dragged the lad from the front door along the street and beat him up.'

While Michael poured himself another drink, Nessa just stared vacantly in deep thought. Everyone could see she was on edge; in fact, no one could tell how Michael would take it.

'Did Tommy *badly* hurt him?'

Nessa slowly closed her eyes and nodded. 'I'm sorry, Michael.'

'I know you are, Nessa. I know you are. But it was my fault. I shouldn't have strayed. I should have remained faithful. The lad never came back, did he?'

The sideways glance told Brodie he had been back.

'Did he, Nessa?'

'I saw him once. It wasn't here, though.'

'Where did you see him, then?' demanded Michael.

'He was in a car, not far from our Tommy's house. I think he wanted to catch a glimpse of you, Michael. Of course, I said nothing because I assumed that he was going away. No one would want a repeat beating, especially from our Tommy. Anyway, he did go away. When I looked out of the window the following day, his car was gone.'

'Did you tell Tommy who he was?'

'No, I just said he was a chancer because I thought it best to let sleeping dogs lie, eh?'

Michael nodded. 'Yeah, girl, it was probably for the best.'

Brodie paused before he said, 'Did he have an accent?'

Nessa replied, 'Indeed, he did. He was posh, very English, not like my Tommy.' She sneered at Michael. 'Considering Tommy and the lad were the same fecking age, and like I said, he was handsome, and you could tell he was well educated.'

'What was his name? Did he say?'

Nessa glanced at her husband. 'He is called Oliver.'

'*Oliver?*' said Michael, as if he was just learning he had a son.

It almost caused Nessa to jump off the sofa.

'He should never have returned!'

'It's okay, Michael. He *has* stayed away. I think it's very likely that Oliver, wherever he is, has nothing to do with all of this.'

'Maybe you are right, love.'

'Er . . . Nessa, what car was he driving? Can you remember?' asked Brodie.

She nodded. 'It was a very expensive-looking car. One of those convertibles, I think.'

'But do you recall the make?' Brodie persisted.

She tutted and then looked to the ceiling while clicking her fingers. 'Michael, what's that car you wanted to buy? It's still in the showroom up the road.'

Mac piped up, 'The Jaguar showroom?'

'Oh,' said Michael. 'The Jaguar F-Type. Yeah, they had a stunning-looking red one in there.' He looked at Nessa. 'He must be fairly well off. That car can cost over seventy grand.'

She nodded. 'Anyway, what does it matter. I mean, our Tommy could have afforded ten of them.'

Michael looked down, just realising he was showing an interest in Oliver when he had made a promise years ago not to.

Brodie could see Michael was sinking lower into his armchair and Nessa was once again in deep thought. He decided it was time to leave them in peace. 'We'll make a move, but would you mind if I come back perhaps tomorrow? I think the deaths of Clifford Jenson-Baine, Tyler, and your Tommy are all connected and Tommy is the key to it all.'

Nessa shrugged her shoulders. 'Oh, Brodie, Tommy was a closed book. He would never let on about anything.'

Brodie smiled. 'Maybe if I give you time to go back and think about everything we've discussed, something might crop up, but, for now, you probably need to rest. Grief, I can imagine, is exhausting.'

'That it is, lad. That it is,' said Michael, as he got to his feet and showed Mac and Brodie to the front door.

'Here,' said Brodie, as he handed Michael his gun. 'I said I would give it back.'

Nessa, meanwhile, hurried back to the kitchen and wrapped a large chunk of the cake for Mac.

As soon as Mac and Brodie pulled away, Mac said, 'Why not stay and ask them more questions, Brodie?'

'Because Michael was hearing things – important things – for the first time. Michael and Nessa need to digest what was said. And she has Oliver on her mind and won't think straight. It's all so consuming, I could see that in her eyes. We should come back here tomorrow and probe into Tommy's life. Because, Mac, there are so many secrets in that family, and I think we have only just scratched the surface.'

CHAPTER TWENTY-SIX

Dixie-Lee was ordered to wait in the interview room. She was baffled by this latest development because she had no idea why she was here, but she couldn't do anything about it. When the door finally opened, she saw two police officers, one of whom was a man possibly in his forties with fine fair hair and perfect veneers. He introduced himself as Sergeant Knight. He spoke softly with a touch of sympathy in his voice. But no matter how he was about to say it, the words amounted to the same thing: 'Dixie-Lee Deacon, you are being arrested for the murder of Tyler Malloye.'

The shock made her stagger back and blink furiously as though she had just entered a nightmare. But it wasn't one. It was all too real. The vision of the two police officers didn't disappear; and neither did the officer's words once he'd charged her with yet another murder. The officer carefully placed her in handcuffs before he escorted her from the prison gates to an unmarked car.

The smaller officer, who remained quiet the whole time, guided her into the back seat. Dixie-Lee couldn't have been more surprised than to find herself sitting next to Officer Brenton.

With a smirk on her face, she followed that up with a nasty greeting. 'So, Dixie-Lee Deacon, we meet again for round two.'

Dixie-Lee stared out of the window, trying to get her head around the fact that they were charging her with Tyler Malloye's murder as well.

During the drive, her stomach was churning like a washing machine; she was continually breaking out in sporadic hot sweats and experiencing what felt like a tourniquet tightening her chest.

After fifteen minutes, Officer Brenton attempted to make conversation with Deacon. She had a particular reason to bait her. 'Looks like you've taken a beating. Prison is a tough place,' she snorted.

Dixie-Lee looked at Brenton for a moment before once again staring out of the passenger window, still trying to understand the fact that they were charging her with Tyler's murder.

'Double murder. Now, that's a long bit of bird. You'll be an old lady by the time you see daylight. Your mother will be in a grave, and you'll come out, if you don't die in prison, to no one and nothing but a probation officer and a bedsit in a hostel with other lowlifes. Sounds terrific, doesn't it, Dixie-Lee.'

Even though Dixie-Lee tried to ignore Brenton, she couldn't help but agree with what the officer was saying. But she wouldn't give her the satisfaction of reacting either.

'I have my bodycam on, Dixie-Lee, and we have a camera in the car. You can talk to us. Look, making a statement will serve you well in court. Judges like confessions because it shows you're remorseful and saves court time and also money, so, believe me, it will go in your favour.'

Dixie-Lee remained silent but she could hear the tension in Brenton's breathing.

'It will be a long, long night, but you know the result will be the same. You'll confess because, let's face it, we have so much on you that no jury in the land would have any doubt you killed Tyler Malloye.'

Deacon's reluctance to speak was getting up Brenton's nose. 'We can hold you for forty-eight hours, you know. Do you have any idea how sleep deprivation works?'

Having spent some time in prison, Dixie-Lee had changed somewhat. It didn't take her long to realise that being kind and sweet, as her mother would say, got you nowhere. She'd learned that some women liked to prey on those they perceived as weak for whatever reason. Knowing she hadn't killed Tyler, her fear veered to anger. She turned her head to face Brenton and smiled with her eyes wide.

'Why are you staring at me like that, Dixie-Lee? Is that your feeble attempt at trying to intimidate me? It's not working because I have seen every expression, so don't try it.'

'Seriously, how can I intimidate you? I'm in cuffs and sitting next to a uniformed officer with two uniformed officers in the front of the car.'

'Did you not comprehend what I was saying to you? I was offering a potential lesser sentence?'

'I am amazed that you think I would make a confession in the back seat of a car while your colleague is driving at seventy miles an hour along the motorway. It's an utterly ludicrous idea. Are we stopping to pick up my solicitor on the way?'

'Hardly!' spat Brenton.

'Then I would suggest you think carefully about what you are saying to me, especially if you say the camera is rolling. You need to get your facts straight. You say you can keep me in custody to interrogate me for forty-eight hours. No, you can hold me for up to ninety-eight for a serious crime, and murder is pretty serious. Officer Brenton, my solicitor will be present, and he's no idiot. You cannot gain a confession when I am sleep deprived because it amounts to torture, and we all know that innocent suspects make false confessions when they've had no sleep. So don't try to coerce me into making a statement and incriminating myself just so you can get down the pub with a pint of lager in your hand and a satisfied smile on your face. All because you have single-handedly secured a conviction. Officer Brenton, understand this: I'm no one's *fucking mug.*'

The last two words threw Brenton. Deacon had spoken to her with articulate grace but then changed to a woman with a fight in her.

'Don't swear.'

'Are you going to arrest me for swearing as well as a double murder? Now, that would be hilarious in court.' She laughed. 'I won't swear, but I will make it very clear that I will not be bullied. So, I suggest you back right off with any ideas of using strong-arm tactics to gain a confession out of me.'

'You watch too many crime fiction programmes. We don't use, as you put it, strong-arm tactics.'

'Yeah, you do. I've witnessed it at first hand, when the police dragged my uncle from the car and beat him, and as you know, he was an innocent man. I don't trust a single one of you, and for good reason, Officer Brenton. Before he was killed, my father exposed the paedophile ring run by a bent copper.' She smiled. 'Remember, Officer Brenton, because you were at the station at the time. I remember seeing you there. In fact, Officer, I recall you sitting in the car outside my house with Carol Lardon. So are you being particularly nasty to me because your friends were locked away in prison for what they did, or is there another reason why you are treating me like a murderer when I've not even been tried yet?'

In a fit of frustration, Brenton retorted, 'They weren't my friends. I had nothing to do with it. In fact, I hardly knew them. They came from Tonbridge, so—'

'The lady doth protest too much—'

'What? Shut up!'

'Oh, I thought you wanted me to speak.'

Brenton looked away. She assumed she had the measure of the girl, but she had been mistaken. Deacon was no fool and she had touched on something she didn't want to visit again. Carol had been a friendly acquaintance, and their developing friendship hadn't been questioned at the time. Lardon and others were convicted and sent down, and she knew that she was lucky not to have been fired for being associated with her since they had shared a few drinks together, and she had accepted a gift, a Rolex no less. She bit her lip and hoped that Lardon would take that information to the grave with her.

Dixie-Lee could see that what she'd said had impacted on Brenton; she had indeed struck a nerve. Even the officer's face had turned grey, almost see-through, which was impossible, since her skin was milk-white and highlighted by ginger hair.

'You didn't allow me my dignity when you came to arrest me, and I thought then, why is this officer of the law treating me in such a vile way? Then I recalled you being in the car with Lardon watching movies on your iPad. I wouldn't call that work, Officer, would you?'

'You are mistaken.'

Sergeant Knight looked over his shoulder. 'You worked with Lardon?'

Dixie-Lee stared at Brenton, waiting for a response, and then she noticed her bottom lip twitching.

'Before I knew, I mean, we didn't know she was . . . a part of that stuff.'

'Hmm, watching what exactly on an iPad?' he probed.

'Colin, leave it out.'

'I was brought over from Croydon to investigate that case. I didn't recall you mentioning you worked alongside Lardon. Was that when you were on house watch duties at the Deacon residence?'

Dixie-Lee answered. 'Yes, it was. I saw her from my bedroom window.'

'Okay, I think we'll discuss this later at the station,' replied Sergeant Knight, firmly.

'And I should bloody well think so. We're bringing in a suspect. I don't appreciate this conversation taking place now.'

'And be sure, Officer Brenton, the conversation *will* take place.'

The moment they arrived at the police station, Dixie-Lee was whisked through the custody suite, where her details were recorded, before another officer escorted her to the interview room. He gently removed her cuffs and stood outside.

She was left alone and she was refused a phone call. The excuse was she could make the call when the line was free. She laughed at them and shook her head, knowing that that was such a pathetic excuse. *Still,* she thought, *waiting in an interview room was no big deal.* However, her legs bounced rhythmically when she thought about the charge, and she bit down on her thumbnail. But moments later, she calmed right down. She surprised herself with how she was so lacking in any form of emotion; but then, there were no more tears to shed. She was, however, angry and frustrated because only she knew the truth, and this, in her eyes, was, without doubt, the police clutching at straws.

***

Detective Sparks was called down to the main reception waiting area, and as he opened the door, he saw Hugh Shields with a briefcase under his arm and a look of indignation on his face.

'Er . . . you wanted to see me?'

'No, I'm here to represent Dixie-Lee Deacon, my client.'

Sparks frowned. 'What makes you think she's here?'

Shields smirked. 'Are you telling me she's not? Because you wouldn't lie about that, would you?'

'I didn't say she wasn't. I asked what makes you believe she is.'

'Stop beating about the bush. Please take me to my client. This charge is very serious, and please don't think for a second that you can interview her without me with her because you are surely mistaken.'

Sparks opened the door, allowing Shields entry. 'She's in interview room one. Tell me, how were you made aware she was here?'

Shields waved his phone. 'I got a call to say as much.'

'Deacon hasn't made a call from the station as yet.'

'Well, anyway, does it matter? I am sure we both want the right person nicked for these murders because, Alan, imagine if you got it so wrong and you have a serial killer on your hands. Now, that would be a right royal fuck-up.'

Sparks said no more and opened the door to the interview room.

Shields stared wide-eyed. 'Bloody hell, who did that to your face?'

Dixie-Lee waved her hands. 'It's fine. Don't fuss.'

Shields sat opposite his client. 'Right, now I have you all to myself, I want a firm word with you. I gather you want to change your plea to guilty.' He looked over his shoulder, making sure no one had crept in. 'Listen to me: I don't know what's going on, but something is amiss regarding the chambers. Cathy shouldn't have met with you without me, and I don't know why she did, but she left a message to say that you've written a statement and you're signing it tomorrow to give her time to get your defence organised.'

Dixie-Lee nodded. 'Yes, but *she's* writing the statement for me. I'm not.'

'If you plead guilty to manslaughter in self-defence, you will live with that stigma attached to you for the rest of your life. You're *not* guilty. You didn't kill him because whoever killed

Clifford Jenson-Baine probably also killed Tyler Malloye, so take this seriously. Once you have made your plea, you cannot change it!'

'Well, her statement can go in the bin as far as I'm concerned. I've decided not to change my plea.'

Shields sat bolt upright. 'Oh,' he said, stunned.

'I'm *not* changing it because I'm *not* guilty of murder or manslaughter. All I am guilty of is fighting with a twat who sexually assaulted me, and that's it. He was still bloody alive when I left him.'

'So why did you say you would change your plea?'

'Cathy suggested it would be a less risky option, or words to that effect. But when I thought about it, I realised that if I pleaded guilty, I could say goodbye to my career as a barrister.'

'Has Cathy ever cajoled you into pleading guilty?'

'No,' Dixie-Lee replied, before biting her bottom lip.

'Has anyone else forced you to plead guilty?' Shields pointed to her bruised face.

Dixie-Lee had intended to tell Hugh about the threat made by Bianca but she decided she had a more pressing issue on her mind.

'No. Hugh, listen, I need to tell you something that might be crucial to the case.'

'Go on.'

'After Cathy came to see me yesterday, I went back to my cell feeling so conflicted, and they say that inside you have plenty of time to think, and that is true, in part, but when other shit is going on, then you get a bit screwed up. So as the day wore on, I became clear-headed. I don't know what it was, but I felt like this fog had dissipated and I was seeing something else emerging.'

Although Shields didn't interrupt, he felt undoubtedly confused.

'So when I was taken to the legal visiting room to meet with Cathy, I heard the officers escorting her along the corridor. Now, the corridor to the legal visits is made of polished wooden floorboards. It's the old part of the building. And that's when the clip-clop sound of her shoes on that floor outside, obviously some distance away from the room, sounded slightly muffled, and at that point, that particular sound triggered something.'

Shields was on the edge of his chair, nodding for her to continue.

'That night, Hugh, when I went to the chambers, I thought I could hear footsteps upstairs, and obviously when Clifford appeared, I mentally dismissed the notion of anyone else being present. And, of course, I was so traumatised by the assault that the memory of the footsteps paled into insignificance. Again, I think the sound was like a muffled clip-clop. It's really hard to explain, but it's not a sound you would make wearing trainers or rubber-soled shoes. Hugh, can you look at any photos of Clifford and Tyler to see what they had on their feet?'

'Are you sure now?'

'Yes, absolutely sure.'

Shields leaned across and clutched her hands. 'So, Dixie-Lee, tell me this. Are you saying that the person you heard at the chambers was Cathy?'

Sucking her bottom lip, Dixie-Lee shrugged. 'That's such a huge question, Hugh. It amounts to a massive allegation. And that comes with so many other repercussions. But, yes, it seems now that it possibly was her.'

'I know, love. As much as we respect Cathy, and she is good – in fact, she's one of the City's best barristers apart from Steve, who, by the way, has buggered off overseas doing some deep-sea diving – we need to keep an open mind about what happened that night. And no one is infallible. Especially where big money is at stake.'

'Thank you, Hugh, for believing me. I thought it would be hard because I know how everyone looks up to Cathy.'

He patted her hand. 'She's admired for her work . . .' He paused. 'Look, I shouldn't really say too much, but I will tell you this because it may make you think more carefully about what you actually saw and heard. Don't, for God's sake, sign any bloody statement. At least for the moment.'

'What is it, Hugh?'

'Rohan has been following Cathy.'

'*What!*' She threw her hands to her mouth.

'Please don't say this to your mum, but we've all known that Cathy has had the hots for Rohan, but she is not his type, and since he has known her for years now, he noticed that recently she has been wearing a watch – not any old watch but a very expensive one. He has also seen her wearing a large diamond in her ears and she's made two trips to Hatton Garden. On the first occasion, he followed her, and then on the second, she asked him to take her there.'

'Oh, I see. Are you thinking about the supposed diamonds that were meant to be in that safe deposit box of Tommy Malloye's?'

Shields nodded. 'But selling a gem to a buyer in Hatton Garden does not a criminal make.'

'No, certainly it doesn't, so I assume you have something else on Cathy. Is that right?'

Shields winked. 'You are a sharp kid, you know.'

Dixie-Lee glanced up at him in a fit of pique. '*Well*, Cathy doesn't think I'll make the grade, that's for sure.'

Shields frowned. 'Really? That's total bollocks!'

Dixie-Lee laughed.

'Rohan asked me because I'm a solicitor to check the visiting records for Tommy when he was away for eight months on remand for an armed robbery in Orpington. When they emailed the details back to me, there was a woman on the list. She visited him in prison regularly once a month before his trial.'

'Don't tell me it was Cathy?'

'Well, that's the thing. I don't know. Whoever she was, she was far too shrewd to use her own name. The visitor's name was Violet Buchannon.'

'Who's she?'

'A woman who died four years ago.'

'Oh my God!'

'I looked her up, and there was only one of the same age and she died in a car crash. Strangely enough, the man who mowed her down was a client of Cathy's.'

'Hugh,' she said pulling up her sleeve. 'I've got goosebumps.'

'Yes, but, Dixie-Lee, this is all conjecture at this moment, so what I need you to do is to stick with your original not guilty plea – just for the moment – and again when the police come in here with their evidence and frightening accusations and tell you how much easier it will be to confess now, etcetera, etcetera—'

'They've already tried that,' she interrupted. 'They tried it on in the car on the way here.' She stopped and stared. 'You know what, Hugh, I can't get my head around all this. So was Cathy having an affair with Tommy, do you think?'

Shields shrugged. 'It's possible, I suppose.'

Leaning back on her chair, Dixie-Lee shut her eyes, now in deep thought. 'A gangster and the barrister. Hey, that would make a great title for a film! So how did they meet? Was Cathy representing him?'

'Oh, there's a lot of history there. You see, Steve represented Tommy, and Cathy and her team represented Bianca on more than one occasion. I mean, I introduced Tommy to them. He was one of my clients. But that was many moons ago. I broke away from them for a while. I had other clients, mainly in Ireland.'

'Did you say Steve has gone abroad deep-sea diving?'

'Yes, why?'

'So, who will represent Bianca now?'

'I don't know. I've handed her over to a colleague because this case is too heavily connected to you, and, of course, you are my number-one client.'

'Hugh, this may or may not be relevant. Bianca is top dog in the prison, you know, and that means—'

'I know what that means. So someone is supplying her with contraband, then?'

'Yep.'

'Well, that's bloody odd because with Tommy dead, who is she seeing?'

'There was a man on a visit. I couldn't see what he looked like. He was facing another way, but from the side, he had a rough beard.'

'That's interesting. I'll get Rohan to look into that if, of course, he hasn't already. Please believe me when I say that we are working hard to get to the bottom of it.'

'The police should be doing that, though, shouldn't they?'

'I think it's more a case of closed minds. They think they've got their suspect. But don't worry, Dixie-Lee, we're on it.'

'And my mum, Hugh. Is she okay?'

'She's your mum. She's tough, resilient, but desperate to get you home, no doubt.'

The door opened, and in marched Sparks and Brenton, who looked less than confident.

Shields got up from his chair and sat beside Dixie-Lee. Moments later, he couldn't believe his ears.

‘So we meet again, Detective Inspector Sparks, and with Carol Lardon’s old buddy Officer Brenton, the iPad movie pals.’

Shields had to laugh. Dixie-Lee was her mother’s daughter all right.

Sparks stared. ‘Sorry, *what* did you say?’

‘Oh, didn’t you know? Your colleague here was friends with Carol Lardon, the infamous, bent, vile copper who was part of the gang that raped my stepbrother.’

‘Miss Deacon, those officers were rightly charged and convicted and are now serving time, so there is no need to deflect the seriousness of your case and the reason *you* are here.’

‘Oh, is that so? Really? And tell me, Detective Inspector Sparks, are you allowing Officer Brenton here to question me when she was seen laughing and enjoying watching a film in the car with Lardon while my stepbrother was being raped – an act organised by Lardon and her brother?’

Sparks turned to look at Brenton, who appeared more than uneasy.

He flicked his head for Brenton to leave the room. She didn’t need to be asked twice; she was gone in a flash.

‘Right, now she has left the room, I will be conducting the interview alone. As you know, you have just been arrested for the murder of Tyler Malloye.’

Shields clocked how Sparks’s tone had softened. Maybe the reminder of the past and what Dixie-Lee had gone through was poking his conscience.

‘Detective, before you turn on the tape, I have advised my client not to answer your questions.’

‘Mr Shields, I understand that Miss Deacon is changing her plea to guilty.’

Under normal circumstances, the shock of hearing that statement would have rendered Shields speechless, but fortunately,

Dixie-Lee had given him the heads-up. He decided, therefore, to pretend he was in the dark about this. 'Who told you that?'

He shrugged. 'I don't know exactly how it came to light today.'

'Well, she's not.'

Sparks sighed. 'Oh, I see.'

Shields grinned. 'Right, let me get this straight. You dragged my client in from the prison and one of your officers tried to get her to confess whilst in the back of the police car. And if my client had pleaded guilty to murdering Clifford Jenson-Baine on grounds of self-defence, you would have reason to charge her with Tyler Malloye's murder as well.'

'Not only that, Mr Shields, but we have a witness saying he saw someone who looked like Miss Deacon wearing a long coat later that evening the night of Tuesday 29th November. We don't have that coat, which will undoubtedly have Tyler Malloye's blood on it, but we do have a witness.'

'Where did your witness see the person they thought looked like Miss Deacon?'

'Walking out of the alleyway, that leads from the back of the chambers building to the street.'

'When it would almost certainly be pitch-black and when your witness showed so much interest that they categorically – without hesitation – confirmed that the woman was Miss Deacon?'

'Yes.'

'Right, so this is where we are. You have my client on remand for the murder of Clifford Jenson-Baine. You have evidence that my client fought him off. She wasn't soaked in his blood. But her clothes were ripped, her injuries evidence of a sexual assault. Now you're saying a witness said he saw Dixie-Lee, when it was dark, wearing a long coat and leaving the alleyway beside the chambers.

Tell me, Detective, did your witness say the coat was covered in blood?'

Sparks shook his head.

'Think about it logically. If you saw a woman in the dark close enough to recognise her face, say from the photo you were shown later, you would also be close enough to see the coat caked in blood, wouldn't you?'

Sparks straightened his tie and coughed nervously.

'Do you have the photographs of the two bodies?' asked Shields.

Sparks opened the files and slid them in front of Shields and Dixie-Lee.

Dixie-Lee gasped at the sight, but she didn't look away. She made a mental note of their shoes. Tyler was wearing trainers, and Clifford had rubber-soled black shoes.

'There's a lot of blood on Tyler Malloye and a wound like that would surely plaster the attacker, and yet your witness didn't notice the blood. Are you sure the witness was close enough to see the woman or possibly even a man's face? Detective, it's not looking good for you, is it? My client will not answer your questions with anything other than "no comment". And when I think you have questioned her long enough, I will request that she gets some sleep after she has had refreshments, and at the very least a hot drink. Detective, you can see she is suffering an injury.' He pointed to Dixie-Lee's face.

Right on cue, Dixie-Lee rose from her chair and lifted her top. Her torso revealed the vast area of bruising.

Sparks's eyes almost popped out of his head. 'Who did *that* to you?'

Dixie-Lee sighed. 'It's prison life.'

At that moment, Alan Sparks felt a need to get to the truth and not force a conviction – particularly when there ought to be more investigation. His promotion could wait. Staring at the photos, he had to agree with Hugh Shields. It seemed ridiculous that with so much blood on the victim, the witness had never once described the state of the coat, whether it was covered in blood or not. And in actual fact, it was now questionable how this witness could have identified her in the dark at all. All he knew was that WPC Brenton had interviewed the witness and she had shown him a photo of Dixie-Lee Deacon. Maybe Brenton had cajoled the witness into believing the woman in the long coat was Dixie-Lee Deacon. *Why did you do that, Brenton?*

CHAPTER TWENTY-SEVEN

Georgie was grateful that Rohan had been more attentive and also relieved that for the first time, she hadn't woken up in a sweat but instead had roused to the smell of bacon and coffee. Her head wasn't thumping either; and yet she was still perturbed about Dixie-Lee because, again, she hadn't phoned her to say she was okay.

Slipping on her dressing gown, she descended the stairs and waltzed into the kitchen to find Rohan frying eggs to perfection and Rodney seated at the breakfast bar.

'Good morning, Georgie,' said Rodney, lifting his mug. 'Want one?'

She nodded and smiled. 'Sounds good.'

'Two sausages, three rashers of bacon, two eggs, and tomatoes,' said Rohan, as he slid the final two eggs onto a plate and presented it to her.

'A bit early for me, Rohan.'

He peered at the clock. 'Early? Darling, it's ten o'clock.'

She was stunned. 'Really? You should've woken me.'

'No way, Georgie. You've not slept properly in ages, you're exhausted, and you haven't eaten either, so get that down yer neck and do something for yourself. Go to the hairdresser's or . . . .'

She shot him a cold look. 'What's wrong with my hair now?' Her mood soured, and she pushed the plate away from her.

'For God's sake, Georgie, I was merely suggesting you go and do something for yourself. I wasn't implying that there was anything wrong with your hair.' He slapped the tea towel down and stormed out of the room.

Georgie felt her heart sink. Why couldn't she see the good in anything? She may not have experienced one of those disturbing dreams to be off kilter, but she still felt less than adequate compared to Cathy, and she was still angry with the world for taking her daughter, locking her up, and putting a wall between them. She glanced across at Rodney, who looked down into his coffee cup. Sensing how this situation was making him feel very awkward, she decided to take her coffee into the lounge away from him.

As she sat on the sofa sipping her drink and gazing out of the window, she heard the front door slam shut. It made her jump. She was just about to get up and check if it was Rohan who had left the house when a soft voice from behind her said, 'It's okay, Georgie. Everyone's tense and naturally so, considering what's going on. But Rohan is right. You need to relax, eat, and slow down a bit.'

She turned to her side to meet Rodney's glazed eyes. 'I think I need to figure out what happened to me as a kid.'

'Yes, maybe you do, but how? Will you go to a therapist or a counsellor or what?'

She shook her head. 'Neither of those, Rod. I'm going back to my old house where I grew up and see if that sparks any memories.'

He nodded. 'Do you want me to come with you?'

She shook her head. 'No, I think I need to be alone, and while I'm out, Rod, would you be so kind as to check out the sensor lights all around the house? I'm not so sure they're all working.'

'Good, that will give me something to do.'

She drank the last of her coffee and left the lounge to get ready.

***

The drive to her childhood home wasn't very far away. Twenty-three minutes, to be exact. However, she had never bothered to venture there even when she lived in her two-up two-down place in St Mary Cray despite being within walking distance of the house. Sidcup was an area she'd never needed to drive through to get anywhere, so she had not been back for well over twenty years; the last time was when her mother died, and she woke up in hospital with disturbing yet murky recollections of that day.

As she turned into the road, her hands felt clammy. She could also feel her heart pumping away inside her chest and had to take a few deep breaths. Knowing that she wasn't far from the house, she slowed down just enough to determine which property it was, and then she slammed on her brakes.

The shock sent her back in time. How could the house be the same? The old Crittall windows hadn't been updated, the front door was still red, although now it was faded to an ugly pink colour, and the cracks in the concrete path were more significant. The only thing that did appear to have been updated were the curtains. Something didn't feel right, though. Surely, the council would, at the very least, have updated the windows? Parking her car directly outside, she got out. It was cold and icy, and the sun was glaringly low in the sky, forcing her to squint.

Scrutinising the neighbouring houses, they looked worlds apart. Their windows were not all the same, but they certainly weren't the old Crittall ones either. Each house had a very different, more personalised look. Many were painted white, some had additional porches, and others had landscaped gardens enclosed by brick walls. Money had been spent on them, highlighting the notion that these weren't council houses anymore, which she assumed her mother's must have been. Whatever the case, her mother's former house was undoubtedly an eyesore now compared to the others in the street. And having looked about, she noticed that the lack of parked cars anywhere would suggest the neighbours were all working. In fact, the street was deathly quiet.

Curiosity got the better of her, so she gingerly walked up the old path. It was so different from years ago when she would often leg it to get out of that house. It was odd because it seemed spooky as a child, and yet now as an adult, it was nothing but rundown; at a pinch, it could even be used in a Halloween film. After all, if there were no curtains, it would look abandoned.

The moment she raised the door knocker, she froze. She needed to take another deep breath and tell herself that she was a grown woman who could handle herself, especially against a man like Bruce Kern, who wouldn't have the strength now that he once had all those years ago. She grimaced because even though that door knocker had always been there, as a child, she had never used it. She'd always gone through the back door and often ran out that way or through a bedroom window. Looking at the overgrown grass beside her, ruined by the icy weather, she wondered how many times she had landed there from her mother's bedroom window. It was amazing that she had any ankles left.

She waited a moment before she used the door knocker. When she was sure that no one was at home, she quickly glanced around before scooting along the side of the house to the back garden. Absolutely nothing had changed except, of course, the bushes were much more extensive and wilder. There was the addition of high fences, more than likely put up by the neighbours to block the view of the untidy garden.

As she approached the back door, she frowned. It was the same; it hadn't been replaced, except for a broken pane of glass. She swallowed hard, recalling images of the fight that night. Naturally, that door would have had to be repaired, the top of which was glass. She stepped closer and put her hands above her eyebrows to block out the sun so she could peer inside what would have been the kitchen. As she looked around, she held her breath: nothing had changed. The old Formica kitchen units with the aluminium strips were still in situ. The Formica had bubbled in places, and there was definitely wear and tear, but other than that, it was as she remembered it. The fridge was different, though; theirs had barely worked and was never full of food – merely tonic water for her mother's gin or Coke for her vodka in the days when she wasn't drinking it neat.

Something compelled her to try the door handle. Mentally, she knew she was trespassing, but because everything looked as it did when she was here last, she felt comfortable entering the property. But it was the framed picture on the wall that really caught her eye. Something wasn't adding up. Why would the present owners keep that same picture? It was so faded that you could barely make out a child's drawing of a little girl and what was supposed to be the mummy. Of course, they were matchstick figures, but, nonetheless, the point was that she had sketched the drawing herself.

A sudden rush of emotion felt like being stabbed in the chest. She remembered that day so clearly. A lady in a suit, who was not her mother, was holding her hand tightly, and as they stood in this very kitchen, she felt safe, loved, and secure.

However, things were about to change; social services had prepared her to meet her real mother. She vividly recalled the meeting. Her mother was beautiful. With her hair piled high in black curls and her pale-pink lipstick covering her plump lips, she smelled like flowers. Dressed in a floral top, flared jeans, and Indian beads around her neck, Georgie was mesmerised by her.

She remembered feeling so excited as her mother reached down and tickled her chin before taking the drawing and beaming. 'Georgie, my little sweetie, I will frame this and hang it where everyone can see it and so they know you are such a brilliant artist.' Georgie remembered shyly swaying her hips and feeling so clever. And there and then, she felt able to trust this woman.

The smile suddenly disappeared when the reality of being handed back to her mother came into play, but again, she'd only been four, and so she knew nothing of what her mother's real life was at the time. She also had no idea that she'd been in foster care in children's homes, but now she was slowly being reintroduced to her mother where she would live with her permanently.

Her mother reverted to drinking, having been sober to get her daughter back purely for selfish reasons. She would receive benefits to pay for her addictions. She'd been very clever and sly about her drinking. Social services would do their checks only between the hours of nine to five. Bang on ten past five, her mother would laugh and get the drinks out, and the fun and games began. Men came and went, many bringing drink, of course, and even a gift. While all this went on, she would be sent to her room with a sandwich, a chocolate biscuit, and sometimes fresh milk, or even sour milk.

As she stared at the picture, she felt the urge to turn the back door handle. It was as if the house was calling her. Maybe this was her way of putting the past to bed or making sense of what really went on in this place. So much was blurred, but the picture on the wall was a vivid memory. *But why was it still here?*

As she turned the handle and slowly pushed the door, it opened. For a second, she paused. Maybe she had not believed it would, but she was inside the kitchen now, and she stood there just taking everything in. It was as though she had stepped back in time. Her hand hovered over a threadbare tea towel, where she could still make out the basket of fruit print. The linoleum on the floor was also worn away by the sink area. The stainless-steel sink was the same; however, it was now thick with limescale.

A low humming sound snapped her out of her gaze. She listened and couldn't work out where it was coming from at first, but then she realised that the sound was coming from the living room. She knew that just a few steps away towards the front door was a room on the right that was the living room-cum-dining room. As she left the kitchen, she recognised the hallway carpet; it was the original red one but this too had faded to pink. And the woodchip wallpaper was still the same. The skirting board was thick with dust, which may have always been that way since her mother hadn't been one for housework.

Creeping closer to the living room, she remained on high alert, just as she had done as a kid. She'd always peered around a doorway to see if the coast was clear. The thought sent her throat tingling as though she was about to be sick, which was how she had grown up – constantly feeling nervous and experiencing a level of fight or flight continually flowing around her body. It was a wonder she didn't have a stomach ulcer or a heart attack. But during her early childhood, she had lived constantly on the run, even if that meant running from room to room, out of the window, or down the road to escape her mother's clients looking for more.

She suddenly felt the scar on her head tingle. *As if that was even possible*, she thought. Biting her bottom lip, she crept closer towards the living room, looking back to ensure the back door was open, ready for her to flee. She shook her head. *How stupid. What would she be running from at this time in her life?*

After another deep breath, she entered the room. What she saw made her momentarily stagger back and gasp; she threw her hands to her mouth in shock. Wearing an old tracksuit and as thin as a rake, a very frail old man was wired up to an oxygen machine. But there was no mistaking who he was. And even though he was propped up with cushions in a nylon-covered armchair, with one foot in the grave, his skeletal face instantly brought back a feeling of dread. She stared, taking it all in.

'Hello, Georgie,' he said, after removing the oxygen mask.

She didn't answer; she couldn't. How was this possible? He was old when she was a kid, and yet here he was in her childhood home, alive, but barely looking any more like a skeleton than before. His skin was paper-thin and mottled, and even as an old man, there was nothing sweet about him.

'I thought you would be long dead,' she managed to say.

'Me? No, I am a lot tougher than you think.' He pointed to the machine. 'Don't be fooled by this. I'm not dying, and neither was your mother when you killed her.'

Georgie stared, not moving muscle. 'And how would you know that?'

His sunken eyes widened. 'And I thought you were intelligent. Your mother wasn't dying. She needed you to come home from the armed services because, you stupid woman, she needed money. She was in debt, and' – he stopped, placed the oxygen mask over his mouth, and breathed before he removed the mask and continued – 'we called your barracks and told them she was dying and that you must come home. But you didn't come back to help her, did ya? No, you came back to *kill* her.'

As if the anger of that fateful day came flooding back, Georgie replied, 'She *was* dying. She had been killing herself for fucking years. And to think I was so terrified of you, whatever the fuck you are, and now, now I want to laugh. I want to relish in your weakness, in your desperation to breathe, and more than anything, I am free of fear, because you can't scare me anymore. You can't invade my dreams, because you're dying, and soon, I will have the chance to dance on your grave.'

His sudden chuckle made her flinch.

'I tell you that I know you killed your mother.' He shook his head. 'But you don't bat an eyelid, do ya. I know what you are, Georgie. I've followed you in the papers and seen the pattern. You are a cold-blooded killer.'

She smiled at him. 'Then you know nothing about me at all. I *might* be a killer. I was in the armed services, but cold-blooded? No. Because you see, if you're a cold-blooded killer, it means without a reason to kill, but sometimes, there *is* a reason. I know what my mother was. She was a fucking drunk, a druggie, a dirty prostitute, who was so selfish to take me from a foster home where the woman loved me, and yet my mother wanted me back here for the social security benefit for this house.'

He pointed a finger. 'This house, Georgie, is mine. It always has been. I let you and your mother live in it.'

'In return for her servicing a string of punters?'

'Yep, that's right. Your mother was a prostitute, a drug user, and a thief. She was all those things, Georgie, but she wasn't a killer.' He pulled the oxygen mask to his face again and took two deep breaths.

'Oh, and that makes it all right, then, does it?'

The old man pushed the mask away, reached for a packet of fags, and lit one, puffing furiously. 'Your mother promised you to me. I had a lot of money on you.' His face screwed up in spite.

Although those words filled Georgie with rage, she held back her violent temper because she felt so much disgust. 'Promised? How the fucking hell can a woman promise me to anyone?' She shook her head. 'She really was quite vile, wasn't she. And you, ya bag of ugly bones, are utterly despicable. I only hope you die a painful death. I can't imagine how many innocent lives you've destroyed.'

He released a plume of smoke. 'I didn't *destroy* lives. Those women on my books were on a path to self-destruction anyway. I just gave them a way out of poverty. They worked for me. I ensured they weren't in danger or selling their arses out on the streets. I kept them safe. I knew the punters. None of my girls were ever brutalised or killed except one – your mother.'

Ignoring his words regarding her mother, she replied, 'Safe? You didn't keep *me* safe.'

He shrugged and took another drag. 'You, Georgie, were the pain in everyone's life. The others—'

'Others?'

'Yes, others. Girls your age. They knew their worth. They liked the drugs. They worked hard for them, and like their mothers, they had a roof over their heads and a minder. One phone call if a punter crossed the line and Bruce would be there breaking bones. But you, you were something else. You didn't need protection.'

Astonished, Georgie took a moment to process precisely what had been going on. This pathetic-looking man had overseen a well-organised sex racket. He had grabbed women off the streets and given them a home in exchange for sex with clients, and when their rent went up, and if they weren't earning enough to cover it, they'd have to resort to selling their daughters or maybe even their sons. Who knew? How could her mother have done that? She thought about Dixie-Lee. She would have died for her daughter.

'You were the one teenager who lost me a stream of clients. You were a prize, a virgin, and even giving you a shot of heroin, you fought it and threw up all over the client. And you knew the consequences, but you couldn't do your mother that one favour.'

So the nightmare wasn't a deluded mix of what Marston-Smith had done to her and what her mother was doing for a living: it was real. They had tried to force her into the same profession by giving her drugs. She had to know if any man had taken her virginity because it had plagued her for years. She'd convinced herself they hadn't because she'd bled on her wedding night with her husband Dixie.

She decided to test him. 'But you got your money's worth out of me, didn't ya?'

He stubbed out his cigarette, began to laugh, and ended up choking on a cough.

Georgie waited until he stopped coughing. She cringed when he coughed up a load of green phlegm and spat it into a clear bag already filled with the gross-looking, thick, lumpy fluids. She looked away, feeling sick.

'You, Miss Frigid, cost me everything. Your mother gave permission for my client to have you. He paid upfront a week before. The money was gone, and yet you, even though your mother begged and pleaded with you to save this house and pay up her debt, wouldn't have any of it. All you had to do was to sleep with one client – fucking one, that was all – but no, your mother had to sleep with a hundred engaging in deviant sex to clear her debt. The poor woman didn't have a vagina at the end. It was your fault, Georgie. All your fault.'

As if his words were hanging in the air somewhere in the distance, visions of the past flooded her mind. She was back in the bedroom. She was fifteen. They were all there: there was the skeletal man, Bruce, her mother, and the man in a suit. She was terrified and lashed out hysterically; but, somehow, she'd managed to escape by launching herself through the bedroom window. She could barely run. Her legs were like jelly, and her feet were numb from the fall, but she managed to reach the end of the street. That was when she stopped and saw the needle in her arm. She was woozy and ready to collapse when someone dragged her into their house. She felt safe there.

Bringing her mind back to the here and now, she found herself gripping the doorframe to stop her legs from buckling.

Oh no, what had she done? She realised now that she had got something terribly wrong, and she was now battling with guilt and anger. But anger got its way. She stared at the man whose face was so smug.

He laughed. 'I know what you did, and, Georgie, you are one phone call away from a lifetime of prison.'

It wasn't what he said that pushed her over the edge. It was that evil dark-eyed expression that did it. His sudden mocking voice chanting 'Get her clothes off' whirled around in her head. Whether at the time that was real or not, she didn't care anymore. It was bad enough that he had colluded with her mother to have her raped by a prepaid client. And she had evidently not been the first, nor probably was she the last.

She noted that he was holding his cigarette lighter, and her eyes darted to the oxygen machine. Reaching inside her pocket, she felt for her own lighter, and before he could put his hand on his phone, she grabbed the oxygen hose, ripped the mask off the end, turned up the dial to full, and flicked her lighter. The flame was like a mini flame-thrower.

His cocky grin evaporated, and genuine fear tightened his skinny face. He tried to push himself further into the chair, but nothing could stop the flames instantly engulfing his clothes. The oxygen accelerated the fire and immediately intensified the flames. He screamed and screamed, unable to get out of the chair.

But Georgie didn't stop; she used it like a water hose. But it wasn't water, it was killer flames. The moment they set the armchair alight, she dropped the hose and saw the man's skin peel from his face, and there it was – his skeletal face – the one that had plagued her night after night. He didn't move, but the flames had now reached the side table.

Hurriedly, she stepped back and looked out of the living room window to see if there was anyone outside. There wasn't: the street looked empty. So, for the first time in years, she ran out of the front door, closed it behind her, got into her car, and drove away. Her hands were shaking while she desperately tried to go back over everything. Luckily, she was still wearing her lambskin gloves. No one would have ever known she'd been there.

CHAPTER TWENTY-EIGHT

In sheer panic, Georgie almost got lost. She had to double back past the house, which was very much in flames. People had gathered, and she could hear the sound of what she assumed was the fire engine in the distance. She had to slow down enough to take a good look. Smoke billowed out from every broken window. Flames licked the outside of the house and mercilessly tore through the roof. The fire had consumed the entire building. A busybody had taken charge and was pushing the onlookers back before there were any explosions.

Once she was on the main road, she knew her way home but her driving was on autopilot. There was too much going through her mind.

When she reached her home, she noticed that Rohan's car wasn't in the drive. In some ways, she felt relieved. She was in too much of a state. In fact, she was constantly gasping for breath and sweating like a pig. Her only place of peace and quiet was in her own bathroom where she could be away from everyone; this would allow her time to get her thoughts in order.

Sliding her key into the lock of the front door, she hoped fervently that Rodney was outside checking that the sensors for the outside security system were now working as they should. Closing the front door, she stood still and listened. It seemed she was alone. Instead of going straight up to the bathroom, she decided to go into the kitchen where she would get a couple of headache tablets and make a pot of herbal tea to calm her frayed nerves.

However, as soon as she entered the kitchen, her plans of being alone and going over everything that had happened at her mother's house were blown to smithereens.

Rodney was sitting at the breakfast bar with blood on his shirt and what initially appeared to be a huge bruise on his cheek. But if that wasn't bad enough, she was dealt with a further unwelcome surprise – when she saw who else was in the room.

'Please, I'm only helping. I didn't hurt him, I swear,' said Sarah, as she held her hands up and recoiled in fear.

'Georgie, I fell off the ladder, trying to check out one of the sensors, and Sarah, here, love her, ran to my aid. She's been patching me up. I'm all right. I only scraped my face. There's no head injury, so don't go making a huge fuss.' He clearly had no idea who Sarah was.

Georgie nodded, but all the while her hands wouldn't stop shaking.

'I'll go. I'm sorry I shouldn't be here.'

Georgie stepped forward, blocking her way.

'Please, Georgie, I don't want any trouble. I came to talk . . . well, to warn you, but I shouldn't get involved. It's not my place. I'm sorry.'

'Wait, please, Sarah. I need you to answer a question for me.'

Sarah stepped back, still wary of Georgie.

'Did you used to live at the end of my road?'

'I, er . . . I did, yes.'

Feeling utterly gutted that she had tried to put the woman's head in the oven, she unexpectedly burst into tears. 'My God, I'm so sorry. What have I fucking done?'

Sarah held out her arms. 'Hey, it's okay.'

'No, no, it's *not* okay. I nearly killed you, and yet you were the one person who saved me.' Her bag dropped to the floor as her shoulders sagged. 'What the hell have I become? Sarah, can you forgive me? I thought you were there when, well . . . when, this man, I mean the two men . . . I, er . . . my mum. My-mu-mum . . .' She suddenly broke off in floods of tears.

Sarah quickly intervened. 'Georgie, it's okay. Come and sit down. May I get you a drink?'

Her soft, sweet voice had Georgie sobbing with guilt. 'I can't believe I wanted to kill you. I genuinely wanted to fucking murder you, and how wrong could I have been. It was you who took me into your house and made me feel safe, wasn't it?'

Sarah smiled and nodded as she poured a glass of water and placed it in front of Georgie.

Rodney knew this was not the right situation for him to be present; this was something Georgie and Sarah needed to talk privately about. Hopefully, Sarah would help sort out this turbulent mess in Georgie's head that was affecting her life. 'Ladies, I hope you don't mind. I'm going to my room.'

Georgie wiped her eyes with her gloved hands and looked at Rodney. 'Are you sure you're okay?'

'Yes, like I said, it's all superficial. Tell her, Sarah.'

'He fell, but it was more of a slide down the ladder and he genuinely only grazed his face. Although it might not look like it, it's more a bloodstain than a bruise.'

Georgie pushed her hair out of her eyes, removed her gloves, and nodded for Rodney to go to his annexe. It was probably best anyway because she wanted to speak privately to Sarah.

'I'll put the kettle on, Sarah. I really would like it if you stayed a while, and please talk about what you remember about me.'

Sarah smiled gently. 'Of course, Georgie. I want to help. More than anything, I really want to help you.'

After filling the kettle and retrieving two cups, Georgie frowned. The phrase *more than anything, I really want to help you* stirred unease.

'Why?' she asked, after dropping a teabag into each cup.

Feeling comfortable enough to take a stool at the breakfast bar, Sarah replied, 'Because I should have done more, with the knowledge I had about what was going on.'

Georgie spun around and looked Sarah over. She noted the woman's jumper was full of bobbles, and her jeans were hanging off her. 'Were you part of it?' she said, in a harsh voice.

'I am ashamed to say it, but, yes, I was.'

Georgie could feel her blood boiling again. 'How?'

'I was a prostitute. Mr Ecclestone, or Skeleton Man, as some of us called him, groomed me as a kid. I was the same age as your mother, and I had a girl just like you.' The blood drained from her face. 'The wicked bastard wanted her. I knew he would 'cos she was so beautiful. Anyway, he put my rent up, and I couldn't pay, but I was buggered if I was going to hand her over. I called the police on him, ya know, but that didn't do me any fucking favours. He had a brilliant brief, and they managed to turn it around on me by suggesting that I was involved in some made-up paedophile racket, and I sure as hell wasn't.' She sighed and picked a piece of loose skin off her finger. 'But mud sticks, so I was treated like a leper for a long time.'

'What happened to your daughter?'

Sarah looked down. 'I gave her away to social services to protect her.'

'Do you see her now?'

'No, she was fostered by a family in Cambridge. I heard she went to university there, and no doubt, she is doing well. God love her.'

'Do you think she hates you for it?'

'As long as she has had a good upbringing and earns enough money to live a decent life, it doesn't matter if she hates me. I hate *myself*.' She looked down again.

Georgie followed her gaze. Sarah was looking at her cuffs that were rolled down to cover a large part of her hands.

'Did you know my mum?'

Sarah's nostrils flared. It was the first time she'd shown any emotion – either anger or remorse. 'Oh yeah, I knew your mother. I'll be very frank with you, Georgie. I didn't like her one bit.'

The kettle boiled, and Georgie made the tea. She handed Sarah a cup, leaned on the breakfast bar, and paid total attention to what Sarah had to say.

'Join the club. I didn't just dislike my mum. I fucking *hated* her. I genuinely detested her. I didn't care when my sergeant said she was dying, and she needed me at home. I told him there was no way I was going, but they insisted.'

'Yes, I remember it well.'

Georgie frowned. 'You do?'

'Of course I do. I was there when that bastard tried to bury the axe in your head.'

Georgie stood up straight, and her bottom lip dropped. '*What?*'

Sarah took a deep breath. 'I assumed your memory would have returned by now. You do remember the fight, don't you, Georgie?'

'Bits come back, but without the missing parts, it's all a blur. Maybe if you can recall it or even some of it. Please will you tell me, and then perhaps I can piece together what happened.'

Sarah sipped her tea and smiled. 'Right. Well, I remember you coming home. I saw the army truck arrive, and you got out. You were so grown up and smart. Your face had changed completely. You looked so confident, not that little wayward mouse that scuttled around as a kid.'

'I wish I could remember you when I was younger. I don't though, Sarah. I truly don't.'

'No, you probably wouldn't. I was different back then, with more hair, for starters. Long, black, and thick, it was, and I wore a lot of make-up. Skeleton Man liked all his girls to be made up, although not the younger ones. He liked them to look like little girls, the sicko.'

She stopped and chewed on her bottom lip.

'Go on, Sarah. Listen, it doesn't matter what you think I should hear, or not. Just tell me everything. My life has been such a fucking mess. I need this. I need the truth.'

'Well, all I remember was that evening when I was walking past the house, there was a lot of screaming and hollering, mainly from your mother's mouth, and then there was silence. I walked on to the off-licence. I was still on the booze – not a drunk like your mum – but I used to like a glass of wine in the evening. It helped me block out the past. As I came back from the off-licence and back past your mum's house, I heard Bruce Kern, the fucking bully, bellowing, "What have you done to her, Georgie? I'll fucking kill you!"'

Before Sarah continued, Georgie quickly asked, 'Do you know what he was talking about?' With her hands now clammy, she was thrown into deep-rooted anxiety that quickened her heartbeat and dried her throat.

Sarah shook her head. 'It didn't matter at the time, but I heard you scream. I thought he was raping you.'

Georgie studied her face, looking for any sign that Sarah might be using this conversation for the purposes of extortion. But Sarah continued in her compassionate tone.

'There was no way I could let him hurt you. I had lost everything. It was probably my way of putting something right. So I ran through the side garden and in through the back door. It was so shocking. Bruce was viciously fighting with you. Christ, I'd never seen anything like it. You, Georgie, were like a wild cat. You jumped onto the kitchen counter and dived on him. You punched and punched him until he hit the floor. Then, he grabbed your hair and swung you around, but by God, you didn't give up. I couldn't get to you because Skeleton Man pushed me out of the way. But Bruce, the fucking bastard, had the strength of an ox. To this day, it still baffles me how you fought him off.'

Seeing Sarah sighing and shaking her head as she recalled the events of the past, Georgie, who was now more settled in her mind, made them both a fresh cup of tea.

'I was outside. As I said, Skeleton Man had pushed me out of the way. But I could see everything through the kitchen window. Bruce was determined to kill you. He wasn't holding back. He threw a punch, and you ducked, and his fist went through the wall. That's when I saw Bruce grab your face and smash your head up against the pane of glass, and, of course, it shattered. I screamed because I assumed he'd killed you . . . But . . .' She laughed. 'Not you, though. You fought back.' She stopped smiling and looked solemn. 'Before I could get back inside the kitchen, Skeleton Man disappeared for a second, only to return with a fucking axe. I used all my strength to open the door, but Skeleton Man was in the way and I couldn't get you out. Bruce swung the axe and caught you. You tried to duck, but it still managed to give you a nasty gash, and, momentarily, it knocked you out.'

Georgie stood with her hands over her mouth. Memories of the fight were now flooding back. So it *was* all real. She'd blocked that out for over twenty years, only remembering snippets and never fully understanding what had happened.

'As you went down, we all heard the police sirens. Then, there was pandemonium as Bruce and Skeleton Man tried to make a run for it. I dragged you out, and, unbelievably, you were staggering about. But I got you away from them and back to my house, where I called an ambulance. I went with you to the hospital. I was so frightened that you'd die because, Georgie, that fight was nothing like I'd ever seen before.'

Georgie smiled ruefully. 'I remember waking up in a hospital. My head was bandaged so they hid all of the stitches, but on the end of my bed was written Jane X. I knew then that however I had gotten to the hospital, they didn't know my name.'

Sarah shook her head and drank the rest of her tea. 'I didn't tell them because I didn't want anyone to know who you really were or where you had come from. Just in case Bruce came for you. The police questioned me, and I decided that no matter what happened to me, Bruce would go to prison, and he did. As you probably know, they arrested him for murdering your mother. A long list of sexual assaults and other evil crimes were added to his sentence. He got twenty years.'

'Do you think he ever loved my mother?'

Sarah nodded and smiled. 'He did, actually. She was the one he did love, even though I could never get my head around the fact that if he loved her so much, why he didn't stop the punters and offer her a decent life.'

'I don't suppose he could because people like my mum and him wouldn't know what a decent life was, and, to be honest, I don't think it would have suited them.' No sooner had the words come out of her mouth than she realised what she had just said. 'Sorry, Sarah, I wasn't including you in that statement. You were trying to turn your life around. But hearing everything this morning, I feel so fucking awful. I should have helped you when I came out of hospital.'

'Don't feel like that. You went through enough shit as a kid yaself.'

Feeling a sudden sense of closeness with Sarah, Georgie asked the ultimate question. 'Do you know how my mother died?'

'Yes, I do,' she said. 'I think we both know she was strangled.'

'Oh.'

'Georgie, I haven't come here to cause you any grief. You probably had every right to end your mother's life. I wanted to end mine. I tried to take my own life and failed.' She looked down at her wrists. 'I was going to save up my pills and try again. But when I read in a local newspaper that Bruce had been given parole, I made it my mission to look out for you. So I took the job in the coffee shop to make sure he didn't come for you.'

'*Really?* Thank you, Sarah. You cannot begin to imagine how knowing all of this helps me. I honestly was beginning to think I was going mad.'

'You don't seem very worried about Bruce, though.'

'He's a lot older now. He doesn't scare me, Sarah, and having listened to your account of what happened that day, I am less afraid of him now. I learned so much more in the Army, so maybe he will come for me, but he'll come off worse this time. In fact, I believe he was watching me from the end of the garden a few days ago.'

'Are you not in the least bit scared?'

'No, I've faced men a lot worse in my life, believe me. I'm glad you told me everything because at least I will be ready if he does come for me.'

'Georgie, about the job in the coffee shop. I could do with the money, and I liked it there. And I would like to spend time with you. I just wish I could have run away with you the day that bastard stuck a needle in your arm.'

Georgie stared. 'Why didn't you, Sarah?'

'Your mum came for you. Bruce was with her. You were asleep on the sofa. I told them that if they ever hurt you, injected you, or raped you, I would go to the police, and if they didn't listen, I would go to the papers. Or kill them one by one.'

Georgie raised her eyebrows. '*Kill them?*'

‘Yeah, it wasn’t an empty threat, but it didn’t do me much good. Bruce broke my jaw, my arm, and two of my fingers.’

Georgie could feel her eyes filling again. ‘Shit, you took that for me?’

‘Georgie, you were a child my girl’s age. It was the least I could do.’

‘Well, you did save me. If you haven’t dragged me away, Bruce would probably have chopped my fucking head off.’

‘Who knows? And . . . er, about the job?’

Georgie chuckled. ‘Yeah, and I think you deserve a fucking pay rise. Call it compensation for a near-death experience.’

CHAPTER TWENTY-NINE

Dixie-Lee was still dozing on the bottom bunk. She'd returned to prison during the early morning hours but she hadn't fallen asleep right away. Patsy had been kind enough to creep around the cell until she dropped a spoon and startled her.

'Cup o' tea, pretty girl?' asked Patsy, when she spotted Dixie-Lee's eyes wide open.

'Yes, please.'

'Right, I've got stuff to tell ya, kiddo.'

Dixie-Lee pushed off her covers and swung her legs around. She stretched and yawned before blinking to focus. 'Go on. Hit me with it.'

'The girls are up in arms, they are. Clucking like chickens, would you believe.'

With a frown indicating that Dixie-Lee didn't know what that meant, Patsy sighed. 'A fucking science lesson, I guess, is needed.' She made Dixie-Lee a mug of tea and offered her a custard cream biscuit. To her delight, Dixie-Lee refused the biscuit, so Patsy greedily dipped it into her own tea and wolfed it down. 'So clucking, then. Look, the druggies have been given an alternative drug. It's called methadone and the medics hand it out every day. It's supposed to help them get off the hard stuff, but, to be honest, most end up leaving prison addicted to methadone and a lot revert to heroin 'cos methadone won't give them that high feeling. So when a heroin addict gets a sniff that there's the hard stuff around, they ditch the methadone and go for the brown powder. When that supply has been stopped, then you'll have a prison full of clucking women.'

Dixie-Lee blew over the surface of her tea before taking a sip. She knew she had to liven up for this information to make any sense. 'So why was the supply chain stopped?' she asked, even though she guessed the reason, but she didn't want to presume anything, especially in prison, because this was a whole other world to her.

'Aha, and there, kiddo, is the crux of the gossip. Bianca has promised the girls that the brown gear is on its way, and believe me, Dixie-Lee, if she is lying, then the screws will have to place her in solitary for her own safety.'

Dixie-Lee clapped her hands. 'Good, fucking good, an' all, the bitch.'

'Well, that's the first time I've seen you seriously react to Bianca! Now you've found your fire in ya belly, d'ya fancy going to the canteen for breakfast? It'll only be porridge and toast, but it gets us out of here.'

'I'll get dressed, and then after brekky, I'll have a shower. I stink, what with the fucking police cell, police car, and those pigs.'

Patsy initially chuckled, then her face turned serious. 'Ya know, swearing doesn't suit ya, kiddo, with your little sweet face and those pretty lips. Nah, swearing and acting lairy doesn't go with your persona.'

With a shrug, Dixie-Lee replied, 'Being sweet doesn't get me anywhere, either. I wanted so much to be a barrister to help the good guys and prosecute the bad guys. But it's all total bollocks anyway. It's like the police are judge and jury and charging a potential villain is number crunching. How could I ever seek to defend or prosecute someone when the police can't even do their job properly? And that's if I ever get out of here.'

'I knew the police had taken you back to the station, but I didn't like to ask about it.'

‘They wanted to charge me with Tyler Malloye’s murder. I didn’t kill him, and I didn’t kill Clifford either. Some random office worker thinks he saw me in a long coat outside near the chambers where I worked. Anyway, the fact is the police have reason to think I may have killed Clifford, but they have nothing substantial to say that I killed Tyler. It seems they want to wrap up the case, so I suppose it’s easier to charge me for both murders.’

‘Shit, Dixie-Lee, so *have* they charged you?’

‘No, because I have the best solicitor in the land. Hugh Shields pointed out a few facts, so they are reevaluating the evidence. Because, let’s be real, if they charge me, and my lawyer gets up in court and runs rings around them, they’ll look pretty stupid, and once again, the media attention will be massive considering I have this huge following since I was attacked all those months ago.’

Patsy smiled. ‘Well, that’s a good thing, ain’t it?’

‘Yeah.’ Dixie-Lee sighed. ‘But I’m still here, and I still have Bianca’s mob ready to—’

‘Oh no, listen to me, kiddo. I know Bianca wanted you to plead guilty. And I know you wouldn’t tell me the nature of the threat, but I assume she threatened to kill you if you didn’t.’

Dixie-Lee’s eyes grew wide, but she remained quiet; she wasn’t going to let on that Bianca threatened to kill her family.

‘My mate Keni, a tough woman, a very dangerous woman, in fact, is in here. Bianca tried to buy her, offering all sorts to instil fear into you to make you plead guilty, but why the fuck she wants you to do that is anyone’s guess.’

‘Maybe, Patsy, because she knows who the killer is and wants me to take the rap to save this other person from jail time.’

Patsy stepped back and opened her mouth in shock. ‘Shit, really?’

‘Well, of course. So this Keni is gonna hurt me, is she?’

‘No, babe, definitely not. Keni is my mate. She owes me, and she won’t hurt you because, as God is my witness, if Keni touches you, there will be another murder, either mine or hers. ’Cos she promised me, and I don’t take too kindly to broken promises. Besides, she thinks Bianca is a plant.’

‘Is she a plant?’

‘No, ’course not, but Keni don’t know that I put it in her head that Bianca is.’

Dixie-Lee slid her tracksuit over her bony hips and pulled the top over her vest.

‘That drowns you. They did that to make you look small and pathetic, ya know.’

‘Do I, though?’

‘Yeah, ya do, actually, but don’t you worry about it, kiddo. You’ve got me, babe.’

‘Yes, Auntie Patsy.’

As they walked along the corridor towards the canteen area, they saw Keni marching their way.

‘What’s occurring, Keni? You don’t look very happy.’

‘I fucking *ain’t* happy. That bitch promised to have someone put money in my account. But she ain’t. She just said to give it a couple more days, and she’ll have it in there. The fucking girls are in a right state ’cos she promised them gear. And I’ve got to fill out my sheet for all me bits and pieces, and with not a bean in my account, I can’t even have a fucking Pot Noodle. That woman’s a right cunt!’

‘Have you bashed her up?’

‘Nah, in case she *does* put a few quid in.’ Keni looked Dixie-Lee up and down. ‘And you’re the one I’m supposed to be terrorising, ain’t ya?’

‘This is Dixie-Lee, Keni, and, yes, she is.’

Dixie-Lee put her hand out to shake Keni's, but Keni just laughed. 'Polite an' all. Don't worry, love, I won't cause you any trouble. Patsy and me go way back.' She laughed again. 'And, see, that bitch, Miss Fucking Rubber Lips. I swear I'll have her if that money ain't in my account. She's playing the long game, though. I'll give her that. She ain't asked me about the bodies yet. Anyway, I'm fucking fuming. I don't have much, do I, the cow.'

'Keni, I was given a bag of bits. Patsy ticked a load of items on my canteen sheet for me. My family have put money in my account for far more than I need. I've got Pot Noodles. I don't even *like* Pot Noodles.'

'Yeah?'

Patsy rolled her eyes. 'Fucking hell, I thought I was getting them.'

'Keni hasn't got anything, Patsy, and I've got a lot.' She smiled. 'Have mine, Keni, and if you need money, I'll talk to my mum. She will help you out, considering you're helping me.'

Keni's face lit up, her cheeks blushed, and her eyes glistened. 'You're lovely, you, ain't ya.'

After Dixie-Lee gave given Keni three Pot Noodles and some biscuits, Patsy and Dixie-Lee made their way to the canteen. 'Keni is right. Ya know, you *are* lovely. Don't let prison change ya. It's changed most of us, but don't let it affect you.'

However, prison life was changing her. Dixie-Lee knew it. At first, she had been terrified hearing Bianca tell Dulcie to cut her ear off. It was so undeserved and wicked, and the fact that she didn't have the strength to fight Dulcie and Blondie frustrated her. But she'd had a lot of time to think and work things out. Now, she was more level-headed than she'd ever been, she had her wits about her, and she had Patsy by her side.

The canteen was busy, and the tables were full because unbeknown to Dixie-Lee, they would have chocolate doughnut day every so often, and today was the day.

Patsy was eager to get to the serving hatch. Her stomach was rumbling and her mouth was salivating because there was nothing better than a chocolate doughnut.

However, Dixie-Lee was watching and studying the dynamics in the room. She saw one of the officers march across the canteen towards two officers who were loitering together and watching the inmates.

Dixie-Lee focused on what the officer was saying to the other two. She observed that their demeanour had changed and then she noticed that when their eyes shot in Bianca's direction, they looked annoyed. The shorter screw crossed her arms and tightened her lips. The taller blonde officer shot her chin forward. Dixie-Lee could just make out the words – *the money didn't arrive, Bianca lied.*

Dixie-Lee looked across at Bianca, who seemed to have a stream of women trying to get her attention, but Bianca's smile was fake. Dixie-Lee knew a forced smile when she saw one, since she had studied body language.

As if Bianca could read Dixie-Lee's mind, she looked up and straight at her. However, she didn't seem too confident because she looked away as soon as she locked eyes.

Dixie-Lee knew this was her chance to act.

Leaving the queue, she stormed towards the table where Bianca was seated. 'Oi, you, ya fucking lying cunt!'

The room fell silent, and Bianca jumped up.

Dixie-Lee turned to see if the officers were going to step in, but they didn't. They weren't backing Bianca now and she knew it.

Patsy left the queue and stood by Dixie-Lee's side. 'I'm fucking missing a doughnut for this,' she whispered in Dixie-Lee's ear.

All her life, Dixie-Lee had seen how her mother reacted to a situation. She would stand her ground and have this immense power to have anyone turn themselves inside out. Being her mother's daughter, she believed if she had an ounce of her mother's gumption and fight, she would sort this shit out herself.

'You're making one huge mistake, Deacon. Now, do yourself a big favour and fuck right off and away from my table. You are enough to give me indigestion, ya silly little prat.'

'Aw, give you indigestion. I'll give you more than fucking indigestion, you fucking bully.'

Patsy stared at Dixie-Lee as if she was seeing another person; the sweet young woman looked like a psychopath. Her eyes were cold and unfeeling and locked on Bianca, her hands were balled into fists, and her face was white, but not through fear but wrath. She'd only seen that look once before, and that was on Georgie's face.

Keni suddenly marched through the canteen and stood a foot away from Bianca.

This gave Bianca a false sense of security and so she upped her game. 'You make threats, little girl, and be prepared to face the fucking consequences. You think you can get away with talking to me like that, yeah?'

'Answer this question, Bianca! Who killed the barrister and Tyler Malloye?'

'You did, bitch! You killed my stepson.'

Dixie-Lee clocked the nervous twitch in Bianca's right eyelid. 'Who killed the barrister and Tyler?' she asked again. This time, her voice was raised a pitch.

'Are you deaf? I said you did.'

‘I’m going to ask you again, Bianca, and if you say “you did” one more time, I’ll . . .’ She paused and looked to see where the officers were, but they were nowhere to be seen.

Bianca jumped in. ‘Ha! It looks to me like you have no protection, Deacon. There are no screws to break up a fight or to wipe your shitty arse. Because you will shit yaself, I can guarantee you that.’ She looked at Keni and grinned. ‘I told you, Deacon, there is a pecking order, and you’re at the bottom. Now, I am not going to repeat myself. I’ll make it clear that you killed my stepson and the barrister. You and I know what you were asked to do and the consequences if you choose not to.’

It was Dixie-Lee’s turn to laugh.

But Patsy whispered, ‘What the fuck are you *doing*?’

Ignoring Patsy, Dixie-Lee carried on. ‘You’ve made a lot of promises to a lot of people, Bianca.’ She waved her hand round. ‘But you lied! Nothing is coming in here for the girls, is there. Just a load of IOUs.’

‘Shut the fuck up. You don’t know what you’re talking about.’

‘Oh, I do. I know how it works. I’ve done my research.’

‘I’ve done my research,’ Bianca mimicked, in a childish voice.

But it didn’t faze Dixie-Lee. She smirked and continued. ‘You see, you are nothing in prison unless you have one of three things.’ She ticked these off one by one by using her fingers. ‘First, notoriety, as in celebrity status, which you haven’t, not even close. Second, if you can fight like, say, Keni there. And third, if you have a supply of contraband, enough to pay for your protection and be able to swan around like the queen bee.’

Bianca narrowed her eyes, now suddenly feeling very uneasy. Shooting a side look at Keni again, she noticed the woman was grinning. *Why was she smiling? Shouldn’t she be tearing across the table and taking Deacon down?*

Seeing the crowd closing in, Bianca suddenly felt as though she was now in a zombie world of characters just like those in *The Walking Dead*. Her table was surrounded by glaring women daring to take a piece of her.

But no one was looking daggers at Dixie-Lee. In fact, a few of them were now standing next to her with crossed arms or balled fists by their side.

Bianca knew that if she didn't stand her ground and show this kid or anyone else she wasn't afraid, her life inside would be a living hell. Besides, she wasn't used to not being at the top. She'd always had money and a husband who had status. Pushing her shoulders back, she said, 'You, ya cunt, you killed them.'

From nowhere, Keni grabbed the back of Bianca's head and smashed her face down on the table. And then, as if Bianca was on a witch's ducking stool, she pulled her head back and glared at her face.

Bianca's mouth had split open, and her nose was pissing blood.

'Not so pretty now, are ya, duck features?' laughed Keni, who was still gripping Bianca's hair.

'Who killed them, Bianca?' said Dixie-Lee, as cool as a cucumber.

The fear enveloped Bianca. She had nowhere to go and no one to protect her; Keni was now her enemy. How the hell this kid had managed this, she couldn't comprehend.

'I don't know. I swear to you I don't know.' Her shoulders sagged and her eyes begged to be believed.

Keni smashed her face down again. '*Liar*, you bitch!' she hissed in her ear.

However, this time, it wasn't Bianca's nose or lip that was bleeding. Blood was pouring from her head. A substantial purple lump rapidly grew from her forehead, while her eyes rolled back.

'Oh shit, not again!' said Keni. 'I think I overdid it.'

Suddenly, Bianca opened her eyes and threw her hands to her face. 'Stop, please stop,' she cried, as she felt the blood dripping down her chin and the cartilage in her nose, which was already fragile since her last nose job, collapse.

'Who killed them, Bianca? You know who they are because you wanted me to plead guilty and threatened to hurt my mum and my family if I didn't.' Dixie-Lee smiled. 'But you have no clout now. No kudos within your family to stand by you. So why, Bianca? Why did you want me to plead guilty?'

Patsy wanted to join in the fight, hearing that Bianca had threatened Dixie-Lee's family, but she had to give it to the youngster. She was bravely holding her own.

Bianca held up her hands in defeat. 'Okay. Let me speak.'

Keni let go of Bianca's head and shoved her between the shoulder blades. 'You'd better tell the truth, or you'll get eaten alive in here.'

'Look, I swear, I don't *know*!' she screeched.

Keni grabbed her hair again.

'Please stop. Let me explain. I thought I knew who killed them, but he came to visit me, and with a Dear Jane letter, he also explained it wasn't him.'

'Dear Jane?' Dixie-Lee whispered to Patsy.

'Yeah, it means he dumped her fake raggedy arse.'

Bianca's eyes welled up with tears as she looked at her hands filled with blood. 'I thought he loved me, but he didn't. He said he didn't need you to take the blame because he didn't kill my stepson or that barrister. He had an alibi.'

'Hang on. A man? You thought it was a *man*?'

'Yes.' She sniffled like a child. 'I thought it was my boyfriend.'

'You'd better tell me why you thought your so-called boyfriend had killed them, then.'

Bianca looked around the room, but there was nowhere to escape. The screws were turning a blind eye, and she knew finally that she was royally fucked. 'Because now Tommy's dead, that file that his lawyers were holding for him containing his last will and testament is missing. If it can be found, it will either make me a rich woman or will fuck me up for good. And also, there is supposed to be a key code to a safe deposit box and in it a load of diamonds worth a fucking lot of money. I thought he would have done anything to get his hands on that will and the diamonds for me. It turns out I was wrong.'

'But you're inside, Bianca, making promises to everyone that you can supply whatever they need, so if he was so innocent, why would he send you contraband? And clearly, he has the power to have officers, no less, eating out of your hand. Oh, and that is past tense, by the way.'

'Fuck off, Dixie-Lee. That's none of your business. You've got what you wanted. Your family is no longer a target, so back off.' The cockiness in her voice was her biggest let-down and today was no different.

'My family!' Dixie-Lee yelled, jumping up on the table and taking two long strides before pulling her leg back and kicking Bianca in the face as though she was booting a football. As Bianca went down, Dixie-Lee jumped on top of her in a frenzy and punched the life out of her. It was Keni who eventually pulled her off.

Out of breath, Dixie-Lee looked down at the mess she had made of the woman's face, and for a moment, she felt glory. The surrounding women had goaded her on with every vicious punch. But this wasn't who she was. It was only when Bianca had reminded her that her family was being threatened that it was like a red rag to a bull.

Looking now at Bianca, Dixie-Lee could see that she was a pathetic, whimpering shell of a woman. She had knocked the bravado clean out of her, and so Bianca would know now what it felt like to be at the bottom of the pecking order.

However, all the fighting hadn't given her the knowledge she needed. Who was it who had actually killed the barrister and Tyler? Before she had a chance to ask more questions, a surge of officers came charging in and broke up the mob of women.

But by this time, Patsy had managed to drag Dixie-Lee and Keni away before they were thrown into solitary confinement.

CHAPTER THIRTY

It was still dark when Steve Elison marched briskly from his car to the chambers. Pulling up the collar of his cashmere coat as protection against the icy wind, he rubbed his hands together, wishing he was wearing his woollen gloves.

He regretted cutting his trip short; he'd told everyone that he'd gone deep-sea diving, which usually meant he'd gone on a long-haul holiday and was not reachable. However, he hadn't. He had driven down to his French cottage in Bergerac and spent two days gardening and shutting the place down for the winter. He'd also removed a photo that he'd had framed, which, at the time, had meant a lot. It showed him on a boat, his face beaming and glowing in the sun; he looked happy. And although she wasn't in the photo, she was behind the camera, merrily laughing and snapping away. It was a reminder of how the two of them had snuck away for the weekend. *Was it the secrecy and sense of excitement that he'd loved, or had he loved her for who she was as a person?* The thrill had certainly added to his plain formal existence. He'd often questioned why he'd worked so hard, and then he thought of his nest eggs – his French holiday home and London apartment.

Combining the profits, he could live abroad in the Caribbean and start a diving school there. He didn't need a woman when he was underwater; the sense of adventure was quite enough. In fact, the thrill of underwater exploring was everything he required to feed his happiness. It was almost like an addiction.

Approaching the chambers, he saw it was in darkness. The street was gloomy and the weather inclement; it was yet another reason to make a change and follow his dream of living in the sun.

As he unlocked the door and tapped in the code, the lights to the entrance came on.

'Would you take these?' came a voice from behind him, which made him jump. As he spun round, he saw the postman, his cheeks red and glossy from the cold.

'Sure,' he replied, relieving the man of a pile of mainly brown envelopes.

'You'd think my load would be lighter, considering most people use emails.'

Steve wasn't the type to engage in pointless conversation so he smiled, nodded, closed the door, and walked across to the reception desk. He'd only popped in to collect Bianca's file before his legal visit. He had intended to put off the visit with her because he was going to be away, but then he decided that he would keep the visiting slot to put a particular issue to bed. He really didn't want to see her again. And he wouldn't after this visit: he would tell her he was done with representing her.

Before heading into his office, he decided to thumb through the mail and save Natalia some work. Most of the letters were addressed to Cathy, but one grabbed his attention. He placed the other letters on the desk and stared at the cream-coloured envelope; the handwriting was so familiar that he turned it over, and there was the prison stamp. But the letter wasn't addressed to him.

Checking that no one had followed him inside the building, he took the letter to his office. He closed the door behind him, drew the blind, and clicked on the desk lamp. The room was warm, and instantly, his nose ran. He used his handkerchief to wipe away the hanging drip and then dabbed his burning eye before he stared again at the handwriting. Curiosity outweighed the legal implications of opening a private letter. But, even so, he bit his lip in hesitation before using the letter opener. He paused, took a deep breath, and unfolded the letter.

It started with **To my forever Ollie,** and before he read anymore, he knew who it was from. Bianca had always started her letters to him with *To my forever Stevie.* He wondered if she actually had any feelings for anyone because, evidently, the sentiment was cloned. *Had she at one time called her husband her 'forever Tommy'?* When her husband was first in prison, she needed Steve's help and she did so again on other occasions. But that was when Bianca had lured him in by her ever inventive flirtatious ways. She was sexy, no two ways about it; she was very seductive, and great fun. He thought back to their brief affair and tried to recall if they'd ever shared an intellectual conversation, but looking back and seeing this letter, he realised that she was just a user. She was nothing more than a prostitute. He'd only recognised her as a master manipulator when it was nearly too late. She had given him false hope by showing him a mental model of their life together if Tommy was out of the way. The vision she painted was without question a beautiful bed of roses, but when she hinted that if he, as Tommy's barrister, made it easier for the prosecution to win the case against her husband, then, with her husband locked up, their lives would be bliss.

He shuddered at the very thought that he had even considered it. It had been a fleeting mad moment while she was performing oral sex on him.

He slammed his fist down on the desk in disgust. How could he have been so pathetically stupid to be tempted by a woman who clearly had no scruples about getting what she wanted – her husband inside while she lived in their mansion spending his money and having enough freedom to fuck around with every Tom, Dick, and Harry?

Steve remembered his very first meeting with Tommy and Bianca Malloye. It was at the behest of Hugh Shields who wanted him to take on a case on behalf of Tommy. That was almost ten years ago.

He had expected Tommy to be a hard-nosed, gruff, and uneducated fighter. But that was not the case. He was actually soft-spoken which seemed somewhat at variance with his vast build, boxer's flat nose, and red hair.

Bianca looked different at that time. She had real natural beauty. Without all the cosmetic surgery she'd gone for in the last few years to keep herself looking younger than she was.

There was only one reason that Steve could think of for why she hung on to Tommy like a leech. It was probably because what Tommy lacked in looks, he made up for in wealth.

By that time, Tommy already had a string of previous offences to his name, but this charge was far more serious. He had assaulted two men with a meat cleaver, leaving them disabled for life.

As it turned out, the trial was over in two days. He had managed to convince a jury that Tommy had acted in self-defence. One of the men he assaulted was a butcher, so it was put to the jury that Tommy had wrestled for the meat cleaver, and in doing so, he had injured the two men.

When Tommy was found not guilty, the press – who were broadly in favour of Tommy Malloye's colourful life in any case – were able to spin to the public that this case highlighted how the police had fitted their narrative to the crime.

A few years later, Tommy contacted Steve for his services again when both he and Bianca were on remand for a serious fraud racket. Evidently, Bianca had gotten too greedy. She'd been a reckless spender of Tommy's cash by blatantly going out and purchasing a flash car – and a different designer handbag for every day of the week. It didn't go unnoticed. Eventually, tongues wagged, and the police arrested them both. Tommy served two years and Bianca eighteen months.

Fast forward to a year back from now and Tommy was arrested and charged with armed robbery. And yet the evidence against him seemed so blatant as if someone had set him up.

He recalled that it was while Tommy was on remand at HMP Belmarsh that Bianca had then charmed her way into his affections. At the time, it was fun, risky, and wrong. He had a legitimate reason to see Bianca when Tommy was in custody being that she was Tommy's wife. However, their meetings, which at first started out as purely professional ones, entered a new phase. While he was advising Bianca on the stages of her husband's case, she was offering far more in return. It was a brief affair – barely a few weeks at that – and only sexual; he wasn't emotionally invested in her, especially when he began to suspect the truth about Tommy's case.

The case was labelled by the press as the Halloween Robbery. It created a lot of attention at the time because it was the infamous Tommy Malloye who was arrested for armed robbery at the local post office in Orpington.

An anonymous call to the police followed by them checking his car barely an hour after the robbery took place had Tommy in heaps of trouble. When the police went to his house and searched his car, they found a gun and a mask in the boot. Only his fingerprints were found on the mask. There were none on the gun. But the implications for him were dire, since being a well-known gangster, he obviously wasn't a stranger to the police.

Tommy's arrest saw him contact Hugh Shields once more, who, in turn, approached himself to take on his case at trial.

When he looked into it, he had a niggling suspicion that Tommy may have been framed, although, at the time, he had to force the thought to the back of his mind.

It was during his final legal visit while Tommy was on remand in Belmarsh awaiting trial that alarm bells rang. Tommy Malloye, the hardened gangster, was dressed in a tatty prison tracksuit. His face was drawn and washed out, and he was frightened. Tommy had put all his trust in him and he made just the one request: to look out for Bianca for him.

After returning from Belmarsh, he immediately went to see Bianca to tell her what Tommy had said. The minute she heard this, she jumped up and down on the spot, clapping her hands in glee. 'Oh my God. That's fucking fantastic! What I need are those diamonds of his put in my name. You *can* make that happen, can't you, Stevie?'

'Sorry, Bianca. Tommy didn't mean he was going to hand over his wealth to you. He suggested I take control of your *spending*. He wanted me to stop all the credit cards and to set up an allowance for you, for your own good.'

How her face changed in that moment was something he would never forget. The sweet and sensual smile tightened to a raging grimace. Her eyes narrowed, and her top lip curled into a snarl. He had never seen anything like it. She'd instantly switched into some kind of monster by grabbing his shirt collar and trying to shake him. In the process, she'd clawed his chin. Even though he was bleeding, she didn't care and continued screaming, 'Why? Why? You're supposed to be *helping me*! I need that money. I need those diamonds!'

Those words, which were imprinted on his brain, made him realise that she'd had a game plan all along.

He suspected it was she who had made sure that Tommy's fingerprints were on the same mask that the police found in the boot of his car. An identical Halloween mask to the one the public recognised in the armed robbery in the post office raid. And to give more credence to the set-up, he assumed that she would have placed the gun in his boot as well. Where she went wrong was to assume her husband's prints were on the gun as well as on the mask.

Whether his instincts about Bianca's betrayal were correct, he knew that he had to be sure of Tommy's guilt or otherwise. So his conscience and diligence compelled him to spend days playing detective, until, finally, he found footage of Tommy in a shop twenty miles away from the crime – evidence that was eventually used to clear his name.

Of course, Tommy had no idea that he had married a wife so callous and cruel. And it wasn't his place to tell Tommy what an absolute arsehole she really was.

So, disgusted with her, he finished their relationship there and then. But for months after, she wouldn't let up. She threatened to expose him for their affair. Having sweated over it, he eventually concluded that she wouldn't dare to do this because then Tommy would know and who knows what he would have done to her. He was aware that Tommy would forgive her overspending and greedy ways, but he wouldn't forgive so easily if she had been unfaithful. That all seemed a lifetime ago, but it was in fact only a year, and now Tommy was dead.

With Bianca in the frame for her husband's murder, he knew in all conscience that he couldn't ever defend her when he was aware she would have resorted to doing this for money.

He shook his head as he stared at the letter. It was obvious that Bianca hadn't changed. Not one bit. Even in the police station she had been trying to seduce him again. When the sexy talk, the smiles, and the licking of her enlarged lips failed, she begged and pleaded with him to reconcile, yet he felt nothing. It wasn't until she threatened once again to expose their affair – and she'd said she had photos hidden somewhere to prove it – that he considered it would not only be the end of his career but it could possibly implicate him in Tommy's murder. How could he run the risk? Bianca was too unpredictable for him to second-guess her moves or even her motives. He had never been wary of anyone, but Bianca was dangerous. She used people and could easily blackmail them. He felt the threat she'd made in the police station was real. After all, now Tommy was dead, Bianca didn't have to worry about him anymore if she exposed their affair.

And, stupidly, he'd acted on it. She had made him take seven grand to a man, a known criminal, who would take two thousand for himself but ensure she had everything she needed to be safe in prison. She had made it sound as though it was the least he could do. And he did it. He took the cash he had kept in his apartment from the sale of his old car and met with the man. A few words were exchanged, an acknowledging nod, and the deal was done.

He leaned back on his chair and rubbed his throbbing temples. He would now meet with Bianca to tell her he would never succumb to blackmail again. She would have to find another barrister because he would be taking a sabbatical. Tucking the letter inside his pocket, he snatched up his briefcase and left the office.

As he was walking down the staircase to the entrance, he saw Cathy entering the chambers. She seemed flustered as she removed her scarf and stormed towards the stairs, not noticing he was even there.

'Cathy!'

She stopped dead and gasped when she saw him. 'Steve, you frightened me. Christ!'

'Sorry, why are you in such a flap? At, um . . .' He glanced at his watch. 'At this ungodly hour in the morning.'

Her shoulders drooped, and a sigh of resignation left her mouth. 'Steve, I am in a bind.' She threw her hands in the air in despair and sat on the bottom of the staircase. 'Everything in my life, everything I have worked so damned hard for, is about to fall down around my feet.'

Steve joined her on the step. 'Cathy, we have worked alongside each other for many years, and if there is anyone you can trust, it's me, so what's the matter?'

Cathy's hair was in a messy bun, a look new for her. She wiped a few beads of sweat away from her forehead.

'I received a letter from the prison from your client, Bianca Malloye. It was sent to my home address.'

'Your home address? How does she know where you live?'

'She's either followed me or had me bloody followed.'

'Go on.'

'She's fucking blackmailing me, Steve. A bloody gangster's moll has the damned audacity to threaten me.'

'With what, Cathy?'

She glared spitefully at him. 'And you had to ask *that question*, didn't you?'

'Cathy, don't get annoyed with me. I'm just trying to help.'

'Are you? Will you really?' she said, with a sarcastic undertone.

He slid his arm around her shoulders. 'Well, let's put it like this. She's blackmailing me too.'

'*What?*' she screeched.

'So, tell me, what does she have over you? Because believe me, Cathy, I won't let her get away with it. She'll rot in hell before I allow her to hurt us anymore.'

Unexpectedly, Cathy McGowan – the formidable London barrister – the hugely respected iron maiden – broke down as she collapsed into his arms in a flood of tears. Steve awkwardly pulled her close and hugged her.

After a moment or so, she gathered herself together, wiped her smudged mascara, and took a deep breath. 'Steve, you need to know something. I am, well, I *was* dating someone. I have been, in fact, for two years. Of course, it was all hush-hush.'

'And Bianca saw you with this person, did she? I assume this person would compromise your position as a barrister?'

She nodded. 'Oh, Steve, I thought when the police charged her with Tommy Malloye's murder that that would be the end of her. Let me go back a step. Bianca met me for coffee, and since I represented her in that fraud case, way back, I assumed it was about business. Anyway, she asked me if I would show her her husband's last will and testament. She thought she had the right as his wife.'

'No!'

Cathy nodded. 'I didn't think much of it at the time. It was a few days before Tommy's murder, and I have no doubt now that it was at the hands of her.'

Steve's eyes widened. 'Shit! She has some bottle, that woman.'

'Anyway, I said to her "absolutely not". And as I didn't even know where the file was being held, I thought no more about it. Being the wife of a gangster and a feral bitch, she was probably used to pushing her luck. When I represented her in that fraud trial, I have to say I didn't like her then. I never have. I could probably have had her acquitted if I had spent more time on the case, but that was one I was happy to lose.'

'So, tell me, who were you seeing? And you can tell me, Cathy, because I will share something with you too.'

She raised her well-defined eyebrow. 'Really?'

'Yes, because we need to help each other now.' He looked around him and pointed to the name on the entrance door of the chambers. 'We didn't build this for the fun of it. I won't have a stupid tart take it away.'

'Okay, Steve.' She sighed. 'The man I was seeing was a judge.'

'Oh shit! Have you any cases with a conflict of interest?'

'I guess so. In a way.'

'What do you mean?'

'The problem is that it's Clifford's father.'

Steve jolted as if he'd had an electric shock. 'Are you kidding me?'

'No, of course I'm not bloody kidding. Why do you think I took the little prick on, eh? I only did it for his father's benefit. Apparently, Bianca saw us together. I can only guess she must have followed me, but I don't know for sure. Anyway, she sent me a letter telling me she knows that it was Clifford's father who I was seeing, and since I am representing Dixie-Lee Deacon, then I will certainly be disbarred.'

'She blackmailed me too because, Cathy—'

'I know, Steve, I'm not blind. You took her out for drinks. I saw you once.'

'It was more than that, Cathy. We had an affair. She used me to try to get her hands on Tommy's money. Look, I'm going to see her in prison. We have a legal visit booked. I think I need to have a conversation with her. And it's going to be the last one. That's for sure.'

Cathy looked at her watch and jumped up. 'Shit, I have a meeting at the prison with Dixie-Lee later today. I spent half the night writing up a statement.'

Steve frowned. 'A bit early, isn't it, for that? Her court case hasn't been listed yet.'

‘She told me she wanted to plead guilty to manslaughter, and I thought that was a good idea. We had enough evidence to get her off on a self-defence plea.’

‘What are you talking about? Dixie-Lee didn’t kill him! She’s not that type of person. Clifford tried to *rape* her. He’s done it before, and it was glossed over. I fucking hated that weaselly little prick. I should never have sent her to the chambers that evening. The file could have waited. And I think it was Bianca who put it in my head that a lot of people would be after the bloody truth, but the only member of the Malloye family who came for it was Tyler. And now, he’s dead. And the file is still missing. So Dixie-Lee’s efforts were all in vain.’ He gave Cathy a serious deep frown. ‘Tell me, what the hell were you thinking in letting her plead guilty?’

‘Because, Steve, she was almost certainly going to be convicted. Although the evidence is circumstantial, the chances of us getting Dixie-Lee off scot-free are almost zero.’

‘And the judge convinced you of this, I suppose?’

‘No, well . . . Clifford’s father is a persuasive man. His influence over the presiding judge would make life very difficult for Dixie-Lee.’

‘And he has that much power over your professional opinion and duty, does he?’

‘No, but you must understand, he is a powerful man. Steve, I know that for sure because he even made his son’s rape allegation disappear. What a mess! I not only liked the man, but I thought it could go somewhere – marriage. I was blinded by his charms. Ha! Me! Who’d have thought it. And I am afraid to say that my feelings may have got in the way of my duty to Dixie-Lee.’

‘Oh fuck!’

‘Yes, Steve, *oh fuck*!’

CHAPTER THIRTY-ONE

When Brodie received a text asking him if he and Mac could return to the Malloye house, he was delighted. There was so much he wanted to discuss with them.

Brodie knocked lightly at Nessa and Michael's door. Mac decided to accompany his brother in case of any trouble because even though they hadn't left on bad terms, Michael and his sons were still potentially dangerous men.

Michael opened the door and ushered them in, and Nessa was quick to greet them. She seemed to have more colour in her cheeks, and her eyes shone, unlike yesterday, when they were dull, much like her husband's.

'Take a seat, the pair of you,' she said, pointing to the three-seater sofa. But it was more like a two-seater when Brodie and Mac sat side by side on it.

'Nessa, make the lads a drink, would you now?'

'Tea or coffee, boys?'

Brodie leaned forwards. He didn't feel comfortable slumped down into a sofa that was past its sell-by date due to worn-out springs. 'Anything for me will be fine, Nessa.'

'Me too, Nessa,' said Mac. 'Any cake to go with it?' Mac beamed, knowing there was because he could smell the baking.

'I've made a coffee cake. It was me Tommy's favourite. I'll fetch a slice. I'll make that a good chunk for you, Mac.'

'That'll be great, Nessa, and I'll happily have Brodie's as well.' He winked. 'He's not a big cake eater.'

Nessa hurried back to the kitchen to give Michael a chance to speak.

Instead, Michael reached into the front pocket of his jeans and retrieved a crumpled piece of paper. 'Here, this may well give you the answers you need.'

Brodie took it, and Mac leaned over his shoulder to see that it was a receipt from a local jeweller.

'I know this place,' said Brodie. 'I bought me first watch from there. I saved up the money from me chores. It was a watch with a leather strap. Until clumsy nuts Mac broke it.'

'Nessa found the receipt in our spare room. Tommy stayed here a little while ago. He came to visit us. I think it was our anniversary or something.'

Mac pointed to the last part of the receipt. Sixty pounds had been added to the bill for detailed engraving.

Brodie turned the receipt over, but there was nothing on the back.

'So the big question is, did he buy the watch for himself or for someone else?' asked Mac.

Nessa entered the living room with a tray holding four cups, a huge teapot with a crocheted cover, and on a separate plate there was a large slice of cake for Mac.

Mac didn't wait for an invitation. He quickly took the dainty floral plate with his shovel-like hands, gripped the cake, turning it around and admiring it, before he took a large mouthful. 'Oh my God, this is delicious, Nessa. Dare I say it now, but it's better than me ma's.'

She lifted her chin and smiled. 'I've always prided myself on my baking. Making and baking, that's me.'

Brodie was still looking at the receipt and reading the details of the watch before he googled it. 'Bloody hell, watches like this one are expensive. A good few grand at least. And the date on this receipt shows Tommy bought it only a month ago. So who was this bought for?'

'Yes, Brodie, you've cottoned on. My son, he didn't buy that watch for Bianca because he was filing for divorce at the time. And so what we need to know is who buys a watch and has it engraved, unless, of course, it was his dark humour and it read: *Bianca, you are a sly old bitch. Wear this watch to remind yourself of the fact.*'

Mac laughed and was joined by Brodie. 'He could have sent a nickel-plated necklace that said the same but that would have given her a right nasty rash.'

'Well, there it is, Brodie. I reckon that is the key to whoever my Tommy was seeing on the quiet. I only hope it helps you to discover who killed our Tyler because we're pretty fecking sure Bianca murdered our son. God love him.'

Mac nudged Brodie. 'Tell her.'

'We got a call last night from Hugh Shields, our lawyer, who is heavily involved in the case. He has a friendly copper on the inside who keeps him updated with developments.'

Nessa sat on the edge of the armchair. 'Go on.'

'I'm not sure how you will take it.'

'Aw, just get on wid it,' said Michael, in his broad Irish accent.

'So the issue with Bianca was the timing. Apparently, when the paramedics arrived, Tommy had only been dead a matter of minutes, not even an hour. So whoever killed him wouldn't have had much chance to leave the house and hide the weapon without the street cameras catching them leaving the house.' He raised his finger. 'Now, her statement says she believed someone had broken in via the back of the house. And as yer know, there are fields at the back of their house – nothing more for miles. So the police searched and re-searched that field and then obtained another warrant for the house. They were right. Whoever killed Tommy either wouldn't have got far, or if Bianca had killed Tommy, then it would suggest that the weapon was still in the house.'

‘And?’ said Nessa, impatiently.

‘All the knives in the house went off to forensics. The results came back with every one of them having been bleached.’

‘I know it was her. That cunt never bleached a thing, the dirty fecking whore. The evil bitch. But why did she have to kill him? He never hit her or abused her. My Tommy was good to her. He gave her everything she wanted. I mean, I know things changed after he was put on remand on a false allegation, and to be honest, he hinted to me that she may have been involved. All the fecking woman wanted was money.’ She broke down and covered her eyes with her tea towel.

‘Nessa, at least we know the truth now. All that’s left to understand is what happened to our Tyler. Then we can properly grieve.’

Brodie nodded. ‘We need to know as much as you do, for the sake of our niece and her case. Maybe whoever Tommy was seeing will provide the answers to this puzzle.’

After they drank their tea and Mac finished his cake, they rose from the sofa and went to the front door.

‘Oh, Michael, not to bring up an obvious sore subject, but what was Anne-Marie’s surname?’

‘Why?’

‘Again, Michael, we are trying to get to the bottom of it, and if we have—’

Nessa was quick to interrupt. ‘It was Minster.’

Brodie frowned. ‘Sorry, did you say *Minster*?’

She nodded. ‘Yes, Anne-Marie Minster.’

‘And you are sure the boy was called Oliver?’

‘Aye, that he was, lad. Oliver Minster, and he drove that red Jag,’ said Nessa, confidently.

Michael grabbed Brodie’s arm before they walked away. ‘Do you know him?’

‘I am not sure. I need to make some calls. I’ll be in touch, I swear.’ He held up the receipt. ‘All right to keep this?’

Michael nodded and waved them on.

As soon as they were in the car, Mac piped up, ‘Fucking hell, Brodie, Oliver Minster? That’s more than a coincidence.’

‘Tell me about it, Mac. There’s no way that’s a coincidence. Nessa said he came looking for his father. She described his posh English voice and commented on how good-looking he was. Oliver, who works with Cathy, is all those things, but he doesn’t drive a red Jag.’

‘And you would know, Brodie, because you know who drives what.’

‘Mac, I love a decent car. It’s my thing. I tell you what he does drive, and that’s a silver Jag. It’s a new car with a red leather interior.’

‘Fuck me, Brodie, no one could ever accuse you of stalking women, but cars? Now that’s something else.’

As they parked outside the jewellers in Saint Kieran’s Street in Kilkenny, Brodie called Rohan and placed the phone on speakerphone.

‘Brodie, what’s up? Any news?’

‘Ro, listen, are you still tailing Cathy?’

‘No, I was following Cathy, but I’m not now. I’ve just been back to the jewellers in Hatton Garden, and it turns out she was gifted a watch and a diamond engagement ring, both of which she had to have made smaller. The ring and watch were bought by a judge, no less . . .’

‘So?’

‘The judge is Clifford’s father.’

‘Fecking hell’s bells. Right, she needs to own up to that. What’s she playing at? We can’t have her representing our Dixie-Lee. That’s ridiculous.’

‘So, anything from your end?’

‘Yep, big, Rohan, big.’

‘I’m listening,’

‘Michael Malloye’s illegitimate son he had with Anne-Marie.’

‘Yeah, go on.’

‘It’s fecking Oliver Minster.’

‘What? Are you joking? Hang on, are you sure it’s the same guy?’

‘Of course, that’s why I am calling. Can you run his number plate? Find out where he bought the car, and check if he traded in the red Jag.’

‘I’ll get Hugh on it now.’

‘Rohan, say nothing for now, okay.’

‘Brodie, that goes without saying.’

‘I think I might have a lead on who Tommy’s girlfriend was.’

***

Steve tapped the table waiting for the officers to escort Bianca to the legal visiting room. He had driven through challenging rush-hour traffic and been spoken down to by a jumped-up screw fresh out of nappies, but he had still managed to go through in his mind the conversation he would have with Bianca. It was one thing to blackmail him because he assumed part of it was down to her being angry with him. After all, he had broken up with her. However, it seemed she was now blackmailing Cathy as well. He wasn’t going to roll over and take it. She had pushed him to the brink, and there was no going back.

Eventually, the door opened and two officers escorted the very forlorn-looking Bianca into the room before closing the door behind them.

For a moment, he felt sorry for her, but only because her face was in quite a shocking state. Her hair was all over the place, and her nose was bent and bruised. It wasn’t too dissimilar from a boxer's nose. Her eyes were black and puffy, and the blood and sticky liquid dripping from her lips made it clear that these weren't old wounds. They were fresh. But as soon as she sat down, the same cocky expression swept over her. She wasn't feeling as sorry for herself as most women probably would have, but he knew she wasn't like most women. She was relentless.

'You fucking let me down. Look at the state of my face. You think I can stay alive in this filthy stinking hole with nothing to barter with? I told you to give Nicki Beaton seven grand and then another seven, and that should last me a few months.'

Steve sat with his hands under his legs, leaning forward, watching every sharp look, and listening to every nasty word she spitefully spat.

'You've seriously let me down. I've got women back there ready to claw me fucking eyes out because they're hooked on smack and have no supply.' She twisted her head and glared. 'Are you even listening to me?'

'Oh, I am listening to you, Bianca. Every fucking word coming out of your murderous mouth.'

She dipped her chin in shock. 'What?'

'Is it my turn to speak, Bianca, or do you still have much to say or rather demand?'

His tone and cold words shut her up, and every muscle in her body tensed.

'I know how you operate, Bianca. I know you killed Tommy.'

He witnessed the shock. It turned her face from pink to a deathly white. Her mouth opened but nothing came out.

'There is nothing about you that is even likeable. You are good for nothing except being devious, conniving, sly, and evil. And in my legal profession, I always go that extra mile, but for you, I promise, Bianca, I will fall short of that. So stop with the threats.'

'Say what you like, Stevie, but I will grass you up. I have the photos, so I think I'm calling the shots. You still have a duty to represent me in court. And I know you, Stevie. You hate to lose, and so you will get me off, or those photos will go straight to the press.'

His satisfied smile unnerved her.

'Why are you grinning, Steve? 'Cos if I were in your shoes, I wouldn't be.'

'I'm grinning because this is entertainment for me, watching you acting like you can get one over me, and Cathy, for that matter.'

'*Cathy?* She told you?'

'Yeah, funny that because you never liked her much. I guess you were always a bit jealous of her, but, then again, she is so much more intelligent than you, and a damn sight more attractive in looks and personality. In fact, I think she is a stunner.'

Those words compelled Bianca to leap up off her seat and attack him, by clawing at his face like a wild cat, until he pushed her back and growled, 'Sit down before I call the officers!'

Raging, she had no choice but to do as he said. Her breathing was intense, and her eyes were dark and wild.

'So I'm here to tell you that there is no jury in the land who will believe you are not guilty of murdering your husband. Add to that blackmailing a barrister, two in fact, and you are most likely going to receive a very hefty custodial sentence. You have nothing on Cathy, just a few photos of a barrister and a judge. None of those are as compromising as you think. Believe me: I know! So, do you honestly think the press or the police would be interested in any of your allegations? You're a woman who killed her husband in cold blood! You have a criminal history and have been widowed twice. Both times now, the finger has been pointed at you. You may have got away with it before, but you won't this time. So,

Bianca Malloye, your version of events regarding Cathy or myself wouldn't stick, and blackmailing us will get you another ten years. You wouldn't be eligible for parole for at least thirty years, and what will you be then, eh, Bianca? I'll tell you what – a fucking ugly old woman.'

She leaned back on the chair and folded her arms. 'You will still fight to get me out of prison, though. You're my brief, Stevie.'

'I'm taking a long sabbatical, so I will have to pass your case on to someone else.'

Bianca showed little reaction. 'Fine, I have someone else in mind, anyway.'

Steve removed the letter from his pocket and held it in front of her. 'It wouldn't be Oliver Minster, would it? Or should I say *your forever Ollie*?'

Her eyes widened and then she tried to reach across the table and snatch the letter from him.

Returning it to his pocket, Steve said, 'You are a user, Bianca. You use everyone, but, see, I don't think you used Oliver. I am wondering if it was the other way around. You see, I'm not blind. The man looks like he has just stepped out of a fucking fashion magazine, but what I read in the letter disturbed me, and it incriminates you in Tommy's murder.'

'Fuck off. That letter is private.'

'Not anymore, it's not.' He waved the letter in her face. 'But it has baffled me, Bianca, because how it was written wasn't like the letters you sent to me. In this letter, you were begging him to stay with you. You promised you would do anything for him and that you had carried out the ultimate act for him. But I think we both know what that meant. You killed Tommy for Oliver. This letter, Bianca, shows you were besotted with him, and I have to say I can appreciate most women would be. He is intelligent, extremely so, so Cathy says, and he's very handsome. So that begs the question: what the fuck would he want with you?'

'Shut up, Steve. Ollie loved me. He worshipped me.'

'Yeah, worshipped you so much that he would do anything for you?'

She nodded. 'Yeah, he fucking would.'

'Even kill Tyler?'

Turning her head to the side, her eyes shot back at him.

'You're in shit up to your neck, Bianca.'

'Ollie will defend me in court. You'll see. He'll get me out of this mess, and then I'll be coming for you, Steve. For *you*.' She poked a finger at his face.

'He won't be representing you in court because he will be in custody for the murder of Tyler and possibly Clifford, the barrister.'

'He didn't kill them,' she replied, quickly. This time her voice was even in tone, not high-pitched and vicious. 'It definitely wasn't him.'

'Oh no, Bianca?' He lowered his voice and spoke calmly. 'Why do you say that?'

She looked at Steve with sadness in her eyes and a tear trickled down her cheek. 'Because I thought he had. I really thought he had killed Tyler—'

'You were so desperate to get your hands on Tommy's will that you were prepared to kill for it. Everything Tommy owned would have rightfully gone to you because the divorce wasn't finalised. But you were afraid he had changed his will and that he would leave everything he had to Tyler or someone else, weren't you?' He laughed. 'So, you killed Tommy for Oliver, didn't you? Did he tell you to? Did he say he would protect you and ensure you didn't go to court?'

She stared unblinkingly.

'Oh dear, and you, in your quest for Tommy's money, believed that Oliver would kill for you so you could both live in a mansion and bask in your dead husband's wealth. Oh, Bianca, you more or less said the same to me when you thought Tommy would go away for a long time. You often said to me if Tommy was out of the picture, how rich we would be.'

She bit her lip to stop the words from tumbling out, but more tears fell. She slowly wiped them away.

'But satisfy my curiosity. Tell me, how are you so sure Oliver wouldn't go down for murdering them?'

'Because!' she bellowed. 'Because he came to visit me. I told him that I would protect him and that I had his back because I'd already convinced Dixie-Lee Deacon to plead guilty to killing the barrister Clifford but—'

'You did *what*? You fucking made Dixie-Lee Deacon change her plea?'

'Look, you don't know what it's like to be in love. I mean, I would have done anything for him, and he would've done the same for me.'

'But he didn't. You just said he didn't kill Tyler or Clifford. But tell me, why are you convinced he didn't or is that just another ploy to try to save his arse?'

She looked away. 'I was going to say, because he told me not to make Dixie-Lee plead guilty as she wasn't guilty and neither was he. He even had an alibi – he was in a pub that night.'

'That says to me, Bianca, that whether Oliver did or didn't kill those two men, his morals have a defining line. Unlike you. You would have let, in fact, forced a girl to go to prison for something she didn't do because you wanted to protect Oliver. And all because you thought he'd killed for you. Ha! A right kick in the teeth for you, wouldn't you say?' He laughed and then mockingly he said, 'And all in the name of love.'

Another tear fell, this time dropping onto Bianca's arm. 'He does love me, but you, Steve, wouldn't know how that feels.'

'I do know how it feels. I did love once before.'

'I know you loved me—'

'Don't flatter yourself. It wasn't you I loved. It was someone else,' he said, before he rose from his seat. 'Goodbye, Bianca.'

He dabbed the blood from the scratches she had left on his face.

'And again, if you try to blackmail me or Cathy or anyone else, I will make sure they add another ten to twenty years to your sentence.'

He tapped the door, and as it opened, the officer gasped. 'Did she do that to your face?'

'Yes, she did.'

The officer shook her head in disbelief. 'Looks like you've lost ya brief, Bianca. Not your best day, is it?'

'Fuck off.'

***

The jewellery shop had changed from when Brodie was a teenager. It had been extended, and the interior was sleek with glass cabinets showing off the latest high-class watches and rotating cabinets displaying gold lighters and diamond bracelets.

Brodie smiled when Mr Moss appeared to greet them. He was Jewish and wearing a kippa or skullcap. Short and round, he was for ever peering over his small round glasses. To Brodie, he looked exactly the same as he had years ago.

'Gentlemen, my colleague said you wish to speak with me.'

Brodie nodded and stared, and when Mr Moss's face suddenly lit up, he was pleased that he recognised him.

'Brodie Deacon, well, it must be a hundred years ago, my friend.'

Brodie offered his hand, and then they both hugged each other.

'My son-in-law, the frugal idiot, tells me you and . . .' He looked at Mac. 'One of your brothers helped him settle a dispute over the little gambling misunderstanding.'

Mac piped up, 'Little? I would hardly call it little. A . . .'

He stopped speaking, following a quick nudge in the ribs from Brodie. 'Yes, Mr Moss, but everything is okay now.'

'Did it cost him big money to settle?' His words were asked gently, knowing it wasn't his business.

'No, nothing he couldn't afford.'

Moss wagged his finger. 'Very diplomatic, Brodie. I see why people go to you. I hope I never need to, but if I do, I hope you will charge me family rates.'

'I will, Mr Moss.'

'Good, good, so are you here to buy a watch? I have a very prestigious collection and for you a family discount.'

Brodie pulled up the sleeve of his jumper and showed his own watch.

Moss nodded. 'I don't think I have one that will match the quality or the diamonds in yours, but I have dress watches for men or a nice diamond ring for the little finger.'

'Mr Moss, I am sure you've heard that Tommy Malloye was murdered in England?'

Moss nodded. 'I only saw him a month ago. Terrible business. He seemed so happy. I believe his wife has been arrested? Yes?'

'Yes, Mr Moss, she has. Look, I've come here to talk about Tommy who bought a watch from you, as you say, a few weeks ago.'

Moss nodded slowly, not knowing where this was leading.

Brodie handed Moss the receipt. 'Mr Moss, it's the engraving that interests me. Can you remember or do you have some record of when the work was done?'

Taking the receipt, Moss stared at it. 'The police didn't ask me for anything. Is it to do with his murder?'

'Not his murder because the police probably have enough evidence that Bianca, his wife, killed him, but his son was also murdered, and this information may help to identify who killed him. Who knows.'

'Mr and Mrs Malloye must be out of their minds with grief.'

Brodie nodded. 'Actually, Mr Malloye gave me the receipt, hoping it would help.'

Moss removed his small round glasses from his nose and placed them on his head. 'Now, I have a record of every sale and of course every engraving. I have had some customers complaining. In fact, they have tried to con me by saying the engraving was wrong, the spelling was wrong, to get a discount. So I always make them write down exactly what they want engraved themselves.'

'Of course you would,' said Mac, grinning.

'Now, let me see.' He pulled out a mini filing cabinet with cards all in date order. He then glanced at the receipt again to check the date. 'Ahh, here it is.'

Brodie took the card, and Mac peered at it over his shoulder.

Three words: **Marry me, Natalia**.

CHAPTER THIRTY-TWO

Having had a remote meeting with Brodie, Mac, Hugh, and Raj until the early morning hours, Rohan was geared up for the event ahead. There was no doubt that he would have to put on his most calming voice. Brodie had once said that he was a natural born hypnotist; he seemed to possess an ability to whisper to the soul, like a horse whisperer, but, in this case, with people. As he showered, he mentally played out how the conversation would go, and he felt confident he could pull it off.

Georgie was up and out of the house before him. She was happier, brighter, and much more like her old self, which lifted his own psyche to a good place.

With no arguments to distract him, Rohan felt relaxed and confident. Dressed in his smart black jumper, black trousers, and fitted camel overcoat, he peered once more in the mirror before adding a splash of subtle aftershave.

Hugh had prewarned Steve what would take place, so when Rohan arrived, both Cathy and Steve were in Steve's office upstairs. The juniors were given duties away from the office, so there would be no disruptions when Rohan entered the building.

Once he arrived outside the chambers, he greeted Hugh Shields. 'I'm ready.' He looked down at the phone. 'And I still have connection.'

'Smooth, Rohan, even I fancy you,' Shields said, chuckling away. He then gave Rohan the nod to go ahead.

Once Rohan was inside the chambers, he fixed a smile on his face, removed his gloves, and approached the reception desk.

‘Hello, Rohan, lovely to see. I didn’t know you had an appointment?’

‘No, I don’t,’ Rohan replied, as he leaned against her desk and looked at her watch. He had memorised it from the photo that Brodie had sent to him. ‘Nice watch, Natalia. Where did you get that?’ His tone was even, and he kept eye contact and maintained a smile. Inside, though, he was angry.

Natalia looked up and immediately saw how close Rohan was. She didn’t mind because he was an attractive man. ‘A jeweller’s shop,’ she replied.

‘Hmmm, that’s worth a lot of money, Natalia.’

Annoyed by the way he was speaking to her, she said, ‘Sorry, Rohan, who did you say you were here to see?’

‘I didn’t. But it’s you, actually.’

Fear played out in her eyes, and he could see her chin twitching as if she was about to burst into tears.

‘It’s hard to keep up a pretence, isn’t it, Natalia?’

‘I-I don’t know what you mean.’

He nodded. ‘It’s okay, love. You can let it all out now. There’s no point in keeping this all bottled up.’

When Natalia noticed her hands were shaking, she quickly hid them beneath the desk. Her eyes nervously darted about.

‘It’s okay, the police are not here yet. But they are at your apartment with a warrant. They’re looking for a long coat, a file, a knife, and anything else that would incriminate you.’

‘If you’re referring to Tommy Malloye’s murder, I didn’t kill him. We were going to get married.’

Rohan sensed the lack of conviction in her voice.

‘I believe you, but I bet it didn’t start off that way, did it?’

Her eyes were like the balls in a pinball machine. ‘I-I don’t understand.’

‘Yeah, ya do. You definitely do, Natalia *Minster*.’

Hearing her real surname made her almost jump out of the chair. 'How did you know *that*?'

'Oh, that was fairly easy to work out. Oliver's Jag was in your name, your *real* name. Hugh Shields, Dixie-Lee's solicitor, checked it out.'

'But why would you . . .?'

It was clear to Rohan that he had caught her off-guard and she was now fishing for clues as to what he knew.

'Natalia, sweetheart, you've known me and me brothers for several years. You know what we do for a living, and you understand the nature of our work.' His smile reached both ears, showing his perfectly straight white teeth. 'And, darling, with our little Dixie-Lee inside on a murder charge, we'd never leave a stone unturned.'

Her eyes glossed over, and her mouth gently parted as she listened, trying to second-guess where this conversation was going.

'The police thought they had their culprit, but, see, here's the thing: we knew it wasn't our niece who should be in the frame. Then, Mrs Malloye, *Nessa Malloye*, found the receipt for a watch, and she thought it might help us. Me brothers followed that up, and the engraving included your name. It's an unusual name, darling.'

'There are millions of Natalias.'

'Yeah, maybe so, but we also investigated the woman who was visiting Tommy, and your name didn't come up. No, it was a Violet Buchannon, a woman who had been dead for four years but whose details this chambers has kept because Cathy had represented the driver who killed her! And you had access to that information, didn't you?'

'And so did Cathy.'

'Yes, she did. You're right. But it was you who was seeing Tommy, wasn't it, darling? But there was nothing wrong in that. In any case, Natalia, the prison has CCTV. It won't take us many minutes to confirm that Tommy Malloye's visitor was actually you.'

Her face glowed bright red, and Rohan could tell she was building up to blurt out something.

Bang on cue, she took a deep breath. 'Look, you couldn't possibly imagine what we went through. Ollie and I never had it easy. I was the product of a rape, not that my mum loved me any less. But Mum was raising the two of us alone. She worked hard to ensure she brought up two decent kids.'

Rohan smiled sympathetically 'I can understand that.'

'Ollie wanted to show his father that he had done good. He wanted to show Michael Malloye that he could be proud of him. Tommy wouldn't accept the truth, and spurred on by his mother, he beat up Ollie. He hurt him so badly that Ollie spent six weeks in the hospital.' A tear fell down her cheek.

'My God, Natalia, I didn't know,' he replied, while showing as much empathy as he could muster.

She stared at him and straightened her shoulders, a subtle sign of annoyance. 'Our mother died when we were young, and social services separated us. I could never tell Ollie what happened to me in care. But, anyway, Ollie came for me and fought for guardianship. You could never understand how hard Ollie worked to keep me out of the system while he studied every waking hour to pass the bar exams. I changed my name and I got the job here as a manager, while Ollie was still in training. I knew Tommy had used Steve before as his barrister. Then I got Ollie the job. We had debts to pay – his university debts – and it was hard, while Tommy' – she flared her nostrils – 'and Bianca were swanning around breaking the law and living the high life. They had money coming out of their ears because Tommy had a head start. He had the support of his dad, Ollie's father.'

'I understand. It must have felt like a slap in the face.'

Natalia looked at him, wondering if he really knew what it was like to be in her situation. 'When Tommy came into the offices to meet Steve, he crossed paths with Ollie, but he didn't even recognise him.' She sighed. 'But then, Ollie meant nothing to Tommy. Six gruelling weeks of hospitalisation, that's how badly Tommy beat him, and then he gave him an indifferent smile when he saw him.'

She gritted her teeth and stared at nothing.

'And you fell in love with Tommy, yeah? How did that feel for you, considering he beat up your brother?'

'I didn't love Tommy. Well, not at first. I grew fond of him, shall we say, but even that wasn't supposed to happen.'

Rohan nodded. 'Oh, I see, so it was all a case of planned revenge on Tommy, regardless of who got hit in the crossfire, was it?'

With shame, Natalia's face turned from red to white. She lowered her head. 'None of this was supposed to happen.'

'What exactly *was* supposed to happen?'

Natalia straightened her shoulders as if she was proud. 'Look, we knew Tommy had invested a lot of his money in diamonds, and when Bianca clapped eyes on Ollie, she was all over him, so he took advantage of the fact. The idea was to have Bianca eating out of Ollie's hand. In other words, part with some of the diamonds. However, as you probably know now, Tommy hid them in a safe deposit box with a key code. Tommy had always been a bit flirty with me and so I decided to push it further. He'd had enough of Bianca and wanted out of the relationship.' She smiled. 'I wouldn't sleep with him until he was divorced and I had a ring on my finger, so he proposed – hence the watch. I thought once we were married, I would screw the bastard to the wall and take him for everything. And I swear to you that I didn't know Bianca wanted my brother so much she decided to kill Tommy. Clearly, she was after Tommy's assets as well, but she also wanted a relationship with Ollie. And why wouldn't she? She assumed he loved her.' She tossed her head, in disbelief. 'But he hated her. So there you have it. The police can't hold me responsible.'

'We know you killed Clifford and Tyler. All I want to know is why?'

'I didn't kill them,' she said, flatly.

'Yeah, you did. I reckon you did it because either Clifford or Tyler had found the file, and you saw it as rightfully Oliver's.'

She glared. 'Well, he should have had *something*.'

'Where is the file?'

She shrugged.

'You killed them.'

'I did not,' she retaliated.

'Who killed Clifford?'

'Tyler did.' She looked around. 'Although you won't believe it, and neither will the police.'

'So who killed Tyler?'

She pulled her hands up from under the desk and rubbed the back of her neck.

'You might as well tell me. If you do, I'll make sure you are dealt with kindly.'

'Oh yeah, and why do you, Rohan, think you have that power? You are not a copper or a lawyer.'

'No, you're right, I'm not, but I am very good friends with the copper who will arrest you.'

Rohan looked down at his phone. 'So the police have secured a search warrant for your apartment. They have just found evidence that links you here at the time of the murder. Tell me about a long overcoat.'

Her eyes widened, her lips tightened, and there was no longer any colour in her cheeks. She looked grey.

'What do you mean? A long overcoat? What are you getting at?'

'I saw you wearing one. It was a few weeks ago.'

'So? So what?'

'Well, as I see it, the person who the police have as their witness saw a woman wearing a long oversized coat leaving the alleyway next to the chambers late that night. The witness assumed it was Dixie-Lee because a photo of her was shoved under the witness's nose. But this is the thing. You are the same size as Dixie-Lee. Your hair is the same style as hers. Can you see where I am going with this?'

'Yes, of course. But everything you are saying is just circumstantial. That's right, isn't it?'

'Natalia, there is more. There is now CCTV footage of you in your car – the black BMW – the car you got when you traded in your red Jag for Oliver's silver Jag. The garage owner told Hugh Shields he was proud of his sale. And you were spotted in that car at five past midnight, near Charing Cross railway station.' He raised a finger. '*And*, darling, your face is visible through the car window.' He raised his index finger again. 'And also your oversized winter coat. Black-and-white check, isn't it? So you may as well admit it. You killed that lad, Tyler.'

'No, I'm not admitting that to you.'

'No, okay, then.' He sighed. 'I was trying to do you a favour because you shared the apartment with Oliver, and so the police will arrest him, since on paper he is probably the most likely suspect. He'd have good reason to kill Tyler, wouldn't he – jealousy, abandonment . . . Shall I go on?'

Rohan saw her shoulders drop, and her face showed a look of resignation.

'Don't arrest him. He isn't as strong as me. It was my idea to date Tommy.'

'It is more likely that Oliver killed Tyler, though, isn't it?'

'No, no, he wasn't even here, I swear. I was here that night, admittedly. I was looking for the Malloye file, and I'd already asked Clifford to help. I said there would be a lot of money in it for him. He was a prick. I had a lot on him, including the details of another rape charge, and he was in debt, a gambler on the side. So he was the ideal fall guy, eager enough to look for the file in return for some renumeration. With neither of us finding the file, I told Clifford I was going home. I was about to leave the chambers, when I saw Tyler lurking outside. He didn't see me, though. I just had a hunch that he might come into the chambers. Well, not knowing if the front door was locked or not, I dashed upstairs out of the way. Anyway, while I was up there, I decided to see if either Cathy or Steve had left any clue as to the whereabouts of this file. It was a long shot, I know. Evidently, Clifford thought I had left for the evening. Then Dixie-Lee showed up, and I knew Clifford had been drinking and being the lecherous wanker he was, it was no surprise when I heard a scuffle. But by the time I came downstairs, Dixie-Lee had long gone.'

Natalia paused to catch her breath and was encouraged to continue by a gentle nod from Rohan, followed by an understanding smile.

'Then, while I was standing right here, I heard loud voices downstairs. When I went down into the basement, to see what was going on, I saw, through the glass panel in the door, Tyler in the filing room. It looked as though he was demanding that Clifford hand over something.'

She sniffed back a tear. 'I crept closer and then I witnessed Tyler take a file that Clifford was holding. I-I . . . I was stunned. But then Tyler stabbed Clifford in the neck. I couldn't believe it.' She paused to gather her thoughts. 'The blood shot out like a pump. It totally covered the file. Tyler jumped back, out of the way, but Clifford slumped to the floor. And that's when I saw Tyler open Clifford's hand. When he planted a brooch in it, I recognised it at once. It is such a beautiful one. I knew, straightaway, it belonged to Dixie-Lee because we'd only been talking about it the day before. Tyler stood there watching Clifford bleeding to death, but Clifford didn't roll around. He lay still, with his other hand on his throat.'

Natalia reached for her lukewarm coffee, now in need of a drink.

'When Tyler saw me in the doorway, he ran out through the door at the end of the room. He was still holding the knife he'd used to kill Clifford. For a moment or so, I was absolutely gobsmacked. But then, I thought: *Tyler's not getting away with this. I want that file. I need that file. I'm not letting him have it. It was for Ollie. Why should the Malloye family have everything of Tommy's?* So, I ran after Tyler. I chased him out of the back of the building, through the fire exit, and along the alleyway towards the bins. At one point, he looked back and saw me. Then, he collided with some bins and dropped the knife.'

Rohan was totally transfixed on Natalia as she was telling her version of events. The way she described them was so vivid, he could easily picture the scene himself. Then he saw her whole body shake uncontrollably.

Natalia looked at Rohan in complete despair. 'Please don't judge me. You don't know everything that has happened to me and Ollie. Life can be so cruel when you are down on your luck. We just needed a lucky break and we thought this was our chance. But we had no intention of killing anyone.'

Despite his initial negative feelings towards Natalia, Rohan could see that she was probably telling the truth. Her account was so visceral, so in tune with her emotions, that he genuinely thought she was giving him an honest version of what happened that night. And it certainly sounded convincing. It prompted him to adopt a gentle tone to his voice to try to calm Natalia down. 'Look, Natalia, it's okay, I understand. So, slowly, tell me what happened next.'

She shuddered as if she had just come out of a trance. 'Everything happened so quickly. He was going to kill me, you know. He was. I could see it in his eyes. Then, we both looked down to where the knife was. I grabbed it first and backed away from him. I was so shocked, I didn't know what to do. But when, like a cornered rat, he lunged at me, grabbed my hair, and tried to take the blade from me, I was scared for my life. So, I lashed out.'

'You cut his throat. You did, didn't you?'

She nodded and avoided eye contact. 'Yes, I did. But I honestly didn't mean to.' She then deliberately looked him in the eye.

They stared at each other, neither not knowing quite what to say. This was an enormous moment.

But quite unexpectedly, it was broken when Oliver charged into the chambers. 'What's going on?' he yelled.

Rohan put his hands up. 'Calm down, Oliver, it's okay.'

Oliver looked at Rohan and then at Natalia. 'There are police outside. They tried to stop me.'

She smiled sadly with a sense of defeat. 'They know, Ollie.'

'No!' he yelled, grabbing his sister and pulling her close. 'I did it. It was me!' he bellowed.

'Oliver, don't, mate. We know it was your sister.'

'No, it was me.'

Rohan shook his head. 'We know it was your sister. And the police have a warrant to search her apartment. They are there now searching the place.'

Natalia looked at him, aghast. '*What?* I thought you said they had already searched it? And I thought you said they have found the evidence?'

'Natalia, they would have been here questioning you themselves. I'm not a police officer, as you also pointed out. However, I have been on the phone with my detective friend the whole time. He has heard every word, love.'

'How did you know?'

He smiled again. 'Because we put it all together, with the help of a few lucky guesses. But what caught our attention was something our niece heard. It was your shoes. The clip-clop sound upstairs. Dixie-Lee thought at first it was Cathy who was upstairs. But it wasn't her, was it? It was you. Sometimes, Natalia, it's the little things that can trip you up. We weren't going to give up until we got to the truth. That's our niece you let take the rap, and for that, I hope you can live with yourself.'

***

Steve and Cathy stood on the landing having listened to the whole thing. Steve put his arm around Cathy's shoulder.

'It's over, Cathy. They have her,' he said, as the police swarmed into the entrance lobby.

'And I thought she was so nice.'

'The sad thing is, Cathy, she *is* nice but she's held on to a lot of bitterness.'

'Steve, I've called it off with the judge.'

'Really?'

'Yes.'

'Cathy, it's been a long time, but do you think we could make another go of it?'

She smiled and leaned closer. 'We had dreams, Steve. We built these chambers for us. Let's not allow stupid disagreements to break us up again.'

'We have work to do, Cathy. You must get on to the courts and the Home Office to grant Dixie-Lee an Executive Release.'

***

Georgie had a big smile on her face as she walked through the coffee shop.

'Well, you look happy, Georgie.' Henry smiled. 'Sarah said she sorted things out with you. She's out the back baking the bread.' He raised his eyebrows. 'Is that right? Did you sort out your differences?'

'Yes, and I've promised her a raise, but please don't ask me to talk about what I discussed with Sarah, Henry. As much as you're my best mate, it's private stuff.'

'Any news from Dixie-Lee how she's coping?'

Georgie straightened the cakes in the glass cabinet. 'She called last night. I'll be honest, Henry, I thought a few days ago that I'd lost my girl. She was not herself then. At the time, she said she was pleading guilty.'

'Guilty?'

'Yes, but, as I said, that was a few days ago. I think she was all over the place and not thinking clearly. I suppose in a panic she thought pleading guilty to manslaughter was an option. Even though we all know she isn't.'

'Georgie, leave the cakes alone. Will you tell me what's going on?'

Georgie stood up. 'Sorry, Henry, yes, so, anyway, Dixie-Lee's barrister apparently went in late yesterday, tore the statement up right in front of her, and said she'd considered her case in more depth and decided she was wrong to advise Dixie-Lee to plead guilty, for a few reasons. One being it would affect the rest of

Dixie-Lee's life if she had that conviction on her record. But Dixie-Lee had already changed her mind by that time. Anyway, Cathy McGowan made it clear she was going fight for her. Her exact words were: "I will work harder than I ever have to get you home with your family."'

'Really? And yet, you didn't like Cathy much, did you?'

'Well, Henry, I do now. My Dixie-Lee sounded so different, and it wasn't put on. She's all right in prison for now, which worried me before because I know she would never murder anyone. She's a good kid and not a jailbird.'

Sarah came out carrying a tray of freshly baked bread. 'Oh, hello, Georgie, er, you still don't mind me working here, do you?'

'No, I've just told Henry we should up your salary.'

The door opened, and Sheila just managed to catch the tail-end of the conversation. 'Well, that's good to hear, and no doubt, Georgie, that includes me.'

Henry rolled his eyes: the café had been very busy since Sheila had started working here. He realised that she was a bit of a novelty act – a total one-off – what with her colourful language and playful banter – and it seemed that customers were coming into the café in larger numbers now for their cake and coffee.

'Did you hear on the news about that fire that burned a house to the ground? It was in Sidcup, the street your mum lived in, Georgie.'

Georgie froze. 'What's that? I didn't hear about a fire, Sheila.'

Henry turned the radio on. 'It's nearly ten o'clock. They'll have it on the local news.'

'Yes, I heard two men were found dead. The house burned to the ground, not a fucking brick standing. I've always said if a house burns to the ground, then evil lived there.'

Sarah looked at Georgie for a moment and clocked that something was worrying her. Quickly, she unloaded the bread into the basket. While Sheila sang along to Sam Smith's latest song and Henry continued working on the accounts, Sarah quietly went over to Georgie, moved a scorched lock of hair away from her face, and whispered, 'Bruce was asleep upstairs, you know. The firefighter couldn't work out why he hadn't woken up and tried to escape, but I reckon it was all the drugs he was using. He probably slipped into a coma.'

Georgie's eyes widened. 'And how would you know *that*, Sarah?'

'Because he came to me for the drugs. He knew I was on opioid painkillers for the pains in my bones from when he broke them.'

Georgie stared into Sarah's eyes. 'But a man like him would have known how much to take to avoid an overdose, surely?'

Sarah grinned. 'If he knew the real dose, yeah, probably.'

Georgie smiled. 'I reckon Sheila's right, you know. Evil lived in that house. Tell me, Sarah, did you ever leave red roses at my mum's grave?'

She shook her head. 'No. But I do know who did. It was Bruce. I even read the note. But he's gone now.' She tapped Georgie's hand. 'No more nightmares, love. You and I can sleep in our beds without waking up in a cold sweat.'

'You as well?'

'Yes, love, me as well.'

A sudden flurry of customers came into the coffee shop, but one in particular caught Georgie's eye. She was roughly twenty years old with long thick black hair. With so much making up to do, Georgie had started with Sarah and had made a phone call in the hope that she could reunite Sarah with her daughter. The call had ended with the girl saying, 'Thank you for letting me know the full picture. I need time to think about it.'

When Georgie looked at Sarah, she knew that the girl who was standing just inside the doorway was Sarah's daughter.

Sarah's eyes filled up. She clutched a tea towel to her mouth and stared. Of course, she didn't know that her daughter was there for her.

But when the girl called out 'Mum?', Sarah ran to her. 'Daisy? My girl!'

Instantly they hugged and cried, and Georgie knew she had to give them space to be reacquainted.

With tears streaming down her cheeks, Georgie slipped behind the counter. Henry, who was also emotional, quickly wiped his tears away before putting his arm around her shoulders. 'You *are* a softy.'

As they watched from a distance, Georgie's phone rang and as soon as she saw it was Rohan, she smiled. Their relationship was back on track, and she hoped he had called to say he loved her.

'Hello.'

'Georgie, it's our Dixie-Lee.'

'Christ, what's happened *now*?'

'It's all over. They've arrested Natalia. She's agreed to tell the police what happened to clear Dixie-Lee's name. So our Dixie-Lee will be coming home, Georgie. She'll be coming home!'

CHAPTER THIRTY-THREE

Nine months later

Feeling on top of the world, Bianca slid her key into her front door. She paused momentarily and her hands trembled. A feeling of dread, one she'd never experienced before, crept through her body. But it was real, all right. Her throat was suddenly dry and tight, as if someone was strangling her. She took a deep breath and forced away the sinister feeling. She turned her thoughts to the enormous amount of money she now had; every diamond that was his was now hers. Although the house was in probate, it would soon be hers. She could fill her bath with his money and bathe in it if she wanted to. That thought should have planted a permanent smile on her face, but something felt wrong. Very wrong.

Her hands trembled again as she gripped the plastic bag that contained all her court paperwork, the pouch full of diamonds, and the note that had been left in the safe deposit box. Her barrister – the numpty – hadn't even bothered to put them in a decent briefcase or sent her home with an escort, considering the diamonds were worth a bloody fortune. Still, she was free and rich, so fuck the lot of them. She didn't need a barrister anymore or anyone else for that matter. The man she'd truly had feelings for had turned out to be a lying wanker who had never loved her and had only used her. But then, the irony of life caused her to utter a tiny chuckle. She'd never even loved *her* husband. He was a meal-ticket, nothing more. And besides, sleeping with such an ugly prick deserved payment.

Glancing back at her husband's car still in the drive and her car beside his, she slowly turned the key and pushed the door wide open.

'Hunny, I'm home,' she said, in an American accent, before cackling to herself like a witch.

All that greeted her was an eerie silence. 'No answer?' She cackled again. 'No, of course not, you ugly wanker! You can't, 'cos you're dead.'

She dropped the bag onto the kitchen table and opened the fridge, hoping to pop open a bottle of champagne to celebrate, but the fridge was empty. In fact, the kitchen seemed different. She glanced at the vast wine rack that had once been filled with champagne. It was her favourite drink. But that too was empty.

A cold feeling swept through her. While she'd been in prison had someone burgled the house? Surely the police would have told her. Then again, if they had been burgled, her neighbours, who were so old and partially blind, wouldn't have reported it. She hurtled up the wide winding staircase to check on her valuables.

As soon as she reached the top, she could smell Tommy's aftershave as if he had just put it on. Her heart began to race, and her throat tightened up. *He was dead. He couldn't be here, not now. Because she had put the knife straight through his heart. She'd killed him, and his body had been taken away in a body bag.*

She slowly crept towards the bedroom and listened, but there was silence. She wondered if being back in the house was playing tricks on her mind. That was until she passed the bathroom. She had to take a step back and look again. Her bathroom was larger than most, with a Jacuzzi bath and white marble tiles on the walls and the floor with not a speck of dust or dirt in sight.

Only it wasn't today. She stood staring and then blinked furiously as if her eyes were playing tricks on her. Everywhere in the bathroom was covered in thick blue plastic sheeting.

A feeling of fear crept up her spine. She knew what covering a bathroom in plastic sheeting meant.

'We know what you did, Bianca, and now you need to disappear,' came the cold harsh words from behind her.

Bianca spun around and stared wide-eyed and terrified.

'But first, you will sign some paperwork, and then we can begin,' said Nessa Malloye, her mother-in-law.

Behind Nessa stood Gilead, her brother-in-law, who looked like a sasquatch ready to eat her alive. As she turned back, desperate to escape, she saw Michael Malloye, her father-in-law, and behind him were Martie and Cameron – more of the Malloye clan.

'Step inside the bathroom. We don't want a mess all over Tommy's house,' Nessa said, as she pointed a crooked arthritic finger towards her.

'Please, please, please, don't do this. I didn't kill him! You can have the diamonds. You can have them all. I don't need them. I beg you. Please take everything.'

Nessa laughed. 'Oh, but we have it all. Yer see, your designer bags paid for my Gilead's house repairs. I have to say my Tommy spoiled you rotten, you fecking whore. We sold your watches and your jewellery. They fetched a reasonable price. And of course, now we have the diamonds. Now, don't make this worse than it needs to be. Here are some papers and a letter, and you will fecking sign them,' she said, as she held up the typed documents.

Bianca couldn't read them: her eyes were blinded by fear.

'No!' she screamed, before she tried to run.

But Michael was too fast. He pulled his fist back and punched her in the face, knocking her to the floor.

Bianca watched as Nessa slapped duct tape over her mouth, passed her some documents, and hissed, 'You should never have killed my son! Now, sign these!'

The last thing Bianca heard in her life was the sound of a chainsaw being started up.

***

As Michael sat at the table inside the visiting room at HMP Peterborough, his knee bounced up and down in anticipation. He was grateful that Natalia Beaumont, formerly Minster, had agreed to see him, but he was nervous all the same.

He recognised her immediately when she entered the room, only because she was the spitting image of her mother Anne-Marie. Her face was thinner and her hair was dull, but he didn't expect any less, having been in and out of prison himself.

The officer pointed at him, and Natalia gingerly approached.

'Thank you, Natalia, love. I've bought you some food from the tuck shop. I didn't know what you'd like, so I filled a tray.'

She looked at the coffee, crisps, and chocolate and tried to smile, but she was emotionally conflicted. While this man had turned his back on her brother – and she couldn't really forgive him for that – she herself had killed his grandson, albeit in self-defence. And yet, it seemed to her that he was the one who seemed sheepish, and for a hardened criminal, she found that very surprising.

'Thank you,' she said, with a wan smile, as she curled her fingers around the cup of coffee and took a mouthful to line her dry mouth.

'Natalia, we have to know, love. My Nessa and me, we are desperate to hear your side of what happened. Did you *mean* to kill our Tyler?'

So this was the purpose of his visit, she mused. With her eyes welling up, she shook her head. 'N-no, I didn't. It was a complete accident. Look, I'll take you back to that night. It might be easier for you to understand what happened. Tyler killed Clifford and stole Tommy's file from the chambers. I witnessed what happened.

Then Tyler fled the scene and I ran after him. I did so because I wanted that file for Ollie. I felt he deserved something for the way he was treated by your family. Anyway, I digress. So back to what happened that night. In his haste, Tyler dropped the knife in this alleyway near our chambers. By this time, I was catching him up. When he saw me, the look on his face told me he wasn't going to let me live. We both looked down at the knife. When he went for it, I beat him to it. Then he lunged at me. Instinctively, I lashed out. I swear, all I was doing was trying to protect myself. But everything just happened so quickly. There was no time to confront him about what had happened downstairs in the chambers or even do a deal. I wouldn't have lashed out if he hadn't gone for me. I just wanted to talk to him, and as I said, see if we could come to some kind of deal. A deal that would give Ollie *something* from your family.'

Michael reached across and stroked her forearm. 'Hey, it's okay. I believe you. All I needed was to hear you tell me this to my face.'

'But how, Mr Malloye, can you be so sure I'm telling the truth? I so want you to know I am. I want you to believe I—'

'Hush, listen, I *do* believe you. I've had the details from Cathy McGowan but I had to hear it from you. You have your mother's eyes, and . . .' He paused to compose himself. 'She was a beauty, that one, so she was. And she was true to herself. Yer see, her eyes never lied, and when she told me she was pregnant with yer bother, I knew she was telling me the truth. That I was his father.'

Michael reached for his cup of coffee and took several large gulps.

'I had to do what I did, all those years ago, and I want you to believe me now. I never wanted to hurt anyone – my Nessa, your mother, or your brother. I was never told that he came back to visit me.' He shook his head and sighed. 'I only wished I had. Because he won't see me now, and I don't blame him for that. Oh, and the knife. We know it was Tyler's, because, sadly, I was the one who bought it for him.'

Seeing the pain in his eyes, Natalia lowered her voice to a gentle pitch. 'Ollie, er Oliver will come around one day to seeing you.' She smiled again. 'I did, and look, you're here.'

'Cathy McGowan tells me they are representing you. She said quite firmly that she will look after her own.'

Natalia nodded. 'Yes, they believe I have a strong case.'

'And you do. You handed back the diamonds – and all of them.' He winked. 'All one hundred and thirty-two.'

'I went to the safe deposit box in London. It turned out it was only around the corner from the chambers, oddly enough. And when I opened the box, there was a pouch with the diamonds.' A tear unexpectedly trickled down her cheek. 'And a note, which said, these are for my son, Tyler.'

She placed the coffee cup back on the table and covered her eyes while Michael patted her arm.

'Hey, it's okay. You've done nothing wrong. First, I know now, you didn't mean to kill Tyler. And secondly, you didn't cash in the diamonds, did you? You didn't hide them. You handed them in.'

'When I saw that note, I couldn't keep them or give them to Ollie. I just couldn't do it. The diamonds were Tommy's. They weren't yours, and they certainly weren't Bianca's. Tyler was his only son. And although my brother and Tommy were half-brothers, Ollie didn't have the right to expect anything from Tommy.'

She drank more of her coffee while Michael stared at her face. She reminded him so much of Anne-Marie, he felt, in a strange way, close to her.

'Anyway,' said Natalia, 'the diamonds have been handed to Bianca. I guess she is having the time of her life. Her case, as you probably know, was dropped because the Crown Prosecution Service couldn't find enough evidence against her.'

'Yes, and that's another reason why I am here. Yer see, Bianca must have had some change of heart because she wrote a letter and signed it, stating that she wanted my family to have the diamonds since they were rightfully ours. She also signed all the relevant paperwork that goes with them.'

Natalia frowned. '*What? Really?*' She narrowed her eyes, not believing a word of it.

His smile lifted his cheeks. 'But there's another reason for my visit to come and see yer today. I want you and your brother to have them.'

She frowned again and her mouth dropped open. 'Us? Really? But why?'

'Because you believed Oliver deserved them, and all my boys, they're living a good life, a wealthy life. Well, they are now. You and your brother should have had the same afforded to you. So the diamonds are for you two.'

'Won't Bianca have something to say about that?'

He shook his head and rose from his seat. 'I don't think you need to worry about that callous bitch.'

As their eyes locked, she suddenly knew what he'd done, and she smiled. 'Thank you, Michael, for coming.'

'The next time, hopefully, when I see you again, it will be when you walk out of court a free woman.'

CHAPTER THIRTY-FOUR

Cathy dropped a file on Dixie-Lee's desk. 'I've had the evidence file sent from the Met's archives for Patsy's case. Oh, and by the way, Officer Brenton has been sacked. It had something to do with accepting a gift from a Carol Lardon, the police officer involved in the paedophile racket. They were friends, apparently. Brenton hasn't been charged with any involvement, but she accepted a watch as a gift from her. And I was told that the witness who described you as wearing a coat had been coaxed by Brenton.'

She pointed to the file spread across Dixie-Lee's desk. 'Patsy was shockingly represented. You have done wonders so far.'

Dixie-Lee looked up. 'You said once, in no uncertain terms, I wouldn't make the grade.'

Cathy sat down opposite Dixie-Lee. 'I know I did. Maybe there was a little bit of jealousy on my part.' She looked at her engagement ring.

Dixie-Lee blushed. 'Thank you, Cathy, for securing my release in record time and I hope I've had long enough to prove my worth.'

Cathy rose from her chair, and, out of character, swore. 'Fuck me, prove your worth? You are an absolute asset to our company. Patsy Dewhurst's case was thought to be dead and buried. That woman was never getting out. But thanks to you, the appeal courts will find it impossible not to grant her her release. You have meticulously picked her trial to pieces, everything that a good barrister should have done the first time around. A lazy lawyer let Patsy down, and you're not that type of person, Dixie-Lee. I can see that. You are doing this job because you care about people. It's a trait I didn't think went well with the role, but you proved me wrong. Anyway, don't work too hard. Tomorrow is your mum and

Rohan's big day.' She clapped her hands with excitement. 'I, for one, am getting my hair done for it.'

'I am so pleased that you and mum get on now.'

Cathy smiled. 'It was hard for her when you were on remand. When she came to the chambers with the wedding invitation, she also apologised for how she had spoken to me in the courtroom that day, although I was probably at fault. She mentioned that she was struggling with a lot at the time and needed first to put her demons to rest. Nevertheless, I had to admit I was rather flabbergasted because a steadfast woman like your mother is pretty scary. I shouldn't imagine there are many demons that would take her on.' She chuckled before pointing her finger. 'But inside that tough exterior, she has a heart of gold, and that's the trait, Dixie-Lee, that you get from her.'

Dixie-Lee watched Cathy leave the room singing. Strangely, she closed the door behind her.

Then, when Dixie-Lee looked up, she chuckled, and a beaming smile spread across her face. Tears – happy ones this time – poured down her cheeks. Her job at the chambers had undoubtedly been cemented by the fact that the partners had secretly etched her name on the glass panel of her office door.

Dixie-Lee Deacon

Printed in Great Britain
by Amazon

43280636R00216